C000174837

Anna Abney is among the
family, former residents of
Derbyshire. She is the autho
the first book in the series.

Praise for *The Messenger of Measham Hall*

'A gripping mystery full of intrigue with wonderful well researched historical detail. A real page turner with a brilliant twist!'   Clare Marchant, author of *The Mapmaker's Daughter*

'The Messenger of Measham Hall is a thrilling adventure exploring complex themes of loyalty, faith and gender against the tumultuous backdrop of the build up to the Glorious Revolution. Both a tender coming of age story and a tense spy thriller, nothing and no-one is as it seems in the mysterious world of Measham Hall. Readers will love it'
Miranda Malins, author of *The Rebel Daughter*

A great yarn...Recommended!
Leonora Nattrass, author of *Black Drop*

'Political subterfuge and family secrets entwine in this tale of historical intrigue, set during the late 17th century tensions between Protestants and Catholics. Meticulously researched and alive with intricate period details to savour, I raced through it, while learning huge amounts'
Lucy Ribchester, author of *The Amber Shadows*

'The history is absolutely right, and so is the mystery: every reader is pretty well guaranteed at least two jaw-dropping moments'   Ronald Hutton, Professor of History at the University of Bristol

Also by Anna Abney
The Master of Measham Hall

The
MESSENGER
of
MEASHAM
HALL

ANNA ABNEY

DUCKWORTH

First published in the United Kingdom by Duckworth,
an imprint of Duckworth Books Ltd, in 2023

Duckworth, an imprint of Duckworth Books Ltd
1 Golden Court, Richmond, TW9 1EU, United Kingdom
www.duckworthbooks.co.uk

For bulk and special sales please contact
info@duckworthbooks.com

A CIP catalogue record of this book is available from the British Library

Typeset by Danny Lyle

Print and bound in Great Britain by Clays Ltd

1 3 5 7 9 10 8 6 4 2

Paperback ISBN: 9780715654798
eISBN: 9780715654804

A Note on the Text

During the time period of the novel the British Isles
were still using the Julian calendar, although most
of continental Europe had moved to the Gregorian
Calendar at the end of the previous century. This meant
that England (until 1752) was ten days behind the rest
of western Europe. The civil year in England started
on the 25 March (at the Feast of the Annunciation),
though New Year's Day was generally celebrated, as
now, on the 1 January, a system I have also followed.

Characters

Derbyshire
Sir William Hawthorne – the
master of Measham Hall
Nicholas Hawthorne – his son
Matthew Harcourt – Jesuit
priest
Crewe – the steward
Abigail – Nicholas's nurse-
maid, servant
Palmes – the butler
Tickell – the cook
John Thornly – the bailiff

Percy Hawthorne – uncle of
William

St. Omer
Father Carmichael – rector
Gilbert Staley
Isabelle Dupont

London and Kent
Lady Jane Pemberton formerly
Sellwood née Calverton
Lord Ralph Pemberton –
husband of Jane
Lord Pemberton's children:
Edward Pemberton
Lettice Pemberton
Dorothy Pemberton
Prudence Pemberton
Richard Pemberton

Isaac Smith – Lord
Pemberton's secretary

Lord Henry Calverton –
father of Jane
Lady Margaret Calverton –
mother of Jane

Jack Fleet
Ellen Liddell
Robin Liddell
Lizzie Tyler
Jeremiah Tyler

Part I
Boy

✦ Chapter One ✦

Derbyshire, November 1678

Concealed by ferns, Nicholas sat watching the narrow path below. He was a good hunter and did not mind waiting. Having learnt to be both patient and stealthy, he was able to observe close up the birds, deer, weasels, voles, squirrels and foxes that inhabited the woodland. He never grew bored, not with these forest creatures for entertainment. Always happier outdoors than in, he loved especially the mossy intricacy of the forest, with its twisted, interlocking branches and hidden dells. This was a better way to spend his time than parsing Latin epigrams under the critical eye of his cousin, Father Matthew.

He took a wild plum from the little store that he'd placed in among the mushrooms in his basket. It was fat and sweet, bursting pleasantly in his mouth to release its juices. Hopefully Matthew wouldn't notice his black fingernails and purple-stained palms. Standing up slowly, he shook out his legs. He would go down to the stream to wash his hands. It would mean turning his back on the path, but he'd hear if anyone approached.

A branch snapped. He dropped down on his heels. A couple made their way hesitantly down the path. Nicholas jumped down before them and introduced himself with a bow. He loved these important errands, or 'missions' as Matthew called them, imagining himself as a sort of latter-day Robin Hood, only he was bringing spiritual succour to the people. On this occasion he had been sent out to guide the Caldwells back to Measham Hall for the baptism of their baby.

The young woman, who carried the infant in her arms, yelped with fright, but the man doffed his hat and gave the customary greeting.

'Good morning, young master. What do you be doing out so early on this Sabbath day?'

'I have been gathering toad's bread.' Nicholas held out his basket of mushrooms.

'Have you indeed? We too come in search of bread, bread and water; perhaps you might lead us to them?'

'I know of someone who can provide what you seek,' Nicholas responded. 'Especially for this Holyday.'

The couple smiled, the woman jiggling the grizzling baby on her hip. She was very pretty; her brown eyes were fringed with long black lashes and her plump lips were the colour of raspberries. The only women at Measham were Nicholas's former nursemaid, Abigail, who now helped in the kitchens and with the laundry, and Lady Jane, who was a frequent guest but usually came alone, without even a maid to attend her.

After the baptism of the baby, which Father Matthew officiated over in the parlour, everyone went into the kitchen for a glass of ale, a slice of game pie and a cheesecake.

'Have you put the articles away?' Crewe, their steward, murmured in Nicholas's ear.

Nicholas nodded. Anxious not to miss out on the sweetmeats and Mrs Caldwell's company, he had shoved the family chalice, holy oil and priest's vestments into the chest under the parlour window seat. They were supposed to be kept in a false step in the staircase. He would hide them away properly once the Caldwells had gone.

'We're very grateful to you all for taking this risk on our behalf, especially given the current times.' Mr Caldwell raised his tankard.

'I was sore afraid little Mary might perish afore she was watered by a priest,' Mrs Caldwell said, her large eyes lustrous with tears.

Nicholas watched her as she took a bite out of her cheesecake. The way her tongue curled upwards to dab at her lips reminded him of Jemima, their kitchen cat.

'Everybody's talking about these night riders that've been heard all over the country. People are saying they should confiscate all papists' horses as well as their weapons.' Mr Caldwell shook his head.

Nicholas was glad Father had taken the precaution of stabling their horses at the Thorntons' farm. He couldn't bear it if Polestar was taken.

'They think all Catholics are like the Jesuits, after the King's blood.' Caldwell looked at Father Matthew with sudden embarrassment. 'Begging your pardon, Father, I know you wouldn't have anything to do with this plot.'

Matthew smiled genially. 'If indeed there is a plot. I wouldn't be surprised if the whole thing is a fabrication. I've heard reports of this Titus Oates fellow and he sounds like a thorough scoundrel.'

'But they've arrested five lords,' Mrs Caldwell said, her eyes wide. 'And a chapman at market yesterday was reading out a newsletter what said Titus Oates can prove the Jesuits and their allies design to enslave England to France and the Romish religion. Them sort of tales make everyone suspect us.'

Mr Caldwell tapped her shoulder and she dropped her gaze to the baby, which lay sleeping in her lap. Nicholas couldn't help noticing how the nape of her neck had turned red. He felt a sudden urge to reach out and place a fingertip on the downy skin, just to see if it was as warm as it looked.

'I hope we can rely on you both not to breathe a word of the baptism or of Father Matthew to anyone, no matter how trustworthy they seem.' Father, a man of few words, removed the pipe from his mouth to speak for the first time.

Father did not like allowing strangers into Measham Hall for Mass, but his cousin was adamant. Matthew could not be a chaplain to the Hawthorne family alone, but must serve the needs of the local people. Nicholas thought this very heroic of him, though Father said it was foolhardy.

The Caldwells swore with such earnestness that they would rather be hanged than betray the Hawthornes; Nicholas had no doubts about their sincerity.

Father looked pensive, however. 'The parish constable told me he's been ordered to draw up lists of suspected papists and hand it to nearest Justice of the Peace. Any that refuse to take the Oath of Allegiance will be gaoled.'

Mrs Caldwell looked up at him with alarm.

Matthew raised his hands. 'We all know what the law says regarding our religion, but it is rarely enacted. Let's not spoil this day of celebration as we welcome little Mary into the one true faith.'

As if on cue, the baby woke and began to cry.

Once he had led the Caldwells back to the forest path, Nicholas took his time returning to the house. At the edge of the wood he stopped to admire some pink and orange berries he hadn't noticed before. He gathered a few to show to Matthew, snapping off a branch complete with leaves as his tutor had told him to.

That afternoon they went through the huge leather-bound herbal kept in the library.

'It is the fruit of the spindle tree, also known as prick-timber,' Nicholas said, pointing to a woodcut illustration. 'Called *Euonymus* in Latin.'

'Good.' Matthew nodded. 'It is poisonous, so take care with it; don't let it touch your mouth.'

'I'm not a baby,' Nicholas retorted, though he was secretly glad he'd resisted eating any of the pretty berries.

Matthew merely raised his eyebrows. 'You should take your inks and make a study of it to add to your collection.'

This was a task Nicholas was only too happy to undertake. He loved drawing plants and had a common-place book devoted entirely to his botanical discoveries.

'When I'm grown I'm going to travel to the most distant lands and bring back wondrous fruits and flowers the like of which have never been seen before. I'll make a present of them to the King.'

'An honourable ambition.' Matthew sounded amused. 'I believe you'll make a fine botanist. Have you shown your drawings to your father yet?'

Nicholas shook his head. 'I don't think they would be of much interest to Father.'

A look of sorrow flitted across Matthew's face. 'William will be impressed by your skilful hand and pleased by your enthusiasm for the works of nature. Why don't you show more interest in our lands here? You know the gardens are your father's pride and joy.'

Nicholas just shrugged. Father hardly seemed to notice his presence and he was convinced he wouldn't want him tagging along as he made his rounds of the land. He had certainly never suggested Nicholas accompany him.

He suspected it was because he was, what Abigail called, his father's 'natural son'. That meant his mother was a whore, or so the stableboy, Jasper, had told him. Abigail said Jasper deserved a whipping. Nicholas's mother had been a good, honest woman and always kind to her. She never understood why his father hadn't married Ellen, even if she was below him in station. He'd always treated her with respect and she was lovely to look at, with her flaxen hair and hazel eyes. Nicholas, being dark, was very much a Hawthorne in looks.

He was always being told how fortunate he was his father had recognised him and managed to make him his heir, despite the circumstances of his birth. It was a great responsibility and he must do everything in his power to ensure he lived up to the Hawthorne name. Whenever he misbehaved, Matthew would warn him to be on his guard against the sins inherent in his flesh.

Only Lady Jane never held his origins against him. The King had at least a dozen illegitimate children, she said; the sons had been given titles and many of them had made good marriages. He had no need to feel ashamed; a child was not responsible for the sins of its parents.

'How old are you now?'

Matthew was studying his face in a way that made Nicholas uneasy. He supposed this was one of Matthew's rhetorical questions since he was sure his cousin knew his age, but he answered anyway.

'Twelve, sir.'

'In a couple of years you will be old enough to attend St. Omers college; how would you like that?'

Nicholas almost leapt up from the table in his excitement. 'I would love it beyond anything.'

Matthew had told him about his own time at St. Omer's: the trips to the countryside, the plays and concerts performed by the students. He said the college excelled at music and drama. Father had also attended briefly, but he never spoke about it. More than anything, Nicholas longed to be among boys of his own age. He would happily endure arduous days in the schoolroom if he could also enjoy the companionship of his peers.

Matthew laughed. 'Well, I will have to persuade your father. I suspect he will prefer to keep you close, but I will see what I can do.' He paused and Nicholas was moved by the warmth and affection with which his cousin spoke to him. 'I didn't know what sort of boy I would meet when I returned to Measham five years ago. If I am honest, I wasn't expecting much, but you continue to impress me, Nicholas. You have an aptitude and enthusiasm for learning and a facility with languages that make you an excellent student. You deserve to be taught by scholars more advanced than me, especially in natural philosophy and medicine.' He closed the book that lay on the table between them. 'You would not be allowed into the priesthood, of course, not without papal dispensation.'

Nicholas didn't care about that. He had no desire to become a priest and the fact that they wouldn't have him made him want it even less.

Matthew gave him one of his wry smiles. 'You will have to come back to look after Measham Hall when your father gets older, but there is plenty of time for travel before then. Perhaps you will bring back a Catholic bride to further the line.'

Nicholas didn't know what to say to this. He couldn't imagine getting married.

'Do you think Father will agree?' he asked anxiously.

Matthew picked at the corner of the book with his slender fingers. 'He wants you to attend Oxford or Cambridge. Presently, of course, that would mean taking the oaths and renouncing your faith, at least outwardly.'

'I could never be such a hypocrite as that.'

Matthew sighed. 'When the Duke of York succeeds to the throne, I believe things will change. He will make it safe for us to practise our religion openly again. Catholics will be allowed to hold positions of office and attend university.' He rose and went over to the window where he stood staring out at the dark November sky. 'That is why so many are stirring up against us; they are terrified England will have a Catholic monarch once more and will do anything to stop it.'

The door opened and Father strode in, enveloped in a cloud of pipe smoke. 'Studying, on a Sunday?' He nodded at the herbal.

'Your son has inherited your fascination with the natural world.'

'Glad to hear it.' Father looked at Nicholas. 'What about the lute? Have you practised?'

Father had said that if he showed some promise, he would get him a music tutor. Though Father did not play himself, he seemed to have a knowledge of the instrument and had tried to teach Nicholas a few chords, encouraging him to sing along as he did so. Nicholas had so desperately wanted to impress his father he had practised until his fingers bled. But he did not have a natural aptitude for music or a good singing voice and Father soon lost interest in coaching him. Nicholas rarely touched the instrument now.

'I'm no good at it,' he said sadly.

'You have to stick at it if you want to improve.' There was an edge of impatience to Father's voice. 'You saw the Caldwells off all right?'

'Yes, sir.'

'Good lad.' Despite his words, Father looked unhappy. He turned to Matthew. 'You will have to lie low for a while, at least until this plot business is resolved and the general panic has calmed.'

'I was about to explain to Nicholas that I may have to disappear for a while. I have been in communication with a Catholic family who have got passes to go to France; they have said I may travel with them.'

'Why on earth would you do that? The ports are being searched and priests arrested. You're safer here — so long as you stop giving communion to every Tom, Dick or Nell that requests it.' Father's sunburnt cheeks looked redder than usual and his high-pitched voice had risen even higher. 'Have you consulted with Crewe?'

Father and Matthew both deferred to Crewe. He was more like a grandfather to Nicholas than a household retainer.

'Of course. It was Crewe who first made contact with them on my behalf.'

Nicholas rushed to Matthew's side, grabbing hold of his sleeve. 'Please, Cousin, let me go with you. I won't be a burden. I can be your groom or your servant and when I am fourteen you can send me to St. Omer's.'

Father jabbed his pipe in their direction. 'What nonsense have you been filling the boy's head with?'

Matthew looked reproachfully at Nicholas. 'I told you I would discuss this with your father. You are too impetuous. And I cannot possibly take you with me.'

Nicholas was so desperate to convince Matthew, he didn't care if he angered the two men. 'I can aid your disguise. We can pretend I am your son.'

'You will do no such thing,' Father snapped. 'You are my son and your place is here. I know how fond of learning you are and am going to great lengths to ensure your entry to one of the English universities.'

Matthew held his arms out to them both. 'Wherever Nicholas completes his education, I am sure he will do well.' He bowed slightly towards Father. 'In my opinion the learning at St. Omers is superior, but that is something we can contemplate later. For now, I believe it may be better for all of us if I go abroad.'

✦ Chapter Two ✦

It was Nicholas who saw them first. Pursuivants, riding five abreast, galloping down the lane that led to Measham Hall. A rider peeled off from either end of the phalanx, heading towards the east and west wings of the house.

'What has caught your mayfly mind now?' Matthew tapped on his desk.

'Soldiers.' Nicholas looked up at his cousin, his eyes round with fear.

Matthew turned to the window. 'Find your father. Warn him,' he said before running from the room.

Nicholas raced down the stairs, through the kitchen and out of the open back door, leaving their cook, Tickell, calling after him. He prayed Father would be on his way home for dinner and he could catch him before he entered the house. As he turned the corner of the walled garden, he collided with a leather-coated torso. His shoulders were grabbed roughly and he found himself staring up into the large, stubbly face of a soldier.

'Where're you off to in such a hurry?' The man's fingers pinched into his flesh.

'Cook needs some eggs.'

The man's lip curled with disbelief. His eyes roamed over Nicholas's fine linen shirt; it was clear he was no kitchen boy. Spinning him round, the soldier marched him back into the kitchen. Tickell dropped the rabbit he was skinning as they barged through the doorway.

'What did you send this boy for?'

Tickell was saved from answering by a thunderous hammering at the front door.

'Let's see who it is, shall we?' The soldier pushed Nicholas in front of him, one hand still clasped around his arm.

Three of the pursuivants stood on the front step. Crewe stepped around the terrified butler, Palmes, to confront them.

'You must have a warrant to enter this house.'

Nicholas was reassured by the steward's measured tone and calm expression. Crewe could handle anything; he always knew what to do.

The captain pulled a roll of parchment out of his jerkin, holding it aloft so that it fell open. Crewe slowly lifted the eye-glasses that hung on a chain around his neck, fixing them onto the bridge of his nose, before extending his hand to take the warrant. But the soldiers pushed past him into the hall.

'The room on the left, that's the one.' The captain pointed to the parlour.

Nicholas's stomach lurched. He felt as though all the blood in his body was draining away into his feet. How did they know where to look? He glanced at Crewe but the old man's face was still as a statue's, his eyes fixed on the opposite wall.

The soldiers, as eager as hounds on the scent of a fox, filled the room with the smell of sweat and mud and leather. It was then Nicholas remembered the chalice and vestments. Matthew's revelations the previous day had distracted him and he'd forgotten to put them back in the concealed step. He bit down on his lip; what were the chances they wouldn't open the window seat?

But the men had moved straight to the parlour walls. They were ripping off the tapestries and knocking on the wood panelling, listening for a tell-tale hollow ring. Nicholas thought of throwing himself to the floor and feigning a fit. Anything to create a diversion, to give his father time to return and Crewe to think up a solution.

One of the soldiers kicked the window seat. He stopped and kicked it again, then pulled the cushions off. Nicholas held his breath. The man felt around the ledge and pushed it up with a creak.

'What've we got here?' As he pulled out the vestments, the gold chalice and chrismatory tumbled out of the silk folds onto the floor.

'Papist trinkets,' the captain said with satisfaction. 'The devil's toys. Put them in the sack.' He nodded to one of his men, who held out a hemp bag.

Nicholas couldn't bring himself to look at Crewe. Instead, they both watched as the soldier dropped the family heirlooms carelessly into his sack.

'Found it!' The soldier who had apprehended Nicholas gave a cry of triumph as he revealed the small door set into the wainscoting by the fireplace.

'Where's the key?' the captain demanded as his men pressed on the wood frame.

'I have no idea,' Crewe said. 'I had forgotten that cupboard was there. It hasn't been used in years.'

Nicholas imagined Matthew curled up on the other side of the wall, praying.

'Cupboard my arse, it's a priest's hole.'

The captain gestured to one of his men and the soldier pulled a small axe from his belt and began to hack at the door, the wood splintering around the concealed lock. Nicholas clenched his fists, the blood drumming in his ears. What if they hacked right into Matthew? He hoped desperately that his cousin had chosen some other place to hide, that they'd find only an empty space.

Father came into the hall as the soldiers were leading Matthew out, his hands tied behind his back. Palmes had put an arm around Nicholas, who was squeezing every muscle in his body in the effort not to cry.

'What on earth are you doing with my cousin?' Father demanded.

'Watch we don't take you away as well. Harbouring a priest is an offence.'

'He's no priest.' Father sounded outraged.

But Matthew looked at Father with a resigned smile and shook his head. Nicholas was shocked to see Father's eyes fill with tears. He had never seen his father cry.

They watched as the soldiers rode off, Matthew slung over one of their horses.

'God help whoever betrayed us when I get my hands on them,' Father said as he pulled the door closed.

'He's being kept in the Cornmarket Gaol.'

Father had left for Derby at first light that morning in search of news about Matthew; now he came storming into the parlour as Nicholas and Crewe sat eating their supper together. The dogs, who had been lying watchfully beside the gate-legged table, leapt to their feet, their tails wagging. Crewe, rising more slowly, gave a stiff bow and Nicholas hastily followed suit.

'Were you able to see him, sir?' Crewe asked.

Father sank down onto a chair by the fire, gesturing for the others to resume their seats at the table. 'He was in better spirits than me. I took him food and ale. He said the gaolers have been respectful.'

'Well, that is good news, sir. We'll soon get him out of there.' Crewe's tone was reassuring. 'No one in Derbyshire will testify against him.'

Father reached for the glass of wine Palmes had set down beside him. 'Times have changed. The sheriff insisted I took the Oaths of Allegiance and of Supremacy to prove I'm not a secret Catholic.'

'And you took them, sir?' There was a faint note of reproach in Crewe's voice.

'Of course,' Father responded briskly. 'Do you want me imprisoned too? I had to convince them Matthew was only staying with us because he is a cousin. Now I have a pass to travel beyond five miles and they gave me back my sword and pistol.' He patted the scabbard at his side with satisfaction. But his face swiftly fell again. 'I only wish Matthew would take the oaths. The sheriff said he will be transferred to Newgate if they connect him to this so-called plot against the King.'

Crewe glanced at Nicholas. 'We can prove Matthew was here. He has never been anywhere near London. We will stand as witnesses.'

'They can still hang him for being a priest.' Father's voice was weary, resigned. He pulled his pipe and tobacco box out of his pocket, packing the clay bowl with the dried, brown leaves. 'They're not deporting priests anymore. They're all to be tried.'

Nicholas stared at his untouched food, his throat clogged with tears. It was all his fault the soldiers had found the family chalice and vestments and now they could be used as evidence against Matthew. Could they also be used to implicate Father? Athena, the older spaniel, came and rested her head on his knee. He fondled her silky ears, knowing she was only hoping for a scrap from his plate, but taking some comfort from her presence anyway.

'What I want to know is who told the pursuivants about the priest's hole?' Father downed the contents of his glass. 'You both said they knew exactly where to look.'

'Do you think it was the Caldwells?' Nicholas thought of Mrs Caldwell's rosy face framed with auburn curls.

'They didn't see the priest's hole. It is never opened in front of strangers,' Crewe reminded him. 'And besides, to inform on us they would have to admit what they were doing here.'

'Who does know of it?' Father refilled his glass from the decanter.

'Only ourselves.' Crewe gestured round the room.

Palmes and Crewe had been at Measham Hall since Father was a child. They were beyond suspicion. Even Nicholas had been ignorant of the hidden compartment until a few months ago, when soldiers had raided the house and Matthew had hidden, successfully that time.

Father inhaled sharply and pressed his fingers to his forehead. 'Jane knows. I alluded to it once. Perhaps she told her mother.'

'Jane wouldn't tell,' Nicholas said indignantly.

'Margaret Calverton is full of wiles. She'd know just how to pick such useful information out of her daughter.'

'But why would she?' Nicholas couldn't help asking, though he knew Crewe thought Father allowed him too much freedom.

'Lady Calverton has a hatred of papists and besides, she disapproves of her daughter's friendship with me.' Father fixed him with a sardonic glare, his eyebrows raised and his mouth twisted into a smile that more closely resembled a grimace.

Nicholas pushed a gristly lump of cold mutton to the edge of his plate then flicked it surreptitiously to the waiting dog. He had always longed for Father to marry Jane so that she might live with them always, but there were various impediments, her husband not being the least of them. Although Lord Sellwood had agreed to a separation, a divorce in the courts was out of the question. Nicholas wished his father would kill Sellwood, just as he had killed a man in a duel when he was a youth. Sellwood certainly deserved it; the man was a monster who had hurled Jane down the stairs, causing her to walk with a limp. To call him out would have been the honourable thing to do, but he feared his father had become something of a coward. Certainly, he was no longer brave, always hiding away in the country, hardly travelling beyond his own lands.

Crewe sighed. 'I did not know you had acquainted Lady Sellwood with Father Matthew's profession.'

'It was impossible to keep it from her with all the traffic to the house for Masses and whatnot.' Father studied the wine at the bottom of his glass, revolving it slowly. 'I can't believe she'd intentionally betray us.'

Nicholas was relieved when Crewe nodded in agreement.

'Lady Sellwood has always shown you great loyalty and proved herself discreet. Though it is possible her mother holds something over her.'

Father tapped his pipe out on the grate. 'Jane will never hear a word said against her parents, but I wouldn't put anything past them if it worked to their political advantage.'

'May I be excused, sir?'

At twelve years of age, Nicholas felt himself too old to give way to tears, but he couldn't bear to sit at the table and hear his beloved Jane disparaged. Father nodded brusquely at him.

As he climbed the stairs, he heard Crewe tell Father, 'It is hard on the lad.'

'We must prepare him for the worst,' Father replied.

Nicholas shuddered. They must find a way to free Matthew from gaol. He and Father could smuggle Matthew's sword in, along with their own arms. Matthew had taught him fencing and said he had a natural gift for it. Father too must be a good swordsman since he had won at least one duel. They could fight their way out and then flee abroad, just as Father had done when he was young.

As soon as Jane got news of Matthew's arrest, she came to Measham Hall. She and Father spent over an hour shut up in his chamber. Nicholas heard raised voices but couldn't make out what they were saying. He studied the collection of miniature wooden knights that were carefully arranged, mid-battle, on the chest beside his bed. Jane had given them to him. She always brought him gifts whenever she visited: spinning tops, sweetmeats, once a singing bird, but it had died. They would pass hours together playing games of cards, backgammon or goose. Sometimes Nicholas could even entice her into the garden for a game of bowls, though she was frail and not much given to outdoor sports.

When Jane was with him, he didn't mind the lack of a playmate so much. He loved her more than anyone else he knew, even more than Matthew, who had earnt his admiration but was a relative newcomer compared to Jane. He worked hard to make her smile and when the dimples appeared in her cheeks and her eyes shone, he felt all his efforts had been worthwhile.

He waited until he heard her uneven tread, accompanied by the familiar thump of her walking stick, pass his door and then ran out after her. She was sobbing quite openly.

'Oh Nicholas, your father won't believe me. I never breathed a word about your cousin, or the priest's hole, not to anyone.'

He threw his arms around her, just as he used to when he was a small boy, and she held him close, leaning her cheek upon his head. He inhaled her smell of geranium and rose-water.

'I believe you.'

She squeezed him tightly. 'I hope the real traitor will be discovered and my loyalty to you all proved.' She drew away from him, holding his face between her palms. 'You know that I love you as my own child and that my home will always be yours.' Her green eyes stared intently into his own. 'You are such a courageous boy. I know you will grow into a fine, noble-hearted man.'

Nicholas was dismayed by the finality of her words. 'I shall see you before then,' he insisted.

She gave him a small smile, her face regaining a little of its characteristic good humour. 'And in the meantime, keep at your lessons as your cousin would want you to. Don't neglect your French either, *mon petit chevalier.*'

Both Jane and Matthew spoke excellent French and had ensured between them that Nicholas was also proficient.

'*Oui, bien sûr.*' He managed to smile back at her.

'*Prends soin de ton papa; il aura besoin de toi.*'

Nicholas doubted his father needed anyone to look after him. 'I will walk you to your carriage.' He held his elbow out and Jane slipped her arm through his.

'I'll write to you; be sure to write back,' Jane said as he helped her up onto her seat, her footman standing stiffly by.

He watched as her carriage trundled away, the dogs bounding after it as far as the gates. When it was out of sight, he ran through the park with them, intending to go into the woods. Beyond the kitchen gardens, Abigail was taking advantage of the dry weather to air some bed-stuff. He stopped, hoping his old nursemaid might cheer him up. But she was as out of sorts as he was.

'It's just like your poor mother all over again.' She gave the coverlet she was holding an angry shake, releasing a cloud of dust. 'I'll never forget the day that carriage took her and little Robin away. Such a sweet chick. My honeycomb, I called him.'

Nicholas glanced around. If Father heard her speaking like that, he might finally send Abigail packing too, just as he was always threatening to do. But only a blackbird hopping about under the currant bushes observed them speculatively. The dogs lay on the grass, panting.

'I'd never been away from home afore I come here to look after Robin. I weren't much older than you are now and terrible homesick, but Robin always cheered me up with his winsome ways.' She pulled a pillowcase out of the basket at her feet and draped it over a lavender bush.

Nicholas had heard her reminiscences a thousand times before: his angelic half-brother, cast out with his mother when Nicholas was only a few months old. He was, as usual, torn between wanting to hear more and being heartily sick of the tale. He had tried quizzing both Matthew and Jane about his mother, but they just referred him to Father, who never told him anything.

All he knew was that his mother had been his father's waiting woman, a common widow Father brought back to Measham when he returned from his travels. Nicholas had spent his childhood longing for a sibling and wondering where his brother was. Had his mother remarried and produced more children? Did they miss him?

'Your mother were too quarrelsome, God bless her. Not with me, she were always kind to me, but she would cross Master and men don't like that, see, especially not in a mistress. A mistress is easily cast off, not like a wife.'

Nicholas wondered whether this was an allusion to Jane. He kicked at a tuft of grass. 'At least Jane said she'd write to me.'

'Your mother were heartbroken to leave you behind. She'd have taken you if she'd been allowed, and written too, for she knew her letters. Master must've forbidden it. She made me promise to nestle you like you were my own. And I always have, isn't that right?'

Nicholas considered the matter carefully. 'Jane is more tender,' he concluded.

Abigail harrumphed. 'She's a lady. I have other chores aside from you, young man.' She jerked her head at the linen spread over various shrubs. Then, looking earnestly into his eyes and lowering her voice, she continued. 'I don't believe Lady Sellwood informed on Father Matthew, not on purpose nohow. And it certainly weren't none of our household. We're all good Catholics here and respect God's servants as we should. Must've been one of them as comes here for Mass, tempted by that twenty-pound reward they're offering priest-catchers now.' She wrapped her broad arms around the laundry basket and hugged it to her bosom. 'I hope your father don't get into trouble. They burnt the Pope in effigy down in the village and it's after the fifth of November. Everyone's up in arms over this so-called plot. No matter if you always pay your tithes and abide by the law, being Catholic makes you a traitor in most people's minds.' She shuddered. 'I fear for us all.'

'We'll be all right because Father makes us go to church and take communion,' Nicholas reassured her, though he had started to question his father's conformity. He couldn't help but think Matthew was the braver man for refusing to renounce their religion or take the Oath of Allegiance, even if it would save his life.

'Your father keeps you safe. He only wants what's best for you.' She might speak with outrage about his treatment of Nicholas's mother, but Abigail would never hear a word said against her master by anyone else.

On 30th November, news reached them that the Duke of York's own secretary, Mr Coleman, had been found guilty of high treason and was to be executed at Tyburn.

'It took the jury less than fifteen minutes to reach a verdict,' Father read out from the newsletter as they sat over their dinner.

'God rest his soul.' Crewe crossed himself.

Since Matthew's arrest, Father had invited Crewe to eat with them. He seemed to take comfort from the familiar presence. Or perhaps it was just that he couldn't bear to be faced with Matthew's empty chair.

Abigail fretted that the master would lose the respect of the other servants by making too much of the old man. Sir William had picked up some odd notions of equalness on his travels, she said, or perhaps they came from Nicholas's mother, who'd belonged to one of them sects, like Quakers or some such.

Nicholas had been stretching across the table to take another ball of veal. Tickell had made extra, knowing how he loved them, but now he laid his spoon down beside his plate. He thought of what Matthew had said about the Duke of York being next in line for the throne and people being scared he would make England Catholic again. Surely they wouldn't dare act against the King's own brother?

'And now a proclamation has been issued offering a reward of two hundred pounds for any information that leads to further prosecutions in the horrid plot,' Father continued. 'That's just asking for every lying rogue with a tongue in his head to come forward.'

'Many Catholic families are fleeing the country, those that can get passes anyhow,' Crewe said. 'If you were so inclined, sir, I'm sure we could find a way of obtaining passes for you.'

'You're not suggesting we abandon Matthew?' Father looked outraged.

'I wouldn't dream of it, sir. Only, it occurs to me that it would comfort Father Matthew greatly to know you and the boy are safe. If he is accused of treason he will not be allowed a defence or witnesses on oath. And then, having no influence in parliament, how will your presence here help him?'

'I could call on Sir Henry Calverton.'

Crewe nodded thoughtfully. 'My associates in London tell me that anyone who expresses so much as a hint of doubt about the Popish Plot is accused of being a traitor. It has become an article of belief no one dare deny. Sadly, I think it unlikely Lord Calverton will prove an ally.'

'I have no friends abroad nor the means to live well there. Where would I go?' Father shifted uncomfortably in his seat. 'And what will become of our household if I desert it?'

They both looked at Nicholas, whose cheeks were bulging with a huge mouthful of bread and trout. He couldn't help it if he got very hungry. Tickell said he must have hollow legs. Abigail said he was growing and would be a fine young fellow someday.

Crewe cleared his throat. 'The boy could be sent to the school in Watten, in preparation for St. Omers college. As Father Matthew always says, there is no better education than that offered by the Jesuits.'

'I don't want my only son turning to the priesthood,' Father said hotly, though they all knew that bastards couldn't become priests. 'Besides, he might drown on the voyage over or sicken from foreign diseases.' He tapped his knife against his plate. 'No, he is much safer here. The parson has vouched for us as Protestants.'

Nicholas was torn between his longing to see new places and his desire to stay close to Matthew. 'Our cousin said St. Omers is renowned for its teaching of natural philosophy. I won't be tempted by the religious life, Father. It's the sciences of the natural world, not the spiritual, that interest me.'

'How can you possibly know that now? Matthew didn't discover his vocation until he was twenty-two. And he entered the college as a young man. You would be going as an impressionable boy.' A look of anxiety crossed suddenly over Father's face. He turned to Crewe. 'The devil behind this plot business, Titus Oates, he claims to have attended St. Omers as an older student. Could he have encountered Matthew there?'

Crewe shook his head. 'Oates was there less than a year ago, sir. I heard that he behaved obscenely and was expelled. The students all hated him. How he inveigled his way in I do not understand; he was far too old to be amongst boys. He had already been thrown out of the college at Valladolid for his mischief-making. Before that he had two counts of perjury levelled against him for falsely accusing a schoolmaster in Hastings of...' Crewe paused, then silently mouthed something at Father. 'And now this fabulist is housed in Whitehall and hailed as the hero and saviour of England,' he concluded with great indignation.

'It is no wonder the people believe his lies when the greatest powers in the land are so eager to swallow them,' Father conceded, pushing his plate away and lighting his pipe.

Part I: Boy

Nicholas wondered what Oates had accused the schoolmaster of that was so terrible it could not be named. But Crewe's expression was impenetrable to him. The old man had ears and eyes everywhere. If he wasn't so pious, Nicholas might have thought him a magician. Matthew had told him the Jesuits had the best network of information in the world, after Crewe.

'Oates is clearly out to line his pockets, and you can be sure he has the backing of the Earl of Shaftesbury.' Crewe sighed. 'It is unfortunate that several priests are using the name Harcourt. Especially since it is the true name of the Father Provincial who expelled Oates and now lies imprisoned with several others in Newgate.' He removed his spectacles and pinched the bridge of his nose as if to relieve an ache. 'Though he goes by the name of Whitbread.'

Nicholas recognised the name. Jasper, the stableboy, had shown him a pamphlet where it was written that Father Whitbread had lashed his accomplice across the arse with a cat-o'-nine-tails as punishment for failing to kill the King. Jasper couldn't read, but he had pressed his blackened fingernail against the illustration of Father Pickering with his breeches round his knees, bending over a bed while Whitbread whipped his raised round buttocks. Each cheek was delineated by a thick black line, making his bum look like a pair of sweet apples, and the eye couldn't help but be drawn to them. Judging by the smudges, the page had passed through many hands.

Jasper had sniggered, 'They say them priests are all buggerantoes.'

Nicholas wasn't sure what a 'buggeranto' was, but thought better of mentioning it to his father or Crewe.

'We have to pray Father Matthew can convince the authorities he is not the Harcourt they seek,' Crewe was saying.

Father gave a snort of exasperation. 'Damme, why did he have to pick such a well-worn alias? I could have come up with a better one for him.'

Though his eyebrows rose, Crewe's voice remained mild. 'I understand the widespread use of the same name can be helpful in

21

putting warrant officers off the scent of an individual, sir. It sows much confusion amongst the pursuivants.'

'Confusing for everyone else too,' Father muttered.

Nicholas could no longer contain himself. 'Why can't we help Matthew to escape? Can't we give the gaoler something to set him free?' He swallowed. 'I could give him Polestar.' Nicholas's horse was the most valuable thing he owned and though he'd hate to part with him, he'd do it for Matthew.

Father looked at him with unexpected affection. 'It's not so easy as that, son. Don't you think we haven't tried?'

'While he is kept in the county, we still have a good chance of getting him released,' Crewe repeated firmly, as much to himself as to the assembled company. 'No one in Derbyshire will testify against him.'

→ Chapter Three ←

December 1678

Nicholas begged to be allowed to accompany Father on his next visit to Matthew.

Father shook his head. 'Derby is eighteen miles away and it's a bad time of year for travel. You've never ridden that far before and neither has Polestar.'

The best present Nicholas had ever received was the bay gelding bred from his aunt Alethea's old mare, Bella Donna. Polestar was named after the white star on his forehead, which Father said was a sign of excellence. Nicholas was devoted to the horse, making sure he had fresh rye-straw each night, mixing honey into his oats and giving him bay-salt and fenugreek to lick. Polestar was equally fond of his young master and had grown into a sleek, well-tempered, fast-paced animal.

'I've been exercising Polestar every day. You can ask John Thornly. He said what a fine horse Polestar is now and he was impressed by how well I ride.'

Father worked closely with their bailiff, John Thornly, on the management of the Measham land and its livestock, often deferring to Thornly's opinions. Nicholas hoped Thornly's praise might convince Father to let him go.

Eventually, somewhat to his surprise, Father agreed, though he said they would have to stop for the night in Derby. Nicholas was delighted. This would be his first proper excursion away from Measham Hall. If only the reason for it wasn't so terrible, it would have been a welcome adventure.

They set off at sunrise. The grass glittered and crunched under its coating of frost and the air was crisp and still, disturbed only by the steam from their horses' nostrils. A pale moon loitered in the sky. The sun glowed back, a fierce white through the pillows of grey cloud. It was a long time since they had ridden out together, though Father had taught him how to ride and Nicholas's earliest memories were of sitting in front of his father on a horse.

After a couple of miles they passed Ashby Place. Behind it lay the old castle of Ashby-de-la-Zouch, which had started off as a royalist stronghold but surrendered to the Roundheads in 1646. Its fortifications had all been destroyed. Nicholas's own grandfather had been briefly imprisoned there before escaping abroad and Father said the late, martyred King had visited twice. Nicholas sometimes snuck into the grounds, he liked especially an area known as the 'wilderness', though the old deer parks had also become pleasantly overgrown. Jane's family were friendly with Lord Hastings, the owner, and he thought he could use her name if ever he was caught trespassing. But he didn't tell Father this.

Near Calke, they stopped for a rest. Everywhere the country rolled gently away beneath great open skies. Only the stark winter outlines of oaks and ashes interrupted the soft gradations of brown earth and golden grass that lay before them.

'Isn't it beautiful?' Father said. 'We're lucky it's such a fine day.'

Nicholas found the wide prospects invigorating, but the carefully tended, hedged-in fields only whetted his appetite for grander vistas and more exotic landscapes.

'One day, can we keep going up to the Peaks? Crewe says the land is rugged and wild up there.'

'Maybe.' Father found a smooth rock to sit on and took out his tinderbox and pipe. 'There's always so much to do at Measham, it's hard to find the time to go travelling.'

'You could leave Thornly in charge of the land and Crewe would look after the hall. If you wanted to go away, that is.'

Father drew on his pipe. 'I know I must seem like an old sit-fast to you, but one day you'll realise it isn't always necessary to go to foreign places to make fresh discoveries.' He smiled as he nodded at their surroundings. 'Every season at Measham reveals something new. The more I make a study of the land, the more I learn. Of course, I understand your yearning for adventure; that's only natural in a boy.' He loosened the knot of his cravat. 'But the truth is, as my only son and heir, your life is especially precious. You need to be conscious always of the role you have been born into, one I have fought hard to keep for you, as the future protector of Measham Hall. You are the guardian of our name and our estate. It is an honour as well as a duty.'

Nicholas wished he could feel as fortunate and enthusiastic as Father seemed to expect. Maybe it was his bastard's blood that yearned to be free of such responsibilities, but every word Father spoke felt like another rock placed upon his back.

'There's a lot of rot in England,' Father continued, his voice taking on a note of bitterness. 'A lot of tub-brained people fearful of anyone who isn't just like them. It sickens me how they lap up every lie Titus Oates tosses them, hailing him as their saviour when it's so obvious what a false prophet he is. His evidence has more holes than a colander and yet the mighty of the land, not just the common rabble, but educated men, are only too eager to believe him. They claim Catholics are growing in numbers and wealth, none of it true. We're no more of a threat to them than dormice hiding away in their nests.'

'Maybe it would be better for us to go abroad, like Crewe said,' Nicholas suggested hopefully.

Father sighed. 'I'm not sure it'd be any better elsewhere. Every country has its mountebanks and their attendant fools. I suppose I've always been a homebird. I never really wanted to leave Measham, even when I was young. Frances, my stepmother, couldn't understand it. She was always on at your grandfather to take her to London.'

'So, you only went abroad because you had to, because of the duel?'

Nicholas watched Father carefully. He never spoke about killing his friend and being exiled – Nicholas had only heard about it from Abigail – but since Father was in an unusually loquacious humour, he thought now might be the time to ask.

'That's right,' Father said brusquely. He studied the woods in the distance, a frown creasing his fine features. 'It's frustrating hearing only bits of stories – I do recall that from when I was young. But sometimes there's a sound reason why you can't be informed of everything. You've an enquiring mind, which is all to the good. Use it for your lessons, not idle curiosity.'

Nicholas was stung by the injustice of this accusation. It was not as if he were some distant relative or prying acquaintance. When so much was expected of him, surely he needed to be well-informed.

Father ruffled his hair. 'You're a good boy and I'm lucky to have you as my son. I don't want you to waste your time hankering after what you can't have, that's all.'

Mollified by this rare compliment, Nicholas remounted his horse in better heart.

A couple of hours later, they were riding over the River Trent across the famous Swarkestone Bridge, which Father told him was the longest of its kind in all of England.

'Watch out for ghosts,' Father said, laughing as Nicholas twisted anxiously round on his saddle. 'They say the causeway was built by two sisters after their lovers drowned trying to cross the river to reach them. The expense bankrupted the sisters and they died in penury. I suppose they want to get their money's worth by haunting the causey for all eternity.'

Nicholas thought it a foolish story. It was more exciting to see the great tower of All Saints church rising up out of the town. He had never seen so many grand houses collected together before. Polestar was not as keen and had to be coaxed along the urban streets. The horse was startled by an approaching carriage and Nicholas had to dismount and lead him by the reins. Father followed suit and they walked companionably side by side until they reached the stables of The Bull's Head, where they had taken rooms.

The inn was larger than The Barley Mow in Measham, its interior dark and cavernous, with tables set back in various alcoves and fires burning in two grates. The smell of beer and men was the same, only stronger.

'Is the occupant of the second chamber coming later?' the innkeeper asked.

'No, no, we're taking a room each,' Father said gruffly, nodding at Nicholas.

'I can put the lad in with my serving-boy if you want,' the innkeeper offered.

To Nicholas's relief, Father said they were both accustomed to sleep alone and would keep the two rooms. The innkeeper raised his eyebrows at such extravagance.

Nicholas was surprised Father was willing to pay the extra; he was usually so careful with money, grumbling when Matthew ordered books to be sent from London or Amsterdam, or when Jane insisted that Nicholas needed new clothes. He wasn't going to complain, however. Despite its austerity, he surveyed his little room with satisfaction. The view from the narrow window was pleasingly different to the greenery he was used to seeing. A variety of roofs jutted out over a narrow lane. Instead of baaing sheep and birdsong, he could hear traders calling out their wares and the town crier shouting that it was twelve o'clock.

His stomach rumbled. He wondered if the food would be different to the sort Tickell cooked. Being covered in mud from the journey, he brushed what he could from his clothes and washed his face before hurrying downstairs for his dinner.

Taking his place beside Father at a roughly scrubbed table, Nicholas was a little disappointed to be given only brown bread, slices of beef and a bowl of pottage. At least the pottage was well seasoned and included a good mix of oatmeal, vegetables and herbs.

'We must buy some supplies for Matthew on our way to the gaol,' Father said. 'I hope they've been feeding him adequately. Last time I saw him he had lost weight and was looking poorly.'

Nicholas immediately felt guilty for thinking only of his own belly. He had been too engrossed in his new surroundings and had let Matthew slip from his mind.

It was a short walk to the marketplace, where there were more shops and stalls than Nicholas had ever seen before. He tried not to get distracted by the variety of wares and to focus instead on the task in hand. They filled a basket with loaves of barley and wheat bread, a thick wedge of green-veined sage cheese, tender slices of gammon and half a dozen sweet Pippins, their peel only slightly wrinkled. Father carried a flagon of ale bought from the innkeeper. The gaol, on the Cornmarket, was close by, which was just as well given all they had to carry. The handle of the wicker basket dug uncomfortably into Nicholas's arm and when Father decided at the last minute to add a jar of honey, he staggered under the weight.

Despite Father's warning, Matthew's gaunt appearance came as a shock. His skin had an unhealthy yellow tinge and there were blue circles under his eyes, which seemed to have sunk into his face. Nicholas set their basket of food down on the floor and rushed to embrace him. The cloak Matthew had wrapped around himself felt damp against Nicholas's cheek and smelt of mould. Next time they must bring him more blankets and a new wool cloak. The few embers left in the fireplace did little to take the chill off the room. Father busied himself in rebuilding the fire with the kindling he had brought.

'Welcome to my hermit's cell.' Matthew stroked Nicholas's hair with a hand so light it was like having the top of his head brushed gently by a bird's wing.

They all ignored the gaoler who stood just inside the door, watching them.

Father turned from the grate and asked sadly, 'Won't you take the oaths, Cousin?'

Matthew only smiled, his skin pulled tight over his jutting cheek-bones. 'Would you have me renounce my faith and all that I have worked for? What is a little suffering in this life compared to eternal anguish in the next one?'

'Many Catholics, and even some priests, are taking the oath of allegiance. Surely it's better to save your life and continue your mission,' Father insisted, ignoring Matthew's pained expression.

'You are my dearest friend and yet you know me not.' Matthew's sonorous voice was filled with sorrow. 'What kind of example would I be if I relinquished my vows at the first sign of danger?' He sighed. 'Even if I took the oath, it would not be enough. They are pushing me to confess to being part of this plot against the King, of which we all know I am innocent.'

The three of them glanced at the gaoler. His eyes were fixed on the small, barred window, which gave a glimpse of the street above. Nicholas hoped the coins Father had slipped him for Matthew's care would also buy his discretion.

'Apparently the authorities are desperately trying to track down another Harcourt who is implicated in the plot. They have already arrested two; one, a Valentine Harcourt, has just been sent back to Shrewsbury from London, or so the informative Mr Cowper, our good constable, tells me. Their determination to prove a conspiracy is leading them on a merry dance.' Matthew chuckled, but Father refused to be comforted. Matthew reached out and grasped his hands. 'Before I left the seminary in Valladolid, the Father Provincial read to us our Saviour's words to his disciples. "Are ye able to drink of the cup that I shall drink of?" I answered without hesitation that I was. "Are you ready to face persecution and calumny? To be reviled and hated?" he questioned us.' Matthew paused to inhale heavily, as though each breath came with effort. Nicholas could hear the phlegm rattling in his chest. 'I am now, as I was then, content to endure an ignominious death for the love of Jesus. To throw myself cheerfully into the arms of He whose own arms were stretched out on the cross for my redemption.'

Nicholas gazed at his cousin in awe and vowed never to cry out over a bruised knee or a cut finger again. He remembered how self-pitying he had been when last he had a fever and felt ashamed. To think he had grumbled about carrying a heavy basket. What a churl he was.

Father was not so impressed by Matthew's stoicism, however. Pulling his hands away from Matthew's, he paced up and down the small cell. 'These grandiose ideas of martyrdom are all very well, but where does that leave the rest of us? Those of us who love and rely on you and do not wish to sacrifice all for an ideal?'

'First and foremost, you must trust in the Lord, and after that you must love and rely on each other.' Matthew gestured towards them both. 'But remember what we have discussed previously.' He lowered his voice. 'There is no sin in you and the boy taking Anglican communion. I have been assured you have nothing to fear from the authorities.'

Nicholas and his father returned to The Bull's Head in silence, both absorbed in their own melancholy thoughts. It was already dark and Nicholas trod carefully, trying to avoid the piles of muck in the middle of the road and the streams of effluent at its edges. The marketplace was empty now, the stalls shut up and the people gone. Only a few dogs sniffed about in the refuse for scraps of food. The place stank of rotten cabbage and stale meat.

He did not want to be a coward when Matthew was so brave, but Nicholas couldn't help shuddering as the image of Matthew on the scaffold forced itself onto his mind's eye. Matthew being cut down from the hangman's noose, still breathing, and then disembowelled. His manhood cut off and displayed. His body hacked to pieces. Such violations could not be inflicted on one so refined, so gracious as his cousin, they just couldn't.

Before going inside with Father, he went to check on the horses, anxious to make sure they had been fed properly. Jasper had warned him that innkeepers often gave horses mash made from old beans and stale bread, which could make them pursy.

The stables had the comfortingly familiar smell of hay and manure. Putting his arms around Polestar's neck, he rubbed his cheek against the horse's downy coat, grateful for the warmth that rose up from the animal's body. Polestar dropped his head onto Nicholas's shoulder and nibbled on a lock of his hair.

When he finally left the stables and crossed the courtyard behind the inn, Nicholas spotted a figure through the archway that led onto the street. A portly gentleman was shouting at the footman who was struggling to help him into his carriage. Lanterns attached to the roof bobbed and swayed as the vehicle shook under its passenger's weight. The footman, clearly reluctant to manhandle his master, stood to one side, holding the door open with one hand and supporting his master's elbow with the other.

'Make an effort. Would you have me fall on my arse, you witless poltroon.'

Nicholas recognised the voice. It was his great-uncle Percy, he was sure of it. He ran stealthily to the shadow in the lee of the arch. He did not want Percy to spot him, for that would only mean a tongue-lashing for himself as well as the poor footman.

Uncle Percy had invited himself to Measham Hall on a couple of occasions, turning up without warning and making his disapproval of both Nicholas and Father very clear. Father did his best to avoid him, but on his last visit Nicholas had overheard Percy exhorting Father to marry and get himself a legitimate heir. Uncle Percy lived only a few miles north of Measham Hall, so what was he doing in Derby?

Leaving the footman to deal with his uncle, Nicholas slipped through the back door to the inn and went upstairs. He encountered Father on the landing outside his room. Pipe smoke hung about his face like a veil.

'Let's get something to eat, shall we?' Father asked, removing the pipe from his mouth for a moment.

Just as he had done for dinner, Father selected a table in the darkest, dingiest corner of the dining room. He ordered a bottle of sack for himself and a small beer for Nicholas.

To Nicholas's disappointment, supper, when it arrived, consisted of further slices of roast beef, only cold this time and served with mustard.

'Did Uncle Percy come to see you?' he asked.

Father looked at him with surprise. 'When?'

'Here, just now. I saw him in the street.'

'Are you sure?'

Nicholas nodded. 'And his crest was on the carriage.' He grabbed an oatcake from the small basket placed in the centre of the table. They were still warm from the frying pan, the batter light and soft. 'Maybe he's going to see Cousin Matthew too.'

'Percy doesn't know about Matthew,' Father said quietly.

'About him being arrested?'

'No, about him living with us at Measham. The man's a blabber, we'd never risk him finding out.' Father gulped a large mouthful of wine, half-emptying his glass.

Nicholas wondered if Father would object to his taking the last oatcake. 'But he met Matthew last time he came to visit.'

Father looked at him as though he was mad 'What are you talking about? Percy hasn't been to Measham in years. I'm surprised you even recognised him.'

'It was only two years ago,' Nicholas said indignantly. 'I was ten.' He remembered this well because it was a few weeks after the birthday when he was given Polestar. 'Cousin Matthew told me to go to my room. He said he would talk to my uncle.' Nicholas slipped the last oatcake onto his plate.

Father had gone deathly pale. 'Matthew spoke to him?'

'Yes.' Nicholas wondered if his father was ill. 'But you must have been there too for I heard you talking to him as well.' Nicholas swallowed. Now he had given away the fact that he had been eavesdropping.

Father poured himself more wine. 'What did I say?' He spoke softly, but there was an edge to his voice.

Nicholas wished he'd never told him about seeing Percy. They had been getting on so well and now Father might not want to bring him on any other trips. But how could Father have forgotten Percy's visit? Was this some sort of test? He took a mouthful of beer to wash down the lump of oatcake that had lodged itself in his throat.

'Can you recall what I said?' Father persisted. 'How did you know it was me and not Matthew speaking?'

Father's and Matthew's voices were similar, though Father's was a little higher in tone. 'Because it was about me, "your son".' Nicholas's cheeks were burning. 'Uncle Percy said I couldn't inherit Measham Hall.' He looked down at the crumbs that had fallen into his lap. 'Because I have base blood. He called me *filius nullius*, a child of no one.'

'That is rubbish. If anything, you are *filius populi*.' Father sounded proud of this, and Nicholas wondered if it was because he had remembered the Latin or because he considered it a good thing to be a child of the people. Father's tone softened. 'Remind me, how did I respond?'

'You said I had all the makings of a noble gentleman.' It felt strange to recount these compliments back to his father. 'You said I would prove myself worthy of the Hawthorne name and that Percy should forget any notions he had about getting the estate for himself.' Nicholas scrunched up his eyes, wanting to impress his father with his accurate memory. 'You have made several cast-iron indentures to your will and I am guaranteed to inherit Measham Hall and all your lands.'

To his astonishment, Father chuckled. 'Well, that was well said,' he noted with satisfaction.

Nicholas was conscious of the fact that his father drank more than anyone else in their household. Perhaps all the wine was causing him to lose his memory. After all, according to his Latin grammar, '*vinum memoriae mors* – wine is the death of memory'. It was a shame Father had not been a better scholar for he seemed to have forgotten most of his Latin. Matthew sometimes suggested he join them in the schoolroom to learn alongside Nicholas, but Father always refused. Father was not keen on book learning, not for himself anyhow.

'Don't you remember how angry Uncle Percy was?' Nicholas asked tentatively. 'He marched out shouting that it wasn't the last you'd hear about it.' This was especially vivid in his memory because he'd had to duck quickly behind a cabinet as Percy stomped out of the parlour, slamming the door behind him. A notion suddenly occurred to him. 'Uncle Percy grew up in Measham Hall, didn't he?'

'He certainly did, and won't let anyone forget it.' Father nodded.

'Might he be the one who told the soldiers where the priest-hole is?'

Father leant back in his chair. 'Percy is the most devout Catholic I know. He wouldn't inform on a priest; he'd be too frightened of being damned. Besides, Percy doesn't know we keep a chaplain.'

'But isn't Matthew Uncle Percy's cousin also? Doesn't he know about his calling?'

Father shook his head vigorously. 'We wouldn't trust him with that information.' He chewed slowly on a piece of beef. 'It must be a coincidence. Percy is probably in town on business. One of his many legal pursuits, perhaps. I doubt he even remembers the priest-hole's existence.'

Nicholas said nothing. He still thought it was more likely to have been Percy than Jane who'd informed on them.

The next morning, they stopped at a baker's to buy hot, sweet buns for Matthew's breakfast. As soon as he saw his cousin, Nicholas felt guilty for the comfortable night he had spent in the soft feather bed at the inn. Matthew didn't look as if he'd slept at all.

It had rained in the night and there were puddles on the floor beneath the window. The chamber smelt of damp and urine. A mouse scuttled across the cold flagstones.

'My companion,' Matthew said. 'I call him Daniel.'

'Perhaps we should get you a cat,' Father said dryly. 'For want of a lion.'

'I would like Nicholas to have my sword. Make sure he has fencing lessons.' There was an uncharacteristic urgency to Matthew's voice. 'Every gentleman must acquire the art of defence.'

He had been teaching Nicholas how to fight and was surprisingly good at it for a priest; boxing, wrestling and sword-play, they had practised them all, much to Nicholas's delight. Father never indulged in such sport with him. Sometimes Nicholas thought Matthew might have been able to escape the soldiers if Father had brought weapons for them to fight with. Crewe was old, but he couldn't see why Matthew and Father had surrendered so easily, even if they had been outnumbered. He could have helped them and would have fought like a lion, even if he was only a boy.

'He would do better to learn how to use his wits. Engaging in combat rarely achieves a desired outcome.'

'True, but it is a useful skill to have in reserve.' Matthew sat on the edge of his narrow bed, gazing up at Father with weary eyes. 'Please, Cousin.'

Father nodded sadly. 'As you wish.'

He generally acceded to Matthew's demands and Nicholas was especially glad he had assented to this one.

They parted from Matthew with prayers on both sides and promises to return soon.

On 17th December, five men, including Whitbread, the Jesuit Provincial, went on trial for conspiring to kill the King. Three of them were found guilty and sentenced to death. Whitbread and another Jesuit, Father Fenwick, were sent back to prison until more proof of their guilt could be found. Matthew remained in prison in Derby. The family's only comfort was that he had not been sent to the capital.

Father was as good as his word and arranged for Nicholas to have instruction in the art of defence from a retired army captain in Ashby. The man was rough and, Nicholas considered, unnecessarily violent. He would return home covered in bruises, which he concealed from Father in case he decided the lessons should cease.

Nicholas was determined to become as expert and noble a fighter as any knight of old or ancient warrior. Then, when he went out to discover new lands, he would be prepared for the most perilous of adventures. For Nicholas could not give up on his dreams of travel, not for some needless apprehensions of Father's. He was as likely to die at home as abroad and he would make a much better custodian of Measham Hall once he had gained some experience of how things were done in other places.

Christmas came and went. It was a sad affair with the household in a state of great anxiety for both themselves and Matthew. There were further trials and executions of those accused of involvement in the plot. When the five Catholic peers who were being held in the Tower were taken to Westminster to enter their pleas, the boats carrying them were almost overturned by a furious crowd brandishing nooses and shouting insults.

'And the lords all elderly men,' Crewe said, shaking his head.

More priests were executed in London, including another who went by the name of Harcourt. But still Matthew was kept in Derby gaol. Nicholas went to see him regularly with his father and though Matthew's health continued to decline, his spirit remained resolute.

It was these visits that kept Nicholas at his studies. Matthew, despite his frailty, would quiz him on what he had learnt, conversing with him in Latin and French and setting him work to complete. Father said there was no need to send Nicholas to school or to find him another tutor since Matthew was still able to teach him.

Just as the trees came into blossom and the earth began to reveal some of its buried treasures, decorating the verges and hedgerows with golden celandine and pale primroses, they heard that Matthew had been indicted and his trial set for the assizes in July.

'At least the waiting will be over,' Father said, though he sounded far from relieved.

'Cousin Matthew is so skilled at rhetoric and logic, he'll be able to convince the court of his innocence,' Nicholas declared confidently.

'Have you read the newsletters? The country is baying for the blood of papists. The King has had to send his own brother into exile. To accuse a man of being a priest is enough to have him hanged.' Father stomped off outdoors. He was rarely to be seen inside the house now.

Nicholas hung his head in shame. Of course, it didn't matter what Matthew said; they had the vestments and chalice for evidence.

'No Derbyshire jury will sentence your cousin to hang.' Crewe placed a hand on his shoulder. 'And they'll be hard put to find witnesses to testify against him, I guarantee it. Several of our Protestant neighbours have expressed their consternation to me at the numbers being executed. They are impressed that so many have gone to their graves insisting on their innocence, when admitting their complicity and naming others could have saved their lives. The tide in the country is turning. It is only the London mobs that continue to be stirred up. The city has always been a hornets' nest; it doesn't take much to set them buzzing.'

Nicholas was comforted by Crewe's assurance. God would not abandon such a virtuous son nor would he deprive them of their spiritual guide and beloved kinsman. He would redouble his prayers to make sure God knew just how much Matthew was still needed on earth.

✦ Chapter Four ✦

July 1679

The day before the trial, Nicholas and his father rode up to Derby. Before they left Measham Hall, Crewe pressed a small parcel into Nicholas's hands.

'A notebook and pencils of black lead. Since I cannot go myself, you must be my eyes and ears. Write down as much as you can of what is said during the trial and most importantly, any speeches of Cousin Matthew's.' His hands trembled and Nicholas saw him suddenly for the old man that he was. Anxiety for Matthew had aged him.

The courthouse was on the far side of town opposite St. Mary's Gate. They stabled their horses before walking over to it. It was set back from the street behind a large courtyard, and both Nicholas and Father slowed their pace as they approached the place where Matthew was to be tried. Though only one storey high, it was an imposing stone building topped with a rail of balusters. Elaborately carved scrolls looped around two enormous black doors. Nicholas felt his belly contract and he almost reached for Father's hand as though he were a small boy. He swallowed down the rising nausea, reminding himself of Crewe's confidence and Matthew's fortitude. He would not disappoint them.

Being the first to arrive, they seated themselves at the front of the gallery. Though Nicholas couldn't understand why Father insisted on sitting at the far end, in the shadows, instead of in the centre with a clear view of the proceedings below.

'You sit in the middle and catch fleas if you wish,' Father said irritably when Nicholas objected. 'I shall remain here.'

Nicholas held up his notebook. 'I need to record everything for Mr Crewe,' he said by way of justification as he slid along the bench.

The gallery was soon full and Nicholas had to jostle for elbow room in order to write. A large, high-smelling woman squeezed herself in beside him. 'Are you an apprentice to one of the newsletters?' she asked with some excitement.

'I am observing proceedings for a private gentleman,' Nicholas replied mysteriously.

'And who might that be?' Her basket dug into his ribs.

'I am not at liberty to say.'

The woman raised her eyebrows, staring down at him with some suspicion, but Nicholas was distracted by a procession of judges, flanked by constables, entering the courtroom. His heart thumped painfully in his chest as he took in the faces of the men below. None of them looked amiable, but he supposed judges were bound to appear stern.

Once the judges were seated, Matthew was brought into the courtroom. Nicholas leant forward, gripping onto the rail, his hands slippery on the cold metal. He just stopped himself from calling out to his cousin. Matthew looked so lean and frail compared to the robust men surrounding him and Nicholas was dismayed to see that he was limping. Still, he managed to carry himself with his customary dignity.

'Hold up your hand,' a small man with a squeaking voice demanded.

'That's the clerk of the court.' The woman nudged Nicholas. She was clearly a regular spectator.

Matthew raised his right hand and though it trembled, kept it raised as the charges against him were read out. These were long and involved many dates, which Nicholas had difficulty in following, but he got down the final words of the convoluted speech.

'How sayest thou, Matthew Harcourt, art thou guilty of this High Treason whereof thou standest indicted, or not guilty?

39

'Not guilty.' Despite his physical infirmity, Matthew's voice rang out clear and resolute.

'How wilt thou be tried?'

'By God and my country,' Matthew answered.

The twelve jurymen were brought in next. Nicholas watched them carefully. None of them seemed pleased to be there. Farmers and yeomen taken away from their flocks and herds, craftsmen whose work had been interrupted, they looked about them uneasily as though fearing they too might end up in the dock.

'Their Honours had three of the jurors changed on account of them being popishly affected,' his neighbour said with satisfaction. 'And see that one on the end there?' She pointed to an ashy-faced man leaning against the side of the jury box as if unable to sit up straight. 'That's Mr Dowds, the cobbler. He's been kept in gaol these last two days to make him lose some nice scruples he had about condemning men for being priests.'

'You are very well informed, ma'am.'

'I'm the constable's wife,' she said proudly.

Despair washed over Nicholas. How could this be a fair trial when they had made sure none of the jurors would risk appearing sympathetic to Matthew?

One of the judges, a broad-shouldered man in a scarlet robe, rose from his chair to stand with his feet planted wide apart, surveying his audience. He looked very pleased with himself, Nicholas thought.

The constable's wife nudged Nicholas again. 'Sir Charles Bullrich,' she whispered. 'Up from London.'

'May it please Your Lords and you, gentlemen of the jury, Matthew Harcourt, the prisoner at the bar, stands indicted for high treason. The offence is not for being a priest only, but that he, being born an Englishman within the King's dominions and having received orders from Rome, did, against the laws of the kingdom, come and abide here.' Sir Charles pointed from Matthew to the ground before him, his voice rising with increasing indignation. 'The indictment is grounded upon the Statute of the 27th Elizabeth, a statute made almost a hundred years since. The leniency of our princes has let this statute lie asleep, but the current times have called for it to be awakened and applied.' He turned to the jury. 'Now we shall prove that this Harcourt hath taken orders from the See of Rome and then we doubt not but you will take that care for the preservation of the government and for the peace and quiet of the nation and give a verdict according as your evidence shall lead you.'

The jury gazed back at him with earnest faces, like schoolchildren wanting to impress their master.

The first witness brought against Matthew was a young man with yellow hair and watery, bloodshot eyes, who stared wildly about him. Nicholas had never seen him before. He wished he were sitting next to Father now so that they could confer. The man, named as Bevil Jenrick, was directed to the witness box and asked what he knew of Mr Harcourt.

'What I do know against him?' Jenrick stuttered nervously.

Sir Charles stepped forward. 'Yes, for being a priest.' He nodded encouragingly.

'When I was a prisoner in Derby gaol back in April, he invited me to his cell to "scour the kettle", as he called it.'

The audience in the gallery tittered.

'Which means to confess and receive absolution?'

'It does, and after I had taken confession with him, he gave me his permission as a priest to go out and get drunk.'

'I have never given this man confession.' Matthew spoke out. 'I can call forth every prisoner in the gaol and they will confirm my innocence of this.'

'Confession must be heard in private, must it not?' Sir Charles addressed Jenrick, who nodded eagerly.

'Yet I was watched constantly by the gaoler,' Matthew interposed. 'If you call him forth, he will tell you of the innocent time I have passed in my cell.'

'It is not for you to call witnesses, Mr Harcourt,' Bullrich admonished.

'If I may, My Lord,' Matthew said more humbly. 'The statute applies the word *credible* to witnesses. It is clear Mr Jenrick is not a credible witness: a man gaoled for disorder and drunkenness, a rogue who has been put in the pillories on several occasions and one who attempted to escape from prison whilst I was there.'

''Tis not his time to make this sort of defence,' another of the judges on the bench said. 'Harcourt should have done it before the witness was sworn, if he wanted to take exception to his testimony.'

'That's not fair,' Nicholas couldn't help exclaiming. 'How was he to know who the witness would be or what he would say?'

Heads turned to look at him and he saw Father lower his hand from his face as he leant forward to shake his head in warning. The constable's wife told him to hush or he would risk their being thrown out of the gallery. But at least he had caught Matthew's eye; his cousin gave him a wan smile, blinking his eyes as if in acknowledgement, or perhaps admonishment, Nicholas couldn't be sure.

Two other witnesses were brought forward, both again unknown to Nicholas. Both insisted that Matthew had said Mass at a house in Derby belonging to a Mr Noakes, two years before. The second witness was a young woman who was clearly not in her right mind. Her testimony was delivered in a wailing sing-song voice and was completely garbled. The third was a weaselly-looking man with thinning hair and an equally threadbare coat and stockings. Nicholas gave up trying to record every word and drew quick portraits instead.

'Upon my salvation, I never saw this man before,' Matthew said.

'But he hath seen you,' the clerk noted triumphantly.

Sir Charles Bullrich surveyed Matthew with contempt. 'It is a strange thing, that you should say "upon your salvation" you never saw him. How many might come into a room and you not see them while you are at Mass?'

'How often have you seen him say Mass, Mr Pursglove?' another of the justices asked.

'A dozen times,' Mr Pursglove answered.

Nicholas's pencil needed sharpening; he pulled out the second one. It wasn't right, surely, that there were so many men ranged against Matthew while he was not allowed anyone to speak up for him.

'I protest, I have never said Mass in any public place,' Matthew said.

'Perhaps you do not count Mr Noakes's a public place,' Sir Charles suggested.

'If it is a private residence, I would know who was admitted there,' Matthew replied.

'No, the truth is, two years ago you were not so cautious whom you admitted to see you in the exercise of what you call your religion, because the execution of the law was not so strict as it is nowadays. Therefore 'tis very probable that you were at Mr Noakes's house, and yet not know all who were there.' Bullrich emphasised each word with such vehemence it was as if they were missiles being hurled at Matthew.

'But I never did say Mass there,' Matthew insisted.

'Here are three witnesses against you, and do you think your bare word will be taken against their three oaths?' Bullrich thundered.

Matthew would not be cowed. 'That I have said Mass, I won't deny,' he continued calmly. 'I would not tell a lie to save my own life, nay, nor would I tell a lie to take away the life of the greatest villain upon earth. But, My Lord, I protest there has not been one true word sworn against me.' He swallowed and Nicholas wished someone would give him water to drink, for his voice sounded dry and cracked. 'I humbly submit that, in accordance with the law, whatsoever is against me must be proved, not simply asserted. They ought to give proofs.'

'You wish for proofs? Here are your vestments and your chalice, as used for your so-called religion.' Bullrich gestured to the items that had been placed on a table in front of him.

Nicholas's stomach lurched.

'Those are heirlooms that have been in my family since before the Reformation.' Matthew looked weary. Would no one allow him a seat?

'Come, when matters are plain 'tis in vain to contend. The witnesses have proved that you executed the office of a priest by saying Mass, which none does but a priest; 'tis enough to guide the jury in their verdict,' another of the judges concluded with satisfaction.

'They are taking the word of three liars,' Nicholas exclaimed to Father, as they waited in the courtyard outside for the jury to return with their verdict.

Father bit down on his lower lip. 'The whole process is rigged against him. The jurors will have to be brave men to go against the direction of Sir Charles Bullrich.' He pulled Nicholas to him in a sudden rough embrace. 'We must be strong for Matthew; do not let him see your distress.'

A pieman was working his way through the crowd, calling out his wares.

'Are you hungry?' Father asked.

But Nicholas shook his head. For once, he had no desire for food of any kind. He hopped from one foot to the other, praying with each leap that the jury would find Matthew innocent. It must have rained while they were inside, for there was a large puddle just to his left. If he could jump over it, he told himself, Matthew would be freed. He almost cleared it, but his heel came down on the edge, sending up a spray of muddy water. A woman nearby gave a little shriek and pulled her skirts away.

Father looked at him with embarrassment. 'Do you need the privy?'

'No,' Nicholas said, looking up.

It was then he spotted Uncle Percy, standing at the back of the crowd, looking around him with evident disdain.

'I cannot bear to talk to that man,' Father said when Nicholas told him. Pulling his hat down low over his forehead, he pushed them forwards into the middle of the throng.

'The jury are back,' the constable's wife declared as she hurried past them and into the courthouse.

'That didn't take them long,' Father said grimly.

Nicholas sat next to Father this time. He noticed Uncle Percy coming in after everyone else and standing at the back, leaning on a silver cane. Father kept his face averted and told Nicholas to do the same.

To his surprise, Father took his hand in his own gloved one and retained it there. They leant forward over the gallery rail and smiled down at Matthew, who was looking up for them. He nodded and gave them a little salute in response.

The inevitability of the verdict didn't make it any easier to hear. Nicholas wanted to leap from the gallery into the court below and whisk Matthew away to safety, hacking down every man who stood in their way. *You're all fools*, he wanted to scream at them.

Father was squeezing his hand. 'Matthew is going to eternal glory,' he whispered. 'Whilst they will all be damned.'

But Nicholas could hear the tears in Father's voice.

The oldest of the three judges pulled himself up to address both Matthew and the courthouse. 'I suppose it is not unknown to any of us that there hath been a hellish plot against the life of the King and to destroy our religion. I would to God I could say the plot was at an end, but the Jesuits have stirred some men up to believe that murder in this world is a certain way to saintship in that which is to come.' He jabbed at finger at Matthew. 'And though you seem to deny it, your practices are a proof beyond all contradiction that the law should now be put in execution against you.' He turned back to the courtroom, gesturing dismissively at Matthew. 'And one thing more I should say to the accused, who pretends to do good services for the public, who enjoins a man to "scour his kettle", as he calls it, handing out the sacrament and then giving him a dispensation to be drunk – this is such a priesthood as is fit only for the Pope and his imps to put in practice.'

There were cheers from the public gallery. Nicholas's hand was shaking so hard his pencil scraped over the page, leaving an indecipherable scrawl. The judge pulled back his shoulders and thrust out his chin.

'Therefore, in the name of the court, I do pronounce this to be your judgement. That you, the prisoner now at the bar, be conveyed from hence to the place from whence you came; and that you be conveyed from thence on a hurdle to the place of execution, where you are to be hanged by the neck. That you be cut down alive. That your privy member be cut off, your bowels taken out and be burnt in your view. That your head be severed from your body. That your body be divided into four quarters, which are to be disposed at the King's pleasure. And the God of infinite mercy, have mercy upon your soul.'

→ Chapter Five ←

Father did not want him to attend the execution, but Nicholas, with a mixture of cajoling, crying and reasoning, persuaded him that being thirteen and therefore old enough to be hanged himself, he was old enough to witness his cousin's demise.

They were allowed to visit Matthew beforehand and he, despite the horrors that awaited him, remained impressively serene. He even joked, when the coffin maker came in to measure him, that it was his tailor come to make him a new suit of clothes. Nicholas and his father did their best to play along, but their half-hearted smiles weren't convincing anyone. Even the gaoler and the constable seemed sorry for the duties they had to perform.

'Look,' Matthew said quietly, laying a hand on Father's arm. 'If I am to be given a coffin, they cannot really intend to quarter me. I believe they will let you have my body. Bury it in our plot, beside my sister.'

Father shook his head wildly, a terrible moan escaping from his throat. His legs buckled beneath him and Matthew had to catch him before he collapsed to the floor. Embracing him, Matthew held Father close, rocking his cousin in his arms, while Nicholas looked on with dismay. His approaching death seemed to have fortified Matthew with renewed strength.

'Remember the stories your mother used to tell,' Matthew told Father. 'Of the sainted Edmund Arrowsmith, whose execution she witnessed as a child. Everyone remarked on the composure with which that priest embraced his death. I hope I might offer a similar example of grace and fortitude. It is an honour to die for our religion. Why would you mourn for me when paradise awaits? You must be strong now, not only for my sake, but for Nicholas.' He held out one arm, inviting Nicholas to join them.

Nestled into his chest, Nicholas could not only hear, but feel Matthew's heart beating against his cheek. He leant into him, absorbing the vitality that would soon be snuffed out. He would carry the rhythm always, drumming through his blood.

'Remember what I have taught you,' Matthew said quietly to Nicholas as he and Father were about to leave.

Drawing him over to the fireplace, Matthew crouched down by the grate and wrote in the ashes with his finger the word 'ἄγγελόν'.

'The Greek for messenger is *angelos* – angel,' he explained. 'By being my messenger, you have acted as God's emissary here on earth.' Placing the palm of his hand against Nicholas's cheek, Matthew stared earnestly into his eyes, his own dark brown eyes huge in his hollowed-out face. 'No matter what your origins, you are one of God's angels. Continue to do His work and be His messenger. There is no greater calling.'

'What did Matthew tell you?' Father asked as soon as they were out on the street again.

'He said I am God's messenger.'

'He should not impose such roles on you.' Father took out his handkerchief and rubbed the ash from Nicholas's cheek. 'I love my cousin, but you see the fate that has befallen him. Do not be a go-between, not for God, or Matthew, or anyone else.' He seized Nicholas suddenly by the shoulders. 'I would keep you always from the infection that is religious zeal. Whatever its hue, it causes nothing but destruction.'

But Nicholas could think only of his elevation from bastard to angel, and was filled with wonder that his cousin saw divinity in him.

They walked up to Nun's Green, where the gallows had been erected, and waited there for Matthew. Nicholas looked around, half-expecting to see Uncle Percy lurking as he had at the courthouse, but there was no sign of him. It was a bright, sunny day and a large crowd soon gathered. Men, women and children stood together, chattering and making merry as if it were a holiday and the gallows were a stage set for a troupe of actors. Nicholas wished that it were raining. Perhaps the heavens would cloud over and darkness would descend, just as it had done when Jesus was crucified.

In the distance, two horses, led by a soldier, could be seen kicking up dust on the dry road. As they got nearer, Nicholas could see the wooden hurdle bumping along behind them. Lashed to it, Matthew lay prone, gazing resolutely up at the blue sky above him. Although his thin body jolted with every stone and rut it was dragged over, his face was calm and he never once called out nor even winced. It was as if his spirit was already halfway to heaven and he could no longer feel the pains and indignities of the physical realm.

They came to a halt beside the scaffold and Matthew was cut loose from the sledge and helped to his feet by two soldiers. Nicholas tried to catch his eye, but Matthew's vision was focused elsewhere. '*Haec dies quam fecit Dominus, exultemus. . .*' he chanted, almost to himself. To Nicholas's amazement Father replied, singing the end of the line, in a low, cracked voice, '*et laetemur in ea.*' – 'This is the day that the Lord has made, let us rejoice and be glad in it.' Matthew looked directly at Father then, smiled and nodded.

The crowd fell silent as Matthew stepped up onto the wooden platform. Nicholas had heard how the London mob hurled abuse and even stones at the condemned priests, but to his great relief, the spectators stood with quietly bowed heads while Matthew delivered his final speech. Crewe had arranged for someone else to do the note-taking this time, a clerk who knew shorthand and would be able to record every word. The man stood beside them, his pencil scratching across the page.

'My dear countrymen, I am here to be executed, not for theft or murder or anything against the law of God. Nor indeed any doctrine against monarchy or civil government. Some of you gathered here may have heard my trial at the last assizes and will know that nothing was laid to my charge other than priesthood. I have never, in my whole lifetime, been guilty of so much as a treasonous thought against His Majesty or the kingdom. I have had no part in this plot that is so much discoursed of. I acknowledge myself as a priest, which I would never deny, because I found it the greatest honour imaginable.'

There were a few dissenting murmurs from the onlookers.

Matthew's voice rose as if powered by divine grace. 'There is nothing in the Roman Catholic faith that is at odds with the laws of the land, monarchy or civil policy. We do not believe that the Pope has the power to depose or licence the murder of princes. I could not sign the Oath of Allegiance because of certain clauses contained within it, but this had nothing to do with my allegiance to king and country.

'So, I take comfort in St. Peter's words: "Let none of you suffer as a murderer, as a thief, or as an evildoer, or as a busybody in other men's matters. Yet if any man suffer as a Christian, let him not be ashamed; but let him glorify God on this behalf."' He paused a moment.

He had the crowd's rapt attention now. Nicholas could see the rise of his chest as he inhaled deeply.

'I have been a faithful and true subject to my King, but I have been a grievous sinner against God. Thieves and highwaymen, had they received as many favours and graces from Him as I have done, would have served Him with greater perfection. I hope, by the merits of His passion He will have mercy on me, who loves Him with all my heart and am heartily sorry that I ever offended Him.'

What could he mean, to compare himself to robbers? Nicholas couldn't believe his cousin capable of a grievous sin. He glanced at the clerk, still busily writing, and hoped that Crewe might remove those words from his account.

'I beg of God Almighty to forgive my accusers, the jurymen and any others who have had any part in my death.' Matthew's arms were

49

outstretched in benediction. 'God bless the King and the royal family. God grant peace to his subjects and that they live and die in true faith, hope and charity.'

All around them, people were crossing themselves and muttering, 'God bless you,' and 'God have mercy.' When the hangman put the noose around Matthew's neck, the crowd surged forwards and people began to shout, 'Hang him until death.' Some men beat on the gallows with sticks and swords until the executioner nodded anxiously.

Nicholas was just able to hear Matthew sing out, 'Sweet Jesus, receive my soul.' And then his body was hoisted aloft and Nicholas and his father heard with relief the snap of his neck before his body was lowered.

When the soldiers went forward to dismember Matthew's body, the crowd began to pelt them with stones, shouting for the priest to be left intact. Eventually, fearful for their own lives, the soldiers conceded to the people and drove the cart with the coffin on it up to the gallows, respectfully laying Matthew's body inside.

Nicholas, despite his anguish, was filled with pride that he had known this man: his close relation and tutor, who had met death with such nobility the crowd would not allow him to suffer more than he had to. He knew Matthew's soul was on its way to heaven, but he was still very glad his body had been saved from butchery.

Father was leaning against him. He had closed his eyes and was breathing heavily. Nicholas, understanding now the depth of Father's love for Matthew, felt a sudden surge of affection and protectiveness towards him. He would be a better son. He would do all he could to comfort Father and fulfil his wishes.

They interred Matthew's body in the Hawthorne family tomb, which lay discreetly at the far side of the local graveyard under the shade of an ancient yew. It was the only tree in the churchyard. In the winter it scattered its red berries across the grass, their poisonous seeds hidden within the crimson flesh. In the summer its moss-covered roots provided a resting place. It was peaceful there, out of the wind, with only the sounds of sheep bleating and birds calling.

The vicar was sympathetic and had no objections to a priest of Rome being buried in his churchyard. They all served the same God, he pointed out. He seemed as troubled as anyone by the slaughter of so many clergy.

Nicholas had always liked the plaque to his aunt Alethea. In the bottom left-hand corner, a caterpillar was carved into the stone; on the top right there was a butterfly. Beneath the name Alethea Hawthorne was an inscription from Corinthians: *Behold I shew you a mystery; we shall not all sleep, but we shall all be changed*. 'You see,' Father had once explained, 'The caterpillar enters the tomb, his chrysalis, and is metamorphosed into a butterfly. So, the butterfly is a symbol of the resurrection, but also it shows us how an earthly creature might be transformed from one thing into another.'

Aunt Alethea had died in London of the plague, the year before Nicholas was born. Because of the turmoil of the times, her body had never been recovered. Abigail said his aunt's bones probably lay in a plague pit somewhere on the outskirts of London, mixed in with the skeletons of strangers. Nicholas suspected her spirit haunted Measham Hall. Once, when he had been sick with a bad fever, he had heard her singing to him. And he had vague memories, from when he was an infant, of lullabies sung softly in that same voice, wafting over him. He knew it must be her because she was known for her beautiful voice and no one else in the house could sing so sweetly. Certainly not Abigail, nor even Jane.

'Why did Matthew ask to be buried beside his sister?' he asked, suddenly remembering his cousin's words in the gaol. 'Do we have another cousin buried here?'

Father looked perplexed. 'Quite possibly, though I don't recall Matthew referring to a sister. He must have meant his cousin.' He stamped his feet, dislodging some mud from his boots. 'I'm just grateful we were allowed to bury his body. Most families whose relatives have been executed for treason are forced to display the head on a pike above their walls.' He shuddered and drew his cloak more tightly round him.

'Father.' Nicholas spoke hesitantly, afraid of distressing him further, but needing an answer to something that had been weighing on his mind. 'Why did Cousin Matthew call himself a grievous sinner and say he was worse than a highwayman? He has never done anything other than serve God.'

Father caressed the stone monument, scraping away some moss with his gloved hand. 'That was just your cousin showing humility, as is becoming of a priest.' He paused to gaze around the churchyard at the huddled gravestones. 'As a very young man, before he discovered his vocation, Matthew was given to gambling and carousing – as are many in their youth. But once he found his path, he led, as you say, an exemplary life.'

Nicholas could not imagine his measured and tranquil cousin being in any way dissolute. Matthew had never seemed troubled by unruly passions or discontents.

'One day Matthew's name will be cleared and the world will see what a terrible injustice was done,' Nicholas declared. Sir Charles Bullrich, with his hectoring, sneering manner came suddenly into his mind and he burnt with hatred. 'When I am a man, I will bring down all those who falsely accused him.'

'Do not dedicate your life to vengeance; you will only bring yourself suffering and it is the last thing Matthew would want for you. Stick to your studies, be a good scholar; that is what he would like.' Father patted the tombstone. 'I am sure he is watching us now from above and noting all we do.' But his tone was forced and Nicholas wondered if he truly believed that.

He would honour Matthew's faith in him and prove himself worthy of the title of God's messenger. Forgetting his earlier desire to please Father, Nicholas promised Matthew he would become a great botanist and natural philosopher. He would make new discoveries and find medicines that could cure diseases like the one his aunt had died from.

Part I: Boy

Looking about him, at the village graveyard and the gently sloping countryside that led to Measham Hall, he felt a terrible longing to be far away, beyond Derbyshire and England, beyond Europe even, to lands where mountains rose in candied peaks and turquoise seas hissed on pearly shores. To lands peopled by the wild and innocent beings he had read about, who cared nothing for a person's religion and had no courts or judges. To be among men who spent their days hunting, called each other 'brother' and had no knowledge of names such as 'papist', 'whore' or 'bastard'.

→ Chapter Six ←

August 1679–April 1680

'Devilish business, devilish.' Uncle Percy stood in the hallway talking to Crewe.

Nicholas was about to creep away when Percy spotted him. 'Don't hide away up there, boy,' he called. 'Come down here where I can see you.' He tapped his walking stick on the stone floor.

Nicholas reluctantly descended.

'By Jove, the boy looks just like my brother.' Percy turned to Crewe with a look of astonishment. 'Nic might have spat him out of his own mouth.'

Crewe bowed slightly. 'The resemblance is striking, sir.'

Nicholas's similarity to his grandfather was much commented on by the older members of the household. The shape of his face with its high cheekbones and firm jaw, his dark brown eyes and wide smile, were all very like the man he had been named for, they said, though Nicholas had never heard Crewe express this opinion before.

'Do you know your catechism, boy?' Percy demanded.

'Yes, sir.'

'Well, go on then, give me the Creed and the Lord's Prayer.'

This was an easy task for Nicholas, who recited them both in Latin.

His uncle gave an approving nod. 'And where is this father of yours? Why has he not responded to my letters?'

'He likes to be out, managing the land, sir,' Nicholas said uneasily. 'He is always very busy.'

'Is he indeed? I take it he eats his dinner like any other Englishman?' Before Nicholas could answer, Percy waddled past him and into the parlour. He reminded Nicholas of a pheasant, with his round belly supported on spindly legs and his jutting chin. Beneath his red face he wore a white cravat tucked into a golden-brown silk waistcoat, as though he were deliberately dressing in the colours of the bird. He only needed a green scarf to complete the ensemble.

Handing Nicholas his cane, he lowered himself into a chair by the empty fireplace, grasping the wooden arms for support and groaning softly. Once settled he looked up at the painting of his brother and then across the room to where a portrait of Nicholas's father hung. He narrowed his eyes, squinting at it.

'Who painted that? It is not a good likeness.' He waved his hand at William's picture.

'Your nephew hired a young artist from London, sir.' Crewe followed them into the parlour. 'I don't believe he is well-known.'

Uncle Percy harrumphed. 'Don't suppose he ever will be neither. The work is no match for Nic's; I would not hang it there to invite comparison.'

Nicholas studied his great-uncle. Could this be the man who had betrayed them? He certainly seemed to resent their presence in Measham Hall.

'Will you be staying for dinner, Sir Percy?' Crewe asked.

'Are there fleas in a beggar's breeches?' Percy chuckled. Met by an uncomprehending silence, he added his confirmation before beckoning to Nicholas. 'It's about time we became better acquainted.'

Crewe went to inform Tickell, leaving Nicholas standing awkwardly in front of his great-uncle.

'So, your father has given you our name and made you his heir. It has taken some damn clever lawyering to manage that, let me tell you. I hope you will prove yourself worthy of the title.'

'I will do my best, sir.'

'I wasn't blessed with sons. Only have one daughter still living.' Percy pulled a handkerchief out of his pocket and mopped his large pink forehead. 'Mary is an abbess, you know, at the convent in Rouen. She is my pride and joy.' His blue eyes brightened when he spoke of his daughter and he looked suddenly more youthful.

'Is Rouen far from St. Omer?' Nicholas couldn't help asking.

'About a hundred and fifty miles, I should think. Why? Are you going to St. Omers College?'

'I would like to, but Father wants me to be educated in England.'

Percy looked scandalised. 'What on earth for? He chose St. Omers for himself as a young man; he must know the education there is second to none. He should get you out of this country while he can. The place has turned into a nest of vipers.'

Nicholas was surprised to discover an ally in his great-uncle. 'Father Matthew wanted me to go to St. Omers next year when I turn fourteen.'

His great-uncle did not appear at all discomforted by this disclosure. 'Well, of course he did. He was also your tutor, was he not? I read his last speech in a pamphlet. Most inspiring.' He felt beneath his shirt and drew out a gold crucifix, which he kissed. 'He will be a martyr now in Heaven, God bless him.'

Nicholas was beginning to think he must have been wrong in suspecting Percy. As Father said, he was clearly a fervent believer in their religion.

'I've been told your father called him a cousin. He must be on your grandmother's side for I've no knowledge of any such relative.' Percy pushed his cross back inside his shirt.

Nicholas was sure Matthew was a Hawthorne, but couldn't remember ever being told as much. Matthew had spoken fondly of both his grandparents and Nicholas had never thought to ask which one was his blood relation.

'Didn't he ever tell you his real name?' Percy asked.

'No.' Again, Matthew's name was not something Nicholas had ever questioned. His cousin was just Father Matthew to him.

'I attended his trial, you know, out of a sense of fellow-feeling.' Percy coughed into his handkerchief. 'He looked remarkably like William, which is odd because your father takes after the Hawthorne side, as do you.' His uncle fixed a beady and somewhat aggrieved look on Nicholas. 'I don't know why William never told me he had a chaplain. I kept one myself until recently. Father Ashby, God rest his soul, was old and died of natural causes. I might have come here for communion.'

'Do you go up to Derby often, sir?' Nicholas asked, hoping to discover what his great-uncle had been doing there when they went to visit Matthew.

'Not for communion.' Percy sounded nettled. 'Though I'd rather go to Derby than London, 'pon my word. You'll find much of the Derbyshire gentry reside there. Was thinking of buying a townhouse in Derby, but I've enough outgoings as it is.' He reached a hand out for his cane, which Nicholas had been absentmindedly tapping up and down on the stone floor. 'Do you know any Greek, boy?'

'I know the word *angelos* – it means "messenger" – and I speak good French. Father Matthew said I would learn Greek at college. He said I am a natural linguist.'

For some reason, Nicholas could not fathom what, Percy laughed heartily at this.

'Well, the Jesuits are the best educators,' he said. 'You should come and stay with me for a bit. You're too old to be at home still. I'd send you to St. Omer. There's even a school in Watten you could attend first.'

While Nicholas was trying to formulate a suitable reply to this surprising invitation, Father returned home.

'William,' Percy called, spotting him through the open door.

'Uncle.' Father's voice was gruff.

'No wonder your son skulks about the house like a deer afraid of the hounds. He has learnt it from his genitor.' Percy hauled himself to his feet. 'I'm beginning to suspect you are avoiding me, sir.'

'Why would I do that?' Father came towards them, carelessly re-tying his neckcloth under his chin, and gave a low bow.

They were interrupted by Palmes, asking whether they would be dining in the parlour as usual or wanting to ascend to the great chamber.

'Don't go to any trouble on my account,' Percy said, leaning on his walking stick. 'In my youth the whole household still ate in the hall, according to ancient custom.'

'In that case, you won't mind Crewe joining us,' Father said, gesturing to the companion standing just behind him.

'Not in the least. Crewe and I played together as boys, when his father was steward here. We got into a few scrapes, didn't we, Crewe?'

Crew gave a thin smile. 'I recall a few beatings being earnt.'

Percy guffawed. Nicholas could not imagine Crewe as a child, especially not a mischievous one.

'I hope you didn't take any beatings on Uncle Percy's behalf,' Father remarked, helping Crewe to unfold the old gate-legged table.

'Do you have a new wigmaker?' Percy was looking curiously at Father. 'There is something different about your appearance.'

Father shrugged. 'Perhaps it is these difficult times taking their toll on me.'

'I did not say you look worse, only different. If anything, you look younger. A veritable *puer aeternus*.' He turned to Nicholas. 'Can you translate that, young man? Comes from some ancient poet or other. My schooldays are long behind me, thank the Lord.'

'Eternal youth?' Nicholas ventured.

'Good lad.' Percy beamed at him. He turned to Father with a more serious look. 'Did you read my letters about the mine?'

'I'm not digging up my land to search for lead or coal,' Father said adamantly.

'I know just the fellow to help you; he's very careful. We've already looked on my fields, but sadly found nothing.' Percy pulled out his handkerchief and flapped it in Father's direction. 'I can manage the whole enterprise for you. You could be sitting on a treasure trove.' He leant forward eagerly. 'Think of the money we could make.'

'We?' Father raised his eyebrows.

'It will be a family endeavour.' Percy smirked. 'I will lend you my men and my wisdom, in exchange for an equal share in the profits.'

Father shook his head. 'The earth can keep her treasures. We've enough bounty from her to live quite comfortably as we are, without hacking her to pieces.'

'You talk like some nature-worshipping heathen.' Percy's face had grown very red. 'One of those fanatics from thirty years ago, the Diggers, or Planters, or whatever they were.'

'Think of the disruption, Uncle. Would you have gangs of free miners taking up residence on the Measham lands, chopping down the trees for their fires and hollowing out the fields? Where would the profit be in that?'

'As I explained in my letter, I know a number of landowners in North Derbyshire who've had the rights of free mining removed through the law courts. Now they can hire men to work for them, accruing great profits. Any free miners that protest with violence find themselves on the gallows, by Gad.'

Father smiled. 'But you see, Uncle, that wouldn't sit right with me. To take away men's liberties and turn them into hirelings. If I were to mine the land, I'd have to maintain the old rights and share the proceeds.'

Uncle Percy looked aghast. 'What are you, a damned Leveller? Is this what your father fought for?'

Nicholas looked from one man to the other. He had never heard of any of these names, Levellers or Diggers, but was impressed by Father's line of argument and glad he didn't want to mine their land.

'I believe my father would be proud of the way I manage these grounds and all the improvements I have made,' Father said stiffly. 'If he had wanted to search for ore he would have done so.'

Uncle Percy couldn't argue with that. He and Father sat at opposite ends of the oval table, while Crewe and Nicholas were placed between them. It was not a comfortable meal, but at least Tickell had managed to make it a larger and more varied one than they usually had when it was just the three of them.

'The lad is a good trencher-man,' Percy noted approvingly as Nicholas took another sheep's foot. 'My wife and daughters all had dainty appetites. A meal was hardly begun before it was over.'

Nicholas's pleasure in the compliment was diminished by Percy finishing off the rabbit stuffed with gooseberries before he got a helping.

'Still, a man needs a wife.' Percy wagged his knife. 'The Hawthorne line depends on you, William.'

'As you have just observed, I have a healthy son and heir.'

Percy lowered his voice, pointlessly since Nicholas, who had the best hearing of the four of them, was sitting beside him. 'I'm glad you've disproved the rumours about your being...' He gave a little cough. 'You know, an effeminate. But now you need to sire a son on the right side of the blanket.' He slurped at his glass of claret. 'As we know only too well, God, in his infinite wisdom, may choose to take our children into his own merciful bosom. Your grandparents always said what a comfort it was knowing that should anything befall their first-born son, they had another to replace him.' Percy pressed a hand to his heart to indicate himself.

Nicholas wondered what Percy meant by 'an effeminate'. Could it be a man like a capon, incapable of producing offspring?

'It is a question of finding the right wife, Uncle Percy. But don't worry, I shall acquire one soon and sire plenty more strapping sons to carry on the family name.'

'I can make enquiries on your behalf.'

Percy sounded somewhat aggrieved, as though he were unsure whether Father was mocking him or not. Nicholas wasn't sure either. He had never heard Father mention finding a wife before. Perhaps, now that he was no longer friendly with Jane, he would want to bring a new woman home.

Abigail said a wife was unlikely to take kindly to Nicholas, given his origins. A Lady Hawthorne would expect her own children to take precedence. He didn't care about inheriting Measham Hall; in fact, he would be glad to hand over the burden of being its custodian to someone else, just so long as he got to keep Polestar. A wife might even encourage Father to send him away to college.

'Sir Wollaton has an eligible granddaughter; not much to look at, but her mother's trained her up to be a thrifty and skilful housekeeper. You can't expect poor old Crewe to perform that task forever.' Percy nodded to Crewe to pour him more wine. 'I can open negotiations for you – Wollaton knows me of old.'

'That is very kind, but I can find my own bride.'

Father's lace cuffs were trailing in the butter. Nicholas wondered why he didn't push them back. He suspected Father was ashamed of his slender fingers, for he always kept them covered with gloves or long sleeves. Was that part of being an effeminate?

'Perhaps I should make enquiries on my own behalf, then.' Percy sniffed. 'I daresay I am not too old to take another wife.'

'If she'll have you, why not?' Father refilled his own glass, finishing the bottle.

Percy gave another harrumph. 'Nay, a wife would be too much trouble at my age. I enjoy an easy life; I couldn't change my ways for a lot of female whims.'

''Tis true,' said Father. 'Women are demanding creatures that put their husbands to no end of tasks and disturbance. When you want to be in the country they want to be in town, they'll have your house and gardens redesigned to the latest, most incommodious of fashions, not to mention needing new wardrobes for every season. Before you know it, you'll have no money left for your cellar or your stables.'

Percy laughed heartily at this. 'I see why a pretty fellow like you remains a bachelor. I suppose you have the best of both worlds by gaining a son without being wife-ridden.' He nodded at Palmes, who had brought another bottle of wine to the table. 'But you are too young to give up on the fair sex entirely.' He leant across the table, ignoring Nicholas. 'I heard about your *amour* with the Lady Sellwood. Mistresses are all very well, but don't waste too much time on strumpets. Find yourself a nice little country wench, uncorrupted by the *grand monde.*' He looked more earnestly at Father. 'You must consider the family name; that duty falls to you, not me.'

'Your admonishment is quite correct, Uncle. Rest assured, I will preserve the Hawthorne name and reputation.'

Nicholas was surprised by Father's placatory tone. Despite their initial discord, by the end of the meal he and Percy seemed to have become the best of friends. Nicholas hoped this new amity might help persuade Father to send him to St. Omer.

Nothing more was said on the matter, however. Instead of finding a wife, Father hired a tutor. Walter Simms was already engaged by a neighbouring family, tutoring their sons, and agreed to come over in the afternoons to teach Nicholas. Mr Simms was an insipid young man who clearly found teaching tedious and only undertook it for want of a better occupation. Nicholas's French and Latin were better than his. Simms, who was ignorant of their true faith and the barrier this created, was surprised Nicholas wasn't at one of the universities already. That Mr Simms was the result of a Cambridge education only made Nicholas more convinced he wanted to continue his education in Europe rather than England. Simms's main occupation at Cambridge had been, according to him, playing games of tennis. He was a poor substitute for Father Matthew and he and Nicholas regarded each other with equal disdain, suffering one another's company only under compulsion. It was no good complaining to Father, who had become ever more reclusive since Matthew's death and had scarcely even met the tutor he employed, leaving all such matters to Crewe.

At the end of April, two weeks after his fourteenth birthday, Nicholas was passing his father's chamber when he caught the tantalising words 'St. Omer'. The door was ajar and he paused to hear what else might pertain to him.

'Did you know about this?' Father sounded indignant.

'I recall Father Matthew mentioning a desire to pass on the annuity the late Sir Nicholas set up for him to attend the college. I did not know he had already made arrangements with the provincial superior.'

Nicholas held his breath. Were his dreams about to be realised?

'Matthew had no right to set up a stipend for my son without consulting me first.'

Nicholas waited for Crewe to answer, but the steward said nothing.

'I'll not have him subjected to any more Jesuitical influences. They've caused our family enough anguish.'

'We cannot hold the Jesuits responsible for their maligners. Think of your dear mother, sir. Of what she would choose for the boy.'

'She never sent us away. It was only after the duel that my—'

Unfortunately, at that moment, a gust of wind blew in through an open window, bringing with it something that irritated Nicholas's nose, causing him to sneeze explosively. The door swung open and he found himself staring up into Father's enraged face.

'What the devil are you doing, loitering there?' Father grabbed him by the ear and dragged him into the room.

Crewe raised his eyebrows reproachfully at Nicholas.

'I'm sorry, Father.' He clapped a hand against his aching earlobe, afraid it might become detached from his head.

Father pushed him away in exasperation. 'Why must you always be sneaking about the place, spying and eavesdropping like some wicked imp?'

'If I am stealthy, it is because you don't like to be disturbed. I cannot help what I hear when voices are raised.' Nicholas was stung by the harshness of his father's words.

'And now I must add insolence to your misdeeds.'

'If you think me so monstrous, why don't you do what Cousin Matthew wanted and send me away to St. Omers?'

'Your beloved Matthew? If I had done as he wished, you would have been adopted at birth. Sent off to be raised by strangers and never acknowledged as my son.'

How could Father tell such terrible lies? Crewe gave a warning cough, which was ignored by both Nicholas and Father.

'Matthew was proud of me. He said I am one of God's angels.'

'One of the Devil's angels more like,' Father retorted.

Hot, angry tears filled Nicholas's eyes. 'You just want me to become as miserable and friendless as you are. I wish you had sent me away with my mother; she at least might have shown me some kindness.'

The air in the room was as thick and heavy as a summer's day before a thunderstorm.

'I will leave you to discipline this ungrateful boy.' Crewe bowed to Father before leaving, without so much as a glance at Nicholas.

He felt utterly bereft. He had no allies here. Why did Father want to keep him at Measham when he had nothing but contempt for him? Was it only because he didn't want to go to the trouble of marrying and having a legitimate son?

'Abigail has filled your head with nonsense about your mother.' Father's voice had cooled to iciness. 'Ellen wouldn't send you to St. Omer's. She did not even want to have you baptised. She was a dissenter who loathed popery even more than she did the established church. She was only too ready to wash her hands of you. You are my burden, and mine alone.' Father turned to the corner of the room, where a rarely used switch rested against the wall. 'So, the duty to teach you manners also rests on me, especially since Matthew clearly failed in that regard.'

The household considered Father overly lenient because he was averse to physical punishment. Perhaps he just didn't think Nicholas worth expending such energy on. Anyhow, Nicholas didn't see why he should wait to be beaten now. He had done nothing wrong. It was Father who was failing to honour Matthew's wishes. His base blood could not be thrashed out of him. He could feel it coursing through his body, driving him on as he ran from the room, out of the house and towards the stables.

'Good Lord, boy, what on earth has happened? You look half-drowned.'

This was not the entrance Nicholas had been hoping to make, but the journey had been arduous and he was so exhausted and hungry, he was only grateful to have found his uncle's house at last.

'You said I could come and stay with you, Uncle Percy. I've left my horse in your stable; I hope he might be given some warm mash, for he is very tired and wet. He took fright in the storm, but carried me here like the brave creature he is.'

Nicholas suddenly felt close to tears. He had had to force Polestar on through thunder and lightning. They had ridden for miles only to find they had missed the turning to his uncle's house and would have to retrace their steps. Then he'd had to dismount and lead Polestar on until he was too exhausted to walk any further and the horse allowed him to ride again. It was a mixture of pride, hope and desperation that had kept him going. He had left home in such a hurry he hadn't brought any provisions and couldn't think where else to go.

'Find him some dry clothes,' Percy told his man. 'And bring him some mutton broth and red jelly. Whatever Cook has to keep fevers at bay.'

'And my horse?'

'Yes, yes, the groom will tend to him. Come, pull a stool up by the fire. You're just like your grandfather, always thinking of his animals first.'

It wasn't long before Nicholas, warm and fed, though in some extremely loose garments, was feeling much happier. He had successfully completed his first adventure as an explorer. Despite getting lost and taking a tumble from his horse into a muddy ditch, he had not been forced to spend the night under a hedge, nor had he been attacked by gypsies or highwaymen as he had feared. He would prove to Father that he was nobody's burden.

The chamber he slept in that night was cold and dusty, but he was so tired he hardly noticed this until he woke late the next morning, all tangled up in one of Percy's enormous nightgowns and sneezing violently.

He stumbled over to the window to survey his new environment. Disappointingly, he couldn't see much beyond the mossy tiles of the sloping roof below. His clothes lay spread across a wooden chest. They were still damp, but he pulled them on anyway, thinking they would soon dry with the warmth from his body.

Despite the clamouring of his empty belly, breakfast would have to wait until he had checked on Polestar. He hoped the groom had looked after him as well as Uncle Percy had promised and that the horse was comfortable in his new surroundings.

Apart from some clattering in the kitchen, the house was quiet. He stood on the landing, wondering which was the best route to the stables, through the front door or the kitchen. A sharp knocking made him jump. Just as he was thinking he ought to go down and answer it, the butler appeared, walking as swiftly as his aged legs allowed.

As soon as the front door was opened, Father rushed in like a gust of wind. Nicholas stepped back from the stairs, his heart contracting.

'Is Nicholas here?' Father sounded breathless.

Percy emerged from his chamber. He stood in the corridor opposite Nicholas. Placing a finger to his lips, he rolled his eyes towards Nicholas's room, before moving to the head of the stairs. Nicholas shrank back against the wall.

'William! Whatever brings you here?' Percy said with feigned surprise, as he descended into the hall.

Father's voice came back frayed and desperate. 'My son. He's run away. I've been searching all night for him. Has he come to you?'

Nicholas felt stricken with a mixture of remorse for having caused his father such anxiety, pleasure that he cared enough to come looking for him, and hope that Uncle Percy might persuade him to change his mind about St. Omer's.

'Haven't seen or heard from the boy. Come into the parlour and sit down; you look quite beside yourself. Lockley, bring us some fortifying wine.'

Although the need to conceal Cousin Matthew's true calling had been explained to him at a young age, Uncle Percy's bold dissembling shocked Nicholas. A lie told to save a life was acceptable, but such dishonesty to Father felt wrong. Should he go down and declare himself? Despite their disagreement, he didn't like to hear Father sounding so distressed.

But then, he reasoned, Percy was only acting on his behalf. He owed his uncle some loyalty in return for his kindness and generosity. And besides, Father had made it clear he only kept him out of duty, when Nicholas was nothing but a burden and a disappointment to him: a miserable worm that should have been cast out. Really, he was doing Father a favour by staying put.

'I've left my horse in the yard,' Father was saying.

'That's all right, the groom will take care of him,' Percy replied.

Nicholas listened to their footsteps receding and the sound of the parlour door closing. If Father spotted Polestar in the stables, the game would be up and he'd be forced back to Measham just because of Father's stubbornness. Should he sneak down to the stables now, while Father was detained with Uncle Percy, and take Polestar out? But where would he go? It would be just his luck to run into Father as he was leaving. No, it was probably safer to remain upstairs and hope the groom fetched Father's horse for him.

Nicholas's stomach gurgled. He wished a servant would come up with some food, but it seemed they had all forgotten him. The morning dragged on and he waited in his room for what felt like hours. There was nothing to do, not even a book to read. What on earth could Father and Percy be discussing?

He was just about to tiptoe down to the kitchens, when Father finally emerged from the parlour. His familiar, swift footsteps could be heard crossing the hall. Nicholas held his breath. Was he making for the stables?

'We have your horse ready for you, sir,' the footman said. 'He's waiting just outside.'

Nicholas raised his fists in the air, shaking them with relief, then castigated himself for being glad to see his father depart. It was just that he was very hungry and if Father found him, all his travails of the previous day would have been for nothing.

'Wouldn't even stay for dinner,' Percy said merrily when Nicholas ventured downstairs. 'He'll be off hunting the county for you.' He chuckled.

'Oughtn't we to tell him that I'm here?' Nicholas asked hesitantly.

He didn't like to think of Father scouring the countryside on a wild goose chase. The rain had picked up again and was being driven against the windows by a rough wind. It was bad weather to be out in, as he knew only too well.

'And have him turn you into some zeal-sick Presbyterian hypocrite? You may be a child of no man, but that doesn't mean you should be orphaned from your Mother Church.' Percy shook his head. 'He doesn't deserve to know. You can write to him once you're safely at St. Omer's, then he'll see sense and realise it was all for the best.'

Over dinner, Percy told Nicholas how delighted he was that his nephew had turned to him for assistance. Angels must have been directing him, for he had arrived at the perfect time. Percy had recently had the honour to entertain as his guest an antiquarian and bookseller – a very learned man, who often conducted business with the English College in St. Omer. He would write to Mr Waddington straight away and ask if Nicholas might travel under his protection when next he made the crossing. In fact, he was sure Mr Waddington was going to France in a week or two. It was divine providence that Nicholas had come to him now – God clearly intended him to be educated at St. Omer's.

⇀ Chapter Seven ↽

May 1680

Nicholas gripped onto the side of the ship, gulping in lungfuls of thick sea air. Seagulls circled overhead, dipping and rising as they rode the air currents. From the dock the grey-green sea had looked more contained, less wild, perhaps because it had been cluttered with boats. Now he stared in awe at the vastness of the water stretching out in all directions. It was terrifying and exhilarating.

He felt better on deck, his nausea subsided. Feeling in his pocket, he was pleased to discover the slice of caraway cake he had wrapped in his handkerchief the day before. He took a bite; it was rather dry and crumbly, but sweet enough to calm his stomach. If this was to be the first of many voyages, he would have to find his sea-legs. Uncle Percy's friend, Mr Waddington, was affected much worse by seasickness than he was and spent the entire journey below deck, even though he said he'd made the journey many times.

Mr Waddington was a lanky, middle-aged gentleman, whose moustache was permanently coated with a dusting of the powdered tobacco he liked to sniff. He said it sharpened his brain, though Uncle Percy called it nose-gunpowder and said it was a filthy Spanish habit.

Poor Mr Waddington looked positively green when they had to climb into a fishing boat and be rowed into the port at Calais. The little vessel reared and dipped alarmingly and Waddington had to lean over the side to empty whatever was left in his stomach.

Even when they were safely on dry land, Nicholas found himself staggering as the earth swayed beneath him. He clutched Waddington's arm. 'Is all of France like this?'

'Like what?' Waddington appeared quite perplexed.

'This shifting ground, is it a permanent feature of French soil?'

'You foolish boy.' Waddington sniggered, his own sickness forgotten. 'It is just the after-effects of being at sea. The sensation of movement will soon wear off.'

Nicholas's relief was tempered by the discovery that the language being spoken all around sounded quite different to the French Matthew and Jane had taught him. Here they talked so fast he could hardly understand a word. He hoped he would pick it up quickly because Uncle Percy had convinced Mr Waddington of his superior grasp of the language and ability to act as a translator. Percy considered the majority of the French to be first-rate villains who would connive to extract all they could from the hapless traveller and had warned Nicholas to be on his guard against such extortions. Not only this, but it was on the pretext of Nicholas being a translator that they had secured him a pass to travel overseas.

His eye was caught by a party of monks, openly wearing their habits and walking in sandals, some even going barefoot. They were entering a church adorned with statues, its bells pealing loudly. Through the open doors Nicholas could see candles burning on a giant golden candlestick. The evocative scent of frankincense drifted out into the evening air. He felt as though a heavy cloak had fallen from his shoulders. Here, being a Catholic was not a dangerous secret but something to be proud of. He too moved towards the entrance, wanting to light a candle for Matthew, but Mr Waddington pulled him on, gesturing to the porter who followed them, wheeling their luggage in a small barrow.

The Maison Rouge exuded dampness and everything in it was sticky, as though, despite being several streets back from the harbour, the whole building had been doused in seawater. As they waited for a maid to fetch the landlord, Waddington informed Nicholas, with a sniff, that this was not his usual abode when in Calais. He was vague about the reasons for the change, but referred, as he had done frequently during the past six days of travel, to the cost of conveying his young companion to St. Omer. Feeling uncomfortable about being such a burden, Nicholas wished he had some money of his own. Uncle Percy had told him that he was paying for Nicholas's passage, but perhaps he hadn't provided adequate funds. What made it worse was that Waddington evidently had no need of Nicholas's services as translator, speaking French quite fluently himself.

Unhappy with the chamber they were eventually shown to, which housed nothing but two very high beds and a rickety-looking table, Waddington complained at length. The landlord shrugged and said it was the best they had. Nicholas, pleased he had been able to follow this exchange, did not mind the sparseness of the furnishings. Staying here would be good preparation for all the different types of accommodation he would experience when he became a voyager, from ship's cabins to tents and private dwellings.

French voices, fluid and musical, came dancing up from the street below. Sticking his head out of the open window, Nicholas inhaled all the intriguing new smells. The salty air blended with the aroma of garlic being fried in butter, which made him eager for some supper, but Waddington called for him to close the shutters on the noisome stench.

Once their baggage was brought up, Waddington checked it over and then departed, saying he had business to attend to. This did not surprise Nicholas, who had become used to Waddington's reserved manner and sudden disappearances. Despite sharing carriages and bedchambers, the man had barely looked at him, retaining a haughty distance that discouraged conversation.

Glancing around the empty room, Nicholas supposed he ought to take this opportunity to write to Father. His departure from Derbyshire had been so rapid, he'd hardly had time to think about those he was leaving behind. Now he was safely across the Channel, he longed to send word that he was secure and well. Only, he hadn't any ink or paper. He looked at Waddington's trunk. He knew there were letter-writing materials packed inside, but Waddington had locked it, carefully pocketing the key. Not that Nicholas would rifle through another's belongings. His father's accusations of a few weeks ago stung him afresh. He was no spying imp. Father would have to wait until he got to St. Omer for news.

Bored and hungry, Nicholas soon gave up waiting for Waddington to return and ventured downstairs. The maid was clearing plates off recently vacated tables and apart from an old man dozing by the fire, the place was deserted. Nicholas asked in French if he might have something to eat and to his delight, the maid not only understood, but agreed to bring him some victuals.

He was less pleased when she returned with a plate of purslane, chicory and dandelion leaves, over which she proceeded to pour a mixture of oil and vinegar. He hoped a more substantial dish would follow, though Mr Waddington had warned him that the French were not so partial to flesh-meat as the English. He did his best with the bitter leaves, washed down with an equally bitter wine, but he must have been making a face, for the maid laughed and shook her head as she brought over a dish of roast fowl.

Just as he was cutting himself a slice of tender, pink meat, Waddington appeared at the table.

'*C'est quoi?*' he demanded of the maid.

She named something Nicholas had not heard of and Waddington waved a hand dismissively at the dish, telling her it needed further cooking. Raising an eyebrow, she lifted the fragrantly steaming meat from under Nicholas's nose and bore it away.

'That woodcock was almost raw. It would have given you terrible colic,' Waddington said as he sat down. 'Glad I ate elsewhere.'

They sat in silence, sipping at their wine, until the maid returned with the bird that had now been boiled until it resembled leather. Nicholas wished he might at least have had a cup of small beer to wash down the chewy meat.

Part I: Boy

Exhausted by the sea voyage, Nicholas fell asleep as soon as he had climbed into his lofty bed. He was woken next morning by Mr Waddington crying out in horror that he had been so mauled by fleas there was scarcely any flesh left on his bones. Waddington's lean frame did not appear significantly diminished, but Nicholas soon became conscious of the itchy red welts on his own legs and arms.

'One of the many hazards of the poorer sort of accommodation in France,' Waddington lamented, 'is the size and the viciousness of the fleas.'

They travelled by post-coach to St. Omer. Waddington insisted on a window seat and Nicholas found himself squashed up beside an old man who snored and farted with equal force. The coach was moving so slowly that after a few hours he begged to be allowed to walk alongside it.

It was easy to keep pace with the creaking wagon as the road was mostly paved and pleasantly firm underfoot. It was also shaded by rows of slender trees whose leaves rustled silver in the breeze. Nicholas marvelled at the vast expanse of land and the huge fields, whose distant edges were framed by dark green forests where, he had heard, wolves roamed. The land seemed entirely given over to the growing of crops and he did not see a sheep or a cow the whole way. He could hear Matthew's voice in his head, asking him questions about the geography of the places they passed, telling him to be observant and to commit to memory all he saw. He hoped that once at St. Omer he would have the opportunity to make some sketches.

There were a large number of crosses and statues of Jesus, the Virgin Mary in her blue cloak, and other saints on the roadside. Noticing how the passers-by openly doffed their hats and crossed themselves at each one, Nicholas began to do the same, which earnt him a smile from an old woman walking in the opposite direction, a black shawl pulled tightly across her shoulders. To his astonishment, he also passed a young woman squatting by a tree and pissing quite freely, unconcerned by her public position. He stored these images in his memory as Matthew had taught him to do, so that he might write them down later.

As they got closer to the city, the land became marshy. Peasants worked on small vegetable plots beside a canal. Rising above the roofs was the square white basilica of the cathedral. Nicholas felt a surge of elation move up from his belly to his chest. Now at last his life was beginning. He sent thanks to both Matthew and Uncle Percy for making this journey possible and promised to prove himself a worthy scholar.

Approaching the college, however, his excitement became tempered with trepidation. The building was intimidating in its size and grandeur. Nicholas stared up at the rows of tall windows, three storeys high. The façade was flat and uniform, its impenetrability broken only by a formidable-looking doorway. Set high above it, he recognised the Jesuit emblem. Could he really belong in such a place, the bastard child of a reclusive Englishman?

The door was opened by the porter, a dour-faced man, who eyed Nicholas with suspicion, but bowed when Waddington stepped forward.

'Father Carmichael is expecting me,' Waddington said and was immediately ushered through the hallway.

Nicholas was about to follow him, when the porter held up a hand and then pointed towards a small door on their right. The sound of Waddington's heels rapping on the stone floor receded into the distance and Nicholas was seized by a sense of abandonment, as sudden as it was absurd.

Filling most of the limited space in his narrow room, the porter opened a huge ledger with an air of the utmost importance, slowly turning the pages until he came to middle of the book. He ran his finger gradually down the list of names, pausing to read each one out loud. On and on went the list, until Nicholas began to fear his name was not included. He felt like a repentant sinner waiting at the gates of Heaven before St. Peter. The porter did not strike him as the sort of man to listen to pleas for admission, no matter how reasonably argued, and Nicholas didn't hold out much hope for Waddington's intervention.

When his own name was finally announced it took him a moment to recognise it.

'*Autonne, Nicolas.*'

'*C'est moi!*' he cried, and was reluctantly directed to the office of the rector.

This was the largest building he had ever entered. Its interior walls, which seemed to stretch on endlessly, enclosed formal and kitchen gardens neatly laid out in a quadrangle. Hundreds of different plants and flowers were releasing their scents into the evening air, attended by a multitude of bees, all buzzing harmoniously. Nicholas stood for a moment, drinking in the gloriousness of it all. Whatever happened next, he could at least say he had got here; he had been inside the sanctified grounds of St. Omer's, like his cousin and his father before him.

There were a great many doors within the cloisters and he tried to remember how many down on the right it was to the rector's. He didn't want to stumble in on a class in the middle of their lessons, which he knew from Matthew continued until six thirty in the evening.

The door he knocked on was opened by Waddington.

'Wait outside, we're almost finished,' Waddington said, shutting it again without waiting for a reply.

At last, Waddington re-emerged. He gave Nicholas a curt nod before walking off without so much as a farewell.

'*Veni,*' a voice summoned from within.

The rector, Father Carmichael, was a tall, stout man with red cheeks and a kind smile. He looked more like a farmer than a priest, though his Latin, when he greeted Nicholas, was fluent and Nicholas found it easier to converse in than the French he had been attempting to communicate with up to now.

'You must be weary after your long journey,' Farther Carmichael said.

'The pace was so slow I did not find it tiring and we stopped for refreshments shortly before arriving here.' Nicholas was keen to impress the rector with his fortitude and enthusiasm.

'Good, I have been assured you are healthy.' Father Carmichael's bright blue eyes were examining him so thoroughly, he felt like a horse at a fair. 'I will hear your confession before we proceed any further.' The rector motioned to a *prie-dieu* in the corner of the room.

Nicholas had not been expecting this. Should he admit to having run away from home? But then Father Carmichael might refuse to enrol him. He couldn't bear to fall now at the last hurdle. And where could he go if he was not allowed in? He didn't want to have to go chasing after Mr Waddington.

Kneeling down, he leant his elbows on the wooden ledge and bowed his head, trying desperately to marshal his whirling thoughts. Uncle Percy had given him his blessing and Father would know soon enough where he was. It couldn't be a sin to resort to desperate means in order to gain a Catholic education. He decided to remain quiet on the matter.

After receiving the sacrament, Nicholas was subjected to a lengthy explanation of the rules and regulations of the college. He would never remember them all; the rector's words seemed to be evaporating in the air between them as Nicholas fought to keep his eyelids from drooping.

When he had finally finished, Father Carmichael opened an inner door and called to his servant to fetch another student. Francis Bedley would show Nicholas around the college and introduce him to the master who would be his tutor for the next six years, Father Carmichael explained. Nicholas hoped Francis would repeat the most important of the many rules so that he could avoid breaking them.

'This arrived yesterday from your father,' Carmichael said, almost as an afterthought, lifting a letter from his desk and handing it to Nicholas. 'You will see that the seal is broken. That is because I have passed the contents. No letters may be sent or received without my permission.'

Nicholas felt dizzy. He held his breath as he took the parchment, almost dropping it in the exchange. How had Father known he would be here? If the rector had read the letter, he knew Nicholas had not made a full confession, yet he said nothing. Father's scrawling hand was compellingly familiar, but Nicholas only had time to glance at the address before there was a knock at the door, heralding the arrival of his guide. Surely the letter couldn't be too awful, since he was being allowed to stay, he consoled himself.

Once they had stepped out of the rector's office, Nicholas, by way of making conversation, asked Francis where he was from. Francis replied in Latin that any boy caught speaking in English would lose their breakfast.

St. Omers was a world unto itself. Everything necessary was contained within its walls, from the granary and the brewery to the apothecary's shop and the printing house. Hearing a whinnying from the stables, Nicholas was struck with a sudden longing for Polestar. It was childish, but he wished his closest friend could be there beside him. He hoped Uncle Percy was looking after Polestar as well as he had promised.

'Boys are only allowed to associate with those from the same chamber, which are designated according to age,' Francis was explaining.

More rules – how many had Nicholas missed?

Francis stopped abruptly in a doorway, beneath a statue of the Virgin Mary, and began to recite the Angelus. Nicholas just avoided bumping into him. Over Francis's sloping shoulder he could see a long room filled with rows of curtained cubicles. When the prayer had finished and Francis stepped into the room, Nicholas followed, peering into the nearest cubicle. A narrow bed and a small cupboard were enclosed within it.

'It is forbidden to enter another boy's cubicle.' Francis's voice grew shrill with alarm. 'This is your bed.' He marched across the dormitory. 'We sleep only one boy to a bed, not in pairs as you may be accustomed to, for it is considered more cleanly and healthful.'

Nicholas was about to tell him that he was used to sleeping alone, but Francis was pulling open the curtain and gesturing at a stack of neatly folded clothes that lay on the bed.

'You must change into the St. Omers' uniform. It is a great honour to dress like St. Ignatius. I will wait here for you.' Francis dropped the curtain and turned his back on the compartment. 'You may call me if you need assistance,' he added as Nicholas hastened to undress.

Pulling on the doublet and breeches of white canvas, rough woollen stockings, black cassock and broad-brimmed hat, Nicholas felt as though he were casting off his old skin and becoming a new person altogether. Now he was truly a St. Omers' boy. He emerged proudly from his cubicle.

'What do you think?'

Francis ignored his question and pointed instead to the straw strewn over the stone floor.

'That is only changed in the summer holidays, but you can ask the apothecary for flea powder if your mattress becomes infected. The window must be kept open to ensure plentiful fresh air.' He puffed out his chest with self-importance. 'I am in charge of seeing that all candles are snuffed out at sleeping-time.'

By the time the bell finally called them into the refectory for supper, Nicholas was so weary he could hardly stand. And still he hadn't had a chance to read his letter.

The vast hall smelt of meat broth, damp stone and tallow candles. Long tables, arranged in neat rows, filled its length. Nicholas had never seen so many boys. He had probably never seen so many people gathered together in one place. Despite the number of youths, the refectory was surprisingly quiet. There was no boisterousness, no shouting or pushing or calling out of names, just the soft shuffling of feet, the scraping of benches and the clatter of pewter.

It was cold in the hall and he was glad of the warm soup set down in front of him. This was followed by a small piece of beef, an apple and a lump of cheese. Jugs of beer and baskets of bread were passed down the table. Nicholas's enthusiasm for this repast was tempered when the boy next to him whispered that he would be given the exact same diet next day for dinner and every day thereafter. Francis raised his eyebrows and put a finger to his lips. The rest of the hall was silent, apart from the clink of knives and spoons.

While they ate, a boy at the head of their long table stood to read from a martyrology. As he recited the names of the English martyrs, 'Campion, Garnett, Thomas Becket and Moore', all assembled removed their hats and lowered their heads. Nicholas imagined Matthew's name being read out with similar reverence in years to come and suddenly understood, in a way he hadn't before, how Matthew's faith had sustained him. It was comforting, in this foreign place, amidst strangers, to know that his cousin and father had been here before him, following the same regimen. Matthew seemed closer to him than he had done at any time since his death. Nicholas felt his heart expand in his chest. He was sure he had acted rightly in coming here and hoped Father might be brought to think so too.

When supper was over, the boys were allowed an hour of recreation before prayers and bed. Nicholas decided to escape Francis by telling him he needed the necessary house. Not knowing the Latin for this, he was about to use the English, but Francis held up one hand and began to hum. Well, if he was not permitted to say it, Nicholas would have to mimic the actions. He stuck his arse out and pulled a face. The boys around him began to laugh. Francis looked utterly disgusted, which only increased their glee. Nicholas extended his performance to an imitation of Mr Waddington in the worst throes of seasickness. To his delight the boys applauded.

Having grown up an only child, he'd been worried the other boys would dislike him; that they would instinctively scent the whiff of illegitimacy about him and find his manners strange. But the pious Francis seemed to be the odd one out and the other pupils friendly enough.

After being directed to the privy, he found a quiet corner behind a box hedge and pulled out Father's letter.

My dear son,

I hope you are now safely arrived at St. Omer. Your uncle forgot to inform me of your departure. It is only thanks to Mr Crewe that I have this information. You can, I trust, imagine the anguish your absence has caused me.

As your loving father, you must know that I have only ever had your best interests at heart. If I have kept a distance from you, it is because that is the way my father conducted himself. There have been many times when I have longed to restore the mother you lost by offering you a more tender care, but I considered it best for both of us to be your protector rather than your nurse or your confidant. However it might appear, I would give the world for you and sacrifice everything I have for your well-being.

It brought me great joy to see the mutual love and esteem held between you and your cousin, Father Matthew. I know he was very proud, not only of your achievements in the schoolroom, but also of the honourable young man you were growing into. His death was a terrible blow for us all. But his example has also shown me not to clasp too tightly that which I hold dear. I trust to God to keep you safe from harm and to your own instincts to follow the right path. Matthew, in leaving you the funds to complete your education at St. Omer's, made his wishes clear. I honour those, as he did mine in life.

Be sure to write to me and tell me of your progress there.

God bless you, my dear child.
Your most affectionate, loving father,
William

Tears started up in Nicholas's eyes. He had expected anger and recriminations from his father, not the love and generosity expressed here. It was true, Father had always provided him with everything he wanted: the best steed ever, books, fencing lessons, the freedom to roam about the countryside.

Father must have known his letter would be read by the rector for he had taken care not to say anything that would be to Nicholas's disadvantage at the school. Nicholas thought uneasily of the confession he had made. Would his omissions be held against him?

Staring up at the stars that had appeared in the blue-black sky, Nicholas felt his spirit expand with equal measures of hope and gratitude. Everything had worked out; Father had forgiven him and he was enrolled at St. Omer's. At last, he was exactly where he wanted to be; he had achieved the first of his ambitions and could see no reason why the rest shouldn't follow on accordingly.

⇥ Chapter Eight ⇤

1st June 1685

My dearest son,

I write to you with details of the trial of Titus Oates, which I attended last month. Thank the Lord, the jury found the villain guilty of perjury and his so-called Popish Plot has now been thoroughly discredited.

What a strange, whining fool Oates is. I have never seen nor heard a less beguiling rogue. His manner, even in the dock, was arrogant and haughty. He must have been assisted by the devil to convince so many. Or perhaps they were only too willing to be persuaded the papists were plotting against them.

Many alumni of your college were there to testify again that Oates could not have met the plotters in London as he claimed, since he was in St. Omer at the time. Though Oates tried to have their evidence dismissed on account of their being papists, this time the judge decreed that a Catholic's evidence was as good as a Protestant's. How times have changed since our gracious King James has come to power.

The bile rose in my throat to hear all those honourable witnesses, judges and politicians, whose testimony helped condemn the innocent, now found they had lost their memories and had no recollection of their previous evidence. Solicitor-General Finch, who himself helped try Whitbread and Langhorne, had the gall to claim it was a strange and wonderful thing anyone had ever believed Oates. 'But how,' said he, 'were they to doubt the word of one audacious enough to lie to parliament and the great Courts of Justice?' Judge Jeffreys told the jury that Oates had drawn innocent blood upon the nation and that the justice of England lay under a very great reproach abroad for this thing.

His words are true, but his real concern is to vindicate the Protestant religion, parliament and the courts of law, so he heaps all the blame on Oates and believes by punishing him he can prove the justice of England to be invincible. No matter that at least twenty-four innocent men were convicted in her courts.

Afterwards I went to see Oates pilloried at Westminster Hall. He was pelted with eggs, but I refrained from such actions as I do not think your cousin would have approved them. It was estimated afterwards that as many as a thousand people were there.

Oates is to be held in prison for the rest of his life and placed in the pillory four times every year. Some consider his punishment too severe, but he gets to keep his sorry life, where better men lost theirs.

All is well here. Crewe, Abigail and the rest of the household send you their service and blessings. Have no fears for Polestar; he continues as healthy as ever and happy to be home at Measham instead of sold off by your uncle Percy.

Your last brought me great joy. Continue to excel in your studies, and on the stage. Your account of playing Saint Thomas Becket had us all transfixed. Abigail cried out in horror to hear that you had been knocked out by an overly eager knight. Perhaps in future it would be better to avoid the role of martyr, though of course it is testimony to your talents to be chosen for the leading part.

Write again soon, my sweet boy, for until I have you home again I must make do with your letters, which, being both witty and informative are a welcome substitute, but cannot replace your corporeal presence.

Your loving and affectionate father,
William

Part II
Youth

Part II

Youth

⇥ Chapter Nine ⇤

May 1687

When Nicholas was called into the rector's office, he thought perhaps Father Carmichael was going to suggest applying for a papal dispensation so that he could join the priesthood. He had been teaching at the college for the past year, having graduated as one of its highest-achieving scholars, but he had no calling to become a Jesuit. He was looking forward to continuing his studies in Paris, where he was going to study medicine and botany. He had assured Father he would not set up practice as a physician or a lowly apothecary; he merely wished to extend his knowledge. In truth, he was more excited by the prospect of living in a great city and seeing all the wonders held there, than in the academic advantages. One of his St. Omer friends was already a year into his master of arts degree in Paris and had written urging Nicholas to join him, claiming it far exceeded any other European city for its elegance and civility.

A sudden sensation of panic gripped his vitals. Had the college found out about his dalliance with Isabelle Dupont? The widowed Madame Dupont was, in fact, the real reason he had stayed on at St. Omers after graduating. Though lately she did not send for him as often as she used to, and to his surprise, he no longer yearned to be with her whenever they were apart. He could now go for whole days without even thinking of her.

Isabelle had become enamoured of him after seeing him perform in the college's production of *Zeno*. Later, she had smuggled him a letter, inviting him to come to her on a Thursday afternoon when the boys were allowed out into the fields to play sports.

How could he resist her summons? She was nine years older than him, wealthy and used to having her own way. She was also a renowned beauty. It was an honour to be chosen as her lover. It wasn't difficult to slip away from a game of boules under the pretext of a meditative walk, though his mind, far from being calm, blazed with a competing mixture of feverish anticipation and terror. He was afraid, not only of discovery, but even more of disappointing this goddess. After their first rendezvous, however, all his fears were assuaged and only his passion remained.

Isabelle's maid would let him in at the garden gate from where he could take the back stairs up to her chamber. Sometimes she would greet him from her bed, dressed in nothing but a satin gown, tied loosely at the waist, the material artlessly delineating each plump contour of her flesh, her round white arms reaching out to embrace him, as graceful as the spreading wings of a swan.

At other times she would be sitting at her dressing table, sipping a cup of chocolate and he would watch with fascination as she pulled the pins from her hair, releasing the thick auburn tresses to cascade down her back. She would tell him that her legs were sore and he would kneel beside her, lifting her heels onto his lap, pressing – as instructed – his thumbs into the sweeping arcs of her narrow feet. Drawing a line up around her tapering ankles and along the elegant curve of her calves, brushing the downy golden hairs with his fingertips and tracing a map around each nut-brown mole. Then, with a leisurely sigh, she would lean over him, pulling his head between her thighs.

When being lectured on the torments that awaited sinners, he would tell himself to resist her next call. But his legs had no such compunctions and would carry him to her door whether he intended to go there or not. It was hard to believe that such sweetness and joy as he experienced with Isabelle could truly be a sin. They were causing harm to no one. Indeed, she often told him that he had rescued her from terrible loneliness. Isabelle said that eventually she would have to give in to one of the many suitors after her fortune. One in particular had the backing of her family and, though she despised the man, she knew it was only a matter of time before she would be forced by her brothers to accept his proposal. While she still had the freedom to enjoy herself, she was determined to do so and if Nicholas was her chosen playmate, who was he to refuse her a little happiness?

He was as good a student in the bedroom as he was in the class-room and learnt swiftly the arts of pleasure from his mistress. And he never had to worry about creating another little bastard, as Isabelle said she knew the means to prevent such an eventuality.

A gentleman in a dark grey velvet suit was standing at the window in Father Carmichael's office. One hand rested on the hilt of his sword. Could this be one of Isabelle's brothers come to call him out? Or would he insist on a marriage? Nicholas wasn't sure which outcome was more alarming. Despite her considerable charms, he felt too young to be tied to the first woman he had had relations with. But if her family insisted, what defence could he offer? It would be a very advantageous match. Matthew had wanted him to marry a Catholic bride. And he supposed Isabelle would be happy to fund his studies and explorations. In return, he would probably have to accept her affairs with other men.

On the other hand, a duel would be disastrous either way. Nicholas, who was noted for his skill at fencing, did not want to be responsible for killing Isabelle's brother, nor did he want to lose his own life.

He was reconciling himself to the idea of marriage when the rector, who remained seated behind his desk, greeted him in English. He hoped this meant the stranger wasn't French and therefore not out to avenge his sister's honour.

The man turned from the window to look Nicholas up and down. There was something familiar about his disdainful gaze, but Nicholas couldn't quite place who he was.

'This is Mister Gilbert Staley,' Father Carmichael said.

Nicholas hastily bowed and Staley inclined his head slightly.

'We have been discussing your future, Hawthorne, and we would like you to alter the direction of your studies,' Carmichael continued. 'His Gracious Majesty, James II, has done you the great honour of obtaining your admission to Magdalen College, Oxford, as a doctoral student.'

Nicholas stared at the rector with a mixture of astonishment and dismay. Could this be Father's doing? He knew Father wanted him to come home, but he didn't think he had any influence with the King. Perhaps Crewe had petitioned on his behalf.

'I am of course deeply honoured and grateful to come to the attention of His Majesty. I cannot think what I have done to merit such notice. But, not having studied at Oxford, I don't believe I am a suitable candidate and, with all due respect, I am already enrolled at the university in Paris.'

The English universities had a reputation for being old-fashioned and limited in what they taught. He'd rather they sent him to Edinburgh than Oxford, which at least was known to be advanced in the study of medicine, even if the weather was inclement.

'Do you love your King, Nicholas?' Staley's voice had a nasal twang that Nicholas instantly disliked.

'Of course, sir.'

'Well then, you will do everything a loyal subject should to protect him.'

For a moment, Nicholas thought they might be asking him to join the Horse Guards.

Carmichael smiled sympathetically. 'You have been selected for this great privilege because of your talents, both as a linguist and an actor. This is also an opportunity for you to spread the faith by proving that a Jesuit education is superior to an Anglican one. Remember, those who teach the best will gain the most students.' Seeing Nicholas's unconvinced expression, he added, 'Oxford has a renowned physic garden too.'

Nicholas looked from one man to the other. 'Please excuse my ignorance, but I still don't see how a post at Oxford will serve the King.'

Staley settled himself into the window seat, gesturing languidly for Nicholas to take the stool opposite. 'I understand that Lady Jane

Pemberton, formerly Sellwood, was a close associate of your father's and that you maintain a correspondence with her.'

Nicholas was too startled to do anything more than nod. It was true, he and Jane wrote to one another, she more frequently and at greater length than he did.

'So, you are aware of her marriage to Lord Pemberton.' It was a statement rather than a question. 'Pemberton is close to the King, but we fear he may be susceptible to external forces most injurious to our kingdom. His eldest son, Edward, is his weakness. The boy is a libertine. We want you to become his close friend. You are older than he is and can influence him for the better. Contrive to be drawn into the bosom of the family. Ingratiate yourself with Pemberton. Find out if he and his son are truly loyal to His Majesty. If they are colluding with the Dutch, one of them at least might be persuaded to reveal their plans.'

'I could propose a visit to Lady Jane,' Nicholas said tentatively. 'She has already extended an invitation.'

Staley wagged his head dismissively. 'She is a useful introduction; her fondness for you will smooth your way. But Edward is the means to his father's heart and all the secrets contained therein. Gain the son's trust and you gain the father's. We need to know if and what he might be plotting with the Dutch and how far his circle extends. A visit will not suffice.'

Jane had made several references in her letters to her stepson being a wayward and difficult youth. Her husband hoped he would calm down as he grew older, but his first year at Oxford had not been promising. Edward spent most of his time at the gaming tables. How was Nicholas supposed to hold any sway over such a headstrong boy?

Staley drew a silver case out of his pocket and took a pinch of tobacco out of it. He placed the brown filaments on the back of his hand, snorting them up with a quick inhalation, then snapped the case shut and exchanged it for a lace handkerchief, which he used to blow his nose. This action prompted Nicholas's memory.

'Mr Waddington!' he cried before he could stop himself.

'Who?' Staley turned back to the window as though Nicholas was calling to someone outside.

'You are the man who first brought me here. An associate of my uncle's. We travelled together from Derbyshire seven years ago.'

'You mistake me for someone else. I hope your ability to recognise people is not always so faulty.' Staley sounded deeply offended.

Nicholas stared at him in bewilderment. He looked just like Waddington, yet his name, his dress and his manner were quite different. Could two unrelated people resemble each other like twins? It was a long time since he'd seen Waddington; he'd been a boy then and now he was a man. Perhaps he was recalling a likeness where there was none. Many men liked tobacco and must take it in the same way.

He turned to Father Carmichael, but the rector, who was gazing serenely down at his folded hands, appeared to have withdrawn from the conversation around him for a moment of contemplation. Certainly, he seemed unperturbed by any similarities between Waddington and Staley.

'Please excuse me, I mean no disrespect, sir.' Nicholas shook his head as if this could clear his whirling thoughts. Were they really asking him to become an intelligencer? 'I am honoured of course that you should consider me, but surely there is someone better placed to discover Pemberton's intentions.' He hesitated before adding, 'I do not like to spy on my friends.'

'You appear to have taught this youth too much disputation,' Staley told Carmichael, and Nicholas was shocked by his insolent tone to the rector.

Moving like a cat, Staley came so close, Nicholas could smell the tobacco on his breath and see the crumbs of it on his moustache. 'Your father has many secrets.' Staley spoke softly, forcing Nicholas, even at this unpleasant proximity, to listen intently. 'Secrets that would destroy him were they to get out.' Staley exhaled heavily and the shreds of tobacco were blown from his moustache to his protruding lower lip. 'We are happy to keep these secrets enclosed within our deepest bosom, provided his son proves his value. Should you disappoint us, however, it is not only you who will suffer; your father too will be punished. If you wish to remain the heir to his estate, you would do well to follow my commands.'

Nicholas felt the blood rising into his face and drumming in his ears. He wanted to strike the odious fellow down. What secrets was he talking about?

'There is no need to resort to threats.' Father Carmichael had also risen from his seat and now extended his arms in a placatory fashion. 'I am sure Nicholas is keen to serve his country and his religion. He has, after all, the shining example of his blessed cousin to follow.' Carmichael smiled at Nicholas. 'Your reticence is commendable. You are an honest, noble-hearted fellow with an affable nature, which is why you are so popular among your classmates and your students. If only all men were as true. Sadly, as we know only too well, there are those who will plot and dissemble, causing untold misery and mayhem.'

Carmichael came over to sit beside Nicholas while Staley retreated to the window seat. The rector's rubicund face was now creased with paternal concern and his sonorous voice had a slight quiver to it.

'Imagine if you had had the opportunity to spy on a man like Titus Oates and by doing so saved many innocent lives, Father Matthew's included. Just as the Bible tells us Paul's life was saved by his nephew, who overheard the plot to kill his uncle... While Mordecai saved the life of King Ahasuerus by informing Queen Esther. And did the Lord not tell Moses to send forth spies into the land of Canaan? When we are called, we must act as the eyes and ears of those who serve God.' He patted Nicholas's knee. 'I am sure you will have no difficulty in discovering whether Pemberton is conspiring against the King and, if so, what his plans might be. I have absolute faith in you.'

Nicholas looked over at Staley. 'If I do this, may I ask for something in return? Will you tell me who betrayed Father Matthew? Someone knew about the priest-hole at Measham Hall.'

Staley returned Nicholas's gaze with a hint of wry amusement in his eyes. 'There are traitors and blasphemers everywhere. I am sure your cousin would rather you worked to safeguard England's future than worried about old scores. But I will see what I can do.'

Nicholas sat in a corner of the physic garden, under the dappled shade of an arbour of hops. The sun never shone so warm and bright as this in England. He was hoping the scent of lavender and rosemary might soothe his disquiet and sharpen his senses. How often he had admired the variety and the richness of the carefully ordered beds. He had even helped plant some of these herbs. He almost wished that morning's visitor had been one of Isabelle's brothers instead of this English intelligencer.

Father Carmichael must have shown Staley his correspondence with Jane. Had he gone so far as to make copies? He was angry with both men, one for his aggression, the other for his flattery. He was not sure he deserved the trust Carmichael placed in him. It was true that, despite his solitary upbringing, he had not found it hard to make friends with the other boys at St. Omer's, but here there were strict rules to follow and a common ethos that united them. Why should Lord Pemberton or his son confide in him?

Father had once accused him of spying and called him an eaves-dropping imp. But he had only indulged in such behaviour because so much was kept from him, not because he was inherently devious.

What on earth could these secrets be, that would ruin Father? What had he done that was so terrible? It must be something more than harbouring a priest or having an illegitimate son. Could that be why he lived so reclusively? Nicholas recollected their trips to Derby and how Father always sat in the darkest corner of the inn, keeping his face averted from strangers and his hat pulled down low. It wasn't just that he was misanthropical; it was as though he was afraid of discovery.

It was also strange how Staley resembled Mr Waddington. If they were the same person, that meant Staley had some connection to Uncle

Percy. Unless he had been deceiving his uncle too. Perhaps Father was right to distrust Percy. Nicholas closed his eyes for a moment and listened to the buzzing and chirping all around him. The insects were as busy as his brain. It all seemed too far-fetched to be true.

A bee alighted on a bright yellow clump of yarrow. Nicholas suddenly longed for a life as simple as the honeybee's, whose days were spent collecting nectar from flowers, whereas he was being sent to extract venom from liars. If indeed Pemberton was working for Dutch interests. They might be mistaken about him. Nicholas hoped so, for Jane wrote of her second husband with great affection and seemed very happy to be Lady Pemberton. At least it would be a pleasure to see her again, though he hated the thought of having to dissemble with her. Father too would be happy to have him nearer, even if he could never tell him the real reason he had returned to England. Both Staley and Carmichael had impressed upon Nicholas the need for secrecy. He must not say anything that would compromise his undertaking.

Crewe must know what Father's secrets were; he knew everything. But surely, if he had maintained his intelligence networks, Crewe would have been able to protect both Nicholas and Father from the machinations of an odious worm like Staley, or at least to warn them. Perhaps age had limited his capabilities and he no longer exercised his former influence. He had not, after all, been able to save Matthew.

Matthew had believed in Nicholas, had seen him not as a fallen angel, but as a messenger of God. And now the rector was telling him to act as the eyes and ears of those who serve God. How could he refuse? He couldn't be so selfish as to resent this change of plans when Matthew had given his life to return to England and nurture his flock. His cousin too would have preferred to stay in Rome or Paris. What Nicholas was being asked to do paled into insignificance in comparison to Matthew's mission.

And yet, with this summons to return to England, he felt as though a net had been thrown over him. A net that was dragging him down into murky, suffocating depths, far from a future that had seemed so full of hope and brightness.

⇢ Chapter Ten ⇠

June-July 1687

'What a fine young man you have become.' Jane held out one arm, her small face almost entirely taken over by a smile of such delighted affection it almost broke Nicholas's heart.

'Lady Pemberton.' He bowed.

'Nay, do not stand on such ceremony with me who knew you when you were still in swaddling-clothes.'

Nicholas took her free hand and she let her cane drop as she drew him into a tight embrace. He hugged her delicate frame somewhat tentatively. Jane seemed to have diminished since he'd last seen her, but she still smelt of geranium and rose-water. The light, floral scent took him straight back to his childhood at Measham Hall and for a second, he wished they really could return to those innocent days.

'You must call me Jane, as you have always done.' She leant on his arm as she turned to introduce the gentleman who had appeared by her side. 'And this is my dear husband, Lord Pemberton. Ralph.'

Pemberton was a large, formidable-looking man, with dark, heavy eyebrows and a bulbous nose. His grey periwig cascaded down his chest almost to his belly, which was gently curved but not overly corpulent. His voice was as rich and warm as his gold brocaded velvet jacket.

'You are most welcome. Jane has spoken of you often, with the same maternal regard she bestows so generously on all the children of her acquaintance.'

Pemberton's respect for his wife was evident in both his tone and his manner. He bent to retrieve Jane's silver walking stick, placing it in her hand with careful solicitude.

'It is an honour.' Nicholas gave a low bow, which Pemberton returned with a slight one, as befitting their different stations.

'You must be fatigued after your long journey. What do you need more, sleep or food?' Jane asked.

'I would like to change out of my travelling clothes.' Nicholas could smell his own sweat and the salty grime of his recent voyage. 'And then perhaps something to eat?'

Jane laughed. 'I'm glad you've retained your hearty appetite. I was afraid your education might have turned you into an ascetic.'

Nicholas wondered if this was a criticism of his Jesuit schooling. 'No chance of that.' He smiled.

'We usually dine late in this household, but you may be used to that, having lived so long on the Continent. My son at least will be glad of an early dinner,' Pemberton said.

'Edward?' Nicholas hadn't expected him to be at home, but this would be a fortuitous introduction.

A stricken look passed over Pemberton's face. 'No, alas, he is rarely here. I meant my youngest, Richard. A boy of a different humour.'

'Richard is a lamb and reminds me so often of you,' Jane said.

'Isaac,' Pemberton called to a young man who was standing at the foot of the stairs. 'My secretary will show you to your room,' he told Nicholas with a wave of his hand. Nicholas was intrigued by the golden-brown colour of the man's skin and wondered if he came from the Americas. Staley had told him Pemberton was the auditor-general of Plantations Revenues, overseeing all the income from the royal colonies, places as far away as Virginia, Jamaica and Barbados in the West Indies.

Ascending the curving staircase behind the secretary, Nicholas took in his surroundings with growing pleasure and admiration. It was a modern house, filled with light let in by tall, rectangular windows composed of large square panes instead of the diamond mullions he was used to. The airy feel was augmented by high, white plastered ceilings and floors tiled like a giant chessboard in black and white marble. He could feel the cool slipperiness of the stone through the worn soles of his boots.

Isaac showed him into a spacious room hung with blue watered silks. Plump pink cherubs smiled down at him from the painted ceiling, garlands of flowers and vines trailing from their outstretched arms.

'Is this my chamber?' Nicholas asked doubtfully.

'Certainly, this room is reserved for guests. They will expect you in the dining room shortly, sir,' Isaac said, with a slight smile and a nod of the head, before pulling the door closed behind him. His accent was as English as Nicholas's, but with a local, Kentish twang.

Nicholas had not been expecting to be given such a splendid chamber all to himself. He spread his arms out and spun round with delight. Any inhabitant of this room couldn't help but feel important. It was certainly a far cry from the austere dormitory at St. Omers or his snug, wood-panelled chamber at home. Of course, he knew that he must be on his guard against the lure of avarice and that this sort of private opulence was offensive to God, but to enjoy such luxury for a short while, in aid of a greater good, could not be a sin.

The dining room was even more impressive. Nicholas felt as though he had entered a classical paradise. Exotic birds adorned the walls while pagan gods disported themselves in the heavens above. Around the high fireplace, acanthus flowers unfurled amid a profusion of carved leaves and branches. He wondered what Father would make of such splendour. Measham Hall certainly lacked a lady's taste.

Three children sat at the table, observing him solemnly. Nicholas introduced himself and the eldest girl replied.

'My name is Dorothy. You may call me Doll.' She gestured to the companions on either side of her. 'This is Prudence, she's ten, two years my junior, and that is Richard, he is eight.'

Richard smiled shyly and Nicholas winked at him.

'And that's Lettice.' Prudence pointed to the doorway. 'She is seventeen.'

Nicholas turned round to see a pretty young woman standing behind him. She bobbed a nimble curtsey.

'Are you admiring our stepmother's designs?' she asked, appearing to have read his thoughts. 'I helped Her Ladyship, you know, in choosing them.'

'They are delightful.' Nicholas bowed.

With her golden curls and rosy cheeks, Lettice rather resembled one of the nymphs smiling winsomely down at them from the ceiling. Though she of course was fully dressed, her breasts just concealed by a low-cut bodice, whereas they were semi-naked, their loose robes draped so as to reveal at least one round, pink nipple per maiden.

'Ready for some fine English beef?' Pemberton entered the room, followed by his wife.

Nicholas felt the heat rising in his cheeks at the lascivious turn his thoughts had been taking.

'I hope now that you're here, we will always eat dinner at noon,' Richard told him, once Nicholas had sat down beside him. 'It is the proper time, but Father makes us wait until two and when Edward is home it's sometimes even later because he never rises before eleven.'

'That's because he's a lazy slug-a-bed,' Prudence said.

Her father raised his eyebrows disapprovingly and she turned her gaze to the table, looking suitably chastened. They sat in silence while Lord Pemberton delivered grace and then Jane stood up to carve the joints of meat that had been brought in. After a nod of assent from her husband, she served Nicholas first, giving him the best cuts. He could see Richard eyeing the chicken breast on his plate and slipped him a piece, earning a look of spaniel-like devotion.

Nicholas was impressed, and a little intimidated, to see not only a knife and spoon beside his plate, but also a small fork. He had seen large forks used for serving food, but never for eating with. When a new arrival to St. Omer's, a boy with an Italian mother, requested a fork to pick up his food, he was asked what he thought God had created fingers for. The other boys had laughed at him and called him womanish.

Nicholas found the use of this dainty implement necessitated cutting his meat into small pieces, otherwise they fell off on the way to his mouth or else were difficult to eat in one bite. He supposed it saved his fingers from getting greasy, but wiping them clean on a napkin was easier than fiddling about with extra silver.

'Lettice.' Jane waved her knife over the various platters. 'What cut would you like?'

'Your Ladyship's choice shall be mine.' Lettice tilted her head demurely.

'A little of each, then,' Jane decided.

Nicholas noticed, however, that Lettice ate very little of what she had been given, despite her father telling her she would be comelier with a little more spread on her. He detected also an element of tension beneath the excessive civility Lettice showed her stepmother and the overt attention Jane gave the young woman.

'My good lady tells me you have turned your back on the superstitions of Rome to embrace the light of a Protestant university,' Pemberton said, giving Nicholas an appraising look.

Nicholas lowered his empty fork, wondering where the piece of beef that had been hanging from its prongs had disappeared to. 'I intend to apply myself whole-heartedly to my doctoral studies at Oxford and am looking forward to learning from the scholars there,' he said carefully.

'Are you still interested in natural philosophy?' Jane asked, coming to his rescue. 'Lord Pemberton is a member of the Royal Society and takes a great interest in the experiments demonstrated there.' She turned to her husband. 'Perhaps you might take Nicholas to see one of them, my love?'

'That would be a dream realised,' Nicholas said eagerly.

'They don't admit any young whippersnapper, you know. Mind you, they allowed a woman in once, back in '67.' Pemberton laughed. 'The Duchess of Newcastle, if you could call her a woman, she dressed in men's apparel and made bows instead of curtseys. Quite insane. They won't be doing that again in a hurry.' But he smiled more jovially at Nicholas. 'Prove your worth at Oxford and we'll see what we can do.'

'Didn't you have a friend who liked to disguise herself as a man?' Lettice asked Jane.

Jane looked quite startled. 'Whatever makes you think that?'

'When we were preparing for the masque at Court and I took the part of Mercury, you showed me many tricks your friend had taught you, to transform me into the other sex. We deceived half the Court, don't you remember? Even Princess Anne took me for a boy.'

'Oh, that.' Jane shook her head. 'Theatrical nonsense fit only for the stage. They were humouring you, my dear.'

'Playwrights love to have women act the parts of men; it's just an excuse to show off their legs.' Lord Pemberton nodded at Nicholas.

'It is different at Court,' Lettice said, her eyes radiant with the memory. 'The masques are the most magical, splendid events ever, with the most fantastical scenery, elaborate costumes, and the very best musicians and dances.' She looked coyly at Nicholas. 'Have you attended Court?'

'I have not had that honour,' Nicholas said, wiping the gravy off his chin.

Lettice sighed. 'I am almost too old now to become a maid of honour.'

'And too sensible, I hope,' her father interrupted.

After dinner, Pemberton retired to his study. Dismissing her waiting woman, Jane said she would take Nicholas for a stroll around the nearest part of the gardens. The children were at their lessons and Lettice chose to remain indoors practising a new ayre on the virginals. Nicholas was glad to have this time alone with the woman who had been so like a mother to him.

As they walked out onto the terrace, he was brought to a halt by the scene before him. Long expanses of lawn bordered a shallow canal fed by a waterfall that cascaded down a hill of at least fifteen feet. The torrent's flow was slowed by successive pools in which it collected before spilling onto the next, finally ending in the calm green waters of the ornamental river. Elaborate fountains featuring nymphs and sea gods were placed at equal distances along the length of the waterway, creating a harmonious symphony of aquatic sounds. Neatly trimmed hedges enclosed the grass, while on the other side symmetrical gravel walkways were screened by trellises over which all sorts of climbing plants – clematis, jasmine and even vines – grew.

Jane laughed at Nicholas's awe-struck posture. 'My husband has spent a great deal of time in the Low Countries and brought back many plants and all the latest ideas in garden design. You must ask him to give you a tour of his hothouses. Being secretary of plantations, he is sent the most marvellous fruits from our colonies. He is currently growing something called an *ananas* or pine-apple. It has never been grown in England before and is said to be the most delicious fruit of all the Americas, though it looks quite inedible from the outside, almost like a giant artichoke.'

'I should like that very much,' Nicholas said, feeling simultaneously delighted at the prospect and filled with guilt for his secret undertaking. He was trying to formulate a question about Pemberton's Dutch connections when Jane asked after his father.

She leant a little more heavily on his arm, looking up at him with an earnest expression. 'I hope he doesn't mind you visiting us.'

'It made sense for me to stop here on the way up to Derbyshire, it being so close to Dover,' Nicholas said uneasily, for the truth was he had not told Father he was going to stay with the Pembertons.

Jane nodded. 'I hope he is in good health. I expect he is glad to have you nearer to him. He used to talk of sending you to Oxford; he must be pleased that you have decided to go there instead of to Paris.' She sounded somewhat wistful.

'Indeed.' Nicholas paused to admire a rose bush, the blooms an unusual shade of fiery red. He still found it painful to think he might have been embarking on a life in the French capital instead of being forced to return to England.

'I will always be grateful to your father for his care of me.' Jane stopped to pull a stalk of sticky cleavers out of a neatly pruned bay tree. 'I was in a sorry state when he first invited me to Measham Hall. A poor sickly plant, battered by storms. William, with patience and kindness, tended to me until I was strong enough to face the world again.' She tried to brush the weed from her hands but it clung to her skirts like a ribbon.

Nicholas pulled it off and rolled it into a little ball. 'When I was a boy, I used to hope that you and Father might marry.'

Jane squeezed his arm. 'Why, if that had been possible, peacocks might fly like swallows.' She nodded at the beautiful turquoise bird that was strutting towards them, followed by two dowdy peahens.

'Of course, you were not widowed then,' Nicholas said hastily, wondering if it was her parents' opposition that made her think marrying Father so beneath her. 'And Lord Pemberton is a nobler match.'

'That is not what I meant.' Jane sounded quite dismayed. 'Your father doesn't understand how much I admire him. The loss of his friendship is a constant source of grief to me. With William I shared the kind of companionship impossible with a husband; he treated me always as his equal. He was the confidant of my heart and my soul. None of my concerns were too petty for his consideration and none of my joys too trivial. That he could think I would do anything that could injure him...' She stopped and swallowed, steadying her voice. 'You can tell him that his lack of trust truly broke my heart, where my first husband could only break my limbs.'

Nicholas was completely taken aback by this passionate declaration and hardly knew what to say.

'Forgive me, it is your likeness to him and not having seen either of you for so long, I have quite forgot myself,' Jane said quickly. 'Ours was a rare friendship, the sort one finds only once in a lifetime, I suspect.'

'He was always happier with you by his side.'

Nicholas remembered watching Jane and his father sitting on the grass together beneath the old chestnut tree, their hands entwined. Father had been laughing with a light-heartedness he did not show again after her departure. Nicholas had put Father's general sombreness down to grief at the fate of his cousin, but perhaps it was not only Matthew, but also Jane, he had been mourning.

'I will try to reason with him. He might leap at the chance to reconciliate.'

Jane shook her head resolutely. 'You must not concern yourself with these old matters. Besides, I am Lady Pemberton now and such a friendship wouldn't do.'

'Of course.' Nicholas hadn't considered their relationship with the eyes of an adult, only with the remembrance of a child. Now it dawned on him just how scandalous their intimacy must have been. He wondered what Lord Pemberton knew of it.

'Your new children are very lucky to have gained you as a mother,' he told her.

Jane led him to a bench overlooking the water. 'The youngest three might agree with you and I have to admit, Richard is my little darling. He was only two when I married his father. His mother died after her delivery of him.' She sat down with a sigh. 'Lettice is in a pet with me because I persuaded her father not to place her at Court.'

'Would it not be advantageous?' Nicholas thought Jane's life might also be more tranquil without her eldest stepdaughter at home.

'To set her up as the plaything of courtly gallants? I am eternally grateful to my parents for preserving me from such a fate: to be wooed, diseased and then discarded by rakes before one is out of adolescence. Perhaps James's Court is not as dissolute as his brother's was, but there are enough little ladies sporting great bellies there and it seems to me tantamount to pandering, to put young girls forward as maids of honour. Our estate is large enough to provide for her; she does not need to enter such perilous places.'

Nicholas watched the rings radiating out from where a fish must be hoping to catch the flies darting over the surface of the canal. A few feet away a stone nymph poured water from an urn into a giant shell. The plashing of the water created a pleasantly soothing sound. The air was filled with the scent of honeysuckle. It was hard to believe anything could be amiss in such an Eden.

'One day, I am sure she will thank you for your care of her.'

'I hope so.' Jane lowered her voice. 'I do not want to increase Ralph's worries; it is bad enough with Edward so addicted to gaming and accruing ever greater debts. He need not add Lettice's welfare to his concerns.'

'Perhaps I might be of assistance.' Nicholas despised himself for seizing this opportunity, but felt he had no choice. 'If I were to befriend Edward, I could try to steer him away from temptation.'

'That is very sweet of you, but I would be more concerned that Edward might corrupt you. I should never forgive myself if my stepson led you into dissolution.'

'I believe my upbringing has fortified me against such vices.'

Jane smiled and patted his knee. 'I hope so, but we cannot be sure until we are tested.'

'Besides, Edward must be still quite young if he is an undergraduate.'

'He is nineteen, only two years your junior. He has always been sickly and was not well enough to attend university at fifteen like most boys.'

'Do you know what he suffers from?'

Jane shook her head. 'The doctors cannot agree; they have tried various remedies and regular bleedings. But he seems much recovered now, suffering only from occasional headaches.'

A feathered missile went whistling past Nicholas's ear.

'Do you want to play at shuttlecock with me?' Richard came running towards them, waving a racket in the air. 'Or we can play tennis if you like it better.'

'Do play with him,' Jane said. 'His sisters leave him out of their games.'

Nicholas jumped up, glad to be released from such tricky lines of conversation. It seemed he might end up befriending the youngest son instead of the eldest.

That evening passed very enjoyably, listening to music performed by the young ladies of the house: Lettice on the virginals and Dorothy on the cittern, while Prudence joined them in singing. The sisters' voices melded in sweet harmonies. Nicholas was quite enchanted. He had spent so little time in female company, apart from his illicit encounters with Isabelle Dupont, which were conducted mostly in her bedchamber. He began to think, despite what he had been told about Edward, that the Pembertons were the most perfect family.

He found the next day equally pleasant, exploring the gardens and grounds. His only disappointment was that Lord Pemberton had been recalled to Whitehall. He had hoped to impress the viscount with his knowledge of the natural sciences and his interest in the rare botanical specimens Pemberton had collected. Instead, he was given a tour by Isaac, who had not accompanied his master to London, and a loquacious Richard.

The greenhouse was as magnificent as the grounds. Huge windows were divided by Grecian columns made of stone and the air inside was as hot and humid as Nicholas imagined the tropics to be. The heat came from two enormous stoves placed at either end of the rectangular building. Nicholas had never seen anything like them; they were covered in green glazed tiles and shaped like cabinets. Lord Pemberton had brought them back from Vienna, Isaac explained; they kept the temperature warm even in the winter.

'We should use these in our homes,' Nicholas exclaimed, thinking of cold and draughty Measham Hall. He was filled with wonder at so many rare botanical specimens all gathered together in this extraordinary place. 'I should like to draw some of these if I may.' Pressing the thick, velvety leaf of an auricula between his thumb and forefinger, he let out a happy sigh. 'I could spend days in here.'

'One of the gardeners has to come in many times every day to open and close different windows and skylights so that Father's plants don't grow too hot or too cold,' Richard said. 'You could take his job.' He laughed. 'You could bring a truckle bed in and sleep here. I'll keep you company; we can watch the stars.'

'These plants are better cared for than most people.' Isaac twisted a yellowing leaf off an orange tree.

'Mother says they are Father's other children, which makes them my brothers and sisters.' Richard ran up and down the corridors between the beds, shouting greetings to the plants whose names he knew.

'Careful, don't slip,' Isaac warned him.

Lucky child, Nicholas thought, *to call Jane mother.*

The citrus trees, which filled the glasshouse with their fragrance, were easily identified, but Nicholas was intrigued by a tall tree with fern-like leaves.

'It's a coco-nut plant,' Richard told him proudly.

'But that is not where chocolate comes from, is it?' Nicholas turned to Isaac. He had seen illustrations of the pods from which cocoa was extracted.

'No, sir, this is a different plant entirely. It produces a large nut from which both food and drink can be derived. The shell too has various uses.'

'Is it native to your land?' Nicholas asked.

Isaac smiled wearily. 'Not unless they grew first in English soil.'

'But I have never seen an Englishman with skin so dark as yours.' Nicholas was even more curious now about Isaac's origins.

'My mother came from the Kingdom of Bornu in Africa. She was lured onto a ship as a child and sent to Barbados as a slave. There she was given to Lord Pemberton's first wife as a gift. Lady Elizabeth took her into her service and brought her back to England. I was born here and raised a Christian.' Isaac recounted the tale as though he had told it many times before.

'And your father was an Englishman?'

'Yes. My mother was married to the footman, Simon Smith.'

'You have done very well then, to rise to the position of secretary,' Nicholas noted with admiration.

Richard grabbed Isaac's hand, swinging it up and down. 'Isaac has always lived in our household.'

Isaac smiled indulgently down at the boy, before addressing Nicholas. 'I attended the local grammar school and though my formal education ended there, His Lordship allowed me the use of his library. I maintain a correspondence with several learned gentlemen and believe you will find me as erudite as any university man.'

'I don't doubt it.' Nicholas would have liked to ask Isaac more about his mother's early life, but sensing his reluctance, did not press him. He had some experience of what it was like to be questioned about one's origins.

After spending several hours making sketches of the plants in the greenhouse, Nicholas was lured away by the children, who insisted he play with them again. In truth, it was no hardship, for he enjoyed their cheerful company. The family introduced him to games of wit, like 'substantives and adjectives' and the sillier 'draw-glove', a favourite of Prue's. This was just how he had always imagined it would be to have siblings.

He couldn't help being pleased, however, when Lettice left off her music and joined in. Though she often seemed distracted, looking down at her fan and counting off its sticks with a dainty forefinger, before turning her gaze towards him and then rolling her eyes away. Whilst in the middle of a game of cards she pressed a hand to her heart, fiddled with her gown, then appeared to adjust her breasts, pushing them up with cupped hands before letting them fall, with a soft sigh. Was this for his benefit? Madame Dupont had been very direct in her attentions and he had no experience of young ladies. Perhaps Lettice was merely practising her coquetry on him. Certainly he found it quite discomposing. She really was extremely pretty. Her creamy skin was perfectly translucent, her cheeks a delicate strawberry. Her large eyes were the colour of forget-me-nots. When she smiled, her full lips parted to reveal two rows of even, white teeth and dimples appeared beside her mouth. Delicate curls framed her round face, trembling every time she shook her head.

'Pay attention, Tilly,' Doll snapped, after they had been waiting several minutes for Lettice to play her hand.

Jane looked at her stepdaughter with a mixture of concern and amusement. 'Have you been reading romances again?'

Lettice flushed, a rich crimson spreading from her bosom, up her throat and across her cheeks. Ignoring her stepmother, she turned to Nicholas.

'Do you like to read, Mr Hawthorne?'

'I do, though you might consider my reading matter rather dull since it is mostly books on natural history and philosophy.' Seeing a look of disappointment cross her face, he quickly added, 'And plays, of course. I performed in many plays at college.'

Encouraged by his audience, Nicholas went on to describe the various dramas they had put on at St. Omer's, the parts he had played, the lavish costumes and sets made for each production and how they had even toured with them to local towns where the gentry and dignitaries came to see them. It was so delightful to have such eager and attentive listeners that, for the first time since he had met Staley, he was able to forget about his more unpleasant obligations.

At breakfast the following morning, Jane told him Lord Pemberton would be gone for many weeks. The King had decided to go on a tour of the West Country and the Midlands. Having dissolved parliament, he was determined to drum up support for his new bills to take off the penal laws and the Test Act. He needed Lord Pemberton close by for counsel.

'Your father must be anxious to see you and though we would love to keep you here, you mustn't let us detain you.'

Nicholas was a little saddened by the firmness with which she spoke and hoped he hadn't offended her in any way. But Jane was right, he couldn't delay returning home for much longer; Father was expecting him and he too was eager to see his childhood home and all its inhabitants once again. After that, he would have to make the most of Oxford to further both his studies and his connections. If Edward Pemberton was as charming as his siblings, befriending him shouldn't be too onerous at least.

⇥ Chapter Eleven ⇤

Father was smaller and less formidable than Nicholas had remembered, though still with the narrow stem of his clay pipe clenched permanently between his teeth and his customary cravat wrapped high around his neck.

Gripping Nicholas's shoulders, Father surveyed him at arm's length with a mixture of pride and admiration. 'I believe you are taller even than Matthew was.'

Nicholas was touched by Father's evident joy in being reunited. He barely gave Nicholas time to greet the rest of the household before giving him a tour of the land. The gardens were flourishing and the farm productive. John Thornly was an excellent bailiff, he said, whose vision for Measham was in harmony with his own.

The Measham gardens were quite muted and rough in comparison to the immaculately cultivated sophistication of Pemberton's park, but Nicholas didn't like them any less for that. Here, the native plants grew in unrestrained abundance and their familiarity made them all the dearer to him.

Walking the land together, he and Father discussed the latest innovations in its management with a shared enthusiasm. Distance had brought them closer. Father was a more effusive and expansive letter-writer than conversant and they had kept up a regular correspondence all through Nicholas's time at St. Omer, so it did not feel as though they had been apart for seven years.

Life at Measham was reassuringly constant. He and Father rode out together most days and Nicholas was glad to discover that Polestar, although getting on in years, was still robust enough to enjoy their excursions around the estate. They set off with fishing rods one afternoon, as Father was eager to show him how plentiful the trout were in the river he had cleared. It ran from the upper lake, which lay on land left to him by his neighbour, Sir Peverell, and meandered down to the smaller lake behind the hall. Father had built a curving bridge over the enlarged stream, from which you could watch the clear waters rolling down a stony incline.

'And if the high-swollen Medway fail thy dish, Thou hast thy ponds, that pay thee tribute fish.' Father nudged him. 'Ben Jonson.'

Nicholas had expected Father to react angrily to the news of his visit to the Pembertons, but on the contrary he was intrigued, wanting to know every detail about Jane and her new family. He was as eager for information about Ralph Pemberton as Staley was and seemed much relieved by Nicholas's assurances that Jane was happy in her second marriage. It was only his excessive interest, as he pressed Nicholas for further particulars, that hinted at the depths of his feelings for her. If he hadn't been such a suspicious, impatient ass, he might have married her himself, Nicholas thought uncharitably.

'Pemberton lives like a king,' Father noted. 'How on earth can he afford such luxuries?'

'I suppose his role as auditor-general of the King's plantations must be very lucrative. He also has wealthy friends in Europe who seem happy to add to his collections.'

'A man with power, then, to command such generosity.'

Nicholas had been so full of admiration for the wonderful rarities that filled Pemberton's house and gardens, he hadn't thought much about how he came by them. Could some of these gifts connect him to more treacherous schemes? Was he being bribed to promote Dutch interests?

Looking at the lake below, a wave of sorrow swept over Nicholas. Matthew had been out in the water every morning when the weather was warm enough, sometimes coaxing Nicholas to join him. It was Matthew who had taught him how to swim. Now he wished he had not been so lazy, but had embraced Matthew's enthusiasm for the activity more willingly.

'Do you remember Master Foley?' Nicholas asked, once Father had selected the perfect place for them to cast their lines.

'The name sounds familiar, but college was all so long ago now. Remind me, what does he teach?'

'He is an apothecary and teaches medicine. He remembers you and how you loved to swim. I said he must have confused you with your cousin for you never swim, but he is quite insistent that it was William Hawthorne who was like a duck, always seeking out water.'

Father watched his line. 'The old man must be confused.'

'Foley is only a few years older than you. He says he showed you where to swim and went with you sometimes. He was surprised you had not become a priest as he thought you had a calling.'

Father had gone to St. Omers late, as a young man, and had left not long before Nicholas was born. Now he reeled his line in and flicked it out again. A sudden breeze shook the branches above them, scattering linden blossom across the surface of the water. The sweet scent was quite intoxicating.

'Was it because of me that you couldn't become a priest?'

Another of the masters had been surprised to hear who Nicholas's father was, having assumed William had entered the priesthood. Nicholas wondered if the loss of his vocation was somehow tied up with whatever it was Staley was holding over them.

'My dear son, I would never have become a priest, whether you came along or no. The masters at St. Omers assume everyone is as devout as they are.' Father sneezed. 'Damn these linden trees, the blossom always sets me off. I'd chop them down if they weren't so handsome.' He secured his rod with some stones and sat down to light his pipe. 'How does Crewe seem to you?'

Where Father remained forever boyish, Crewe had grown older and frailer. Nicholas had been disturbed by his decline.

'I think perhaps you need to look for a new steward so that Crewe can retire,' he suggested.

Father drew on his pipe, releasing puffs of smoke. 'Who could possibly replace Crewe?'

Nicholas agreed it was hard to imagine Measham without Crewe at the helm. 'Could he train someone up?'

'He's been training you since you were an infant. When you come home for good, we can manage the manor between us.'

Though flattered Father now had such confidence in him, Nicholas was perturbed by the absolute assurance in his voice. Measham Hall was everything to Father, his idyll and his refuge; how could he tell him its ownership was under threat?

'I have to complete my studies at Oxford first. Until that day, what about John Thornly?'

'John doesn't have the time or the disposition to manage the household as well as the farm.' Father sat staring into the water.

Nicholas hoped he wasn't lonely. 'Uncle Percy hasn't found you a wife yet, then,' he joked.

'She'd have to be a particular sort of woman to marry me,' Father said.

Every night Nicholas promised himself he would question Father the following day, but when in his presence, he found it impossible to find a way of broaching the subject. He couldn't just come out and ask Father whether he had any terrible secrets he'd like to share. Especially not when Father was so pleased to have him back in England and out from the influence of the Jesuits. Crewe, being so aged, was no easier to approach. Nicholas didn't want to cause him any anxiety.

The few possessions Nicholas owned had been sent directly from St. Omer to Measham Hall. Unpacking them, he came across some sketches he had made of his first impressions of France. One of them was of a thin man whose lips, beneath his lanky moustache, were pursed in an expression of disdain. Despite his lack of experience, the drawing was well executed, good enough at least to be a clear depiction of Mister Gilbert Staley. Underneath the portrait he had written '*Mr Waddington sends back my meat*'. He had not forgiven the man for ruining his first French meal. Folding the paper, he slipped it into his current notebook.

That evening he tried to draw Father and Crewe out by asking them about their salad days, but they preferred to discuss more recent matters, like the cost of wool at market and the King's proroguing of parliament.

'If James keeps suspending parliament, people will accuse him of tyranny,' Father said. 'I fear another civil war.'

Crewe agreed. 'And it is doubtful whether the King would be able to carry the army with him. His attempts to convert those in power are only breeding resentment. We even have libertines like Admiral Herbert discovering his conscience and resigning from the navy.'

'Aren't you both pleased the King has suspended the penal laws and the Test Acts?' Nicholas said with surprise. 'Now we have the same freedoms and rights as Protestants.'

But Father shook his head. 'He goes too far, too fast. It is the common Catholics who will suffer for his policies. As if there isn't enough hatred of us as it is.'

It was hard to imagine what his father could have done that was so terrible it might mean losing everything. Despite his furtiveness among strangers, Father was not a schemer, nor was he a violent or aggressive man. His desires were modest and his manner retiring. Could his humility have been bought at the cost of some former act of depravity? There was the man he had killed in a duel, but he had been pardoned for that and, though outlawed, duels were not dishonourable.

After a few glasses of wine, Nicholas almost confessed everything. He wanted, in a momentary return to childishness, for Father and Crewe to rescue him from Staley's coercion. But, observing the two men chatting softly over supper, he couldn't bear to distress them, especially not after all they had suffered.

Instead, he rode out early next morning to visit Uncle Percy, determined to discover what he knew about Gilbert Staley. He found his great-uncle asleep in the parlour, the folds of his chin sunk onto his chest, a newsletter spread out over his knees. After waiting a minute, Nicholas gave his arm a gentle squeeze.

'Nic?' Percy regarded him with bleary-eyed confusion.

'It's Nicholas, your nephew.'

'Thought for a moment you were me brother.' He pushed himself up in his chair. 'How are you, my boy?'

'Very well, thank you, Uncle.' Nicholas pulled up the one chair that didn't look as if it might collapse if sat upon.

'Why aren't you in Paris?' Percy asked, picking at his nose with a long, yellow fingernail.

'His Majesty gave me a pass to study for a doctorate at Magdalen College.'

'Good for you.' Percy pulled a greasy-looking handkerchief out of his waistcoat pocket and used it to continue his excavation of his nostrils. 'Well done, my boy, I'm proud of you. Things are looking up here, eh? Now we have a monarch with the manfulness to return England to the old religion. The abbey-mongers will be squittering in their breeches.' He erupted into a barking laugh.

'Or perhaps the King means to tolerate all faiths equally, without prejudice to any,' Nicholas suggested.

'Pish!' Percy's face went from red to scarlet. 'They didn't teach you that sort of drivel at St. Omer's, did they? I'd never have sent you there if I'd known you'd end up some cow-baby preaching atheisticalness.'

'Peace, Uncle, you have no cause to question my devotion,' Nicholas said quickly.

'Damned glad to hear it.' Percy thumped his cane on the floor.

The aged butler appeared at the door. 'Did you require anything, sir?'

'Bring us two brimmers of claret. Damme, I need a drink.'

The butler shuffled off. Nicholas wondered if there was anyone in the house under the age of sixty. Every surface in the parlour was thick with dust and the stale air was laden with tallowy, vinegary odours.

'Uncle, when you so generously arranged for me to travel to St. Omer, you sent me with Mr Waddington. Are you friends with him still?'

'Waddington? Good God, I don't believe I've seen him since then. Certainly it's been years since we last had occasion to meet. Why? Are you going into the book trade?'

Nicholas had forgotten Mr Waddington had been a bookseller whose business was importing printed matter. Now he realised Waddington had probably been smuggling Catholic texts into England.

'That is not an occupation I wish to pursue. It's just that I'm sure I encountered him recently, only he was going by a different name.'

'Has he got into debt? Trying to avoid his creditors, eh?' Percy cackled. He often enjoyed others' misfortune, especially if the cause was financial.

How much should he risk telling his great-uncle? Nicholas couldn't imagine the old man had much power or influence, dozing away in the country. 'He was visiting Father Carmichael, the rector at St. Omer's.'

'And why shouldn't he? Was probably supplying them with primers, or manuals or suchlike.'

'Yet he was introduced to me as Mister Gilbert Staley.'

Percy looked offended. 'Must've been someone else. Father Carmichael wouldn't use the wrong name. Unless' – his face brightened – 'Waddington's taken holy orders. Though you'd think it'd be safe for English priests to use their own names now we've a Catholic king. Better to play it safe, I suppose. Anyway, I've never heard of this Staley.' Percy hammered his cane on the floorboards again. 'Damned snail, should've brought us in that wine by now. My throat's as dry as a crone's cunny.'

Old age had not improved his great-uncle's manners. The conversation for the remainder of Nicholas's visit centred on Percy's various physical ailments, from gout to heartburn, for which he was trying numerous remedies, all to no avail. Only the subject of Measham Hall could divert him. He was still adamant Sir William should exploit the land's potential for lead or coal.

'You must impress upon your father the great riches he might accrue if he were to allow mining at Measham.' Percy pressed one hand against the great ball of his stomach, as though having to raise the subject was also bringing up his dyspepsia. 'William should never have made John Thornly his bailiff. The Thornlys are farmers, always have been. The only digging they like to do is for vegetables. Your grandfather never allowed old Mr Thornly so much authority as that bacon-slicer of a son now exercises.'

But on this issue, Nicholas was in agreement with Father. Their land was far too beautiful to be excavated and he was proud of Father for prizing the riches of nature over those of the marketplace. As to Thornly, he thought his uncle overestimated his influence. He had always found Thornly to be a kind and honest man, but it was Father who gave the orders.

As he was taking his leave, his great-uncle seized his hand, pulling Nicholas down towards him so that their faces were level. His strength took Nicholas by surprise.

'Don't forget, it was I who sent you to St. Omer's. You are the standard-bearer of our family and owe me some allegiance.'

Nicholas stepped back, reclaiming his hand from Percy's grasp. 'And I am grateful for my education, sir.'

Percy looked away, shuffling his feet on the floor in front of him. 'Your father's a milksop of a man and don't even venerate our religion as he should. I saw potential in you. You put me in mind of me brother.' He dabbed at his eyes with his grimy handkerchief. 'I've no heirs, as you know, only my daughter, the abbess. If I leave the manor to her, she'll only turn it into a convent and I can't abide the thought of my home being overrun with women.' He pointed a meaty finger at Nicholas. 'If I'm to make you my heir I expect something in return. You must change your father's mind. Bring me in as your partner and we can get the excavations underway.' Raising his fists in a sudden outburst of enthusiasm, he cried, 'We could make a fortune, my boy!'

Nicholas bowed. 'I will do everything I can to uphold the honour of our family. But I will not cross my father.'

Percy harrumphed, tucking his chin in towards his chest, like a bird taking refuge against the cold. 'You'll find you need the money for the upkeep of Measham. Mark my words, a demesne like that don't run on air alone.'

By the time he returned home, Nicholas had decided that if Uncle Percy knew anything he could use against William, he would have exploited it long ago. His uncle was not a subtle man and Nicholas could not imagine him being involved in any Machiavellian plots. He was aggrieved that Father would not make him a partner in a mining venture, but that was all. As for Waddington, perhaps his uncle was right and he had become a Jesuit. He was a very different sort of man to the masters at St. Omers and absolutely nothing like Matthew, but it was possible, he supposed. All this didn't bring Nicholas any closer to discovering Father's secret, however.

✦ Chapter Twelve ✦

October 1687

Once at Oxford, it wasn't difficult to become acquainted with Ned Pemberton. He was one of a group of self-styled wits, infamous for their antics in both the town and the university. Ned would gladly play at dice or cards with any gentleman.

Peering through the window of The Greyhound tavern, Nicholas could see a group of young men gathered around a table in the centre of the room beneath a large wooden candle-branch. He could hear their raucous laughter from the street.

The tapster nodded at him as he walked in and Nicholas got himself a tankard of ale before joining the fringes of the group. They were busy watching the players, shouting out various words of advice, derision and support, and hardly noticed his presence. He elbowed his way in until he was able to observe the game.

Ned was a loud, flamboyant young man dressed in a gold-striped waistcoat; his lace cravat hung loose around his neck and his cheeks were flushed red from the champagne he was drinking. He had inherited his father's large nose, though unfortunately for him it dwarfed the other features on his younger face. His small blue eyes were trained on his competitors, roving quickly from their faces to the cards on the table with an intensity that belied his jocund manner. When the players revealed their hands, Nicholas was not surprised to see Ned had a flush with two aces.

Taking advantage of the end of that game, Nicholas leant across the table to introduce himself, hastily explaining that he had only recently been a guest at Pemberton Manor.

'And how do their gravities?' Ned asked disparagingly.

'Your parents? They are both well. Lady Jane is an old family friend.'

Ned was less impressed by this than he had hoped. He gave Nicholas a withering look. 'I hope you haven't been making love to my sister, Hawthorne. All the fellows would like a taste of my little Lettice, but she's out of bounds.'

'I wouldn't dream of it,' Nicholas replied, startled both by Ned's careless accusation and its perspicacity.

Ned laughed at his consternation and looked around at the other young men. 'The pretty fellow is a maid. We'll have to show him the kind of education the square-caps won't give him.'

The others joined in with strident guffaws. 'We'll make a man of him,' one said, slapping Nicholas's shoulder, a little too hard.

'I had a mistress in France,' Nicholas declared indignantly, irritated by the assumptions of this choir of undergraduates, some of whom he might be required to teach.

''Well, who's the coxcomb, then? And how did you find yourself a French mistress?' Ned scoffed. His thin-lipped mouth remained permanently open, either speaking or drinking or breathing heavily as he counted his winnings.

'I was educated there.'

'Are you a papist?' Ned asked, more with curiosity than antagonism.

'I was raised so.' Nicholas hadn't anticipated such an interrogation.

'Well, so was Sir Denis here, but we don't hold a man's religion against him, so long as his wit is sharp and his pocket long.' Ned gestured to a narrow-faced youth in a luxuriantly curled, yellow wig. 'We all know what smell-smocks the Frogs are, though, so monsieur had better keep his hands off my sister.'

The assembled company sniggered.

'I would consider it beneath my honour to attempt to seduce my host's daughter,' Nicholas said, a little more primly than he had intended.

'Would ye now? I trust you don't think yourself too good for her?'
Ned reached a hand to his sword hilt.

'Quite the opposite,' Nicholas said quickly. 'Besides, Lady Jane
was as good as a mother to me when I was small; I would never abuse
her hospitality so.'

Ned examined Nicholas speculatively and the youths around him
fell silent. 'Ambrose, give the man a seat,' he said eventually, waving a
hand at the fellow on his right, who immediately stood up and offered
Nicholas his chair with an ostentatious bow. 'D'you know how to play
primero?'

'I am acquainted with it.' It was just as well Gilbert Staley had
spent an afternoon teaching him the rules of various card and dice
games. Though it struck him now that Staley's knowledge of gaming
was unusual for both a bookseller and a Jesuit.

'Let's test your mettle, then.' Ned began to deal. 'What's your wager?'

Picking up his hand, Nicholas surveyed his cards uneasily. They
did not match in suit or kind. 'Two shillings.'

The assembled company erupted into jeering laughter.

'Poor little country mouse, only willing to play for crumbs,'
Ambrose said.

'You'll have to up it to five shillings minimum to play with us,'
Ned told him.

'Fair enough, I've been abroad so long I've forgotten the values
of English coin,' Nicholas said light-heartedly, deciding that the only
way he was going to get along in this company was by taking on a
character, just as he would when performing in a play.

His education at St. Omers had honed his already capacious
memory and by concentrating carefully, Nicholas was able to memorise
the cards played, just as Staley had shown him. His new comrades were
soon impressed by his skill and what they took to be his experience.
He won two rounds, but seeing the discontented expression on Ned's
face, he made sure he lost the third.

Nicholas's good looks and obliging manner soon commended him to Ned, who liked to be surrounded by beautiful things. Being allowed into his inner circle was not without its challenges, however. Money was required, large amounts of it. Staley had given Nicholas five guineas and Father was also paying him a small annuity to cover his living expenses, but after losing two pounds in one night, he was afraid of going through it all before the first term ended.

Keeping up with his studies and Ned Pemberton's band of rakes didn't leave much time for sleep either. He was determined to advance his knowledge of natural philosophy and to make the most of his time at Oxford, but this meant rising early, while his friends slept off the previous night's drinking. He surreptitiously worked in the library and attended lectures, activities that would have been mocked by his new companions, who thought all knowledge worth attaining could be found in taverns and whorehouses. Nor did they show any interest in affairs of state. Being a traitor to the King would have required far too much effort and proved an unwelcome distraction from the pursuit of pleasure. Whatever Lord Pemberton's affiliations might be, they did not extend to his son and his friends.

Nicholas also had to work hard to win over the tutors and students of Magdalen, who resented him as another papist foisted on them by the King. The fellows of the college had recently been stripped of their offices for refusing to elect His Majesty's choice of president and now many of them were said to be quite destitute. Nicholas had to prove he had the intellectual right to be there and wasn't a covert Jesuit working to turn the college into a seminary. He had hoped his association with Ned might help in this respect, but it only fuelled their suspicions that papists were all debauched hypocrites.

After seven years of strictly regulated living, part of him enjoyed the revelry. It wasn't just the wine that was intoxicating; it was the camaraderie and the freedom of living for pleasure, with no thought of the next day. It was only when he was having to run to the privy to void his stomach of all the wild liquor he had drunk the previous night that Nicholas feared Gilbert Staley's mission might end in his own demise. Still, the discipline instilled at St. Omers forced him up and out of his bed most mornings.

One Saturday towards the end of term, Ned decided they would all walk out to a country tavern where he had heard cockfights were held. At first the afternoon unfolded in a similar vein to most of their excursions, in drinking and gambling. Ned was disappointed that there were no fights taking place that day and drank more wine than usual. As it grew dark, he and his closest circle became increasingly rowdy, beating time on the table as they sang lewd drinking songs.

A black and white puppy that had been lying, curled up asleep by the fire, was woken by the men's shouts. Terrified by their wild cheers, it ran beneath a neighbouring table.

'What's that? A rat?' Ned pulled out his sword.

'It's my dog, sir.' The innkeeper's son, a boy of about seven, rushed over. 'She's a good girl really.' The lad crouched down by the table, calling softly to the frightened animal.

Ned took a piece of meat from Denis's plate and knelt down by the boy. 'I know how to get a bitch to come to me,' he said, to the laughter of his fellows.

The puppy, sniffing cautiously at the meat, came gradually to Ned's hand. He picked the little dog up and stroked it. 'What's her name?'

'Posy,' said the boy, looking anxiously up at Ned.

Since he had spoken fondly of his little brother, Nicholas didn't think Ned would do anything to distress the lad. He was pleased to see a gentler side to Edward, as well as being grateful for a respite from the tuneless singing. Excited by the attention, Posy pressed her forepaws against Ned's chest and licked his neck.

'Damn creature's pissed on me!' Grasping the puppy by the scruff of her neck, Ned held her aloft, revealing a wet stain on his shirt. 'Who's got a dog?' He looked around the room as he shouted out, 'Let's bet on how long Posy lasts in a fight.'

Most of the other customers had left by now and the few regulars who remained shook their heads disapprovingly. Only an old drunk sitting alone in the corner declared that his hound would swallow the whelp in one mouthful. Ned's friends immediately began laying wagers on the time it would take for the puppy to be slaughtered. Sobbing, the innkeeper's son begged for the return of his pet.

'What sort of cow-baby are you, snivelling over a farmyard cur?' Ned teased, swinging the whimpering dog in the air.

Leaping to his feet, Nicholas grabbed Ned's arm. 'For God's sake, Edward, give the boy back his dog.'

Pouting at Nicholas, Ned dropped the dog to the floor and the boy scooped her up, racing from the room as fast as he could.

'Time for you gentlemen to pay up and depart.' The innkeeper stood, arms crossed over his chest, glowering at them.

'I haven't finished my wine,' Ned replied sulkily.

'Finish your wine and leave,' the innkeeper insisted.

Nicholas thought they were going to comply. Ned's 'band of merry roisterers', as he liked to call them, made a noisy show of knocking back whatever was left in their cups and making for the door.

'You haven't paid the reckoning yet.' The innkeeper, a stout man with brawny arms, moved to block their way.

'Why should we pay when we've been denied the entertainment we came for?' Ned demanded. 'And you owe me recompense for my defiled clothing.' He tugged at his shirt.

'Give us our dog fight and we'll pay you for the wine.' Another of his band pushed forward to stand nose to nose with the innkeeper.

'He should be paying us for elevating the standing of his establishment,' Sir Denis drawled.

'Let's pay what we owe as any gentleman should.' Nicholas pulled out his purse, but the fellows were all shoving towards the door where the innkeeper stood and he found himself pushed to the back of the group.

Afterwards he couldn't say who started the fight. Perhaps the innkeeper had thrown the first punch, though he was outnumbered half a dozen to one. Nicholas was joined by the man's wife and two other customers in dragging back those undergraduates they could get hold of. As he wrestled with one of the Roisterers, Nicholas was horrified to see Ned and another student pummelling the lifeless body of the man on the floor.

'My boy's gone for the constable,' the innkeeper's wife screamed. 'He'll have the lot of you in irons. You won't get away with this.'

'Come on, Ned, let's go.' Sir Denis pulled on Edward's shoulders.

Nicholas felt hands against his back and he too was propelled along as the Roisterers ran from the tavern and out into the night.

Catching up with Ned, he shouted, 'I must go back and see if that poor fellow is all right.'

'Don't be a simpleton.' Ned thrust his arm through Nicholas's. 'You'll be arrested and then you'll get the rest of us into trouble too.'

'We can't leave him for dead.'

Nicholas tried to pull away, but coming up beside them, Denis took his other arm. The two men leant heavily on Nicholas, forcing him on, stumbling together down the dark and rutted road.

'A man like that has a skull so thick it'll withstand anything.' Ned gave a shaky laugh. 'God, I need another drink.'

'You should go back to your rooms,' Nicholas warned them. 'If the constable is looking for you, he'll start with the inns.'

To his relief, Denis agreed. Once he was certain the Roisterers were going to retire for the night, Nicholas, having managed to extricate himself, turned round and walked back to the tavern. It was risky, he knew. He might be set upon by the locals and taken prisoner by the constable, but he couldn't forget the poor innkeeper, spread out on the floor, blood seeping from his head. What sort of man would he be if he hid like a coward in his bed?

'There's one of 'em.' An elderly man pointed a shaking finger at Nicholas as he re-entered the inn.

The constable put a hand to his sword, but to Nicholas's eternal gratitude, the innkeeper's wife vouched for him.

'He saved Posy from the bad men,' her son piped up.

This caused some confusion as the constable assumed, with an uncalled-for degree of excitement, that a young lady of the house had been abducted. He was not impressed to learn Posy was merely a dog.

The innkeeper had been moved beside the fire and though he still lay on the ground, cushions had been placed beneath his bloody head.

'How does your husband?' Nicholas asked the woman.

'We're still waiting for the surgeon, but his breath is steady.'

Examining the man, Nicholas was fairly certain he would recover, but he stayed at the inn until the surgeon at last appeared and confirmed his prognosis. The innkeeper would be confined to bed for at least a week, but he should not suffer any lasting damage, the surgeon assured them.

Nicholas paid his fee and promised the woman she would be recompensed for the trouble caused.

'They must pay their reckoning too,' she said, her mouth a tight line. Though her fierceness was undermined by the tears in her eyes. Nicholas had no money left, but promised their debts would be honoured.

Waking early the next morning, he went straight over to see Ned, who was not pleased to be roused from his slumbers. Forgetting in his anger the need to make himself indispensable, Nicholas rounded on the younger man, telling him he was a disgrace to his family and his nation, that his behaviour had been barbarous and he should be thoroughly ashamed.

'Damme, you're worse than my pater.' Ned put his hands over his ears. 'It was just a bit of fun. If the innkeeper hadn't been so damned bellicose it would never have got violent, but I had to defend myself.' He sounded somewhat repentant, but Nicholas wasn't sure if that was just his ale-sickness talking.

In the end Ned agreed to send his man, Geoffrey, over to the tavern to see how the innkeeper fared and to pay damages, as well as their reckoning.

'You're too damned serious, Nicholas. A pox on morality; I only want people about me who know how to enjoy themselves.'

Reminding himself of what was at stake, Nicholas affected a careless air and suggested they went out for a breakfast of champagne. From then on, he had to force himself to play the part of a libertine, but he had come to dread the evenings spent in Ned's company.

At least he found solace and companionship in the study of botany. Father Carmichael had been right about one thing: Oxford had an impressive physic garden. Its superintendent, recognising Nicholas's abilities and dedication, enlisted his help in compiling the latest volume in a great history of plants, which had been many years in the writing and was still far from complete. Mr Bobart was another outsider. Not having attended the university he was denied a professorship, though he gave lectures and was an expert in his subject. With his muddy face and black fingernails, Bobart never received the respect he deserved, but he warmed to Nicholas as one who was as happy to dirty his hands with soil as with ink.

'We are going to have to get you a new suit of clothes,' Ned told him one afternoon as they sauntered through the quadrangle. 'I can't have fellows about me so shabbily dressed.' He lifted Nicholas's collar. 'You'd think your French education might have put you at the front of fashion, but sadly not. It's almost the end of Michaelmas term; return to London with me and I'll send you to my tailor. You can stay at ours since your people don't have a townhouse.'

Nicholas's heart lifted at the prospect of staying with the Pembertons. Here was an opportunity to insinuate himself more closely with Lord Pemberton. Late one night the previous week, a messenger from Staley had appeared at his door, wanting to know if he had any reports to pass on. Nicholas had told him he was making advances and would write soon, using the cypher Staley had given him, but in truth he had no information on Pemberton's possible schemes. Ned was always vague about his father's business, his interest extending only as far as his personal allowance. Nicholas hoped that allowance might cover the tailor's bill, but feared it would have to come out of his own pocket.

He couldn't help wondering if Lettice would also be in London, but didn't like to raise Ned's suspicions by asking. At least he no longer feared having offended Jane; they had exchanged several friendly letters and she had told him he was most welcome to stay with them again.

❖ Chapter Thirteen ❖

December 1687

Although he had passed through the outskirts of London before, Nicholas had never spent any time in the capital. What little he could see of it was a disappointment. Everything was obscured by the clouds of seacoal smoke that filled the streets. Not only that, but there was so much traffic no one could move beyond walking pace. On one particularly narrow street, their coach had to wait for close on an hour as the way was so congested with carts and carriages. The air was filled, not only with the sulphurous smell of smoke and the more earthy odours of the dung of both animals and humans, but also with foul language as the drivers of hackney coaches hurled abuse at everyone in their path. Nicholas would have got out and walked, but Ned was asleep and he was afraid of losing his way.

The Pembertons' townhouse was a more modest, sedate building than the lavish Kent residence, but the tall brick mansion was still impressive to Nicholas. Inside it was as beautifully decorated as Pemberton Manor, if a little less ornate. A calm orderliness prevailed over the freshly swept floors and polished wooden furniture. Standing bathed in the golden light of the large hall, Nicholas found his fatigue and anxiety slipping away.

Despite Ned's warnings, he couldn't help being pleased to discover Lettice was also there. She was receiving guests when they arrived and he could hear her light, musical laugh escaping through the parlour door.

Lord Pemberton was at Court but Jane received them warmly, evidently pleased to see Nicholas. After some refreshments, Ned took himself off to bed to recover from the two-day journey. Jane ushered Nicholas into the drawing room, eager to hear about his first term at Oxford.

'And Edward?' she asked after he had given her a brief, carefully censored summary. 'His father has received some worrying accounts of his behaviour, not to mention several applications for further funds, even though Edward is very well provided for.'

Once again, Nicholas found himself in the uncomfortable position of go-between. He could not deny Edward spent most of his time gambling, whether it was on dogs, horses, cards or tennis; anything that could have a bet placed on it was fair game. But neither could he afford to alienate Ned by getting him into trouble with his parents. Though the truth was, if he weren't acting under compulsion, Nicholas would have broken all ties with him. He could not say any of this to Jane, of course, but she recognised his unease.

'Take care, my dear, remember how I warned you. You do not have to be a friend of my stepson's to remain close to me.'

'He is a good fellow really.' Nicholas gave her a lukewarm smile.

'But you promised me, Ned.' Lettice's eyes glowed with unspent tears and the pyramid of brightly coloured ribbons on top of her head quivered like flowers beset by a breeze. 'Lady Jane will not go because she's fearful of the crowds and my maid is ill. I have been looking forward to this for weeks.'

Nicholas looked at Edward. 'Do not put your sister off on my account. I should hate to be the cause of her disappointment.'

Ned swallowed another oyster. 'You will have to come with us to the tailor's and wait patiently while Nicholas is measured,' he told his sister sternly. 'And we are not going to spend hours being bubbled by every little wagtail with a toy to sell.'

'Of course, brother,' Lettice said meekly. 'I am desperate for a new pair of gloves and a little lace to trim the sleeves of my dress, but that is all I shall buy.'

'For Gad's sake don't buy any more ribbon for your top-knot; you've already got an entire milliner's shop up there.'

Lettice gave an injured sniff and took a sip of chocolate. 'It is the fashion,' she said, as though this made it compulsory. She turned to Nicholas. 'Have you visited the Royal Exchange before?'

Nicholas shook his head. 'I am yet to have that pleasure.'

Her face glowed with anticipation. 'It is the most wondrous place. Merchants from all over the world gather there to sell the best of everything.'

Ned snorted. 'Foreign crooks, whores and charlatans gather to fleece the innocent Englishman, more like.'

Because Lettice was with them, Edward had the family coachman drive them to his tailor's on Cornhill, close by the Exchange. Ned was especially proud of having a French tailor who could keep him attired in the latest Parisian fashions.

Monsieur Benoist shook his head sadly, lifting Nicholas's jacket with the tips of his fingers, as though the cloth were soaked in poison. He tutted at the waistcoat beneath.

'So short!' he exclaimed. 'Were you dressed by your grandfather? No one is wearing flowered silk this year; it must be stripes, in gold or silver.'

'Is that true for ladies as well?' Lettice asked anxiously from her chair in the corner.

Benoist gave her an indulgent smile. 'I am told Indian sprigs will be the pattern of the next season.'

'Jean,' a querulous voice called from the next room.

An interior door was pushed open and an old man, bent almost double, shuffled into the shop.

'*Pas maintenant, Papa,*' Benoist called out in alarm.

The tailor attempted to usher his father from the room, but the old man had taken a strange fancy to Nicholas, who was standing nearby. Seizing hold of Nicholas's hand with his bony fingers, he began to sob.

It was a heart-rending sight and, crouching down so that he was on eye level with the stooped gentleman, Nicholas asked in French how he might be of assistance. In response, old Monsieur Benoist begged him to save the lives of his daughter and her children. Horrified, Nicholas asked where they were.

'*Les soldats les ont pris*,' the old man cried.

'Please excuse my father,' Benoist interposed, grasping him by the shoulders and forcibly removing him from the room.

Nicholas caught sight of the tailor settling his father back onto a narrow bed, before he returned to the shop, shutting the door firmly behind him.

'Have your relatives been arrested?' Lettice asked. 'We can petition Father to intervene. He's had to get Ned out of hot water on a couple of occasions.'

Ned glowered at her.

'*Merci, ma demoiselle*.' Benoist bowed. 'Your gracious father is doing his best for us poor Huguenots, I am sure. It is the tyrannical Louis XIV who is determined to murder every Protestant in France.' He lowered his voice. 'Be careful good King James does not do the same here. He is not sympathetic to us, despite what he says publicly. I am told he has forbidden ships carrying French refugees from docking in English ports.'

'God damn me, we're here to turn this country bumpkin into a beau of the town, not to talk religion,' Ned said impatiently. 'Let's get you measured and find ourselves a dining room at the Exchange; all this French talk is giving me a headache and an appetite for a glass of Burgundy.'

'Let's not forget to visit the shops too,' Lettice said.

She clearly knew her brother's habits. Once Ned had settled down to taste the wares of an obliging wine merchant in the vault of the Exchange, he lost all interest in visiting the arcades above. In fact, he was quite happy to let Nicholas escort his sister around the shops and stalls, while he sat below tasting various vintages.

Nicholas was as enthralled by the Royal Exchange as Lettice was. The central courtyard was filled with men buying and selling, haggling and debating in Italian, Dutch, Spanish, French and other languages whose origins were alien to him. Nicholas had never heard so much noise; it was as though a dozen different winds were blowing through the place all at once, bringing with them smells of coffee beans, frankincense, ambergris, tobacco, exotic fruits and homespun wool. There were men with great black beards and turbans, others in thick fur coats, chains of beads hanging from their wrists. A group of Spaniards in flat-crowned hats and short cloaks turned to gaze admiringly at Lettice. Nicholas felt for the hilt of his sword, hoping he wouldn't be called upon to use it.

'The shops I need are in the arcade above.'

Lettice tugged at his arm and Nicholas felt instinctively for her hand, afraid he might lose her in the maelstrom. To his surprise she had removed a glove. She pushed her naked fingers as far inside his own loose leather glove as they would go, tickling his palm with her soft fingertips. He curled his fist around them, the blood beating almost as loudly in his ears as the cacophony of voices around them.

She drew him forwards past a row of pillars plastered with advertisements for everything from love potions to acrobats, and into a cloister where a large man with the stance of a sailor eyed them curiously.

'This is known as Kidnappers' Walk.' Lettice spoke into his ear, her breath warm against his cheek. 'You'd better watch out, or you might be stolen away and forced to work on a plantation in Jamaica, or so Ned tells me.'

Nicholas wanted to put his arm around her waist to secure her to him, but it would have meant letting go her hand, and anyway Lettice didn't appear the least afraid. She laughed, one of her deliciously throaty giggles.

'There's no need to be alarmed. Father oversees all the plantations in the West Indies; he wouldn't permit any harm to befall us. The governors are much obliged to him and always sending gifts. They wouldn't do anything to offend him.'

Reminded of his purpose there, Nicholas asked what the tailor had meant about Lord Pemberton helping the Huguenots.

Lettice shrugged. 'Father has the ear of the King; I suppose he does what he can to promote the cause of Protestants. You must know better than I how people dread the sway of France.' She laughed. 'They fear we will all be made to worship the Virgin Mary and eat garlic.'

'And you are not afraid?' he asked curiously.

'Everyone decries France and yet longs to be dressed in its newest fashions. And young ladies who can't speak a little French are considered terribly *démodées*. I'm told by those who've been that the popish churches are quite beautiful, filled with ornaments and pretty pictures, which must make the time spent in them pass more quickly. Better than having to stare at plain, drab old walls while some reverend drones on. Half the time the sermon might as well be in Latin for all I take in.' She paused and looked up at him, her pretty face framed by the dark folds of her hood. 'Do you think me dreadfully wicked?'

He smiled back at her. 'No, I think you impressively free-spirited.'

She pressed his palm and he could feel the sharp edges of her fingernails. 'Well, don't tell Father; he would not be so approving.'

'Is he so zealous an Anglican?'

She frowned. 'He is a good Protestant, as I suppose we all should be.' She seemed struck by a moment of contrition for her previous words. 'And, of course, the French King's slaughter of his Protestant subjects is monstrous.'

With this, Nicholas could only agree. He was certain Matthew would never have condoned forced conversion or considered the persecution of Protestants acceptable and he did not believe King James would pursue such policies either, however close he was to Louis XIV.

They had arrived upstairs and Nicholas did not feel he could pursue the subject any further. He was surprised to see a long line of square, pen-like enclosures from which young women called sweetly to them to view their wares.

'Look here, Your Honour, I've knives, scissors, toothpicks – all top quality, you won't find none better nowhere.' A girl who, judging by her height, could not have been more than ten years old, held up a tray of wares. 'Eight shillings for this here ivory-handled penknife.

Just what a gent of your quality needs. You won't get a better price in London.' Her small face was pinched and there were dark shadows under her narrow eyes. Seeing his lack of interest in the knives, she picked up another tray, thrusting it towards him with skinny arms. 'How about a tortoiseshell comb?'

Nicholas was about to buy one out of pity for the poor child, but Lettice seemed oblivious to the desperate entreaties echoing round them.

She pointed to a stall at the far end. 'There! She does the best gloves.'

A wench of about thirteen with painted cheeks and a face covered in heart-shaped patches, probably covering pimples, presented a tray of delicately embroidered gloves trimmed with lace.

'Which do you like best?' Lettice asked him.

His eye was caught by a pair in cream leather with birds and flowers embroidered in silver, blue and pink thread on the backs. The girl immediately held one up. The ends were trimmed with a blue fringe and each finger outlined in fine stitches. The birds looked a little like swans. Removing his own gloves, Nicholas felt the softness of the leather. They had been perfumed with something sweet and floral, jasmine perhaps.

'These might do justice to your fair hands,' he told Lettice.

'I can let you have them for eleven shillings, sixpence, sir,' the girl said quickly. 'They cost more than that to make, I tell you no lie. But seeing you with your sweetheart there has made me soft as this here leather.'

Nicholas felt his cheeks burning at the reference to 'sweetheart'. Lettice, however, was studying a pair of deerskin gloves with elaborate gold and silver cuffs.

'Now, I can see you're a lady of discernment.' The girl dropped the first glove back into its box and proffered the darker one. 'These are the finest doeskin I have. See how they're lined with silk taffeta and the thread and spangles is pure gold, not painted, not even gilt.'

Nicholas swallowed. The first pair had been costly enough; these were bound to be even more.

'Thought I'd find you here.' Ned thumped him on the back. 'How now my pretty maid, that's a fine set of wares you have on display.' He gave the girl a wolf-like grin as he stared down at her bosom.

She curtseyed demurely. 'I've gentlemen's gloves too, the best you'll see in London.'

'I'll wager you fit as snugly as a glove too, hmm?' Ned leant across the narrow counter.

The girl pushed a pair of hunting gloves in front of him and gave a resigned smile.

'How much for these?' Lettice said impatiently, giving her brother a disapproving look.

'One pound, two, mistress.'

'The deuce they are,' Ned cried. 'That's as false a price as the roses on your cheeks. Your charms aren't that beguiling!'

'On my life, sir, that's a fair price. You try anywhere else you like, you won't find a better.'

'Come, minx, d'ye take us for rooks?' Ned pulled at the ribbon round her bodice, but the girl stood firm, seemingly undaunted.

'I'll give you fifteen shillings for them,' Lettice said.

'I can't take less than a pound.'

'Seventeen and sixpence.'

Nicholas was somewhat taken aback by Lettice's ability to haggle.

'Nineteen and I'm selling them to you at a loss.'

The women around them called out their own prices, offering gloves, stockings and lace for fifteen shillings or less, but it was clear Lettice had set her heart on this particular pair.

'Eighteen, take it or leave it,' she said decisively.

The shop girl looked questioningly at Nicholas. Ned guffawed. 'Don't turn to him. He's not such a hoddypoll as that, are you, my man?' Nicholas could smell the wine on his breath. 'Besides, he has to save his pennies for the gaming tables.'

Lettice had placed her money on the counter. The girl sighed and swept it into her hand. Lettice pulled on the gloves triumphantly.

'*Bien gantées*,' she said, admiring them on her hands.

'She took you for a cull,' Ned told her as they left. 'Little hussy.' He turned to Nicholas. 'Probably has the pox anyway. Never trust a strumpet with patches.' He winked.

'She looked little more than a child,' Nicholas said uneasily.

'You have to understand, these city harlots aren't like your country wenches. They teach 'em young here.' Ned waved a hand around the hall. 'Whole place is a damned bawdy-house.'

After taking some dinner at a suitably respectable eating-house, they went to a playhouse on Drury Lane, where they took a box. Musicians played as they waited for the comedy to start and Nicholas gazed eagerly at the deep stage and the heavy curtains. He was looking forward to witnessing some of the more spectacular theatrical devices he had heard about, such as the use of real fire, waterfalls and vanishing actors. Having delivered many fine speeches in honour of queens, mothers and saints, Nicholas was also intrigued to see a play where women characters would appear, in the flesh of actual women. For there were no female parts in the dramas at St. Omer's, only off-stage goddesses.

Ned turned immediately to flirt with a masked woman in the adjoining box. Before long he went to sit beside her, leaving Nicholas and Lettice to themselves. Though he enjoyed the painted scenes that glided across the stage, transforming the setting, Nicholas was as entertained by Lettice's witty conversation as by the performances. She seemed to know all the gossip, pointing out various members of the audience and recounting amusing anecdotes about them. She guessed that the lady Ned was so intimate with was probably the Earl of Derby's latest mistress. Ned had danced with her last season and become completely smitten.

'I am told you kept a mistress in France,' she said, glancing up at Nicholas from beneath lowered lashes.

Nicholas didn't know how to answer and cursed Ned for giving him away, but to his surprise, far from being shocked, this seemed to raise him up in Lettice's estimation.

'I can't abide the sort of sheep Jane would have me consort with,' she told him, fluttering her fan.

A short while later she pulled suddenly on one of his long curls, causing him to gasp and put a hand to his head.

'It is your own!' She laughed. 'Such beautiful locks, you'd make a fortune if you sold them to a wigmaker. I should have bought you that comb.'

'I am not so desperate that I must sell my hair,' he said, somewhat affronted.

'Of course not. Though you could have it made into a wig for when you are older and that fine chestnut has turned grey.' She smiled mischievously. 'Father has strands of silver woven into his now, says it gives him a dignity befitting his age.'

The play, called *The Rover*, was bawdier than Nicholas had expected and full of references to rape and fornication. It was certainly nothing like the dramas they had performed at St. Omer's. A young lady, destined for the life of a nun, fell in love with a libertine and fought off her rival, a courtesan, by disguising herself as a man. When the maiden expressed her determination to know love before taking her vows, he cast a furtive glance at Lettice, but she was laughing along with the rest of the audience. She was very worldly, but then with a brother like Ned perhaps that wasn't surprising. He just hoped her parents wouldn't object to the choice of entertainment, which Lettice informed him, to his astonishment, had been written by a woman.

While in London, Nicholas was determined to fulfil a long-held promise. Hearing that Titus Oates, who was still a prisoner at the King's Bench prison, was having one of his quarterly visits to the pillory, Nicholas went to Tyburn to see the man he held responsible for Matthew's death.

The enduring celebrity of Oates's name ensured a large crowd. Men held children on their shoulders so they could see the famous creator of 'the horrid Popish Plot'. Women stood in knots, their shawls pulled tightly round their shoulders. Rotten eggs and mouldy vegetables were being sold by street vendors at the edge of the crowd, but Nicholas considered such missiles too pathetic for the enormity of Oates's crimes. Even to throw stones would have been to engage with the man in a way that could not do honour to Matthew's memory. Nicholas would have preferred to pull out his sword and decapitate the villain. He pushed his way through to the front of the eager audience.

Oates was indeed a strange-looking creature. A huge chin rested on his chest as though his head grew straight from his body with no neck in between. A small pair of eyes stared out into the distance from beneath a large, flat forehead. To Nicholas's disappointment he did not look contrite nor even fearful. He looked as though his mind had retreated to some hidden place that neither the insults nor the foul projectiles of the mob could reach.

He stared at Oates's mottled grey skin, at the red lines criss-crossing his cheeks and nose. Here was the man who had dressed himself up like a bishop and claimed to be the saviour of England. The man who had hounded his betters into their graves, who had deliberately stirred up the people until they were filled with terror and hatred against those who meant them no harm whatsoever. The man who lined his pockets with blood-money and hoodwinked judges and juries.

'The whoreson still maintains everything he said to be true,' a man next to Nicholas remarked.

'It's a papist conspiracy. Oates says they want to silence him so he can't tell all he knows about the popish intrigues, but he'll expose them one day, if the King doesn't have him murdered before then,' the man's companion said.

'They could easily have killed him before now if that were true,' Nicholas couldn't resist telling them.

'They don't want to make it obvious, though,' the first man said. 'They want it to look like he died of natural causes.'

'There are too many papist vermin crawling through the corridors of Whitehall,' said his friend. 'Sly, bloodthirsty snakes. Oates will uncover them, if he gets the chance.'

Nicholas turned away in disgust. To think he might have been living in Paris, instead of having to return to this ignorant place. He felt no satisfaction on seeing Oates, had no sense that justice had been done or the innocent exonerated. The man still exerted his malevolent influence, even from the stocks.

❖ Chapter Fourteen ❖

The following afternoon, Edward insisted Nicholas accompany him to a gaming house in Lincoln's Inn Fields.

'I used to play at Court,' Ned grumbled. 'All the fashionable young blades go to the groom-porter's apartment. You should see how fast they play at backgammon and dice there and the sums they play for. But the pater has forbidden it and they won't let me in now.'

'I should like to go to Court.'

It wasn't only that he needed to discover more about Pemberton's associates; Nicholas was also keen to see the Court of James II, whose reign Matthew had held such high hopes for.

'You should ask Pater; he might take you.'

'Wallfleet oysters, will you have any oysters?' A young woman passed them, calling out her wares.

Ned waved her over. 'I know how obliging you oyster-wenches are, but how fresh are your goods?' he asked, looking her up and down.

'They've come straight from Essex.' Ignoring Ned's innuendoes, she reached her arms up to lift the basket from her head. 'I got 'em fresh from Billingsgate before the sun was up.'

'I like to taste before I buy.' Ned put one hand to her waist, attempting to kiss her before she had time to dodge.

But the girl pulled her oyster-knife out of her pocket and held the blade between them. 'Fie on you, sir! I'm an honest maid.' She backed away, hugging her basket to her chest.

'Then what are you hawking about on the streets for?' Ned demanded, drawing his sword. He struck her basket with the tip and several oysters went tumbling into the road.

'Come away, Ned.' Nicholas stepped between them and both lowered their weapons. 'How much for the spilt goods?' he asked the girl, nodding at the shells on the ground.

'One shilling,' she said gruffly.

Despite knowing he could have bought twice as many for the same price, he passed her the coin and they left her picking the oysters out of the gutter and wiping them on her apron. 'You should learn to treat women more civilly,' he told Ned.

'Those harlots? Whatever for? If her fish is as foul as her breath it belongs in the sewer anyway, along with the rest of her.' Seeing Nicholas's expression, Ned laughed. 'I know how to behave with a lady, damme.' He laid a hand on his arm. 'Listen, Colley.' He had begun to apply this nickname, which Nicholas didn't particularly like. 'Don't be getting any ideas about my sister. Don't think I didn't notice how intimate the pair of you were yesterday, quite the honeys.'

'My feelings for her are purely fraternal,' Nicholas insisted.

'Good, because the pater is negotiating a match for her, one that will be very advantageous for our family. He was none too happy about our taking her to the theatre yesterday. Doesn't want her seen gadding about with young men. She's a forward young maid and the sooner she's married off the better.'

Nicholas thought this rather unfair, since it was Ned who had left her to his charge. He hoped he hadn't alienated Lord Pemberton. He'd hardly seen him since arriving in London.

'You father is very taken up with the King's business.'

'The Dutch ambassador is visiting; Pater is hoping he might persuade the King to more sensible courses.'

'Such as?'

'Well, not papist ones for a start.'

They had reached The Phoenix. It was a smart establishment with a green-painted front and a large sign depicting a bird rising up out of the ashes of London after the Great Fire. Ned sailed past the bar and up a narrow staircase. Nicholas followed him into a large, elegantly decorated room where men and a few women sat playing various games at small tables. No one looked up as they entered; all attention was fixed on the game at play. The air buzzed with suppressed excitement as the players placed their bets or declared their score.

'Over there.' Ned pointed to a young man at a far table who was waving a lace handkerchief at them.

Nicholas recognised him as one of the Oxford circle and his heart sank. Ambrose Mount was a vain, foolish man who encouraged Edward's worst excesses. Leaping to his feet, Ambrose kissed Edward on both cheeks, ignoring Nicholas, much to the latter's relief. If anyone had foul-smelling breath, it was Ambrose, but he was too cowardly to have the offending tooth pulled.

'Allow me to introduce you.' Ambrose flapped a hand at his companion. 'The honourable Edward Pemberton, Mr Clements.'

Mr Clements, who remained sitting, inclined his head and extended his hand across the table. He was a plump, genial-looking, middle-aged man with a lively, amused look in his blue eyes.

'Mr Mount tells me you are skilled in the art of dice,' he addressed Edward.

'Like most ladies, Dame Fortune seems to favour me.' Edward sat down opposite him, obliging Nicholas to sit across from Ambrose. 'Shall we play hazard?'

'Certainly.' Mr Clements reached for the dice.

'I've brought my own.' Ned slipped a hand into his jacket.

'Sorry, good-fellow, only the house dice allowed here. Prevents cheating, don't you know.' Ambrose grimaced apologetically.

'I always use these dice.' Ned dropped the ivory cubes onto the table.

'Can't play with those,' Clements said firmly, shaking his head.

Ned scowled but returned his dice to his pocket.

'But at least the wine is good,' Clements added amenably, nodding at the empty bottle.

Ambrose jumped to his feet. 'I'll order another.'

As if by magic, a diminutive man in a green wool jacket appeared beside them. 'Can I be of assistance, gentlemen?' he asked.

'We'll take another bottle of claret, if you'd be so kind, Mr Fleet,' Clements said.

'By all means, I'll send a servant over right away with a bottle of our best claret and a plate of Cheshire cheese. Always best to take a little food with your drink, I find.' He nodded at them. Catching Nicholas's eye, he gave him a quizzical look. 'You're not a regular, are you?'

Nicholas shook his head. 'Never been here before.'

'Ever been to The Red Hart in Highgate?'

When Nicholas answered in the negative, Mr Fleet just shrugged and moved away to chat to another table.

'Who was that impertinent fellow?' Ned asked.

'Mr Fleet is the proprietor of this venerable establishment,' Clements explained. 'Like the groom-porter at court games, he ensures fair play and arbitrates in any disputes.' Rising from his chair, Clements asked them to excuse him for a moment.

A maid arrived with the cheese, wine and a basket of bread. Ned was about to proposition her when she gave him such a withering look, he thought better of it.

'You'd have to take her from behind.' He laughed. 'Or her face would turn you to stone.'

Withdrawing to the window, Nicholas saw Clements talking to one of the linkboys waiting in the street below. The boy nodded earnestly, before passing his torch to one of his comrades and running off down the road, his short legs racing as though his life depended on it. Nicholas wondered what the errand could be, that was so urgent, but Mr Clements returned to the table with the same light-hearted countenance as before.

'Happy for me to continue as the setter?' he asked.

The other three agreed he should act as the bank and Ned called the first dice.

Nicholas was comforted by the fatherly presence of Clements, hoping he would prove a calming influence and at first this proved to be the case. They won and lost in equal measure while exchanging stories of their amorous conquests. Clements, though, as he admitted himself, now running to fat, had enjoyed a variety of women in as many different countries. He had in his younger days been a merchant, travelling often to the Levant. Nicholas would have liked to hear more about the lands he had seen, their geography and customs, but Ambrose and Ned had no interest in this, dominating the conversation with their own boastful talk, which grew louder and more extreme the more they drank.

'D'you know Lady Easterly? Only been married three months.' Ambrose asked Ned. 'I swived her in St. James's Park last night. She lifted her skirts for me right there, under the trees.'

Ned guffawed. 'I had her when she was still betrothed. You've probably got my crab-lice in your breeks right now.' He reached under the table and made to grab Ambrose's groin. Ambrose squealed and pushed him away. 'She must've been with half the town since I first ignited the fire in her privy parts,' Ned boasted.

Nicholas refused to describe his own exploits with Isabelle Dupont no matter how they provoked him. Let them doubt the existence of his French mistress; he didn't care. He doubted the veracity of half their claims of seduction. He thought of Lettice, her vivacity and openness, and hoped no one discussed her in the sort of terms Ambrose and Ned were using about the ladies of their acquaintance. He wondered, with even more discomfort, what they would say of his mother and was grateful that Jane had not disclosed the details of his parentage to the Pembertons.

Gradually, Ned began to lose more than he won back. When he was in debt by twenty-five pounds, Nicholas tried to get him to stop.

'You go home if you want to,' Edward responded angrily.

'Poor country Colley, sums which are mere trifles to us seem vast to him.' Ambrose smirked. 'I've been told that in Charles's Court, the Duke of Ormond once won a thousand pounds at dice.'

'We can switch to cards if you like,' Clements said amicably to Ned. 'A game of basset, perhaps?'

'The dice are usually lucky for me. Let's stick with them for now.' Ned looked around the room. 'Don't they have champagne here? I need something to clear my head.'

'I'll ask.' Nicholas got up, needing to use the privy.

He was tired of the game, which had become repetitive, and even more tired of the company, which had become equally so. But as the Pembertons' guest, he couldn't abandon Edward, who was already in his cups.

As he left the room, Nicholas almost tripped over the boot of a huge man who was sitting beside the door, watching the players vigilantly. The man glanced at him, his face impassive. He had enormous hands, which were resting, motionless, on his knees. A long scar ran across the left knuckles. Instead of a wig, his bald head sported a woollen cap like a sailor's.

'I beg your pardon,' Nicholas said, not wanting to offend such a fearsome-looking giant. The man inclined his chin slightly in response, his eyes still fixed on the room in front of him.

Emerging from the privy into the dark backyard, Nicholas felt a hand grasp his arm. He reached automatically for his sword, the hairs on the back of his neck bristling. His first thought was that it might be the giant from upstairs.

But then a familiar voice spoke in his ear. 'We are still waiting for news.'

He turned to find Gilbert Staley, with a hat pulled down low over his brow and his mouth twisted in a vicious frown. His heart lurched. How had Staley known where to find him?

'Lord Pemberton is seeing the Dutch ambassador,' he whispered.

'That's no secret.' Staley kept his hand encircled around Nicholas's wrist, pinching it tightly. 'You need to discover what they discuss in private.'

'How can I do that?'

'Ask Pemberton if you can wait on him. Convince him you are indispensable,' Staley said impatiently. 'Have you searched his rooms for letters? Checked his closet, his study, his bedchamber?'

Nicholas shook his head.

'Carmichael assured me you'd make a capable intelligencer.' Staley twisted Nicholas's arm behind his back. Despite his foppish appearance, he had a grip like a vice. They were nose to nose and Nicholas could feel the heat of Staley's breath on his face and smell the tobacco he still inhaled. 'It would be a shame to see your father thrown into a house of correction and to lose that fine home in Derbyshire.' Nicholas blinked as Staley's spittle sprayed his cheeks. 'Keep your focus on the task at hand. And keep an eye on that blackamoor of Pemberton's. We think he's been carrying messages to Holland.'

The back door opened and Mr Fleet stepped out into the yard, a lantern in one hand and a cat under his arm.

'Go on, out you go, Puss, catch some mice.' He dropped the cat, who stalked off towards the wall, tail held erect. Straightening up, Fleet surveyed the two men. 'Gentlemen.' He gave a small bow.

'I give you three weeks, Hawthorne,' Staley muttered, pushing past Fleet and back into the tavern.

Through the open door, Nicholas could see his cloaked form as he marched out into the street on the other side of the bar.

'Mr Hawthorne, is it?' Fleet asked.

'It is,' Nicholas replied warily, rubbing his wrist.

'Don't mean to pry, only you look very familiar and I once had a friend called Hawthorne. Miss Alethea Hawthorne. Don't suppose you know her?'

'I had an aunt by that name.' Nicholas wondered how his aunt could have been acquainted with such a man, but her name was not a common one and it seemed unlikely there would be two who shared it.

'Had?' Mr Fleet said with a note of sadness.

'She died before I was born, in the plague of '65.'

'Then, perhaps it was a different lady. Apologies for troubling you.' Mr Fleet held out an arm, beckoning Nicholas back inside.

'Can you send some champagne up to my companions? They'll be getting impatient.' Nicholas thought anxiously of Ned. He didn't like to wait for his drink.

'Certainly.' Mr Fleet followed him inside, calling to the potman, 'Champagne for table six.'

Nicholas was at the foot of the stairs when he heard crashing and shouting from the room above. He recognised the sound of Ned's voice swearing. He and Mr Fleet hastened up the stairs. When they got into the gaming room, they found Ned with his feet off the ground and his arms pinioned behind his back. He was being held aloft by the giant who had been stationed by the door. Ned was bellowing and cursing for all he was worth, while Ambrose demanded in vain for his release.

'Causing trouble, was he, Mr Clements?' Fleet turned to their companion, who was looking as serene as ever.

'Unfortunately so, Mr Fleet. The young gentleman, tired of waiting for his friend' – Clements gestured to Nicholas – 'decided to relieve himself in one of your wine flagons.'

Nicholas stared in horror at the vessel on the table and the yellow liquid splashed over it.

'Never seen anything so scandalous in my life,' a woman at the next table complained. 'These colts think they can behave however they please with no respect for anyone.'

'Perhaps you could see our guest out, Moses,' Fleet said to the giant.

'Do you know who my father is?' Ned demanded.

'I do indeed and I will be informing Lord Pemberton of your conduct here and the damages owed.'

Fleet nodded at Moses, who made for the door, carrying Edward in front of him like a wet coat.

'Do something, Colley, for God's sake,' Ned shouted, writhing and kicking his feet helplessly, while Ambrose flapped and squawked beside him.

Nicholas had no more desire for Pemberton to find out about this than Ned did. He had promised Jane he would keep Ned away from the tables; now it would seem as though he were encouraging him in his libertine ways. They might send him away. Certainly it would not get him any closer in Pemberton's confidence.

'Mr Fleet, perhaps we might talk this over. I am sure we can come to an amicable resolution without needing to involve any third parties.' He looked hopefully at the landlord.

Mr Fleet appeared somewhat disconcerted. He shook his head as if to clear it. 'You do have the look of her,' he said wonderingly. 'And the voice.' Then, turning to Moses, said more forcefully, 'Take the young man outside. He is barred from this establishment henceforth. I will discuss what compensation might be made with Mr Hawthorne, here.'

The unhappy maid was summoned to clean up the mess and drinks were offered, at the establishment's expense, to the offended parties. Mr Clements joined some acquaintances at another table, his equanimity seemingly undisturbed. Mr Fleet led Nicholas into a booth downstairs. Nicholas hoped Ambrose would see Ned got home without any further altercations.

'I'm sincerely sorry, Mr Fleet,' Nicholas said as soon as he was seated. Having to apologise for Ned's behaviour was becoming an unpleasantly frequent experience.

Fleet waved a hand dismissively in the air. 'Call me Jack.' He smiled approvingly as the potman set glasses and a decanter of wine down on the table. 'If you can ensure everything is paid for, and I won't overcharge, but I will have to include all costs accrued, then there'll be no need for me to involve Lord Pemberton.' He filled their glasses. 'I'll draw up a list.'

Nicholas took a sip of wine. It was a lot smoother than the claret they'd had upstairs. He took another mouthful. 'You have my word, the reckoning will be paid in full and all damage accounted for.' Nicholas knew by now that fear of his father finding out and cutting off his allowance would ensure Ned paid up, even if he had to sell his new gold earring to meet the expense.

'You strike me as an honest fellow, Mr Hawthorne, well-bred as I would expect any of your name to be, so I hope you won't take it amiss if I offer you some advice. Only, I know how easy it is to fall in with the wrong sort, and the company you're keeping…' Jack shook his head slowly. 'If it ain't too late, I'd find myself a new circle of acquaintance. Nearer home, maybe?'

'Edward is young and high-spirited, but as you are aware, he comes from a very good family,' Nicholas replied, irritated at being condescended to. Did the man think him some country bumpkin?

'I don't mean him.' Jack paused. 'The cove outside, in the yard. An unsavoury fellow if ever I saw one. Are you in his debt?'

'That is none of your business.'

'Apologies, apologies for my impertinence.' Jack held up his hands. 'It's only your strong resemblance to my esteemed friend Miss Hawthorne that compels me to speak out. If you did happen to be a near relation, well, I wouldn't forgive myself if I didn't do right by you.'

'Then please forget you ever saw the gentleman outside.'

'Saw who?' Jack winked and topped up his glass.

Somewhat placated, Nicholas took another drink. He had not tasted such good wine since last he drank with Isabelle and it would be a shame not to savour it. 'So, who was your Alethea Hawthorne?'

'Ah.' Jack gazed out across the room, a wistful smile playing over his lips. 'Now there was a lady who was all romance – noble-spirited, proud and passionate. She might have stepped right out of some old tale of chivalry.'

'How so?' Nicholas couldn't help being amused by the landlord's fanciful humour.

'When I first encountered Alethea – for we was on first-name terms,' Jack explained with a note of apology, 'she was being attacked on the street by a plague-crazed wretch. I rescued her.' He tapped his chest, holding his small frame up proudly. 'She'd been cast out by her so-called friends and left to fend for herself. It was during the last great pestilence, when people was reduced to all sorts of wickedness. Even great folk like the Ca— well, I won't say who as you may be acquainted.' He smiled and nodded. 'I then had the great privilege of accompanying Alethea for a time as she made her way home to Derbyshire. We had some adventures.'

'Where in Derbyshire was she going?'

Jack scrunched up his eyes. 'Something Hall. Begins with an M.'

'Measham?'

'That's it.' Jack nodded enthusiastically.

'Why, then your friend and my aunt must be the same person, for that is my home. I will write to my father straight away; he'll be most interested to hear any information relating to his sister.'

'Except, my Alethea survived the plague. Her and Ellen, they paid me a visit, up at my tavern in Highgate.' Jack studied Nicholas's face carefully. 'Must be at least twenty years ago now. You'd have been an infant.'

'Ellen?' Nicholas suddenly felt a little dizzy. Surely Jack could not be referring to his mother?

'That's right, Mrs Ellen Liddell.' Jack coughed. 'She lives back in London now.'

'Do you know where?'

Nicholas had resolved long ago to forget about his mother. She was, after all, a sinner who had relinquished her child. It was better he did not know her. St. Omers had become his second parent and he had been so caught up in life there, and now with his mission in England, that he had not given her any thought for a long time. But Jack's words rekindled that earlier desire to know her. Perhaps his mother could provide some clue as to his father's secrets. No one at home had ever said his aunt and his mother were acquainted. His aunt was supposed to have died before his parents returned to Measham. Either Mr Fleet was mistaken or Nicholas had not been told the truth.

'Last I knew of Ellen, she was living in Whitechapel with her sister's family. Lizzie Tyler, she was a warm-hearted soul, for all she was a puritan. I think their dad left them his draper's business and they set up a shop together. Always meant to look them up, but never found the time, not between the Red Hart, this place and a wife and eight children, bless 'em.' He shook his head. 'There aren't enough hours in the day.'

When Nicholas finally walked out of The Phoenix, he almost tripped over Ned, who was lying by a pool of vomit in the gutter. There was no sign of Ambrose. To Nicholas's relief, Ned opened his eyes and mumbled something in response to his name.

A hopeful linkboy appeared, holding his smoking torch aloft to illuminate the scene.

'Beware.' Ned lifted an arm to gesture in the linkboy's direction. 'They're often in league with footpads, you know.'

'I ain't,' the boy declared indignantly. 'I been watching out for him, like Mr Moses told me to.'

Hoping Ned had cleared the contents of his stomach, Nicholas lifted one of his arms over his shoulder. 'Come on then,' he sighed, staggering slightly as he raised Ned to his feet. He nodded at the linkboy. 'It isn't far.'

As they stumbled slowly home, their path lit by the boy's torch, Nicholas recalled Mr Clements's much swifter errand earlier that evening. He asked the boy if he or any of his friends had been sent on urgent business by a gentleman from the Phoenix, but the boy denied any knowledge of it and Nicholas had too many other concerns weighing him down to pursue the matter. When they got to Pemberton House, he handed the boy sixpence. The lad touched his cap and ambled off, looking for other customers.

'Hey,' Ned called after him. 'Fancy a bit of buggery?' He laughed, slapping Nicholas's chest. 'You know what they say: if you can't find a woman, a boy will do.'

The linkboy hastened across the road, his light bobbing in the darkness.

'You want to watch your mouth,' Nicholas told him.

Ralph Pemberton must have heard them arrive, for he came hurrying down the stairs in his nightgown as Nicholas staggered across the hall, half-carrying his inebriated son.

The colour drained from Pemberton's face. 'Is he injured?' he asked as he rushed to Edward's side.

When it became apparent that Ned was merely drunk, while Nicholas, in comparison, appeared quite sober, his concern turned to anger.

'You promised me you would curb your debauchery,' he told his oblivious son, with a mixture of weariness and disgust. 'I'm grateful to you for getting him home,' he said to Nicholas. 'There have been occasions when I've had to fetch him from the gaol and even less salubrious places.'

'That's quite all right,' Nicholas said, relieved both to be freed of his burden and to have gained some approbation from Lord Pemberton.

He barely had the energy to undress, before falling into bed and straight into a heavy sleep. He woke only a few hours later, his head buzzing with a swarm of questions. How could it be that Jack Fleet, tavern and gaming house proprietor, knew not only his aunt, but also his mother? He had the uneasy sense that Jack knew more than he'd let on, which made him even more determined to find a way to visit Ellen for himself.

And now, according to Staley's instructions, he also had to search Lord Pemberton's apartments. Nicholas felt especially bad about this given how solicitous his host had been last night, offering him possets or soup or anything else he might desire from the kitchen. Not wanting to wake the kitchen maid, Nicholas had declined, but now his stomach rumbled hollowly.

Perhaps he could invent some harmless information to give to Staley. It would have to be convincing, though, and what did Nicholas know of Court intrigues or foreign affairs? He wished he was back at Oxford, taking refuge in some book on natural philosophy or in the physic garden. Ned was becoming an increasingly odious companion. He consoled himself with the thought that at least here he could enjoy the more sympathetic attentions of Jane and Lettice.

⟶ Chapter Fifteen ⟵

14th December 1687

Hearing the front door slam, Nicholas rose and hurried over to the window. He was just in time to see Lord Pemberton entering his carriage. The coachman cracked his whip over the horses and it rumbled off down the street. Nicholas stood outside his chamber door. The only sound he could hear was some distant clanking in the kitchen below. The house was still dark, the pale winter sun only just rising. Knowing their habits, he was confident no one else in the family would be up for some time yet. It was the perfect time to search Pemberton's study.

After tapping lightly on the study door as a precaution and receiving no reply, he tried the handle. To his relief it turned easily and he slipped inside, carefully closing the door behind him. The large room smelt of beeswax, woodsmoke and something richly aromatic that he couldn't identify. His slippered feet sank into soft carpet.

An elaborately carved cupboard stood on his right; this too was unlocked and contained neat stacks of pamphlets. Nicholas flicked quickly through them. Some were written in support of the King; others, however, attacked James's policies. One, by a Dutchman, claimed to be a genuine account of the Prince and Princess of Orange's thoughts concerning the repeal of the Test and the Penal Laws. Notes had been written in the margins of several of the pamphlets. Nicholas was tempted to take a few, but didn't want to arouse Pemberton's suspicions, for, given what were surely his annotations, he must have further plans for them.

Needing to work quickly in case a maid came in to set the fire, he moved over to the imposing desk at the far end of the room. The top drawer was locked but the next slid open easily. Perhaps here he might discover some correspondence with the Dutch ambassador, or an account of Pemberton's conversations with him. He pulled out a manuscript.

'What are you doing?'

Nicholas leapt up, his mouth dry and his heart pounding. Pemberton's secretary stood by the open door.

'I was just looking for some parchment. I need to write a letter,' Nicholas stammered.

'If you had asked, I would have brought some to you, sir,' Isaac said coolly, pushing the door shut before strolling across the room. 'And what's that in your hand?' He pointed at the sheaf of papers clutched in Nicholas's fist.

Nicholas looked down at them. 'Oh, those.' He flapped the pages carelessly while searching desperately for some plausible reason why he might be holding onto them. His head was still too clouded by the previous night's drinking for him to think swiftly.

'Can you read Dutch?' Isaac studied his face appraisingly.

The papers, which he hadn't had a chance to look at properly, were indeed written in a language unfamiliar to Nicholas. 'No, unfortunately not,' he said, feeling like an idiot. A condition made worse by the fact that he was standing in his nightclothes, while Isaac was fully and impeccably dressed.

Isaac held out his hand for the manuscript, scanning it quickly when Nicholas passed it to him. 'It is an order for plates, bowls and tiles from Holland. I helped Lord Pemberton draw it up. Have you a particular interest in earthenware?'

'Not especially.' Nicholas managed a watery smile and then, remembering Staley's warning, asked, 'Does Lord Pemberton send you back to Holland for such items? That must be a pleasant errand.'

Instead of replying, Isaac opened a cabinet and took out a bottle and two dainty glasses, which he proceeded to fill. 'You look as though you could do with a hair of the dog that bit you last night.' He handed a glass to Nicholas.

The dark brown liquid was strong and syrupy. The first mouthful almost made Nicholas retch, but the second did indeed help clear his head and settle his stomach.

'It's rum.' Isaac smiled. 'Comes from Barbados.' He gestured round the room. 'Just as those juniper floorboards came from Jamaica and this black walnut panelling was a gift from the governor of Maryland. The fine carpets, the ornaments, all sent from or bought with money from our royal colonies. More impressive, I think, than clay-work.'

'They are very fine.' Nicholas finished his drink. 'I should like to visit such places one day.'

'Perhaps, if you prove loyal, Lord Pemberton will send you on foreign errands.'

'Of course Lord Pemberton has my loyalty, for he serves our King. It would be an honour to act on his behalf,' Nicholas said carefully. Isaac was addressing him as an equal, if not as an inferior. Did he suspect Nicholas of spying?

'In the meantime, however, he would like you to attend on Sir Edward Petre,' Isaac continued briskly. 'This Jesuit has become the King's closest adviser. Since you are both graduates of St. Omers, Lord Pemberton believes Petre will look favourably on you.'

This was an unexpected and potentially advantageous request. Did it mean that Pemberton was no longer one of the King's favourites? Nicholas knew of Father Petre by reputation; he was Dean of the Chapel Royal and had recently been made a member of the Privy Council. He was also loathed at Magdalen for being behind the removal of those fellows who had refused to vote in the King's choice of college president.

'Make sure you enquire, on your own behalf, after the Queen's health, paying particular attention to the priest's response.' Isaac took the glass Nicholas had been revolving absentmindedly between his fingers and placed it on a silver tray. 'You are to assure Petre that Lord Pemberton, far from being an enemy of the Romish religion, is an admirer, one who would be grateful for instruction from such a learned and esteemed cleric.'

'He has changed his opinion of Popery, then,' Nicholas couldn't help exclaiming.

'You will find many courtiers are becoming more catholic in their sympathies.' Isaac returned the bottle to its cupboard, locking the door with a key from the collection he always carried attached by a chain to his belt.

Nicholas was never sure whether Isaac was being satirical. There was often a note of mockery in his words, but he was always too subtle to be pinned down and Nicholas couldn't tell whether it was himself or the world that was being ridiculed. Still, here at last was something that ought to please Staley.

As if reading his thoughts, Isaac said more sharply, 'I'm sure I don't need to impress upon you the need for absolute discretion. You are not to speak of this matter to anyone other than Petre and myself, and Lord Pemberton only if he raises the issue with you directly.'

'Absolutely.'

'You will not speak of it to Lady Jane.'

'You have my word,' Nicholas said, finishing the sentence in his head – *I will not speak of it to anyone else other than Staley* – an act of school-boy equivocation that at least gave him some comfort.

'When you call on Petre, Lord Pemberton also desires you to take note of whoever else is present and report back to him.'

'How will I recognise anyone? The Court is unfamiliar to me!'

'I've seen you with your drawing-book. Why don't you take it and draw whomever you find there, and bring the pictures back? Be discreet about it, of course.'

'Very well,' Nicholas replied curtly, resentful of being treated like a servant, or a child.

Isaac managed to disconcert him again with a charming smile and a bow. 'Lord Pemberton will be indebted to you.'

So, now he was gathering intelligence for both Staley and Pemberton. Perhaps he should take some lessons from Isaac in how to play one man off against the other. The secretary seemed to know exactly how to read men's humours.

Despite his initial excitement about the opportunity to attend Court, it turned out to be less impressive and more tedious than Nicholas had anticipated. He tried taking out his notebook during the long wait in Father Petre's antechamber, but he was too closely crowded in by other petitioners, who darted hostile looks in his direction, nudged his elbow and tried to peer at what he was drawing. Like him, everyone else was also busy trying to determine which families were represented and what favours they might be hoping to gain. A few wore the livery and badges of great houses, but most appeared to be private gentlemen. After standing for several hours, Nicholas alighted on a vacated window seat and fell into a fitful doze, from which he woke with a start at the sound of his name being called.

To his relief, Father Petre, despite the number of visitors he had already received, was both enthusiastic and charming. Beneath his square cap, a Roman nose and strong jaw gave his face a classical authority, offset by lively, enquiring eyes. He was keen to hear all about St. Omers and its inhabitants and they spent several minutes discussing the college. The rector was an old friend, Petre said. He then moved on to the topic of Oxford and the recalcitrant fellows there. He was pleased to know that Nicholas was doing well at Magdalen and hoped that soon he would be joined by others of their faith. Though of course it was all nonsense, these rumours that he was planning to turn the university into a Jesuit seminary.

'Perhaps you also know of Mr Staley,' Nicholas ventured, hoping the dean might exert a benign influence over Staley. 'He too is a friend of Father Carmichael.'

Petre gave him a genial smile, but his voice turned colder and there was a glint of ice in his eyes when he replied. 'I am sure the rector has many friends; I cannot be acquainted with all of them.'

'No, of course not, Father,' Nicholas replied, chastened.

A large painting of the Madonna and Child hung high up on the wall. Mother and infant stared out with earnest, mournful expressions, reminding Nicholas to ask after the Queen's health. There was a brief silence as Petre followed Nicholas's gaze to the picture of the Virgin Mary and the baby at her breast.

'The waters at Bath, along with the King's pilgrimage to Holywell, have proved most efficacious.' Petre pressed his palms together in front of his chest. 'The soul of our country may yet be saved.'

'Her Majesty is with child?'

'Her Majesty has not had her courses since the end of September and her ladies are certain of it. An announcement will be made soon.' Petre beamed. 'His Majesty is confident of an heir and I am sure you will join your prayers with ours for a healthy boy child.'

'Of course, Father. That is joyous news indeed,' Nicholas said. He understood, as the priest did, that England's long-term salvation depended on a Catholic prince. 'I also have good tidings to relay.' And he passed on Lord Pemberton's message. 'He would welcome a private audience with you, Reverend Father.'

'I rejoice that His Lordship's spirit has been opened to Divine Love. Is it possible that God has been speaking through one so young in years, and that you have discovered and enlarged this chink in his heart?'

'I wish I could own such an honour, Father, but my influence with Lord Pemberton is not so great.'

Nicholas felt the heat rising into his face. Was this a missed opportunity? Ought he to take credit for Pemberton's sudden interest in Rome? It was quite possible that Staley worked for Father Petre, despite his denial. Even so, Nicholas had not been sent to convert Pemberton and the dean did seem genuinely interested in his education and work.

'I expect I shall see Lord Pemberton in my congregation on Sunday. Perhaps I might speak to him then,' Petre said as Nicholas was being shown out.

It was unfortunate he had not been able to secure a private meeting. Petre clearly wanted some proofs of Pemberton's new faith. Perhaps he suspected the viscount's motives were political, rather than spiritual. But at least Nicholas had spoken personally and warmly with the King's favourite adviser; that was surely some achievement. To think, one of the most influential men in the kingdom was a Jesuit priest, and there might be a popish heir to the throne. That would surely convince the people of God's true purpose. He could almost see Matthew smiling approvingly down on him from the heavens.

He would offer to accompany Lord Pemberton to the Chapel Royal on Sunday and provide any assistance he might require with the unfamiliar Romish rites. It would be the perfect opportunity to discover more about his real allegiances.

It was dark by the time Nicholas got back to Pemberton House and, having missed dinner, he was looking forward to his supper. But Isaac met him in the hall and he was ushered straight into the study. Lord Pemberton was sitting back from his desk so that his face was in shadow. Nicholas, in contrast, was fully illuminated, for Isaac was holding a branched candlestick so close to his head Nicholas could hear the wicks hissing and feel the warmth from the flames on his cheek. He was compelled to stand as Pemberton subjected him to such a thorough disquisition on his meeting with Petre he began to feel as though he were a prisoner in the dock.

'So, the rumours are true,' Pemberton muttered when told of the Queen's pregnancy. 'At least now we have confirmation.' He sighed and rubbed his chin. 'I suppose it's evens on the child's sex, but I would not take the odds on it surviving, given her losses so far.'

'It might be safest to assume she succeeds this time,' Isaac murmured, placing his candlestick on a side table and sitting down on the only other available chair.

'True, true.' Pemberton nodded at his secretary. Nicholas was beginning to wonder what it was that gave the servant so much power over his master. Pemberton leant forward, placing his elbows on the desk. 'What was Petre's manner when he conveyed this news to you?'

'Why, he was very pleased, sir.'

'As are we all, but: do you think his pleasure went beyond mere duty, to resemble something akin to a paternal joy, for instance?'

'His joy was that of a priest for his sovereign. The King believes his pilgrimage has been rewarded.'

'Of course,' Pemberton agreed, but Nicholas was left with the uneasy feeling that his interpretation was rather different.

'Did you manage to make any drawings?' Isaac asked.

When Nicholas explained why this had not been possible, both men looked disappointed.

'Go down to the kitchens and the cook will find you some supper,' Pemberton told him peremptorily and Nicholas understood that he was dismissed.

As he was returning to his chamber after his solitary repast, Nicholas heard the front door close. Stopping a footman in the hall he asked who had departed at so late an hour.

'Mr Isaac has gone on an errand for His Lordship,' the man replied.

'Will he be back tonight?' Nicholas asked, affecting a casual air.

'I doubt it, sir. He has to oversee some cargo down at the docks, and must be travelling too, for he had me pack his trunk. I'd say he'll be gone at least a week.'

Nicholas wondered if Isaac might be on his way to Holland to tell Prince William that his wife's claim to the throne was now threatened by the possibility of a brother. He thought of the Dutch pamphlets in Pemberton's cupboard. Pemberton might have seized them in order to stop their circulation, or conversely, he might be circulating them himself. Considering the notes of rebuttal on the English letters, he might even be helping to write them. Either way, Nicholas had plenty to share with Staley now.

Not wanting to trust a letter to a third party, he went, early the next morning, to the address Staley had given him. It was neither a house nor an inn, but a Jesuit school in Fenchurch Street. There was no sign of Staley so he left a long, coded account with the schoolmaster, Mr Northleigh, who seemed, by his impassive expression, to be accustomed to receiving such missives.

As he was leaving the building he almost collided with Mr Clements, who was coming up the front steps.

'Hello, dear sir. What a delightful surprise to encounter you here.' Clements grinned roguishly at him.

'Indeed, I— I was just enquiring about an old tutor of mine,' Nicholas said quickly, the excuse formulating itself as he spoke.

'Splendid.' Clements leant towards him. 'Can you recommend the school? I am making enquiries on behalf of my godson.'

Nicholas glanced over his shoulder. 'My tutor is no longer there and I have no personal knowledge of the establishment, but the Jesuits are known to be the foremost educators.'

Clements looked gratified. 'Precisely.' He patted Nicholas's arm. 'I have an appointment with the headmaster, otherwise I would invite you to a coffeehouse; there's a rather good one round the corner. But perhaps we might meet again at The Phoenix.'

'I think I should keep Edward Pemberton away from the gaming tables.'

Clements's blue eyes twinkled. 'But I am sure you would always be welcome there. You appeared to strike up very cordial relations with the honourable Mr Fleet.'

'Mr Fleet was pleased by my assurances that all costs would be repaid,' Nicholas said warily.

'As any hosteler would be. Well, my good fellow, I must bid you adieu. May Lady Fortune smile upon you.' With a sweep of his hat, Clements bowed low. 'If you fancy a game of cards or dice, you know where to find me.'

At the corner of the street, Nicholas turned, expecting to see Clements still standing on the steps, watching him, but the imperturbable gentleman had disappeared inside.

→ Chapter Sixteen ←

'**M**y parents are coming to dinner; will you be joining us?' Jane called to Edward as she followed him into the parlour. There was an uncharacteristically sharp edge to her voice, but then, it was already eleven o'clock and Edward had only just emerged from his chamber.

'I haven't the vigour to go out, so we might as well stay for some fodder, hey, Colley? The cook always serves something special for Jane's genitors.'

Edward sauntered over to the desk where Nicholas sat writing. He had been halfway through a long-overdue reply to a letter from Father. Blotting his work, he folded the parchment and slipped it into his pocket. He didn't want Ned reading it out to the assembled company – something the fellow was only too capable of when on the hunt for entertainment. Not that the letter contained anything incriminating, it was just an account of his impressions of London, but he could hear Ned's snide tone as he recited Nicholas's enquiries after the Measham household, especially of Crewe, who had been suffering from rheumatism, and Abigail, who, to everyone's astonishment, had rejected an offer of marriage from the local blacksmith.

Dorothy and Prudence were sewing by the fire and the warm room had been agreeably tranquil, but now the calm was disrupted by Ned's overbearing presence and Jane's evident agitation. Nicholas looked over at her uneasily. Conscious of the rift between his father and Lord and Lady Calverton, he wondered if he ought to absent himself. Jane, however, smiled affectionately back at him, making him suspect it was Ned she was most concerned about.

'You are welcome to dine with us, Nicholas,' she assured him.

'Thank you,' he said.

Edward pulled Prudence off her seat and, ignoring her remonstrations, flopped down onto it himself.

'Go and see if Lettice has finished dressing and make sure Richard is presentable,' Jane told the disgruntled girl.

Rolling her eyes, Prudence moved towards the door just as her sister came through it.

'My toilette is complete,' Lettice announced triumphantly, extending her arms and revolving slowly for all to admire.

It was impossible not to be impressed by her appearance. A pearl necklace and pendant earrings drew the eye to her slender neck, while a stole of grey fox fur, lying snugly across her shoulders, set off an exquisitely intricate hairpiece interlaced with ribbons.

'Oh, Tilly, you must allow your maid to dress my hair.' Dorothy joined Prudence beside their eldest sister. She pushed her little finger into one of the dainty ringlets at the nape of Lettice's neck. 'What do you call these again?'

'*Crèves-coeur*,' Lettice said, and her eyes met Nicholas's. 'Heart-breakers. Don't ruffle them, Doll.' She moved away from her sisters and towards the fire.

Ned began to sneeze. 'Damme, how much powder did you put on that confection of curls?'

'I'm not sure my parents require such an ostentatious display,' Jane said, raising her eyebrows.

'But isn't she pretty?' Prudence hung on Jane's arm. 'The curls by the ears are known as *confidants*,' she explained, evidently proud of her knowledge.

'Hmmm.' Jane caressed Prue's head. 'I think you are just as pretty without such adornments.'

'I hope I won't incur Lady Margaret's displeasure,' Lettice said, a note of defiance in her voice.

'Her Ladyship will tell you soon enough if you do,' Ned pointed out.

Nicholas could see Jane's jaw tighten and wished he could help ensure the good behaviour of her stepchildren. He had always assumed his father's accounts of Margaret Calverton's monstrousness were exaggerated. And then it occurred to him – Jack Fleet must have meant the Calvertons when he spoke of the so-called friends who had abandoned Aunt Alethea, for she had been staying with them when she died. Now he was more curious than ever to meet Jane's parents.

'So, you are Sir William's son?' Lady Margaret peered at Nicholas across the table.

'That's right, madam.' He found her scrutiny of him quite unnerving. In contrast to the spongy folds of her face and the softly curled periwig above it, her narrow eyes were shrewd and flinty.

'I don't understand why your father hasn't married. Such an odd, reclusive fellow. How on earth does he manage his household without a wife to organise it?' She sounded personally aggrieved, but perhaps that was because of Father's familiarity with her daughter.

'Now, now, Peg,' her husband warned.

Henry Calverton had a more amiable manner than his wife. His voice, whenever he spoke, was reassuringly soft and measured, as were his observations.

But she continued regardless. 'You would think Sir William could find favour with our gracious monarch given their shared religious affiliations. Doesn't he wish to attend Court now?'

'My father is a country mouse. The city does not agree with him, too much noise and smoke.' Nicholas attempted to push some fish and a preserved nasturtium seed onto his fork with his knife. A spoon would have accommodated all elements quite easily. He still thought forks an unnecessary affectation.

Margaret harrumphed. 'And are you seeking an introduction at Court?'

Nicholas lowered his fork and glanced at Pemberton, but he was watching Edward, who appeared to be falling asleep over his plate.

'I am more interested in pursuing a scholarly life,' Nicholas explained. 'But of course I would be most grateful, if the opportunity arose, to be presented.'

Margaret pursed her thin lips. 'Well, I suppose the King has fathered plenty of natural issue of his own. Still, he may have had enough of other men's bastards. He certainly put down Monmouth's rebellion with gusto.'

'Mother!' Jane exclaimed.

Charles II's illegitimate son, James Scott, Duke of Monmouth, had been executed a few years previously for attempting to overthrow his uncle. King James had been much commended for his swift and merciless action against the rebels.

'There are many more natural sons who are loyal to the crown – the Duke of Grafton, for example,' Nicholas said quickly. Since it was evident they all knew about his illegitimacy, he refused to be shamed by it. Most of Charles's base-born sons had been made dukes, and there were plenty of them.

'I know Henry FitzRoy well, a most commendable young man,' Pemberton said, belatedly joining the conversation.

Nicholas felt immediately grateful to him for his inadvertent support, even if Pemberton had been too distracted by his son to heed Margaret's jibes about bastards.

'And what about you, young man?' she said, turning on Edward. 'Shouldn't you have finished with university by now?'

Opening his half-closed eyes, Ned gave her a lazy smile. 'I went late, don't ye know, due to a period of ill health. I shan't stay much longer; it's beginning to bore me. Think I might try the Inns of Court.'

This was welcome news to Nicholas. If Ned left Oxford, he would be free to devote himself to his studies. Then it occurred to him that he might be forced to leave as well, to follow Ned to the Inns. Surely Staley couldn't do that to him?

'Are you going to train him up in overseeing the royal plantations, Ralph?' Calverton asked.

'Perhaps, if he shows some aptitude for such work,' Pemberton answered warily.

Edward yawned in response and gestured for his glass to be refilled.

'It is certainly lucrative,' Calverton remarked, nodding at the huge blue and white vases on the mantlepiece. 'Impressive chinaware.'

'Ralph brought them back from Holland.' Jane's normally cheerful disposition seemed subdued in the company of her parents. She had barely spoken a word during the meal. 'They are made for displaying tulip flowers.'

'You must have made many interesting acquaintances during your time in the United Provinces,' Nicholas ventured, hoping to discover something more about Pemberton's Dutch associates.

'Ralph is a great virtuoso; he has a wonderful collection of rarities.' Calverton pointed to Jane with his fork, a piece of chicory suspended on its prongs. 'The most beautiful being, of course, my daughter.'

'But Lettice outshines us all.' Jane motioned to her stepdaughter, who had been equally reserved throughout dinner, though she was always more demure in her father's presence.

'Yes, she is growing into a fine young woman,' Margaret observed more kindly. Lettice's efforts with her appearance had paid off, it seemed. 'You must play for us after dinner,' Margaret commanded Lettice. 'I am told you have made great progress in your study of music.'

Lettice shook her head modestly. 'No, indeed, ma'am, I am but an indifferent musician, though I hope I might offer some little entertainment, especially if my sisters accompany me.'

Dorothy and Prudence smiled shyly, nodding their heads in acquiescence. Nicholas's spirits lifted at the prospect of hearing them in concert again. Jane must be pleased too, he thought, to see her stepdaughters behave in such an exemplary fashion. He grinned at Richard, who was too busy eating his way through a pastry swan to misbehave. Ned had been right about one thing: the food was delicious.

'Where is that blackamoor of yours?' Margaret demanded, looking around the room. 'Have you finally sent him back to the West

Indies, Ralph? They make pretty pets as children, but I wouldn't retain one past adolescence.'

'I have no desire to lose such a faithful and capable servant,' Pemberton replied testily. 'Besides, he was reared in England and is as true an Englishman as your husband or myself. He wasn't bred to hard labour.'

'He's part of the family, isn't that right, Pater?' Edward said languidly, mopping up the sauce on his plate with a slice of pheasant.

Pemberton gave his son a warning look. 'He is an excellent secretary,' he declared, somewhat too forcefully.

'Another of your rarities, eh, Ralph.' Calverton chuckled. 'You won't part with anything from your collections, isn't that right?'

'Are you going back home for Christmas?' Margaret asked Nicholas.

'Yes,' he said, startled by her frequent changes in topic.

'I thought you were spending Christmas with us in Kent,' Lettice said with evident disappointment and the three youngest Pembertons fixed their eyes longingly on him.

'Nicholas's father will be expecting him,' Jane said firmly.

'You are welcome to a ride in our carriage. We're travelling up to our place in Nottinghamshire next week.' Lord Calverton broke off a piece of Spanish candy from an elaborate arrangement in the centre of the table and popped it into his mouth.

The thought of two or three days spent travelling with the Calvertons filled Nicholas with dread. But then, it might prove fruitful in gaining further insights into Pemberton's position with the King, and Calverton's too, come to that. The two men had spent some time before dinner talking privately in Pemberton's study and they appeared on very good terms.

'I'm sure this young man will keep us amused during the journey, eh, Peg?' Calverton said, extracting a bit of candy from between his teeth with a silver toothpick.

'I hope so.' Margaret sniffed. 'Watch you don't break another tooth; you don't have many left.'

⇥ Chapter Seventeen ⇤

The following day, a boy delivered a message from Monsieur Benoist. His suit was ready and if Nicholas would come to the shop, Benoist could make sure it fitted correctly. It had rained that morning, washing away the worst of the smoke clouds and now the sun was shining crisply; it was the perfect weather for enjoying the sights of the city. Nicholas had grown accustomed to the dirt and din of the capital, though the bad air still bothered him. Walking slowly along Fleet Street, he paused to watch a group of tumblers performing tricks, marvelling at their agility as they leapt onto each other's shoulders to create a human pyramid. He spent some time looking through the wares of the booksellers by St. Paul's Churchyard, finally buying a pamphlet of songs by Henry Purcell that he thought Lettice and her sisters would enjoy. He hoped Lettice would not be upset that he had slipped out alone. After Ned's warning about her betrothal, he felt he should put some distance between himself and Pemberton's eldest daughter.

They had been rebuilding St. Paul's ever since the original burnt down in the Great Fire and still, almost twenty years later, hadn't finished it. Nicholas thought the pillars very large and ungainly but Lord Pemberton had told him they were that size because the architect planned to top the cathedral with a mighty dome, of the kind built by the Saracens in places like Turkey. Pemberton didn't know what was wrong with the old cathedral spire; it could be seen from miles around and was a more fitting Christian image. When Jane pointed out that St. Peter's Basilica in Rome had a cupola, Pemberton retorted that that was even worse. Was London's greatest cathedral going to be turned into a shrine for heathens and papists? This was before his avowed change of religious sympathies, of course.

Nicholas decided, since it was nearby, to take a look at the famous pillar on Fish Street. As he weaved down towards the river, he could see the monument to the Great Fire from several streets away, towering over the new brick houses and empty lots. He stared up at the flaming copper orb surmounting the two-hundred-foot-high stone column. It certainly was impressive. Pemberton had told him that the great Robert Hooke had intended the monument to function as a giant telescope. This plan had not come to fruition, but they had built an underground laboratory in its vaults where Pemberton had witnessed experiments performed by the Royal Society. Nicholas hoped he might get to see one there.

In the meantime, he paid his toll and began to climb the three hundred and eleven steps that curled their way up the interior of the pillar. At about halfway he began to feel a little dizzy but forced himself on until he arrived at the balcony near the summit. Gripping the guard rail, he gazed down at the city below him with exhilaration. The boats ploughing across the Thames were reduced to the size of toy vessels crossing a stream. He felt as he imagined an eagle might, gazing down from its eyrie on the miniaturised world below. To the east he could see the Tower of London and to the west the top of the Old Bailey. All the instruments of English justice were down there below him. How solid they appeared and yet how susceptible they were to the fickle currents of public opinion.

Once back at ground level, he read the inscriptions around the pillar. One side described the devastation wrought by the fire, which had incinerated thirteen thousand Londoners, two hundred houses and four hundred streets. The final sentences had been recently plastered over.

The monument keeper, observing his interest, ambled over to him. 'The present king may have ordered them lines to be covered, but plaster can easily be removed. He should've had them taken out with a chisel if he didn't want them seen again.'

'What did they say?'

'Well, there you are, see, even when they're defaced, there's those of us what've inscribed them words on our memories, so as to warn them that come after us.' The keeper cleared his throat, staring at the strip of plaster as though he could see right through it. '*On the third day,*' he recited, '*Heaven stayed the course of the fatal fire and it everywhere died out.*' His voice rose. '*But popish frenzy, which wrought such horrors, is not yet quenched.*' The man clearly relished his role as truthteller.

'Catholics did not start the fire,' Nicholas snapped. 'That has been established.'

The keeper eyed him belligerently. 'Course they did; everybody knows it. Since they can't have their way and burn all good Protestants at the stake like they did during popish times, they sneak about fireballing houses. They all stick together.' He spat in the gutter. 'A French Jesuit was caught with fireballs, but the King, then Duke of York, pretending to arrest him, had him spirited away to escape justice.' He shook his head. 'I fear for England, that I do. London is crawling with the slaves of Rome and the French are only waiting for the signal to invade. When that happens' – he jabbed a finger north-westwards – 'we'll wake up to the smell of our children frying in Smithfield, you mark my words.' He nodded sagely.

Nicholas felt nauseated. Everything in him shrank away from the Monument now, as though the column itself was consumed by fire. Why hadn't those hateful words been scored out permanently? Nicholas had hoped King James's rule might convince the English people they had nothing to fear from Catholicism, but it was clear he hadn't won over all his subjects. It would be a waste of breath arguing with such a man, he thought. Instead, he nodded stiffly and set off in search of the tailor's.

'Cast your eye up Smithfield direction,' the keeper shouted after him. 'And picture your nearest and dearest tied to a stake, screaming for mercy as the flames lick their bones. Such things ain't far away, I'm telling you.'

Nicholas shook his head as if he could dislodge the man's furious polemic from his ears and marched up Fish Street towards Cornhill.

A young boy sat cross-legged on a large table in front of the tailor's window, stitching buttons onto a coat. He looked up and smiled when Nicholas entered the shop. He was the same boy who had delivered the message earlier that day. Carefully laying down his work, he slipped from his perch and bowed.

'I will fetch my father for you, sir,' he said as he sped off into the backroom.

Nicholas looked down at the coat. The embroidery was exquisite, gold silk thread looped and scrolled in intricate patterns around the cuffs and buttons. This could not be the boy's handiwork, surely? The child didn't look more than eight or nine years old. Nicholas tugged on a button; it was neatly and securely stitched.

'Good afternoon, monsieur.' Benoist came in, carrying a rich red velvet jacket over one arm.

The boy hovered by the table, waiting for permission to return to his work.

Nicholas stepped aside, waving a hand over the coat. 'I was just admiring this fine needlework. Can it be your craftsmanship?'

The boy grinned. 'I did this bit' – he held up a cuff – 'but Papa did the rest. I just followed his line.'

'Well, I can see you are going to be as fine a tailor as your father.' Nicholas turned to Benoist. 'You must be very proud of him.'

Benoist bowed. 'I am fortunate in being blessed with such a dutiful son.'

As if to illustrate his parent's words, the boy had resumed his seat and was diligently applying his needle and thread to another button.

'And your father, how is he?' Nicholas glanced towards the backroom.

A look of pain crossed over Benoist's face. 'We still wait for news of my sister and her family. It causes my father great distress; he fears the worst. I tell him it is a sin to give way to despair. We must trust in the mercy of God. But then we hear of more French Protestants massacred.' Frowning, he raised his hands in a gesture of helplessness.

'I will pray for you,' Nicholas said. After all, they worshipped the same God.

Benoist lowered his voice. 'I am making arrangements for my family to remove to Holland. I do not think it will be safe here for us much longer.'

'But King James is offering liberty of conscience to all,' Nicholas exclaimed.

'I beg your pardon, sir, I did not mean to cause offence,' the tailor responded quickly.

It saddened Nicholas to see the fear in the man's eyes, as though he would do anything to add to their persecution.

'Anyhow, we must not dwell on sorrows when I have made this beautiful habiliment for you,' Benoist said with forced gaiety, holding out Nicholas's new suit of clothes.

Standing in front of the tailor's looking-glass, Nicholas found himself entranced by the figure reflected back, dressed as it was in a fine silk waistcoat, matching jacket and breeches. These would certainly be the most beautiful, well-fitting garments he had ever owned. He couldn't help speculating on how impressed Lettice would be to see him in such fashionable attire. Not only were they cut to the latest style, the clothes also showed his figure off to its best advantage, making him look quite the gallant. Though, of course, he did not wish her to admire him in that way. It was just that, like her brother, she held it so important to be in the mode.

'You look like a king,' the boy exclaimed.

Nicholas grinned at him and Benoist ruffled his son's hair affectionately.

'I'm sure it is all thanks to the cut of the cloth,' Nicholas said, moving behind the screen provided to change back into his old clothes.

If his mother had taken him with her, would he, like this boy, have spent his childhood with a needle and thread in his hand instead of a quill or a pair of reins? Perhaps she had done her best by him in leaving him at Measham Hall and he ought to be grateful for her sacrifice.

'I don't suppose you've come across a female draper by the name of Ellen Liddell, have you?' he asked Benoist. 'I believe she runs a business with her sister, a Mrs Tyler.'

'There is a linen-draper's shop off Cheapside run by two sisters, by the sign of the Black Raven. But if you need cloth I can purchase it for you.'

Nicholas shook his head. 'That's quite all right, thank you.'

Benoist wrapped the suit of clothes carefully, tying the package with string. The cost was even more than Nicholas had anticipated, but he couldn't refuse it now. Despite his depleted resources, he pressed a shilling into the boy's hand on his way out, earning a look of gratitude that outdid even Artemis, his spaniel.

The Black Raven was only a few minutes' walk from the tailor's – back towards St. Paul's, on the corner of Goose Lane. It was a narrow brick building, another that must have been rebuilt after the fire. The glass-fronted shop was on the ground floor, with two storeys above. Nicholas imagined the sisters and their families lived there. They must be doing well to own such a property.

He stood on the other side of the street, watching as a man emerged carrying a large packet. The man was whistling; he looked pleased with himself. Nicholas didn't have to go in. It might not even be his mother's shop. And if she was inside, he didn't want to distress or embarrass her. He hoped she might come out so that he could see her, but would he be able to recognise her?

'You all right, sir?' A hunger-bitten woman loosed her dirty shawl to show him her sunken breast. 'Maybe I've got what you're looking for.'

Recoiling, Nicholas hurried across the road and into the shop. A plump matron was leaning on the counter. Behind her, another woman was folding up a bolt of linen.

'How may we help you, sir?' The larger woman smiled at him. She had friendly, pale blue eyes. Greying ginger curls were escaping from her linen cap and she tucked them back up inside it with deft fingers.

'We're closing shortly,' the other woman said, without turning.

'I'm looking for Mrs Ellen Liddell.'

The woman turned round. She was handsome still, her flaxen hair and hazel eyes fitting Abigail's description. She looked at him questioningly.

'I'm Sir William Hawthorne's son, Nicholas.' His voice sounded strange to his ears, but it was stranger still to be introducing himself to his own mother.

After a moment of surprised silence, the older woman beamed. 'Why, Ellen, it's Alethea's nephew.' She nodded at him. 'I can see the resemblance. You've got her eyes.'

So it must be true, what Jack Fleet had said, about his mother knowing his aunt. 'May I speak with you alone?' he asked Ellen.

The cheeks of her pale, oval face flushed red and she stood, gripping the counter and regarding Nicholas with a mixture of alarm and tenderness. 'Will you mind the shop for a bit, Lizzie?' she said, turning to her sister.

'Of course,' Lizzie said, looking with puzzled concern from one to the other.

'Come upstairs.' Ellen held open a door at the back of the shop.

He followed her into a small parlour. The room, though sparsely furnished, was neat and tidy. She sat down on a high-backed wooden chair and indicated for Nicholas to take a seat. Between them stood a circular table with a bible on it.

'You've grown up into a fine young man,' she said. Her hands were tightly clasped in her lap and her voice was guarded.

Gazing at her, Nicholas was filled with a sad and resentful longing, though he was no longer sure whom he should blame for her absence from his life. It was clear she wasn't overjoyed to see him.

'Abigail, my nursemaid – you might remember her – often speaks of you and Robin.' Now he was sitting opposite her, he felt he had to edge around the fact of her maternity. 'Abigail was very fond of you both,' he added when she didn't reply.

'She was a proper maid,' Ellen said curtly. 'I knew she'd take good care of you.'

'Not like a mother would, though,' Nicholas said, somewhat nettled.

'And your father, William, how does he?' she asked hesitantly.

'He is well. I shall be returning to Measham in a few days. I see your sister doesn't know about me. I suppose Robin doesn't know he has a brother either.' A note of bitterness crept into his voice.

Ellen held his gaze with a look that was both earnest and reproving. 'Robin doesn't have a brother.'

The sense of dizziness came over Nicholas again. He was winded by the cruelty of her words.

'I am not your mother.' She spoke more gently now.

'How can you say that?' he exclaimed.

'Because it is true.' Ellen sighed and smoothed down her skirts. 'I was your wet nurse and you were like a little brother to my Robin. But you did not come from my womb.'

Nicholas's head was reeling. Ellen got up and went into the next room, returning with a jug of beer and two cups. He drank a little from the cup she poured for him.

'Then who is my mother? Why would my father lie to me?'

'You will have to ask him that. Only he can tell you.'

'But you must know who she was.'

Ellen looked pained. 'It's for your own good, please believe me. Your father has your best interests at heart.'

How sick he was of being fobbed off with that excuse.

The staircase creaked under the weight of rapid footsteps and the door was opened by a robust, broad-shouldered young man with fair hair and dark blue eyes. He set two loaves of bread down on the table.

'Evening, Mother. Lizzie said the son of one of your old Epping Forest friends was here.' He brushed his right hand on his trouser leg before extending it towards Nicholas. 'Robin Liddell, pleased to meet you.'

Standing, Nicholas shook his hand. It was rough and flecked with dust.

'Not the son, the nephew,' Ellen quickly corrected him. 'I was Nicholas's nursemaid; you were too little at the time to remember him.'

Whether she was really his mother or not, Ellen was more than just a nursemaid, Nicholas thought, but said nothing.

'Does your aunt like to talk about their time in the forest? Mine certainly does.' Robin laughed cheerfully. 'She and Uncle Jem will be up shortly; I'm sure she'll bend your ear about it then.'

As he spoke, the door opened again and a tall, muscular man with grey hair and a lined face came in, followed by Ellen's sister. The man touched the rim of his hat, but did not remove it.

'There's no sad news, I hope,' Lizzie said, smiling anxiously.

'No indeed. All is well at Measham Hall, thanks be to God,' Ellen replied quickly.

'Oh, I am glad to hear that.' Lizzie clasped her hands together in front of her chest. 'By your long faces I feared some calamity had befallen your good father,' she told Nicholas. 'Will you stay for a bite to eat?'

Nicholas looked at Ellen, but she didn't meet his eyes.

'That's very kind, but I ought to be going,' he said.

'There's plenty of stew in the pot,' Lizzie said insistently. 'I was ever so fond of your auntie, you know. She sang like an angel; must be why the Good Lord took her so young – he wanted her for his choir.' She sank down onto a chair with a sigh.

'How did you become acquainted?' Nicholas couldn't resist asking.

'Hasn't Ellen told you? We met her and her companion, a man by the name of Jack Fleet, on the road. They was strange times during that Great Plague. So many of us forced from our homes. We all set up camp together. How long were we living together?' She turned to her husband. 'Must've been a year at least.'

'Not that long, nay, it were only a few months.'

'We wanted Alethea to stay on with us, but she was eager to get back to her family and Ellen would accompany her.' Lizzie gave her sister a slightly disapproving nod. 'I suppose at least Alethea got to see her home again before she passed out of this world.'

'Hush, sister,' Ellen said quietly.

'I regret to tell you, but my aunt died in London,' Nicholas said.

Lizzie and Jem looked at Ellen, their faces creased in confusion.

'That is what my father believes, anyhow,' Nicholas added, less certainly.

'Why'd he think that, then?' Lizzie asked her sister.

'I couldn't say.' Ellen picked the loaves up and took them into the kitchen.

'Well, there must be a good reason.' Lizzie smiled at Nicholas. 'Is your father in London with you? Please send him our thanks for all he's done for our Seth.'

'Seth?'

'Our son. Sir William paid for his apprenticeship. Seth is a joiner now and has set up his own household. He's getting married in a few weeks to a fine young woman, the daughter of a master carpenter,' she said with great pride.

'That's right, that's right.' Jem nodded. 'Seth's a finer craftsman than I am, knows all about geometry and suchlike. I'm just an old workhorse.'

'You're too modest, Uncle.' Robin gestured to Jem. 'He's as fine a carpenter as any you'll find in the city. It's an honour to learn from Jeremiah. Have you seen the work on St. Paul's?'

'I walked past it earlier today,' Nicholas said, trying to marshal his thoughts.

'We've been working on that for years. My first job. I can show you round if you like.'

'I'd like that very much.' Robin's warmth almost made up for his mother's reticence.

'Now I won't hear of you rushing off. Come and have a bite to eat,' Lizzie said firmly.

Nicholas was ushered into the kitchen where Ellen was stirring a large pot that hung over the fire. The smell of slow-cooked stew set his mouth watering.

'You can take Seth's place,' Lizzie said, patting Nicholas on the back.

So he sat down at their table and bowed his head as they said grace. Their thanksgiving was stated in plainer terms than he was accustomed to and he enjoyed the simplicity of it. To his surprise, they all toasted King James, but then the King had, as they pointed out afterwards, freed many friends from gaol and had even forced those informers who had profited from the arrests of dissenters to reimburse their victims. They were as enthusiastic about the King's campaign for religious toleration as Nicholas was, even if they were less keen on sharing that liberty with papists.

As Robin had predicted, he was regaled with tales from their time in the forest and heard more about his aunt in the next hour than he had in all his life before: her character, her beautiful singing voice, her willingness to humble herself and live as an equal among poor folk, were all commended in the warmest terms.

Ellen maintained her story about accompanying Alethea back to Measham and her manner was so sincere, Nicholas was inclined to believe her. They had clearly set out together. And yet, he reminded himself, Ellen had also been his father's mistress, something she had evidently concealed from her family. He could hardly blame her for that, considering their puritan leanings, but Ellen was not so trustworthy as she appeared and he still did not know whether to believe she was his mother or not.

Why had Father shown such generosity to them, paying for, it transpired, both Robin and Seth's education, if there was no tie other than through his sister? Father had always been so cautious with their finances, apparently resentful of any expenditure that wasn't on Measham Hall and their land. Could Nicholas have underestimated his benevolence or was Father acting out of a sense of obligation? What other sins might he be making amends for?

After leaving the draper's establishment, Nicholas walked down to Queenhithe Stairs, thinking he might get a boat home. He stood for a while, wishing his thoughts were as calm as the icy waters below. If Ellen wasn't his mother, then who was? He had missed the chance to find out if she knew anything about the secrets Staley held over Father, but they had not been alone together long enough to ask.

He would certainly question Father about Aunt Alethea when he got home. It was so strange that no one at Measham Hall had ever mentioned his aunt returning to Derbyshire. Had she lived there secretly with Ellen? But why would she do that? And what about Jane? She too believed Alethea had died in London. None of it made any sense.

Hearing rapid footsteps behind him, he put a hand to his sword.

'Nicholas, you left this behind.' An out-of-breath Robin pressed a package into his arms. 'You wouldn't want to lose that. Mother says Benoist is one of the finest tailors in England.' He nodded at the label tucked under the cording.

'What a blockhead I am and how kind of you to come after me. How did you know which way I'd gone?'

'Lad on the corner told me.' Robin grinned. 'Good to see you're on your guard.' He motioned to Nicholas's hand, which still rested on his sword hilt. 'There are plenty of footpads hereabouts and no sign of a boatman. I can walk you up to Ludgate Hill if you like; you can get a chair from there.'

He clearly thought Nicholas quite the pampered gentleman.

'I don't want to take you out of your way,' Nicholas said, though in truth he welcomed Robin's company.

'I don't mind. It's a beautiful night for a stroll.'

Nicholas had to agree. The sky was clear enough for a great fat moon to cast its milky light across the black Thames, picking out the broken shards of ice in silver. You just had to ignore the foul smells of refuse, excrement and decay that issued up out of the river and the streets.

'Have you ever been to a frost fair?' Robin asked.

'No, but I heard about the one in '84. I was told they raced horses over the ice. Now that's something I'd like to see.'

So far this year, only the birds risked walking across the Thames and its fragile skin of ice was easily broken by the wherrymen's oars.

'The Blanket Fair, that was a marvel for sure. I skated all the way down the river to Westminster. You should have seen the fires burning on the ice and the children and dogs sliding between puppet shows and bakers' stalls. There was even bull-baiting.'

It was hard to imagine such things now, but it was only December and there was still time for the weather to turn colder. The stillness of the night was fractured by a woman's voice, raised in drunken anger. A man's, equally belligerent, soon followed.

'Have you spent any time in the country?' Nicholas was prompted to ask. 'That's the place for a moonlit walk. You can listen to the owls and the nightjars, or nightingales, depending on the time of year, and the air is always sweet with blossoms or berries and fresh with dew.'

'I like to go for rambles on the Sabbath day. Across the fields and through the woods, away from the smoke of the town; it does the soul good. Mother says it's because I spent my infancy in a forest.'

'You would be welcome at Measham Hall, should you ever wish to visit. I'm sure Father would be pleased to meet you.'

Abigail would certainly be overjoyed. He almost told Robin how Abigail doted on him and was always holding him up as an exemplar of infant goodness, but realised that could lead to awkward questions. If he did come to stay, though, it might force Father into revealing the truth.

As they passed St. Paul's, Robin told him more about the work on the cathedral, promising him a tour of it when Nicholas was next in London. They chatted together as easily as if they had been childhood friends. Nicholas rather wished they were related. Even if they did inhabit completely different spheres in society, he'd rather be Robin's brother than Ned's, that was for sure.

Chapter Eighteen

Nicholas had to rise early the next morning to present himself at the Calvertons' house before first light. He waited in the hall as they finished their preparations for the journey, finally emerging swathed in cloaks and scarves. Margaret's waiting-woman, Winifred, followed behind her mistress, carrying such a weight of blankets she could hardly walk. Nicholas rushed to relieve her of her burden, an action that earnt him a grateful smile from the elderly woman.

The Calverton coach was far grander than any he had travelled in before, with glass windows and the family crest freshly painted on the doors. It was much better sprung than the creaky old carriage his father kept. The huge wheels moved lightly over the rutted roads, pulled by six Flanders mares, whipped on by the coachman and the armed postilion who trotted beside them.

Feeling rather grateful to be riding in such a comfortable vehicle, Nicholas gazed eagerly out of the window, hoping the view would become clearer once they were out of London. The Calvertons, tucked up under their blankets, sat facing forward while he sat opposite, next to Winifred, whose neat frame took up little room.

The sun rose as they travelled over Highgate Hill and he wondered if they would pass Jack Fleet's tavern. This put him in mind of his aunt. She had been part of the Calvertons' household when she died, so they must know where her death took place. He was about to raise the subject when Lady Margaret spoke.

'We have left it very late in the year to travel, but My Lord had business to attend to at Whitehall.' She sighed and pulled her cloak more closely round her. Despite the elegance of the carriage, it was almost as cold within as outside. 'We might as well have stayed in town.'

Her husband patted her knee and Nicholas wondered whether this was a sign of affection or a warning.

'Do you, like Lord Pemberton, work closely with the King, sir?'

'I do my best to advise him.' Calverton smiled.

'There seems to be some hostility towards him in London,' Nicholas said, thinking of the monument keeper.

'His Majesty's insistence, since Monmouth's rebellion, of keeping a standing army has not made him popular. The soldiers are poorly disciplined and are costing the country a fortune.' Calverton sighed. 'The King might also exercise his religion with more circumspection.' He raised his eyebrows. 'There are so many Irishmen in Whitehall now, many fear Ireland will be given up to the papists.'

'And the Queen has become most intolerant, flying into rages with those of her Ladies who refuse to convert to Rome. One of her maids-of-honour recently suffered a cut to the face when the Queen threw a hairbrush at the poor woman.' Margaret looked at Winifred, who tutted and shook her head.

'Perhaps it is the Queen's condition that makes her peevish,' Nicholas said, assuming the Calvertons would have heard the news, if not at Court, then from Pemberton.

They exchanged glances. Margaret turned back to Nicholas. 'I believe the Queen has taken to her bed. She has suffered some bleeding,' she said pointedly.

'I am sorry to hear that, ma'am.' If the Queen miscarried, the prospect of a Catholic heir to the English throne was significantly diminished.

Calverton frowned at his wife. 'We must not pay attention to gossip. The Queen may prove fruitful yet.' He looked at Nicholas. 'Lord Pemberton tells me you are not overly rigid in your beliefs.'

Nicholas shifted uncomfortably in his seat. The quality of the road seemed to have deteriorated. 'Like the King, I believe in toleration.' He thought suddenly of Benoist's family. 'I sympathise with those who fear the influence of the French King.'

'Indeed, those who love our King will steer him away from the counsel of Louis. But you have more knowledge than most of the Jesuit mind. You were not tempted to join them?' Calverton regarded him probingly.

This was more easily answered. 'I do not have a religious vocation. My interests are in the natural world. What I should dearly love is to travel to remote places and discover new breeds of plants.' Staley's interference in his life had made Nicholas long more than ever to escape to lands beyond the reach of politicians. 'But first I must equip myself with a thorough understanding of our own native species,' he added, realising he had to justify his return to study in England.

Calverton chuckled. 'So you are both a scholar and a would-be Columbus. My son-in-law can certainly be of assistance there.'

'I would be most grateful to him. But I think at present his time is also taken up at Court.'

'Have you been to Holland?' Margaret asked suddenly.

'No, My Lady.'

'You could certainly further your pursuit of botany there. The Dutch are some of the foremost collectors, as Lord Pemberton can attest.'

'Indeed, he has many Dutch connections, I believe,' Nicholas said cautiously.

Margaret coughed. 'This fog lies heavy on my lungs.'

They were passing along a tree-lined road, the branches meeting overhead to create an archway. It would be beautiful in the summer, but shrouds of winter mist lent the dark trees an eerie aspect. This sinister ambience was heightened by the heavy thud of hooves galloping towards them.

'Who can that be?' Margaret leant forward, squinting out of the window.

Winifred disappeared even further under her blanket, so that only the top of her head was visible.

The carriage slowed and they fell into an uneasy silence. When the driver rapped quickly on the roof, Calverton, despite his age, drew his sword out of its scabbard and Nicholas, assuming this was some sort of warning, followed suit. Winifred gave a little squeak. Margaret freed her hands from the sable muff that had been keeping them warm, pulling it in under her cloak. Nicholas wondered if she kept money or jewels inside it.

The postilion was riding in close beside the coach window. Something was yelled, Nicholas couldn't make out what, but he saw the postilion cock his pistol, his reins wrapped round one hand. There was a crack and a blast and the man was keeling backwards, a ragged, bloody hole in his chest. His horse reared, its eyes rolling, and as the reins fell from the postilion's hand it cantered away, leaving him lying on the road. The carriage ground to a halt, the horses stamping and neighing in distress. All around them, birds rose from the trees, cawing in alarm.

'God save us.' Margaret gripped her husband's arm, but to her credit she did not scream or swoon.

Calverton pulled her away from the window. Winifred threw herself against Nicholas, smothering him in her blanketed form. Fortunately he had lowered his sword. The carriage was rocking so violently he thought they would be overturned. Someone must have climbed up onto the box beside the driver. The voices of two men could be heard shouting instructions to one another and at the driver.

'They're taking the trunks. Hopefully they won't bother with us,' Calverton said quietly.

They sat in silence, listening to the thumping on the roof and the clatter as their luggage was thrown to the ground. Nicholas hoped the robbers had left the driver unharmed. He didn't think it possible the postilion could survive his wound. The poor man had probably been killed instantly as the bullet tore open his chest. Taking a deep breath, Nicholas thought of all Matthew and his French fencing master had taught him about remaining calm and alert.

The carriage door on Lord Calverton's side was yanked open and a man's voice called up for them to get out.

'We had better do as he says.' Calverton rose from his seat. 'You will have to pull the steps down for us to disembark,' he told the highwayman below, with a composure fitting for an old cavalier.

Shielded by Winifred's woollen form, Nicholas was sure he had not been seen by the robbers. Peeking out from behind her, he managed to catch Lady Margaret's eye and put a finger to his lips. She dipped her chin, indicating, he hoped, that she understood his intention.

'Come on, Winifred,' she said loudly. 'These brigands will hardly murder two defenceless women and an elderly gentleman.'

Hidden by their skirts, Nicholas dropped to the floor as the women disembarked. He reckoned, from all he had heard, that there were only two highwaymen holding them up. He hoped to God he was correct, since all their lives might depend on it. As the Calvertons were blocking their door, Henry pausing to help his wife and Winifred alight, Nicholas pushed down on the handle beside him, opening the door a crack. He peered out. There was no sign of anyone on this side of the coach. He pushed the door a little wider and lowered himself to the ground, praying neither robber was looking at the underside of the carriage where they would be able to see his legs emerging opposite.

The postilion lay a few feet away, his gun still on the road nearby. From between the wheels Nicholas could just make out the highwaymen's horses, tethered to a gate on the other side of the road. He could hear the men assuring the Calvertons they would come to no harm so long as they followed their orders.

'Anyone who can afford such a grand carriage can afford to lose a few guineas,' one of them said.

Nicholas crawled towards the postilion.

'I must ask you to remove those heavy cloaks so we can see what you've got beneath,' the second voice asked with surprising deference.

'Will you have us freeze to death?' Lady Margaret's voice rose querulously.

'You've enough flesh to keep you warm,' came the less polite reply.

Nicholas picked up the gun. He had little experience of pistols but would have to assume this one was loaded and primed. The postilion's mount stood not far off, cropping the grass between two trees. If this didn't work, he would end up like the poor postilion, in a bloody heap on a country road. Thankfully, Margaret was keeping the highwaymen distracted with her argumentativeness.

'You will suffer for this ill-treatment of a lady,' he heard her say.

The fog was as useful a shield for him as it had been for the highwaymen. Thrusting the gun into his belt, he ran, bent double, to the front of the coach, peering round to see what was happening. One of the footpads had laid his musket down in order to search through the trunks. He was busy pulling out anything he considered worth taking and stuffing it into a sack. The other was standing in front of the Calvertons and their driver, his pistol cocked.

'Get a move on,' he told his accomplice.

Taking a deep breath, Nicholas ran as lightly as he could to the trees behind them. One of their horses whinnied but the men were too intent on the robbery to pay any mind.

Seeing Nicholas, Margaret began to wail. 'My gold, my pearls, take anything but them. They belonged to my late mother.'

'Where are they?' The pair of land-pirates looked at her.

'I cannot tell you with a firearm aimed at my heart.'

'I am not so careless as my friend. Give us the jewels and we'll be on our way.' The highwayman lowered his gun so that it was pointing at the ground.

Nicholas seized his chance. He ran with all the speed he could muster, over to the crouching man. Before the ruffian could get to his feet, Nicholas thrust out his rapier. Stopping just short of piercing the man's flesh, he held the tip to his neck. At the same time he raised the pistol, pointing it towards the back of other. He hoped they wouldn't see how his arm was trembling.

'Move and I'll run you through,' he said as he kicked the musket along the ground towards the driver.

The second robber spun round, a look of amazement on his face. The driver seized the musket and then, before the highwayman had the chance to put his match to the barrel of his gun, launched himself at the man, beating him about the head with the musket. Calverton, showing some sprightliness for his age, joined in the fight, wrestling the pistol from the robber's hand and tying his wrists together with his own cord.

The positions were now reversed, with the highwaymen prostrate on the ground before the travellers.

'We meant you no harm,' one of them cried. 'We're driven by desperation to feed our families and only rob them as clearly has ample.'

'We share our spoils with them as needs it most,' his companion insisted.

'What of poor Andrews, whom you've shot to death?' Calverton retorted.

'My gun misfired. I never meant for to kill him.'

The man sounded genuinely sorry, Nicholas thought. And it was true, they were a miserable-looking pair of wretches, their threadbare clothes only just covering their wasted limbs. No wonder it had been so easy to overcome them.

Once the highwaymen's hands and feet were secured with rope, Nicholas asked what should be done with them.

'We'll have to bring them into town and hand them over to a constable,' Calverton said.

'Drag the filth behind the coach,' Lady Margaret demanded. 'Strip them of their clothes and let them shiver before they burn in Hell.'

The highwaymen were spared this fate by the arrival of a farmer with a cart. After some initial reluctance, he was persuaded to carry their well-trussed criminal cargo, along with their unfortunate victim, into the next town where, Lord Calverton promised, he would be paid handsomely for his trouble.

Winifred repacked the luggage and the Calvertons' driver tied the highwaymen's horses behind the coach, while Nicholas coaxed the postilion's mount out of the orchard he had wandered into.

'I can take the position of the outrider if you like,' he offered.

'That is an excellent idea.' Lady Margaret even bestowed a thin smile on him.

By the time they had reached Dunstable, handed over the highwaymen to the local constable and arranged for the postilion's body to be transported back to his family in London for burial, it was too late to travel any further that day. Besides, they were all shocked and weary and in need of refreshment.

There were several inns set along the broad main street and Calverton secured rooms at the best of them, telling the innkeeper to bring a bottle of his finest sack to their private dining room as fast as he could. Nicholas had never been so grateful for a brimmer of wine, especially since this one had plenty of sugar to sweeten it.

'I admit, I'm astonished that fellow with the cart delivered those ruffians up,' Lady Margaret said. 'Highwaymen are often in league with the locals. That is how they get away with so much. I wouldn't be surprised if the cart was intended to transport their plunder.'

'The carter could hardly abscond without our noticing, given he was leading the way,' Calverton said wryly. 'As for you, young man.' He raised his glass. 'Those were some heroics you performed today.' He looked more sternly at Nicholas. 'While I applaud your daring, it was also foolhardy. Better to lose a few valuables than our lives.'

Nicholas felt rather crestfallen. Mixed with the fear and the horror had been a sense of elation at his morning's successful adventure. He'd been hoping to win the Calvertons' esteem and gratitude. He was sure they'd all have been murdered if he hadn't acted as he did. To his surprise, Lady Margaret came to his defence.

'For shame, Henry,' she cried. 'It was exactly the sort of bravery you displayed as a young man.' She turned to Nicholas. 'I'd come to believe the youth of today were more interested in cards and women than honourable combat – a flock of hen-hearts, the lot of them. But you have shown both courage and a noble command of strategics, bravo.'

'You are quite right, of course, my dear.' Henry Calverton chuckled as he refilled their glasses. 'We are indebted to you, young Hawthorne. To judge by your riding today, you would make a fine cavalry officer. If you are interested in a military career, I can recommend you to Lord Churchill.'

'Thank you, it would be an honour, sir.'

Nicholas didn't want to become a soldier, but he needed to stay on the right side of Calverton and he had heard Pemberton refer to meetings with Churchill. Entering the cavalry would be one way of seeing the world and escaping the demands of Staley, if a rather desperate one.

'I suppose it was your father who taught you how to handle weapons,' Lady Margaret said.

Nicholas hesitated. How best to play this in order to extract the most information? 'My cousin Matthew first taught me swordsmanship.' He watched her face carefully, but she showed no signs of guilt. 'It was he who left provision for me to attend St. Omers college and to study fencing. He said I must know how to defend myself if I was to go travelling.'

'Father Harcourt was clearly a strong influence on you, and I imagine on your father too.' She took a sip of wine, her expression impassive.

'We were both heartbroken when he was wrongly seized and so unjustly executed.'

His words elicited no pity from Margaret. 'But he was a Jesuit priest?' she demanded.

'He never denied it, but he had nothing to do with any plots against the King.' Nicholas tried to keep his voice as measured as hers was.

'The horrid plot aside, Father Harcourt must have been prepared to forfeit his life by entering this country illegally.' Margaret spoke calmly, but adamantly. 'We are a Protestant nation after all.'

Nicholas took a gulp of wine. 'Does that mean you would applaud anyone who turned priest-catcher?'

'Most certainly not.' Henry Calverton spoke on behalf of his wife. 'We were both sickened by the perjuries of Titus Oates and his cronies. Besides, having enjoyed the hospitality of both France and the Spanish Netherlands when we were forced into exile after the late civil wars, we would never inform on a popish chaplain who was serving in a Catholic household.'

'So long as he restrained his ministrations to his own parishioners and did not attempt to convert good Protestants to Romish superstitions,' Lady Margaret said defiantly.

'My cousin had no interest in proselytising,' Nicholas insisted, the choler rising in his blood. 'But I know you had other reasons to resent my father. His friendship with your daughter, for example.' There it was, he had said it and damn the consequences. He felt almost as daring as he had done in facing the highwaymen.

Margaret's eyes glinted. 'Jane's intimacy with your father was certainly ill-advised. She was fond of your aunt and that led her to befriend Alethea's brother. Fortunately, she has made a very good second marriage. Though we would never have married our only child to a man with so many heirs, had it not been for the injuries inflicted on her body by her first husband and to her reputation by your father.' For the first time Margaret's voice betrayed her rising emotion.

Henry coughed. 'Where is that man with our food?' He looked eagerly around as though the innkeeper might be hiding in a corner of the room.

Margaret continued, ignoring her husband. 'Jane told us of your father's baseless suspicions.' Her small, dark eyes remained on Nicholas's. Her voice had regained its composure. 'It is not healthful for the spirit to be so splenetic; I hope your father has a good physician. I can recommend one in his county if you wish.'

'That is very kind, but Father has little faith in doctors. Leechmen, he calls them.' Nicholas responded with equal lightness of tone.

Henry laughed. 'Quite right too. With so many quacks about, one is safer trusting to nature for a cure.'

The innkeeper momentarily diverted the course of their conversation by arriving with a saddle of mutton.

'Exactly what we need,' Henry said with hearty enthusiasm.

When their plates were nearly emptied, Nicholas said, 'I should be interested to hear more about my aunt. I understand she was a member of your household before she died.'

'She was a companion to Jane; you'd best ask her,' Margaret replied brusquely.

Henry licked his fingers. 'Such a beautiful singer. But rather fond of gadding about.'

'Is that why no one knows where she died?'

'She died at her friends' house. Where was it again, my dear?' Henry looked at Margaret.

'Somewhere near Vauxhall Gardens, I believe.'

For once Margaret did not look directly at Nicholas and he noted curiously that her voice had lost some of its confidence. He would almost say she looked as though she had something to hide. Still, he did not want to hound the elderly couple, especially since they were his beloved Jane's parents. Nor did he want to bring Ellen and her family into the conversation, so he let the subject drop.

They spent a third night in Leicester before parting ways. Servants of the Calvertons had ridden down with fresh horses to accompany them back to Rufford Castle. Despite their affectionate farewells, Nicholas had to hire a horse from a local stables to take him to Measham Hall. He had thought the Calvertons might give him their postilion's fine stallion out of gratitude for his actions on the road. But instead, he was lumbered with a slow and obstinate nag, who paused every few steps to explore the hedgerows.

At least his mare didn't mind plodding through the mud. A coach would have struggled to get over the roads to Measham. Once he got home, he would have to send someone with a cart to return the horse and collect his trunk. Nicholas was cheered by the thought of the Christmas presents it contained – gifts he had bought for everyone at the hall, which might otherwise have ended up in the hands of the highwaymen: a green mohair shawl for Abigail, parcels of the best quality tea and chocolate for Tickell, cinnamon-flavoured pastilles for Palmes, a silk cravat for Crewe and a fur sash for Father. The last had cost him dearly, but he thought it would look very well over the long coats Father liked to wear.

The rain, which had started that morning as a gentle drizzle, was getting heavier and at the rate he was going, he had at least another hour's riding ahead of him. He decided to take a detour into the Measham woods to wait out the worst of the rain. There was an old, uninhabited cottage by a stream that Father sometimes used when he went fishing. He would shelter there awhile.

After spending the last four days on the road, it would be pleasant to amble through the trees. He also wanted some time alone to think through all the unsettling information he had received over the past few weeks. The conflicting stories about his aunt's death and, more importantly, who his mother was, were competing for attention with Staley's threats and Pemberton's machinations.

He had to lead his unwilling mount by the reins and it took him a while to locate the dwelling. The trees had grown so much since he was last in these woods that what had once been familiar now looked strange. The bridleway had shrunk to a narrow track, but at least the lack of bushy summer leaves made the overgrown branches easier to navigate.

By the time he spotted the ivy-clad cottage, Nicholas was beginning to think he had imagined its existence. As a boy he had been warned not to come here, for the place was said to be haunted by the ghost of a murdered woman. A she-devil who sought vengeance on any male who crossed her path. This had been enough to keep him from the door, but now the wind was shaking the rain from the trees, causing cold water to cascade down his back and the desire for shelter outweighed any childish fears.

The horse was only too happy to be left tied to a tree by the stream, though by now Nicholas felt less keen to be free of his only companion. Treading carefully so as not to ruin his new boots, he made his way round a clump of brambles. Just outside the dilapidated building, he stopped short. There were sounds coming from within, a groan and then a cry. The hairs on the back of his neck bristled and a clammy dread rose up through his belly. It was just the wind, he told himself, though it had sounded uncannily like a human voice. He crossed himself, sending a quick prayer up to St. Benedict for protection against evil spirits.

Just as he was putting his hand to the door latch, however, he heard a distinctive moan, reminiscent more of pleasure than distress. He crept to the window. Through the grimy panes he could make out two figures entwined on a low bed. The profile of the man on top was clear enough through the dusty glass. Nicholas almost laughed out loud. It was John Thornly, their bailiff. The old dog, this must be where he brought his lovers. Well, Mrs Thornly would never venture out here, so the place was well-chosen.

Thornly rolled off his paramour to reveal the figure beneath. The clamminess in Nicholas's belly turned to nausea. This was surely sorcery at work; his eyes must be deceived. That could not be the face of his father rising up from the pillows, his shift loose about him. But there were his coat and breeches thrown over a chair. That was his sword propped up beside them.

Nicholas turned quickly away before he was seen. As he made his way back to his horse, he heard laughter coming from the cottage, low and familiar. He was scarcely aware of his movements as he untied the reins and, throwing an arm over the animal's neck for support, steered her through the trees and back to the road.

Though he had often felt unloved as a child, Nicholas had always esteemed his father as any child should. During his time abroad their correspondence had drawn them closer and on his last visit he had discovered that he could enjoy Father's company, for they shared, as Matthew had always pointed out, many interests and similar passions.

Some of the boys at St. Omers had snuck into each other's beds at night, despite Francis's most vigilant efforts, and Nicholas had never really thought them sinful. At least not mortally, for they were young and lusty. He had dreamt of girls and woken to damp sheets, so was guilty too of venial sins.

But to be tumbled by their bailiff, he could not believe it of his father. Was he so infatuated with Thornly he was willing to risk the gallows? To cast himself into the abyss of eternal damnation, to act against the laws of God and man – how could he be so weak? And to think, he had decried Matthew for risking arrest for the purest of motives.

Now Nicholas knew what it was Staley held over them. The intelligencer must have obtained proof of Father's crime. Could he have been so foolish as to declare himself in letters or had a servant once caught sight of him in flagrante, just as Nicholas had done now?

He went through everyone who could possibly have discovered Father's proclivities, his thoughts bolting like wild horses. Uncle Percy's remarks came back to haunt him with new meanings – Father's effeminacy, his disinclination to marriage. He remembered the sly way the stable boy, Jasper, had shown him that pamphlet about the Popish Plot, his grubby finger pointing at the illustration of Father Pickering's bare arse raised over the bed. Was Nicholas the only person ignorant of his father's true nature?

As soon as he got to Measham Hall, he handed his nag over to Jasper, dealing curtly with the man's amusement at the sorry horse he'd ridden home on. Surprised by Nicholas's uncharacteristic bad temper, Jasper led the mare silently to the stables. Nicholas was equally terse with Palmes and Crewe. Telling them he was unwell, he retired to his chamber for the night.

Curled up on the window seat, his arms wrapped round his bent knees, he watched through the descending darkness for his father's return. A barn owl must have been flying nearby; he could hear its territorial screech. The clouds had cleared and the familiar figure of the chestnut tree stood outlined against the blue-black sky, stars twinkling as if suspended between its branches. That tree had always been such a comforting, reassuring sight; he felt it was as much a part of his family as any human or animal creature and a more dependable one at that.

He thought wistfully of Ellen's family, in their modest city residence. They seemed to live such moderate, wholesome lives, their warm affection and respect for each other evident. Even if Ellen had strayed from their path, she had returned to their hearth and their hearts. It must be hard for her to keep secrets from them. And then it occurred to him that perhaps she didn't, or at least, not completely. Robin had referred to him as the son of her friend and Ellen had quickly corrected him, but what if he was the son and not the nephew? What if Alethea was his mother and had died as a result of his birth? That would explain the conflicting stories about her demise and Ellen being his wet nurse. His uncle had adopted him, raising him as his own son in order to make Nicholas his heir, for William had such an aversion to women he could not bear to marry and produce children of his own. Nicholas's real father either did not know or refused to acknowledge him.

The sound of hooves clattering across the courtyard rang out in the still air. His father, or his uncle, was back. Despite waiting up, he felt suddenly overcome with exhaustion. He could not face Father now. Tomorrow, with a clearer head, he would not flinch from demanding the truth about his parentage. He climbed into bed, grateful for the warming-pan that had been placed beneath the covers and eager for respite from his teeming thoughts. Closing his eyes, he welcomed the oblivion of sleep.

→ Chapter Nineteen ←

'**A**re you merely lovesick, or should I send for the physician?' Father asked humorously when Nicholas finally joined him for dinner the next day. They were eating alone, Crewe having discreetly absented himself.

'Perhaps I should ask you the same question.'

Nicholas had never considered before how womanish Father's voice was. Really it was quite mincing. And yet Jane had such a passion for him; how could this be?

'Was it your journey with the Calvertons that has made you so out of sorts?' Father asked with more solicitude.

Nicholas shrugged and immediately felt foolishly childish. He took a draught of wine and picked up a quail from the serving-plate. 'I paid a visit to Ellen Liddell.'

Father pressed on his moustache with his fingertips, a gesture he often made when discomforted. 'And?' The word came out almost as a groan and Nicholas remembered with a shudder the sounds he had heard the previous day.

'She says she is not my mother.' He laid his meat down on his platter and stared at his father.

'I am sorry she denied it.' Father's tone was peremptory and his countenance so hard and shut-off he might as well have lowered a visor over his face.

'I believed her. Are you saying she is a liar?' Nicholas would not be abashed.

'What does it matter who your mother was?' Father erupted with exasperation. 'Am I not parent enough for you?' He reached for the wine bottle, emptying the contents into his depleted glass.

'Doesn't every child deserve to know its origins?' Nicholas looked over at the portrait of his grandfather, the man he was said to resemble so closely. Jack Fleet had been struck by his similarity to Alethea in both looks and voice, but there were no pictures of her in the house, not even in a family portrait. 'Ellen's family all swear my aunt returned here, to Measham. So she cannot have died in London.'

Father's face had lost its habitual rosiness. His skin looked grey and his eyes empty. 'Alethea died of the plague. Her body lies in London. I don't know why they should think differently.'

'Because Ellen travelled here with her. They lived together in Epping Forest. They all remember her well. She was hale and hearty when she left London in 1665.'

'Are you training for the law now, that you attack me like some barrister, throwing out false statements? I told you to stay away from those people for good reason. They will lead you astray with their delusions. I never thought you'd be so ungrateful as to disobey me in this, the only thing I have forbade you.'

'They were as sane as you or I. Good, honest men and women, dissenters or no. Alethea was their friend and they remembered her with great affection.'

Father swept his plate so violently from the table it clattered to the floor, sending sauce and meat flying in all directions. The dog rose swiftly, lapping up this unexpected bounty. Staring fixedly ahead, Father marched from the room without another word.

Nicholas sat for a minute frozen with disbelief, before leaping up from his chair, knocking it backwards in the process. Father couldn't just walk out on their conversation. He would force a confession from him if he had to.

But Father was already out of the house, running across the court-yard, bellowing for Jasper to saddle his horse. Where was he racing to as if his life depended on it? Was it into the arms of his lover, John Thornly?

Nicholas watched, too disturbed by his father's agitation to pursue him further. If Father was so desperate to avoid answering his questions, the truth must be terrible indeed.

He turned to find Crewe making his way down the front steps.

'Whatever has passed between you to make Sir William ride off like that?' Crewe's quavering speech was both anxious and accusatory. 'I heard raised voices.'

'He has lied to me and now he evades my questions.'

'Your father will tell you what you need to know when you need to know it.'

Nicholas was sick to death of that old line. 'Now is the time. Now, when I am being forced to spy on the Pembertons in order to save him from the same fate as my cousin.' He spoke bitterly, tired of being cast as the wrongdoer and no longer able to restrain himself.

'Come inside, sir,' Crewe said, linking his arm with Nicholas's, partly for support, partly in order to guide him back into the house.

Nicholas allowed himself to be led into Crewe's chamber. They continued through to his closet, the only room where they could talk without fear of being overheard or interrupted. Crewe moved the piles of papers and account books off the table and onto a shelf, before taking a seat and gesturing for Nicholas to do the same. Nicholas picked up a quill and tapped it rapidly but absentmindedly against a bottle of ink, until Crewe leant over and removed it from his hand, placing the inkbottle out of reach, just as he used to do when Nicholas was a boy.

It was a great relief to tell Crewe about Gilbert Staley, Pemberton, Sir Edward Petre and also his encounter with Ellen and her family, leaving out only what he had seen in the woods the previous day. The old man listened attentively, nodding occasionally and patting his hand whenever Nicholas faltered.

'I will find out what I can about Staley. He is working either for the Jesuits on the King's behalf, or else for the French. I would be surprised if Father Petre doesn't know of him.' Crewe removed the spectacles from his nose and rubbed his eyes. 'God forgive me for saying it, but Father Petre is overly ambitious. He is a Jesuit so of course the Pope refused to make him a bishop; the King was foolish to ask for such a thing. Even the Queen dislikes Petre and resents his influence.' Crewe leant forward, staring intently into Nicholas's eyes. 'Information is currency in the world of spying; it is what both Staley and Lord Pemberton are after. Make sure you know its worth and hoard it well. From what you say, I fear Pemberton may suspect you. This errand to the dean sounds like a test. We must not allow Staley to expose you to danger.'

'But what is it Staley holds over Father?' Nicholas asked.

'Nothing that would merit a death sentence.' Crewe loosened his cravat. 'Though certainly the inheritance of Measham Hall might be questioned.'

'That is where you are mistaken,' Nicholas burst out. Being of an open and honest nature, he found it extremely difficult to keep secrets. Staley had picked the wrong person for an intelligencer in this respect. 'Father is guilty of such things as would have him hanged.'

Crewe raised his eyebrows. 'What crime do you think your father has committed?'

Nicholas swallowed. Despite his longing to unburden his mind, he hesitated to reveal Father's sin, especially to one who loved him so dearly. Yet Crewe was wise and had been a worldly man, apprised of everyone's secrets. Surely, he could not be completely ignorant of an affair taking place right under his nose?

He stared down at his boots. The right one was already scuffed and they needed polishing. He would have to ask the new kitchen boy to clean them. He plucked at the cloth of his breeches. It was still impossible for his mind to comprehend what his eyes had seen in the forest. Perhaps the place had been bewitched by the murdered woman, so that men who trespassed there were subjected to devilish illusions.

'Why do you think Father has never married?' He looked up from his feet to meet Crewe's gaze, and swiftly looked away again.

'Sir William is content with his life as it is. He has no need of a wife.'

'Or he has an unnatural aversion to women.' There, he had said it.

'Well, he may have had an unfortunate experience of the female sex.' Crewe's voice was measured but wary, as though he were explaining something beyond the comprehension of a slow schoolboy.

'How so?' Nicholas drummed his fingers on the table. What sort of heartbreak could drive a man to buggery?

'I think his life is better led celibate,' came the enigmatic reply.

'Sadly, though it may be better for him, he is not chaste, far from it,' Nicholas retorted with some irritation.

Now it was Crewe's turn to be taken by surprise. His forehead became furrowed with apprehension, his eyes almost disappearing beneath their hooded lids. 'What have you heard?'

'It is not what I have heard, but what I have seen.' Nicholas turned away. 'Yesterday, in the cot by the river, I came upon Father and John Thornly. They were lying together.'

'The fool.' Crewe wrung his hands in distress. 'To risk everything for a weakness of the flesh. I knew they were too much together. Sir William has allowed Thornly dangerously close. I should have suspected, should have sent Thornly packing years ago.'

'It isn't your fault.' Nicholas regarded the old man with concern, wishing he hadn't told him. In his vexation he had forgotten their steward was no longer the invulnerable figure of his childhood.

'Whatever his faults are, I don't believe Thornly would betray Sir William,' Crewe continued as though to himself. 'They probably fancy themselves in love, like the shepherds in one of those ridiculous poems Sir William likes to read.'

This was unexpected. 'So, you know that Father is a sodomite?'

Crewe looked outraged. 'You must never use that word. Have you any notion how dangerous it is?'

'Of course I do. I'm the one having to act the fly to save him from the scaffold.'

'You have misunderstood.' Crewe lowered his head into his hands and massaged his temples. 'It is their connection to Matthew; that is how the Jesuits would know,' he muttered to himself, before sitting upright again, his expression resolute. 'I am surprised at Father Carmichael. I suppose he believes he is acting for the good of the country, otherwise he would never have coerced you into scouting.'

'Know what?'

'That, you will have to ask Sir William.' Straightening, Crewe lifted his spectacles, dangling on their chain around his neck, and placed them back on his nose.

Nicholas ground his teeth in frustration. 'Please don't treat me like a child. You know full well Father refuses to tell me the truth about our past. He'd rather run away from me than answer my questions.'

'It is not my place to speak on these matters. It is not my history to relate.'

Nicholas pressed his fingernails into his palms. 'Tell me this at least, was Alethea Hawthorne not my aunt, but my mother? Is Sir William really my uncle?'

'You would question why the sun shines instead of enjoying its warmth. Lay aside this frantic questioning and appreciate all your father has given you. You are the heir to an honourable title, a noble seat and fruitful lands. Go and walk around them now, thinking not why they are there, but thanking God for their creation and for all the bounty he has heaped upon you.' Crewe paused, his severe expression melting into a kindlier smile. 'Try to forget what you saw and I will speak with your father.'

It was clear he would get no more information out of Crewe and his father was still nowhere to be seen, so Nicholas took Crewe's advice and went for a walk, hoping to bring some comfort to his heart and clarity to his mind.

Was Crewe overly complacent in thinking Father safe from the executioner? Nicholas was glad at least that he had told him about Staley, though not so happy with his advice. Since worming appeared to be his fate, perhaps he should sneak into Father's closet and search for documents relating to his true parentage. Crewe might think him fortunate, but he was heartily sick of the lies and deceit that seemed to characterise his family. Whatever Lord Pemberton's loyalties or Ned's shortcomings, the Pembertons seemed a far happier lot. Perhaps that was Jane's influence. Crewe could not think it was Jane who had driven Father to other men, could he? Whatever she might have done, it was surely not so extreme as that.

He leant against a stile, observing the sheep. A ram had been put in with the ewes. He wore a raddle-harness to leave a chalk mark on the sheep he had tupped. Father had talked about his experiments in breeding sheep last time Nicholas was here. He wanted to enrich the bloodline by crossing his purebred Border Leicesters with a hardier hill breed.

Nicholas couldn't escape the knowledge of his base-blood; it pumped through his veins, preventing him from ever feeling he was worthy enough to be a true gentleman. Was it to protect his sister's honour that William had raised Nicholas as his son instead of hers? He was almost of age now; why the refusal to tell him his true parentage? Was it so shameful? His appearance testified to his Hawthorne descent, while the evasive behaviour of Crewe and Father convinced him that his supposition about Alethea was correct. Had she been raped by some lowly rogue, someone they did not want recognised? Is that why Matthew had wanted him sent away for adoption as a baby?

He climbed over the stile and walked across the field. The ewes scattered at his approach, but the ram stood his ground, guarding his flock. A horrible concept had taken root in Nicholas's mind and was busily growing. Could that strong family likeness, so widely noted, be due to a doubled bloodline? Was he the creation of an incestuous union? Surely his father was not so depraved he had copulated with his own sister? If this was the case, he might as well throw himself in the lake and put an end to such a monster as he was.

Matthew had called him an angel, but perhaps he was ignorant of Nicholas's true origins. Unless – could it be possible that Matthew was his father? Was that why he had called himself worse than a highwayman? He had seduced his cousin and got her with child. This was at least preferable to being the son of his uncle.

Determined to look for answers in the house, he ran back the way he had come, anxious to conclude his search before Father reappeared. Watching from afar, the sheep stood baaing in alarm.

There was no sign of Father's horse in the stables. The house too was quiet and Nicholas was able to ascend the stairs without any of the servants seeing him. The corridor to William's bedchamber was empty. Nicholas tapped on the door and waited for a few moments. No one came. Pushing the door open, he slipped inside.

The tapestry that covered the door to Father's closet was half-drawn. He tried the handle only to discover, to his dismay, that it was locked. He imagined Father carried the key with him, but searched his room anyway, looking under pillows and in cupboards.

At the back of a drawer in the dressing table he found a folded paper, tied with a green ribbon. He glanced out of the window. There was no sight of anyone outside, but he ducked down onto the floor just in case. Leaning against the bed, he unwrapped the little parcel. A collection of milk teeth tumbled out into his lap. Besides them, all the wrapper contained was a lock of hair so fine it must have belonged to a baby. The colour was a match for his own as a child – before it had grown darker. It moved him, to see these keepsakes of his infancy (for they surely could not belong to any other child). They spoke of a devotional love. An uncle would not treasure such trinkets, nor, he thought, would a man ashamed of his offspring.

He had been so absorbed in his discovery he hadn't noticed the footsteps on the stairs, but now they could be heard outside the door. Nicholas just had time to roll under the bed, the packet scrunched in his hand, as the wooden latch lifted. Two pairs of boots crossed the floor. He tried to slow his breathing. There was so much dust under the bed it took a great effort not to sneeze. How shameful it would be to be caught out again exactly as he had been at the age of fourteen, only hiding under his father's bed this time.

He could hear keys rattling and the closet door being opened.

'I am not such a slave to my passions as you think,' Father was saying. 'Of course I wouldn't risk doing anything that might result in another conception. Fine gentlemen take lovers all the time and are not judged for it, nay, often they are applauded for their gallantry.'

Was Father consorting with women as well as men?

'You have placed yourself at Thornly's mercy,' came Crewe's voice. 'Hazarding everything for some fleeting pleasure.'

'I trust John with my life. He guessed my secret soon after I returned to Measham and has kept it faithfully. We have loved one another for many years, though it is only in the past few that we have allowed ourselves greater intimacy. Do you think I would not restrain myself while Nicholas was living here?'

A spider crawled past Nicholas's nose. To his relief it scuttled away towards the wall. The men's voices had grown fainter; they must have pushed the door to.

What was he doing here, lying in the dirt like a worm while Father boasted of his sodomitical love? He refused to skulk in the shadows any longer. Wriggling forward until he was able to stand, he brushed himself down. Then, before he could think twice about it, he thrust open the door to Father's closet.

William was standing by the window, smoking his pipe. Crewe was sitting with his head propped up against his fist. Candles glowed on the table and in the wall sconces. They both jumped with alarm as Nicholas burst into the small room.

Pushing his shoulders back, Nicholas looked his father squarely in the face. 'Put me out of my agony on one score at least. Am I the hideous creation of an incestuous union?'

Crewe started back in his chair, regarding Nicholas with horror. 'How could you imagine such a thing?'

'You may have been born out of legal wedlock, but your conception was no more depraved than that,' Father said.

Somewhat relieved by their reactions, Nicholas refused to relinquish his righteous anger. 'If you think me fit to be your heir then you must trust me too. I am a grown man now and will keep your secrets just as well as John Thornly. How can I protect this household and the land when I am kept in ignorance about my parentage?'

Father nodded. 'I have come to the same conclusion,' he said, taking the wind out of Nicholas's billowing sails. 'Forgive me for behaving in such a cowardly manner earlier. I did not know what to say to you. I used to think, if I only kept you at a distance, you would see me always as your father.' Putting down his pipe, he crouched down to open a cupboard, withdrawing a decanter of aqua-vitae and placing it on the table, along with three small glasses. 'But my hand has been forced and I do not wish to deceive you any longer. It has become too onerous a burden.' He poured them each a drink. 'Here, I think you will need this.' He held one out to Nicholas. 'You'd better sit down too.'

Nicholas took a sip from his glass. The fiery liquid burnt his throat and he was surprised to see Crewe, as well as Father, knock his drink back in one, before Father refilled their glasses. His stomach contracted with apprehension. Good news did not require such strong liquor.

'Crewe has told me what you saw yesterday and I am truly sorry for it. I would give the world to have preserved you from such a sight.' Father pressed his palms over his eyes as if acting out his words. 'You want to know who your mother is.' He lowered his hands. 'You have known her all your life. She is standing before you.' He lifted his arms, holding them out so that he looked almost Christ-like. 'I am your mother and father both.'

Nicholas was aghast. Father's madness was worse than he had imagined. Now he blasphemed doubly against God. How could Crewe be so complaisant about these delusions?

Father took up his pipe, tamping down the tobacco with a stopper. 'I started out my life as a girl, Alethea Hawthorne, but at the age of nineteen I was forced to renounce my sex.' He stared up at the ceiling as he spoke, as though seeking inspiration for his story, or perhaps it was because he could not look Nicholas in the eye as he recounted his lunatic tale. 'I had been abandoned in London by the Calvertons and, as you heard from my former friends, found sanctuary with a group of dissenters in Epping Forest.' Cupping the bowl of his pipe in his hand, he carefully relit the tobacco with a taper and puffed out a shield of smoke between himself and Nicholas. 'There I was seduced and fell pregnant with you. I travelled back here on foot, with Ellen as my only companion and during the journey discovered it went much easier for us if I disguised myself as a man. I meant, as soon as I got home, to become Alethea once more, but I found my parents and younger siblings all dead of the plague and my brother, William, still abroad. Everyone assumed I was William, so I continued the pretence. If I had not, Uncle Percy would have taken Measham Hall for himself and had me shut up in a convent. Ellen would have gone unrewarded for her loyalty and you would have been given away, goodness knows where.' At last Father found the courage to look directly at Nicholas. 'I gave birth to you in secret, with Ellen's help, and then we returned here. Again, it was just accepted by the people hereabouts that Alethea had died, and that Ellen was your mother. I never said she was, but neither did I contradict it.' Father sucked on his pipe.

'When William finally came back, he too was a new person. A priest called Father Matthew Harcourt. We eventually agreed that I should live as William to secure Measham Hall and aid him in his ministry.'

Nicholas wanted to laugh. It was as if Father was putting on a play for him, acting out some arsy-versy drama for a Twelfth Night celebration. All of a sudden, his cousin was his uncle and his father was his mother. He looked questioningly at Crewe. He wasn't sure if they should call for a doctor or a priest.

'All this strange information will take some time to comprehend, I am sure.' Crewe's expression was apologetic. 'I can only confirm the truth of your father's words.'

Nicholas pointed at the person now leaning against the window frame. He mustn't succumb to the insanity that had clearly infected them both.

'Except, in that case, he cannot be my father.'

Staring at the man standing before him, Nicholas tried to imagine Father as a woman. It was impossible to picture him in a bodice and skirts. There couldn't be breasts beneath his jacket. And yet, he couldn't recall Father ever in his shirt only, without an overgarment of one kind

205

or another. Where his Adam's apple should be was always covered, as now, by a high tied cravat. And then there was his boyish appearance. But he carried himself like a man. He spoke like a man. Though it was true, the pitch of his voice was light and somewhat high; his words, his pursuits, his interests were all those of a man. Everyone knew and accepted him as a man.

'I am your father and have been from the day you were delivered from my womb. I renounced the role of mother in order to keep Measham Hall, not only for myself, but also for you. Now I am so thoroughly a man I scarcely know what it is to be female.' William sounded weary, almost sorrowful. He slapped a hand against his hip. 'Only this body trips me up sometimes. But I have trained my mind to become entirely masculine. There is not a womanish thought left in it.'

'Yet you have female desires,' Nicholas said slowly.

Father took another drink. 'I must be Venus's plaything, she enflames my heart with such invincible passions. Don't you think I fought against my love for John Thornly with all my strength?' He shook his head reproachfully. 'Sometimes I wish the gods would make a swap of my sex and John's, but of course, there would still be his marriage and the difference in rank to obstruct our happiness.'

'But you are not a god. You could not create me on your own.' There was a sour taste in Nicholas's mouth. He had no patience for Father's self-pity.

William turned back to the window. It was dark out now, with just a sliver of a moon visible as the clouds were blown past it by the wind. An ivy-owl could be heard calling to its mate.

'The man who sired you was a sectarian preacher. I thought we would marry, but it turned out he had a wife still living. He was a self-serving hypocrite and you are better off without him. Besides, he no longer lives in this country and may be dead for all I know. Certainly he is dead to me.'

It occurred to Nicholas that he had acquired enough relatives in the last few minutes to be cured of the desire to seek out more, especially one so unsavoury. 'But how can you be a woman and I not see it?' he burst out. 'Everyone knows you as a man – at least, most people do.' He looked again to Crewe for some reassurance.

Father shifted to face him again. 'It is hard to have all one's beliefs upended; I know this first hand. We are taught to trust implicitly those with power and authority over us, not to question, not to look our betters in the face, not to see things any differently from how they are presented to us.

'I keep myself mostly among my subordinates because they will not question the man who employs them, who owns the land they live on. But even my equals are not going to challenge what is universally held to be self-evident. What fool would suggest I am a woman in disguise? Oh, I know there are those who call me effeminate, a she-man, a will-jill, but none would dare call me out to my face.'

Of all the secrets his father might have harboured, such as could cause his downfall, being a woman was the last thing Nicholas could have anticipated. He felt as though his life had become a drama written by Shakespeare or Lyly. Except their women in disguise fell in love with noblemen, not itinerant sermoners or farmers. He wasn't sure if it was better or worse that his father, instead of being a buggeranto, had put on the other sex.

'You have deceived me all my life. Both of you and Matthew.' He looked accusingly from Father to Crewe.

'No, son, we have not. As I said before, I am your father, the only one you will ever need.'

'Then you have denied me a mother.'

'Well, there you are not alone. Mothers die all the time, especially after childbirth,' Father said with an impatience that made Nicholas feel like a boy again. He responded in kind.

'Is that really your moustache?'

Father gingerly pressed the hair on his upper lip. 'It is my hair. I glue it on with mastic.'

'Does Abigail know?'

Nicholas had once seen her scrubbing bloody clouts, which, when he asked, she said were from a woman's visits. Jane had been staying at the time and he'd asked with alarm if she had been injured, but Abigail had shooed him away. Later, he learnt that women produced a bloody flux that turned to milk in the womb in order to nourish any child within. If there was no child, the blood must be evacuated. He had read in his Pliny that a dog that tasted a woman's terms would run mad and a woman who went near wine during her monthly visit would turn it sour. Palmes had even shouted at Abigail to keep away from the claret in case she soured it. If Father had the body of a woman, he too must produce that monthly evacuation that could ruin a good wine and yet he drank all the month round. Perhaps his female purgations had ceased. That might explain his aberrant behaviour, since the blood, if it was not spent, ran to the head, causing melancholy and strange fancies.

On one of Nicholas's visits to Isabelle Dupont he had found her being bled from her foot for just such a reason. Her physician was concerned that she often missed her terms and would grow ill if the blood wasn't drawn down, away from her brain. When her husband was alive the doctor had prescribed much vigorous copulation as the best remedy. This was why she needed to take lovers, she had told Nicholas with a smile; her health depended on it. Could this be why his mother-father sought out John Thornly?

'Abigail is too much the tattler. I wouldn't confide in her. Besides, I pay all my servants well enough to keep them loyal.' Father spoke with his customary authority.

Nicholas had never met a woman with such masculine confidence and couldn't imagine any women of his acquaintance who would have the audacity to live as a man. Yet he had heard of women who went off to war disguised as soldiers and even rose through the ranks to command armies. So it must be possible for women to be as bold and bloodthirsty as men. Isabelle had complete dominion over her household, but she used more feminine wiles to maintain her rule. Would she ever turn man to avoid another marriage? Nicholas longed suddenly to be lying in her arms, unburdening his soul to her. How amused she would be. Isabelle was so liberal in her thoughts, she was the only person he could imagine believing his story, let alone understanding it.

'There are other, more pressing issues.' It was Crewe's turn to become impatient with William. 'Not everyone is so reluctant to expose you.'

When he and Nicholas explained the position they were in with Gilbert Staley, Father sank onto a chair, looking as though he'd just been punched in the stomach.

'Are you certain the villain knows my original identity?'

'What else could it be that would see you imprisoned and Nicholas disinherited?' Crewe rubbed his cheek wearily. 'I believe I have worked out who must have told Staley.'

'Not Ellen?' Now it was Father's turn to sound incredulous. 'She would never conspire with the Jesuits.'

Crewe shook his head. 'You'll recall Matthew's companion from St. Omers, Lawrence Gascoigne. The man whom he intended you to marry?'

'How could I forget?' Father pulled a drawer open and rummaged through it. 'I have Gascoigne's portrait somewhere. A miniature, in a locket. I came across it among Matthew's belongings.' He grimaced as if caught by a spasm of pain, then shook his head. 'I'll find it later.

Between them, Father and Crewe explained that when Matthew was living in France, Crewe had sent him messages, keeping him abreast of all the news at home, including his own apparent return to Measham Hall. Crewe had soon realised that the counterfeit Sir William was Mistress Alethea in disguise. On hearing that his sister was still alive, Matthew arranged a marriage for her to his bosom friend, Lawrence Gascoigne; a man who was willing to take the Hawthorne name and manage the Measham estate on Matthew's behalf. Alethea however, having enjoyed the independence of a man, had no wish to become a wife. In order to dissuade her brother, she enlisted Crewe's assistance and through his contacts in France, Crewe compelled Gascoigne to confess to Matthew that he had returned to his old vice of gambling. Matthew, accepting that Measham Hall was safest under Alethea's sole stewardship, gave up any idea of reclaiming his sister and called the wedding off. Unfortunately, however, he had already confided the story of his sister's disguise to Gascoigne.

'Matthew was amused at first by the imposture and wanted Gascoigne to know what sort of wife he would be marrying.' Crewe polished his spectacles with his handkerchief. 'I believe the pretence was rather appealing.'

'But why should Gascoigne tell Staley?' Nicholas asked.

'Revenge,' Father and Crewe replied together.

'Because you didn't want to marry him?' Nicholas looked at Father.

Father and Crewe were silent for so long, Nicholas was about to repeat the question, when Father finally answered. 'Because we damaged his reputation with Matthew.' He nodded his head thoughtfully. 'I was simply the means for him to live at Measham, close to his beloved friend. I ruined their plans in that respect.'

'We must hope Gascoigne doesn't share what he knows with anyone else,' Crewe said matter-of-factly. 'If the knowledge that William and Alethea are one and the same person is held only by the Jesuit order, I don't believe we have too much to fear. It is, however, unfortunate that Staley has stooped to extortion.'

They passed a very strange evening, acting as though nothing had ostensibly changed. Father was Father and that was that. Nicholas joined him in drinking too much wine and both vowed undying affection and loyalty to the other.

By the time he went to bed, Nicholas had concluded that since Matthew and Crewe, both devout Catholics, had colluded in this hare-brained folly, it could not be such a wicked sin. Certainly it was not so depraved as incest. It seemed God had smiled on Father too, for he had successfully maintained his disguise for the past twenty-one years. Indeed, Nicholas felt a new admiration for his extraordinary parent. It took skill and bravado to carry off such an audacious masquerade.

He slept until the late morning sun prised his eyes open. Above him, miniature huntsmen chased their embroidered prey. Little brown does sat placidly behind spiky green bushes. How often he had invented stories for the comfortingly familiar scene woven into his bed-hangings. Sometimes Jane had sat on the bed with him and they would invent tales together. Now he felt like Descartes' captive sleeper, longing to remain in slumber, dreaming that he was free.

Certainly Descartes' theory that the senses were not to be relied upon had been proved true. How could he not have seen through his father's disguise? What else might he be mistaken in? Whom and what could he believe? Yesterday's revelations seemed so fantastical he thought perhaps Father and Crewe had been fooling with him.

Forcing himself up, he splashed cold water on his face, dressed and made his way downstairs, his head thumping with every tread. Father was in the hall dressed to go riding. Nicholas had a sudden urge to rip the hat and wig from his head and the jacket from his back, to expose him for what he really was. But then Father turned to him and smiled.

'Will you come up to the graveyard with me? We can walk if you prefer.' He held up his flask. 'I've cherry-water if your throat is dry.'

The sun was low but bright and the sky was a pale, wintery blue. High above them a buzzard was mewing to its mate. The birds were probably circling some luckless rabbit in the field below. Artemis bounded off up the lane, her tail wagging. Her mother, Athena, had died while Nicholas was at St. Omers. He missed the old dog.

The sharp air helped clear his head. He breathed in deeply, appreciating its sweetness after the coal fumes of London. Casting a sidelong glance at Father (for he could only think of him by that name), he asked, 'Does Jane know?'

'She suspected who I really was when I first met her as William, and then, when she came to visit on her own and my trust in her grew, I admitted the truth.'

'And still she conceived a passion for you!'

Father looked rueful. 'I wish I could have returned her affections with equal ardour, but I always saw her more as a younger sister than a lover.'

An image of Lettice came into Nicholas's mind. He kept telling himself his feelings for her were fraternal, but never having had a sibling, how could he truly know what that love was like? Love, it seemed, could take on many forms and travel in multiple directions. If a woman could become a man, why shouldn't another woman fall in love with them? Or even a man for that matter?

'Jane's visits here brought me great joy. I missed female company and it was such a relief to have a friend to confide in. When I was sent to be her companion, she was scarcely more than a child and overindulged by the household. Her marriage forced her to grow up. Sellwood tried to beat the compassion out of her, but she never allowed him to succeed. Instead, she only grew kinder and wiser.'

'She said it was you who nursed her back to a healthy state again.'

'That is generous of her.'

They were approaching the village and Father whistled to Artemis to come to heel. 'Jane had always been a little in love with William, or her idea of him, and I embodied that ideal. She said if she ever became a widow, she would marry me, and though flattered, I thought it too dangerous. We would have been sinning against the Church and the State and I did not want to risk coming under greater scrutiny.'

'But you are willing to sin with John Thornly,' Nicholas said. Though he had always liked Thornly, he would have preferred it if Father had succumbed to Jane instead.

'I am not like Matthew. I cannot suppress my desires and live celibately as he could. One day you may meet someone who draws you to them with a pull so strong you cannot resist it. I hope the one who calls to you will be a good person, with your best interests at heart, someone eligible. And if they are not, then I hope you are stronger than I am.'

Nicholas had never actually attempted to resist Isabelle's charms, but that had been a delightful dalliance, nothing more. He was drawn to Lettice and keenly aware of her physical beauty, but would never attempt to seduce her or behave in any way that would damage her reputation. He was not so arrogant as to think himself an eligible match for her either.

'Were you ever going to tell me?'

'Not unless I had to.' Father shrugged. 'What good does the knowledge do you?'

They had reached the back gate into the churchyard. Fortunately, it was empty of people. Neither of them was in the right frame of mind to be sociable. Artemis had caught the scent of something and went snuffling across the long grass. A rabbit bolted out from behind a gravestone and the dog sped after it.

'You suspected Jane of telling Lady Margaret about the priest's hole; weren't you afraid she would also let slip about your real identity?'

Father nodded. 'Jane thought her mother had guessed, but none of them have ever spoken of it. How could they? Lady Margaret arranged for me to be sent on a wild goose chase in search of my brother and then told the rest of the family I had contracted the plague. Jane always insisted her mother did not intend to have me killed, but I am sure the man she presented as my brother's messenger was really an assassin hired to murder me. I think it was only a sense of pity that prevented him.'

Now Nicholas understood why Father hated Margaret Calverton. Still, his suspicions were extreme. Before he could ask why Lady Margaret should want Alethea dead, the sexton appeared.

'Watch that dog,' he said. 'We've a newly dug grave over yonder; don't want him digging there.'

Father whistled the dog up and Nicholas observed, with new curiosity, the easy way in which he spoke to the sexton. They chatted affably of local affairs as any squire and countryman might. The sexton was by far the more garrulous of the two but there was nothing unusual in that. Indeed, there was nothing that might overtly distinguish William Hawthorne from any other rural gentleman. He was less effeminate in his speech and manner than many city gallants. His clothes were as plain and dull as any rustic, male or female. He stood with his feet planted solidly some distance apart, his gloved hands held loosely by his sides. His legs were muscular, well-shaped perhaps for a man of his age, but then the only female legs Nicholas had seen uncovered were Isabelle's. Her thighs had been deliciously round and plump, the flesh soft and dimpled. He shook such thoughts from his head and went in search of Artemis, who had wandered off again.

Fortunately, she had not discovered the new grave, but was lying panting by their family tomb. Nicholas traced his finger over the engravings of the caterpillar and the butterfly that had captivated him as a boy. As he read the inscription again, he began to understand how his mother had become his father. It was not merely some elaborate act; Alethea really had been transformed into a new version of her brother. She had taken the mould of William, abandoned by Matthew, and filled it anew.

Behold I shew you a mystery, said the carved words. *We shall not all sleep, but we shall all be changed*. Next to these words was a more recent engraving, added in memory of Matthew: *IHS* with a *V* below it. It was subtle enough to escape the gaze of the uninitiated but Nicholas knew what it stood for: *In Hoc Signo Vinces* – 'In this sign, you shall conquer'.

What or whom had Matthew conquered by his death? His fellow priests were using what they knew about his family to coerce his nephew into spying, hardly an honourable method to achieve their ends. Nicholas had always considered Father's religious conformity an act of cowardice, but now he understood why Matthew had endorsed it. Previously, English hostility towards papism had made him feel more protective, more proud of upholding the old religion, but since his return he had been made painfully aware of just how few shared his faith. And not only that, but some of their fears were starting to seem justified. King James claimed to be promoting toleration, but refused to condemn the French king's persecution of Protestants. And Nicholas couldn't help but sympathise with those Oxford scholars who had been deprived of their livelihoods. They too had made a stand for their religion and suffered for it.

Was a society where everyone was free to live and worship as they chose an impossible ideal? Perhaps he had absorbed Ellen's dissenting views with her breast milk, or perhaps it was his puritan father's blood, but the symbol on the tomb no longer inspired him as it might once have done. Instead, he came to the dizzying realisation that he knew nothing. His only consolation was that at least, like Plato, he knew that he knew nothing.

Part III
Becoming a Man

⤳ Chapter Twenty ⤶

January 1688

I t was a relief, after the twelve days of Christmas, to return to the orderly quiet of his rooms at Oxford, where everything was exactly as he had left it before his world had been turned head over heels. Nicholas spent the first week of Hilary term buried in his studies. The library became his refuge. Here he could push his extraordinary father-mother out of his mind for a while.

By the second week, he kept catching himself staring out of the window, lost in reveries of life at Measham Hall. Though he tried to do as Father and Crewe advised, resuming his previous conception of William Hawthorne and thinking of Alethea as his aunt only, it was impossible to banish his parent's revelations from his consciousness.

Instead, he resolutely turned his mind to philosophy. Which was more powerful, the intellect or the body? Could the very atoms of his mother-father's corporal being have rearranged themselves into a masculine form? Such a thing must be heretical. Unless free will could be extended into the organical parts of the body. But if Plato was right when he argued that the soul had no gender, what did it matter if his father was male or female?

Father was right on one matter, Nicholas decided: it was better not to question his origins. Having two parents in one was quite enough. Besides, his natural father sounded like a scoundrel. Nicholas was grateful to his parent for naming him and keeping him when he could so easily have been fostered out elsewhere. And yet, although it was true that many people grew up without a mother, he couldn't shrug off the sense of melancholy that had descended on him.

He felt especially anxious and protective towards William. Father might insist he could look after himself, but as far as Nicholas was concerned, he had multiple layers of vulnerability: his religion, his lover, his forged identity. Being so reclusive, a ruined reputation would not hurt him, but Nicholas could not imagine his father existing outside of Measham Hall and the thought of him being forced into women's clothing and cast into prison or a house of correction was unbearable.

His fears were not assuaged by a letter that arrived from Staley. It thanked him for the news of his 'cousin' and his 'cousin's servant', by which Nicholas understood Staley meant Pemberton and Isaac. The servant had been arrested at Gravesend under suspicion of spying. He was currently being questioned, but was proving particularly stubborn. Nicholas must sound out his 'cousin's son' to discover where his cousin's affections really lay. For his cousin was fickle and likely to send him on whimsical errands.

Nicholas had not seen Isaac since the evening in Pemberton's study after his audience with Father Petre. In his letter to Staley, he had mentioned Isaac departing on a journey. Was that the basis on which Isaac had been intercepted? The thought made the bile rise in his belly. Even if Isaac had been on his way to Holland to tell the Dutch prince about the Queen's pregnancy, Nicholas did not wish him any ill. They were both only doing their masters' bidding.

Setting aside his studies, he went in search of Ned Pemberton. He had been half-expecting Ned to come knocking on his door, but there had been no sign of him since the beginning of term. If Ned had grown bored of his company, Nicholas would have to work hard to revive his interest.

He tried a few of the usual haunts before spotting some familiar faces in the Golden Cross. Ned's Roisterers were gathered round a table playing at dice with their accustomed rowdiness, but he was nowhere to be seen.

Sir Denis was standing at the back of the crowd, calling out what he took for witticisms. Nicholas caught hold of his elbow and asked if Ned was with them.

'Don't you know?' Denis said with surprise. 'He's seeing some quack in Tunbridge Wells. Got a bad dose of the pox. Ambrose Mount says he's lost his nose. We wrote him a poem about it, but haven't heard back yet.' He let out a snorting guffaw. 'He's been there since after Christmas. Hope he comes back soon, isn't half so much fun here without the pretty rogue.'

Disturbed by this news, Nicholas returned to his rooms to write to Jane. He didn't mention what he had learnt about his father; he wouldn't commit such dangerous information to paper. Nor did he refer to the specific nature of Ned's illness.

Her reply came a week later. After making some initial progress, Edward's health had declined. He had now been seen by Pemberton's own physician, who thought he would find the waters at Bath more efficacious than those of Tunbridge, but they would wait for better weather before undertaking such a journey. In the meantime, he was taking regular mercury baths, along with purgatives and bleedings. They did not believe his illness to be entirely caused by his own weaknesses, but would, of course, appreciate Nicholas's discretion. The family were all praying for his recovery. There was no reference to Isaac, and Nicholas wondered whether Pemberton was keeping news of his arrest from her.

There was nothing for it, but to travel to Tunbridge Wells. Nicholas wrote to Staley, telling him that he would discover all he could from his cousin's son, but that the servant was an honourable man who did not deserve rough treatment. It was essential too, he emphasised, that Isaac did not suspect his involvement.

He had read a treatise by an Italian physician decrying the use of mercury and claiming it was as likely to kill as cure the patient. If the Italian was correct, Ned's health would only worsen. With this in mind, Nicholas consulted one of his lecturers in medicine. Doctor

Paterson assured him that mercury was the only effective remedy for the French pox and should be taken internally. Though, of course, one must be certain of the diagnosis.

'Has your friend been frequenting the garden of Venus?' Paterson gave him a probing stare. 'Close proximity with the poxy steams of an infected womb is all that is required to contract the disease, you know, even without full carnal contact.'

Realising the professor thought he was the one with syphilis, Nicholas felt the colour rising to his cheeks. 'I couldn't say, sir. But I will be sure to enquire as to his exact symptoms when I see him.' Despite Ned's reputation for loose living, Nicholas did not like to reveal his identity.

Doctor Paterson pulled sagely on his beard. 'If only the authorities would treat venereal evil with the same seriousness as the plague. It is my opinion that transporting all whores to the West Indies could solve this blight upon society. The heat of those islands would soon cure the women of the pox and many innocent Englishmen would be saved much suffering. I am currently writing a paper on the matter. Perhaps you would like to read it?'

'It would be an honour, sir,' Nicholas assured him, though he doubted the practicalities of such a scheme.

On the road from Oxford, Nicholas's coach was stopped and searched by soldiers looking for copies of the latest pamphlet from Holland. Despite the government's efforts to suppress it, this pamphlet appeared to be making its way across the country, for it was the topic of conversation in every hostelry Nicholas entered.

While taking his dinner in Maidenhead, he listened to the talk of the men seated at the far end of the same table. They were discussing a pamphlet that had been left there.

'I've read this afore,' an old man with a face as brown and wrinkled as a walnut informed his companions. 'If the Princess of Orange comes to the throne, she'll keep the Test Act and put an end to all this promoting of papists over Protestants. They won't be allowed in parliament nor any other public office.'

'Princess Mary is all very well, but what about her husband? D'you want to be ruled over by some republican water-rat of a Dutchman? My brother died fighting the Dutch for this country.' A thin man with a hunched back spoke sharply.

'Times have changed, Peter,' the old man said gently. 'The Prince says he's all for toleration and will respect our ways. It wouldn't only be him ruling over us anyhow, for all he's the King's nephew, not without the Princess, and she's as English as you or me.'

Nicholas stretched over towards them. 'Might I take a look at that letter?'

Ignoring the wary expressions of his friends, the old man pushed the beer-stained sheet over to Nicholas. 'A Letter writ by Mijn Heer Fagel' – he recognised it immediately as one of the pamphlets from Lord Pemberton's study. Perhaps Pemberton had been composing a rebuttal to it, he thought, remembering the handwritten notes on the front page. He hadn't had time to read what they said and wished now that he had taken Pemberton's copy. He could have given it to Staley, though that would hardly have prevented the pamphlets being shipped around the country. Unless, of course, it was Pemberton who was organising their distribution.

'You can keep it,' the man said with a note of apprehension. 'It's not mine. I just found it here.'

Thanking him, Nicholas folded the pamphlet and shoved it into his pocket. Once in his room, however, recalling the search of their coach, he dropped it into the fireplace and watched as the flames reduced the incendiary claims to ashes.

Arriving in Tunbridge Wells, Nicholas went straight to the house of the physician where Ned was lodging. Greeting Nicholas from his bed with a raised hand, Ned appeared uncharacteristically dejected. The pale skin of his face was covered in livid, weeping pustules and the disease had already begun to eat away the corner of his mouth. At least Ambrose had been wrong on one score: his nose was still intact.

'I can't endure much more of this.' A tear trickled down the side of Ned's ravaged face. 'The pain of the treatment is the worst part. I'd stop it entirely but the doctor says I must continue with the mercury salivation for another two weeks in order to complete the cure.'

'That's not so long.' Nicholas did his best to sound cheerful. 'When you are restored to health it will all seem worthwhile.'

'I'll only be touching virgins from now on,' Ned vowed. 'Passing water is agony. There's a carbuncle on my yard that they might have to remove with a knife.'

Ned offered to show him the chancre on his penis, but Nicholas, being more interested in botany than physiology, declined the opportunity to view what Ned insisted was a gargantuan specimen.

'I sent word to your stepmother that I would stay with you until you recover. Their Lord and Ladyship asked me to convey their good wishes,' he said.

Ned merely rolled his eyes in response.

'How about a game of cards or dice?' Nicholas asked, hoping to distract Ned from his suffering. He placed the pack of cards he had brought with him on the bed and Ned's expression brightened somewhat.

After a few rounds of piquet, Nicholas returned to the subject of Lord Pemberton. 'I am sure your father has great plans for you at Court. I believe he would even change his religion to ensure his place by the King.'

Ned snorted. 'Only if the King keeps his crown, and from what I've heard that ain't likely. Sorry, Colley, but most people don't want to go back to Rome.'

Keeping an eye on the door in case the doctor or nurse returned, Nicholas asked, 'Did Lord Pemberton tell you that?'

'Father knows how to back the winning horse. How else do you think he grew so rich? It isn't all inherited, you know.'

'And the winning horse is orange?'

Ned gave a wheezing laugh. 'It's certainly looking that way. Your beloved Jane's parents have been grooming that horse too, you know.'

'Is that so? But Lord Calverton fought for King Charles. He has always been loyal to the Stuarts.'

'Princess Mary is a Stuart and so's her husband come to that – William is James's nephew after all.' Ned shrugged. 'Not that I give a damn either way.'

Changing tack, Nicholas asked if Ned had seen the latest Dutch pamphlets and wondered out loud whether Lord Pemberton had any interest in such matters, but Ned's eyes were closing and his hand had flopped open to reveal his cards.

Leaving Ned to sleep, Nicholas went in search of an inn and, having secured a room, wrote to Staley with this new intelligence. Father had warned him that Calverton was a wily dog and his wife made her enmity to Rome quite clear, so he supposed their support for the House of Orange should not surprise him. Yet Calverton had offered to put in a word for him with Churchill, one of the King's highest officers. Could they be trying to turn him too? When it came down to it, it didn't really matter what the common people thought about James, so long as he had the army and the navy behind him. If the King lost their loyalty, however, there was little chance of him holding onto power.

Despite the emetics and bleedings, Ned's health did not improve. Each day he seemed a little worse. Nicholas spoke to the physician, who assured him they were doing all they could, applying tried and tested remedies. The problem was the patient's inherent frailty: his body could not, it seemed, endure what most others could and a cure rested now in the hands of God.

Although he didn't much like Edward, Nicholas hated to see anyone in pain. When Ned wasn't raving and cursing all women, Nicholas tried reading to him. Since the Bible only made Ned cry that he was suffering the torments of Job and didn't need reminding of his sins, he bought a couple of Shakespeare's comedies from a local bookseller, which Ned seemed to find more calming. When a letter arrived from Lord Pemberton, he read that out too. It was a disappointment to both of them, being too pious for Ned and not political enough to interest Staley. Nicholas had hoped there might be some reference to Isaac, but though Pemberton wrote of the family and household in general terms, no mention was made of the secretary.

'Isaac holds a great deal of authority in your household, does he not?' he asked Edward instead.

'Pater's black bastard, you mean. Father wishes Isaac was his legitimate heir instead of me.' Ned sounded resentful, but then admitted, 'He's a more upright fellow, 'tis true.'

Now Nicholas understood the familiarity between Isaac and Lord Pemberton, as well as Isaac's elevated position in the household. Though that position hardly compared to his own as heir of Measham. Still, if Isaac resented his treatment he did not show it.

'Shocked, are you? But you're base-born too.' Ned tittered. 'Don't look so mortified. I daresay I've sired a few whoresons myself.'

'Does Jane know?'

'Pater might have told her, but he likes to keep it quiet. I only know because Mother confided in me once. Isaac's dam was lucky to be married off to the footman. Mother didn't want her in the house and Father refused to sell her.'

Nicholas was disgusted by the brutality of Ned's words and besides, he was sure it was illegal to buy and sell slaves in England. He couldn't press the youth any further, however, as Ned had begun to retch and he had to grab the bowl that had been left by the bed.

'You're a good fellow, Colley. When I die you can have my clothes,' Ned told him when he had finished vomiting.

'That's most generous, but I'm sure we'll be old men when that time comes,' Nicholas replied as soothingly as he was able.

By the fourth day, however, Ned was refusing to eat even the broths or jellies the cook sent up. Consequently, the vomits and enemas had little effect, except to cause him greater agony. Anxious for Ned's chances, Nicholas was about to write to Lord Pemberton, when the fever passed. Only his slow and laboured breathing suggested that, though the disease had been driven out, Ned's body had not recovered.

A nurse came in to sit with Ned, ordering Nicholas back to his lodgings to get some sleep before he succumbed to sickness too.

When Nicholas returned the next morning, the grave-looking doctor told him that Edward was now in the happiest of conditions, peaceful at last in the arms of his Maker. Hiring a horse, Nicholas rode with all speed to London to tell Lord Pemberton that his son was dead.

Chapter Twenty-One

February 1688

Edward Pemberton's funeral was the most impressive ceremony Nicholas had ever attended. The streets in Covent Garden were blocked with carriages. A long procession of mourners, carrying sprigs of rosemary and wax tapers, followed the coffin on foot to the church where Ned's body was to be interred in the aisle. The night was filled with the sound of bells tolling for each year of his short life.

The abundant candles did little to warm the frosty church and the congregation's breath could be seen hanging in the still air like clouds. Despite the cold, the stench of putrefied flesh and old bones rose up from the opened crypt. The mourners clasped their bunches of rosemary to their noses while the rector delivered his sermon.

From the minister's eulogy, anyone unacquainted with Ned would have thought him the most exemplary youth. His lifelong battle with illness, which he'd endured with Christian fortitude, was emphasised. The nature of his final sickness was not referred to. Nicholas thought of the pain Ned had suffered at the end and wondered if he should have done more to encourage Ned to repent and seek forgiveness. For it was not in Nicholas's nature to believe that those of different faiths were precluded from God's mercy.

He had ended up near the back of the church with Sir Denis and Ambrose Mount.

'You were given a mourning ring,' Ambrose noted with indignation, spotting the ring on Nicholas's gloved finger.

'Only close family get rings,' Sir Denis said.

'I am a close family friend,' Nicholas explained.

Jane had given him the ring. Realising he didn't possess one, she had also provided a mourning suit, to Nicholas's relief. He didn't like to mention the deathbed bequest of Ned's clothes in case it seemed covetous.

Ambrose was only partially mollified. 'Considering we were Ned's most intimate companions, I thought we might have merited a ring.'

Nicholas suspected Lord Pemberton held Ned's friends partly responsible for his demise, but refrained from voicing this suspicion. He was simply grateful not to be considered similarly culpable.

Outside the church, children fought for the pennies that were tossed to them by wealthy members of the congregation. One of the mourners was robbed of his candle and several gentlemen had to beat the crowd back with their swords. In the affray Nicholas almost lost the black crape hatband he had been given to wear.

The disturbance meant he was one of the last to arrive back at the house for spiced wine and cake. Richard, who had travelled up from Kent with his sisters, squeezed his way through the guests and flung his arms around Nicholas.

'I'm so glad you're here,' he cried.

Touched by this enthusiastic reception, Nicholas bent down to return the embrace. 'I'm very sorry for the loss of your brother.'

'I am the heir now.' Richard gazed solemnly up at him with wide eyes. 'I will have to look after my sisters, as well as all our land and property, and Jane too if Father dies before her.'

'It is a great responsibility,' Nicholas agreed.

'Well.' Richard put his hands on his hips. 'Lettice, Doll and Prue should all be married by the time I come of age, so I won't have to worry about them too much.'

'You will just have to find them good husbands.' Nicholas couldn't help being amused by Richard's precocity.

'I'll leave that to Father,' Richard said, aghast.

'Very wise.' Though Nicholas had always longed for siblings, perhaps having a duty of care for only one relative was preferable, especially when that one proved so onerous. 'Where are your sisters?' He had been wondering how Lettice was.

'Tilly's over there.'

Richard pointed to a couch where his sister sat, already flanked by Sir Denis and Ambrose, who were attending to her with lavish solicitude. Remembering Ned's defensiveness regarding his sister, Nicholas was dismayed by the freedoms they were taking. He was about to intervene when Jane appeared by his side.

'My mother would like to speak with you,' she said quietly.

He looked around the room for Lady Margaret.

'She is upstairs resting. The footman will take you to her.' Jane squeezed his arm before moving off to talk to other guests.

The footman was nowhere to be seen, so Nicholas had to find his own way to Lady Margaret's chamber. The room was in semi-darkness, lit only by the candle beside her bed and the flames from the fireplace. Bowls of flower petals and herbs had been placed around the room and their perfume merged with the faint odour of sweat and urine. Winifred, her waiting-woman, sat dozing in a corner of the room. Nicholas supposed sleep must be a welcome refuge from such an oppressive apartment.

'Come, sit here beside me.'

Margaret was propped up on several pillows, a heavy shawl wrapped around her shoulders. Her wig appeared overly large on her diminished face and the glossy brown hair only heightened the pallor of her unpainted skin. Nonetheless, her voice still carried the expectation of obedience. Nicholas sat down on the chair placed next to the bed.

She dismissed his condolences for her step-grandson with a wave of her hand. 'He refused to listen to his parents. It is fortunate for them the boy died before he had a chance to squander all their wealth. If he had continued to gamble and lose such monstrous sums, he would have left his poor sisters without dowries and Richard would have been lucky if there was enough over for an officer's commission.' She sniffed. 'How is your father?'

'Very well, I thank you.'

Margaret tugged at the bedclothes fretfully.

'Is there anything you require, ma'am?' Nicholas was becoming quite adept at tending to the sick, though the experience made him grateful he did not need to pursue medicine as a profession.

'You can refill my glass. My mouth is dry.' She gestured to the jug that had been placed on a table in front of the fire.

Glad of an excuse to move away, Nicholas poured the wine out slowly, inhaling the warming aromas of cinnamon and aniseed that rose up from it, masking the foetid air of the chamber.

'I do not expect to live long,' Margaret said as he handed her the glass.

He didn't attempt any platitudes because he knew she would see through them. She was already into her seventh decade; not many were fortunate enough to reach such an advanced age. Though he wondered if their encounter with the highwaymen and being forced to remove her cloak on the road, had contributed to this sudden decline.

Holding the glass in both hands, she drank as if to quell some pain. 'I hope our merciful God will forgive me my sins.' Her voice had lost its certainty. 'The worst of them is that I am too easily moved to jealousy. I have suffered such torments because of it. I hope the Lord will pity my weakness and spare me further anguish.' She passed the glass back to him and began twisting the quilt, blue veins standing out like ribbons on the backs of her hands.'

Nicholas pitied Margaret in her distress, but at the back of his mind was the possibility that she might be a traitor to their King. Even more pressing were Father's accusations and the knowledge that she might have betrayed Matthew. He leant in a little closer.

'Here's the truth, young man. I suspected my husband of harbouring a fondness for your aunt. I once found his handkerchief in her bed.' Margaret pulled on her own lace cuff as if to demonstrate. 'I thought she had lain with him. Or, if she had not, that it was only a matter of time before she allowed herself to be seduced. I couldn't bear to lose control of my household, to be pushed aside by some chit, to see her belly swell with his child.' Margaret's voice had grown agitated and she stared fixedly into the dark room, as if the scene was being enacted before her.

Suddenly overtaken by a coughing fit, she brought up a lump of black phlegm, which she spat into a napkin. Since he had often observed this expectoration among London residents, it didn't cause Nicholas any great alarm. He was more concerned by the way she seemed to be reliving so vividly events that had happened long ago and he feared her mind was wandering. He wondered what else might be in the wine, besides spices. He looked over at her maid, but Winifred was snoring softly, her head lolling against the back of the chair.

'Lord Calverton loves and honours you; that is plain for anyone to see,' he said gently.

Father had been adamant that the preacher was the first man Alethea had lain with and Nicholas could see no reason for him to lie about this. Besides, Father had declared himself confounded by the source of Lady Margaret's animosity towards Alethea; if Calverton had taken advantage of her, he would have known exactly where it sprang from.

'He has been a good husband, better sometimes than I deserved. I ought to have trusted him.' Leaning forward suddenly, Margaret grasped Nicholas's hands. 'I had contacts – men who owed me their allegiance for favours I had done them when Cromwell was in power. I used to carry messages, you know, between the royalists in exile and those in England who were plotting to restore the King. The Great Trust and the Sealed Knot, I had access to all their agents. Cromwell's men never suspected a lady like myself of being an intelligencer.' Catching sight of Nicholas's startled expression, she gave a throaty chuckle, which turned into another bout of coughing. 'I thought it might shock you to learn this. I hope my service for His late Majesty will earn me his thanks when next we meet.' She sat up a little higher against her cushions, a haughty pride bringing dignity to her crumpled face.

'Did you also inform against my cousin, the priest, ma'am?' Nicholas asked, taking his chance while she seemed in a confessional mood.

'No I did not.' Margaret shook her head irritably, annoyed by his interruption. 'As I told you before, that is merely your father's distrustful mind.' She put a hand up to her wig to check if it was still correctly positioned. 'Of course, he has reason to be wary.' She gave Nicholas a searching look.

Glad to have his hands released from her grasp, he sat back in his chair, eyeing her with equal caution. She seemed to have regained some of her strength, and with it her customary imperiousness.

'Your father resembles his sister to an unusual degree.'

There was a silence as each waited for the other to reveal what they knew. Margaret won.

'I have never met my aunt so I cannot judge her likeness.' Nicholas pressed down on his knee to stop his foot from tapping on the floor.

'Are there no portraits of her?'

'No, I have never seen one,' said Nicholas and for a moment he wished there were. He would like to have seen what his mother looked like when she was a girl.

'Alethea did not die while staying with friends, as my husband believes. I sent her to Deptford in the company of a man I had employed before. He was supposed to ensure she did not return, but later I learnt from my neighbour that she turned up at our London house the next day. We had already left for the country by then. What became of Alethea after that is a mystery.' Lady Margaret stared combatively at Nicholas.

'You were prepared to have my aunt murdered?' So, Father's suspicions had not been excessive.

Margaret looked suddenly stricken. 'I was driven out of my mind with fear. Henry refused to leave London even when the bodies were piling up in the streets. The girl was likely to have died anyway, along with the rest of us. By telling Henry that Alethea had contracted the plague, I was able to persuade him to depart. I convinced him we would have to be shut up in our house otherwise, because the people looked to him to set a good example. I know it was a wicked thing to do. I think I must have been possessed by devils.' She began to cough again, but this time Nicholas found it hard to summon any sympathy for her. 'In any case, Alethea survived, so at least her death is not on my conscience.'

'How do you know she survived?'

Margaret looked shifty. 'Jane once alluded to Alethea as though she were still living. I suspect she has had some communication with her.'

'Lady Jane's friendship with my father must have been very distressing for you,' Nicholas said, determined to persevere in his line of questioning.

'I can assure you I have never again taken any actions so drastic as those I resorted to with your aunt.' She reclined against her pillows.

He suspected now that Margaret didn't know William and Alethea were one and the same, or at least, if she was fishing he wasn't going to take the bait.

'Do you know of a man by the name of Gilbert Staley, ma'am?' he ventured.

She shook her head absently, gazing into the darkness of the chamber once again. 'Why, who is he?'

'Someone interested in Lord Pemberton's allegiances.'

Margaret turned and raised an eyebrow. 'My son-in-law is a loyal subject; you can assure anyone who asks of that.'

'I have, of course.' Nicholas hoped he had not divulged too much.

'You are a fine young man, Mr Hawthorne. I respected your grand-parents and I'm glad to see their noblest traits in you.' She smoothed the quilt out over her knees. 'You might want to think carefully about where the best prospects for yourself and our country lie. For myself, I am glad the King raised such worthy, Protestant princesses.'

'Indeed, Mr Fagel's "Letter" seems to have convinced much of England that our interests are best served by Princess Mary and her husband. I expect you have read it.'

Margaret did not respond immediately. Nicholas was trying to think up something that would draw more information out of her, when the door opened and Jane stepped in.

'How do you fare, Mother?' she asked with forced cheer.

'Well, I shan't return home this evening. The jolting of a carriage would be too much for me,' Margaret said querulously, though her London house was only a few streets away.

Winifred woke with a start and stumbled to her feet. Seeing Nicholas, she bobbed a quick curtsey, then moved hastily to the bed and began brushing down the covers as if anxious to show she was taking care of her mistress.

'Winifred will stay with me. I expect Henry will want to go home.'

Nicholas pitied the waiting-woman having to spend a night in this noxious chamber.

Margaret looked pointedly at her daughter. 'When my hour comes, I hope you will be by my side.'

'Of course I will. But you seem to have rallied a little. Has conversing with our young friend proved restorative?' Jane smiled wearily at Nicholas.

She looked exhausted, he thought with concern. Standing, he offered her his seat, but Jane shook her head.

'Indeed.' Margaret studied Nicholas speculatively. 'He has eased my mind somewhat. I hope I can trust in his discretion.'

Nicholas bowed. 'Utterly.' Feeling every inch the duplicitous rogue, he pressed his right hand to his heart.

It was a relief when Jane ushered him out of the room.

'She often believes herself to be close to death,' Jane whispered as they stood at the top of the stairs, gulping in the slightly fresher air.

'Lady Margaret does seem poorly.'

'She is worse this time,' Jane conceded. 'What did she want to say to you?' She leant heavily on her stick. The candlelight emphasised the dark shadows under her eyes, making her face look almost spectral.

Nicholas didn't want to add to her unhappiness so he said nothing of Alethea. 'She wanted to know what I thought of the King.'

'I see.' Jane frowned. 'Your heroics on the road certainly won her admiration. It was very brave of you to tackle two highwaymen.'

'It was an honour to be of assistance,' Nicholas said.

Much wine appeared to have been imbibed during his short absence from the great hall. The sound of voices amplified by drink filled the large room. Sir Denis and Ambrose were engaged in a rowdy conversation with two middle-aged gentlemen and all four of them broke off to laugh loudly over some shared witticism. A group of city aldermen were in the middle of a heated dispute over taxes. Nicholas wondered what Ned would have been up to had he been there and whether he would think this a grand or fond enough farewell. He'd probably have left for a gaming house or a tavern by now, so perhaps the lack of tearful reminiscences was fitting. To spend the night eulogising him would have been an affectation anyhow.

'We have been waiting to speak with you all evening.'

Nicholas found himself suddenly in the midst of Edward's sisters. Prudence slipped her arm through his, while Lettice fluttered her fan, peeping at him over the top of it, her large eyes full of mischief.

Richard fought his way through the forest of legs and into the family circle. 'You must tell us all about the highwaymen and how you dispatched them,' he cried, pulling on Nicholas's jacket. 'I wanted to ask you earlier, but Mother interrupted.'

To his bewilderment, Nicholas had gained a reputation for heroism with the younger Pembertons, who gathered eagerly round him, demanding a first-hand account of his courageous exploits. Their brother's recent demise seemed far from their thoughts.

'Let the poor man have a cup of wine and a biscuit first, at least,' Lettice commanded. She looked around for a servant, but none could be seen in the crowded room. 'I hope Isaac returns soon, he may be Father's secretary, but Her Ladyship struggles to control the household without him,' she sighed.

Doll dutifully went to fetch some refreshments, which Nicholas, who was tired and hungry by now, consumed gratefully. It was very flattering to have won such admiration and he couldn't help enjoying the rapt attention of his little audience. Even if it did mean eclipsing Ned's memory for a moment.

Waking early the next morning, Nicholas thought at first he must be at sea, the bed was heaving and tossing so. A pair of small feet appeared in his line of vision, disappeared and then landed with a thud, perilously close to his face. He looked up to see Richard, with whom, because of the number of guests, he had had to share a bed. Groaning, he rolled over to his other side, but it was impossible to ignore the boy jumping up and down beside him.

'Awake, awake, the sun has arisen!' Richard chanted breathlessly.

'All right, you win.' Nicholas heaved himself out of bed and over to the wash basin.

'Hooray,' Richard cried, leaping from the bed and running round the room. 'Shall we go to Hyde Park to see the riders?'

Pemberton had told them the previous night about the ambassador of Morocco who was visiting the King; he and his retinue liked to exercise their horses in Hyde Park, where they rode with extraordinary skill, standing upright at full speed, throwing and catching their spears, to the amazement of all the onlookers.

'This afternoon, perhaps.' Nicholas was also eager to see such impressive horsemanship, but wasn't sure it was a suitable pastime during mourning.

After breakfast, having managed to shake off Richard, Nicholas was pleased to discover Lettice alone, reading in the little parlour. It was a bright, airy room with white calico curtains and Lettice looked as though she might be a figure in a painting, sitting as she was in a large, red-striped chair with her feet tucked up beneath her woollen skirts. Her sable mourning clothes set off her fair complexion to good effect. Despite the previous night's burial-feast, her skin looked fresh and rosy. Her golden hair, beautifully curled, was piled high on her head and adorned with black ribbons.

'What are you reading?' He nodded at the slim volume on her lap.

'It is a new work by the woman playwright Aphra Behn, whose play we saw at the theatre.'

'Is it another drama?'

Nicholas put a hand on the back of her chair. Leaning over her shoulder, he could see the pale down on the back of her neck and a red mark where the clasp of her necklace had dug into her skin.

'No, it's quite different to her other writing. Bishop Burnet called her poems obscene.' Lettice paused for a moment, then added with a sly note to her voice, 'Father was not pleased to find my stepmother reading them.'

Taking the book she held up to him, he read out the title as he walked round to face her: '*Oroonoko: or the Royal Slave, A True History*.'

'If it is as honest an account as she claims, it's most shocking. The noblest of African princes and the most beautiful maiden, a "black Venus", are taken as slaves to the West Indies where they are treated despicably.' Lettice studied him artfully for a moment. 'All the men, of every nation, fall in love with Imoinda. Behn says she is more charming than any white beauty. Could you imagine giving your heart to an African lady?'

'I read a history of the Antilles by a Dominican missionary when I was at St. Omers,' Nicholas said, ignoring her question. 'He describes how many of the slaves were lured onto traders' ships under false pretences and then clapped in irons. One, a former queen bought in Guadalupe, carried herself with such a regal air that all who met her were impressed by her dignity.'

'That is just like the heroine of this tragedy.' Lettice clapped her hands together with renewed enthusiasm. 'Their fate is more terrible than any spectacle I have seen on stage, or at a public execution.' She leant forward, her eyes as round as buttons. 'Both choose death and Oroonoko is subjected to a most brutal and gruesome end.' She lowered her voice. 'Whipped and bound, his shameful parts are cut off and thrown in the fire, then they sever his ears, his nose and each of his limbs, one by one. He endures this torture with the utmost nobility, smoking his pipe as if oblivious to the pain and indignity, until death finally claims him.'

That would be Father, Nicholas thought, smoking his pipe until the end. Except, he realised with a shudder, should such a fate befall

Father, his true sex would be exposed. He forced this disturbing image from his mind. At least Matthew had been spared similar humiliations, though he was sure his uncle would have borne them with equal courage.

'Your father owns many slaves in Barbados, I understand,' he said, more sharply than he had intended.

'His Negro servants are quite content. They would never consider rebelling against their master like the slaves in *Oroonoko*.' Lettice sounded quite affronted.

Suddenly irritated by her complacency, Nicholas couldn't help saying, 'Perhaps you should ask Isaac his opinion on the matter. His mother was your mother's slave, was she not?'

Lettice looked at him with astonishment. 'That is quite different. Isaac's mother was not an African queen. She was born a slave.'

Nicholas rapped his knuckles on the book on his knee. 'The history I read tells of a common slave woman who refused to be married off. When asked for an explanation, she shocked the holy fathers by saying she never wanted to conceive a child if it were to endure such miseries as she did. The punishments meted out to slaves are recorded as cruel in the extreme.'

'Father says other European nations treat their slaves much worse than we do. I'm sure the French use their Negroes barbarously.' Lettice shifted in her chair, rearranging her skirts with an injured expression.

'That,' said Nicholas, 'is what is known as a *tu quoque* form of argument.' He drummed his fingertips on the arm of his chair. 'I have no experience of the trade in slaves, only it seems to me, as a principle, to go against all that is Christian. No matter where it takes place. For how can one man own another?'

'Well, of course I haven't had the benefit of a masculine education and can't avail of your sort of rhetoric.' Lettice sniffed. 'All I have been taught how to do is entertain guests.' She dabbed her nose with a handkerchief.

Nicholas couldn't bear to see her looking so aggrieved. 'Which duty you perform with great skill and elegance,' he said hastily. 'Forgive me, I am more used to the company of students than of ladies.'

'Behn's book is not flattering to the English settlers, to be sure,' Lettice conceded, smiling cautiously at him. 'One day I should like to preside over private assemblies like the Parisian ladies do. To host entertainments where men and women will be able to discuss all the topics of the day quite freely. They say Madam Mazarin's house, by St. James's Palace, is such a place, but Father won't allow me to go there because he does not consider it respectable. He is all for Mrs Middleton, though there is gossip about her establishment too.'

'Who is Mrs Middleton?' Nicholas asked.

'Jane Middleton, one of the most famous beauties in London. Don't tell me you've never heard of her?' Lettice shook her head at him with mock incredulity at his ignorance. 'There are portraits of her all over the place.' Lettice leant forward in her chair. 'She was thrown out of the Queen's drawing room recently for arguing with Her Majesty. Mrs Middleton is not afraid to criticise the Court, for which she gains much praise.'

'And what is the nature of her criticism?'

Lettice shrugged. 'The same as most people's: the King's tyrannical, papist tendencies.'

'And your father approves of her stance?' He leafed through the pages of *Oroonoko*, feigning indifference.

Lettice was not to be drawn. 'You will have to ask him about that.' She got up and retrieved her book from him. 'For my part, I'd rather visit Lady Mazarin's, even if she is French and a Catholic.' She wrinkled her nose. 'It is said Mrs Middleton gives off a sour smell, which gets worse when she grows warm.'

Nicholas laughed. 'That is unfortunate; I was going to offer to accompany you – if we are allowed to visit her.' If Mrs Middleton was such a public critic of the King, it might be the place to pick up more information on those with Dutch allegiances.

Lettice looked delighted. 'Will you ask Father?'

'Certainly. I was intending to ask him if he would like me to stay on in London. That is, if I can assist him in any way.'

Lettice gazed at him with uncharacteristic earnestness. 'Father esteems you highly. You have been a great comfort to him. We're all very grateful.'

Lettice would despise him if she knew the truth. And yet, if he was bringing the Pembertons some solace, his mission was not entirely without virtue. Nor were his motives wicked, for besides protecting his own parent, he did genuinely desire to comfort them in their grief.

'I wish I could have been the bearer of happier tidings.'

'I hope Ned did not suffer at the end.' There was a slight tremor in Lettice's voice. 'He was always prone to sickness, but I did not expect it to carry him away so soon. He seemed quite well last time I saw him.'

Nicholas thought of Edward's emaciated, pox-ridden body and did his best to smile reassuringly. 'He is at peace with his Maker now, I am sure.'

'God bless his soul,' Lettice said dutifully.

Looking up from his desk, Lord Pemberton gave Nicholas a wan smile. In contrast to his daughter, the dull black of his mourning suit drew all the colour from his face, turning it an ashy grey. He had aged by a decade in the week since Nicholas had informed him of Edward's death. His plump rosy cheeks had fallen in and the skin hung in folds beneath his leaden eyes.

'The good Lord gave me two sons and He saw fit to take one away.' Pemberton shuffled the papers on his desk into a neat pile. 'Richard admires you, Nicholas. Help me to keep him free of his brother's temptations. Set him a good example.'

'I will do all I can, sir.' As Nicholas bowed, he couldn't help but think of Pemberton's third son, who had also been taken away.

Pemberton nodded. 'It is good to have you here; you've raised the spirits of Jane and the children.'

'I am glad to offer whatever service I can, sir.'

'Come, let us sit by the fire.' Pemberton rose from behind his desk, waving Nicholas towards a seat in front of the huge fireplace.

Nicholas glanced at the cupboard as he passed it, wondering what seditious material it might contain now. The fire was almost out, but Pemberton seemed oblivious to how cold the room was.

'Shall I throw a couple of logs on?' he asked.

'Yes, do,' Pemberton agreed absentmindedly. 'That wretched page should have been in to see to it.' Reaching for the decanter placed on a side table, he poured them each a glass of port-wine before sitting down.

'Have you had any further communication with Father Petre, sir?'

'I attended one of his Masses,' Pemberton said with studied nonchalance. 'How gaudy they have made the Chapel Royal; everywhere you look there are statues and paintings. It was entertaining, I suppose, and the dean was gracious enough, but he was too taken up with the Earl of Melfort to spare me more than a few pleasantries.' He took a mouthful of wine. 'I received a death threat, you know. Some anonymous coward wrote that if I cared for my life, I'd go over to Rome.'

Appalled, Nicholas wondered if Staley would stoop to such measures.

Pemberton was watching him through narrowed eyes. 'It's set me against papism altogether. I shan't be coerced.'

'Of course not, sir,' Nicholas replied quickly. 'A lot of people have been discussing a pamphlet; perhaps you have heard of it – it was written by a Heer Fagel. It has convinced many that Prince William and Princess Mary would make better monarchs than King James.'

'And you?' Pemberton stretched out his legs. 'What is your opinion?'

Nicholas thought of Benoist and of the promises for toleration made in Fagel's 'Letter'. 'I believe true Christians should show each other mercy,' he said quietly.

'Amen to that.' Lord Pemberton raised his glass and Nicholas also took a sip of the sweet wine. Pemberton immediately topped his glass up. 'Perhaps, in the spring, you might carry a letter for me to an old friend of mine in the Low Countries. A great collector of botanical specimens.'

'I would be honoured, sir.' At last, he might have something tangible to offer Staley. Hopefully it would be enough to keep Father safe.

'I don't want to interrupt your studies at Oxford.' Taking the wrought-iron poker that was leaning against the wall, Pemberton pushed a burning log back from the edge of the grate. 'Usually Isaac is my messenger, but he is currently detained elsewhere.' He stabbed at the log, releasing a flurry of orange sparks. 'The contents concern personal transactions only. But now all letters are opened and so much post is being seized at the ports, it is hard to get anything through, no matter how innocent.'

'I'd be happy to take the risk,' Nicholas said, trying to temper his eagerness. 'My colleagues at Magdalen will understand. I'll promise them a paper on your friend's collection, with his permission of course.'

'I am sure Mr Van Dorp would be delighted to give you a tour and share his knowledge of the botanical world with you.'

Was Pemberton testing his loyalty? Despite being told what a comfort he was to the family, Isaac's arrest weighed heavily on Nicholas's conscience. Perhaps this errand to the United Provinces was a trap, a means of vengeance for Isaac's detention.

Hoping to draw his host out further, he asked if Isaac was expected back soon, adding, 'He is so much a part of your household, his presence must be missed.'

Pemberton's countenance, which had lifted momentarily, sank again, and he held Nicholas's gaze with a mixture of sorrow and distrust. 'I hope he will be home before long.'

'Of course.' Nicholas nodded vigorously.

There followed a lengthy silence and, desperate to fill it, Nicholas asked if he might take Lettice to visit Mrs Middleton. This at least had the effect of rousing Pemberton from his reverie.

'That is quite out of the question. If you understood society better, you would never have asked it,' he said irritably. 'When Lettice is married she may visit such establishments with the permission of her husband. It is not a place for young ladies.'

'I beg your pardon, sir. I didn't mean to cause offence.' Nicholas was dismayed to have squandered any good standing he might have with Pemberton so quickly.

'Oh, I don't blame you.' Pemberton held his glass up to the fire, observing the illumination of the red-amber liquid. 'I know my daughter. She has planted the idea in your head no doubt, the little minx. I ought to have married her off years ago, but Jane talked me out of it.' He swallowed another mouthful of port. 'My first wife was fourteen when we wed. I was only twenty-five. She needed an older husband, really, a man with the patience to train her to his hand. She was headstrong like Lettice and I was a bit of a rake back then, didn't have much interest in my young bride. But you must have sown a few wild oats yourself. The priests can't have kept you locked away the whole time, hey?'

Nicholas thought of Isabelle and blushed.

Pemberton raised his eyebrows. 'Good lad, I hope you took advantage of the French *demoiselles*. We may not like their king but they breed fine fillies.'

Pemberton was starting to remind Nicholas of Edward. 'Your first wife was raised in the West Indies, I understand?' he asked, thinking of Isaac.

'I didn't meet her until our wedding day in England. It was a relief she was almost as pretty as her portrait showed her, only not half so cheerful-looking.' Pemberton's lips curled into an ironic smile, then dropped again. 'Elizabeth proved an excellent mother in the end. Until her sad demise, of course. Thank the Lord she was spared the trouble her first-born has caused us.'

'God rest his soul,' Nicholas answered automatically.

Pemberton nodded, but he did not look as despondent as he had when speaking of Isaac, and Nicholas wondered if he had been attributing Pemberton's grief-worn appearance to the wrong son.

Once back in his room, Nicholas wrote a coded letter to Staley, care of the Jesuit school in Fenchurch Street. He would find an errand boy to deliver it when he went out to Hyde Park with Richard. Spending a few hours in the company of the guileless and cheerful little lad would be a welcome relief from the manifold intrigues of his adult life.

Just as he and Richard were leaving, however, Lettice appeared in the hall.

'We are going to see the Moorish riders,' Richard told her excitedly.

'Perhaps I will accompany you.' She looked expectantly at Nicholas.

Richard tugged Nicholas's hand, his face creased with anxiety. 'If we don't go now we will miss them.' He knew only too well how long his sister took to get ready for any outing.

Nicholas was torn between wanting Lettice to join them and knowing that her inquisitive presence would make it much harder for him to dispatch his letter. 'Perhaps, given the circumstances, it would be better if I take the boy on his own,' he said, gesturing to her mourning attire.

She looked surprised and wounded by this unexpected rejection. 'Very well. I am sure you are right,' After an elaborate curtsey, she returned to the parlour with a sweep of her skirts.

Nicholas sighed. It was hard to relinquish her company, but besides the letter in his pocket, he also had her father to consider. He could not risk angering Lord Pemberton. At least her father's Dutch errand guaranteed further visits to the Pemberton household and the possibility of continuing their friendship. When he was back in Oxford, he would look for some books that might interest her. Lord Pemberton would surely not object to a philosophical correspondence; one where Nicholas might act as tutor in a purely Platonic exchange. Cheered by this prospect, he smiled down at Richard.

'Come on, then,' he said. 'What are we waiting for?'

✦ Chapter Twenty-Two ✦

April 1688

He had been assured Staley would arrive soon, but Nicholas had already been waiting for at least an hour. Rising from the low wooden stool he had been directed to, he wandered over to the window where he stood easing out his cramped legs and watching the narrow street below. If Staley didn't get here within the next half-hour, he would have to ignore the instructions he had been sent and hurry to Gravesend. He couldn't risk missing his ship. How would he explain that to Lord Pemberton?

He felt for the letters in his pocket. One was an introduction to Mr Van Dorp, the plant collector; the second, a private missive, was sealed. Pemberton had told him to guard it carefully and put it only into the hand of Mr Van Dorp himself. An order he was about to betray.

It had taken Pemberton so long to write with arrangements for this journey, Nicholas had begun to think he had decided against sending him to Holland. But he was very glad to be travelling in late April, now the weather was better and Mr Van Dorp's gardens would be coming into bloom. He was only sorry that he had missed Lettice, who was out of town, visiting friends in the country. He had sent her a treatise on the value of Seraphic friendship and received a very witty reply, one he had hoped to respond to in person. Perhaps she would be back in London when he returned and they could resume their discussions then.

'I hear you're doing well at Oxford.' Staley strode into the classroom, tossing his hat onto the schoolmaster's desk and dropping onto the seat behind it.

Nicholas forced himself to bow. He hadn't realised his academic advancement was of any interest to Staley. 'I have received some praise for my work and am making progress on the classification of plants for Mr Bobart's encyclopaedia.'

'Very good.' Staley held out a gloved hand. 'So, you may have something significant at last.'

Nicholas could smell the musk and ambergris used to perfume the leather. For a moment he wished he had his sketch of Waddington to slap down on the upturned palm. That would disconcert the knave. But Staley's watery blue eyes were regarding Nicholas with a mixture of boredom and contempt, and he realised it would take more than a childish portrait to unnerve the man.

Crewe had told him not to refer to Lawrence Gascoigne until he worked out the best use for such information, so Nicholas would have to bite his tongue on that matter too.

Staley scanned the letter of introduction and passed it back to Nicholas. He held the second letter up to the window, looking at it from every angle.

'The folding doesn't appear too complicated. I don't think it is designed to tear if opened incorrectly. But that in itself might be a ruse to make the letter look innocuous. We will know more when we prise the seal off.'

Staley pulled off his gloves, finger by finger, then removed two phials of liquid and a small bowl from a wooden box. Mixing a couple of drops of liquid from each bottle, he applied them to the seal with a brush. Nicholas watched with fascination as the seal softened enough for Staley to lift it from the paper without destroying it.

Staley spent so long reading the letter, Nicholas resumed his seat. 'What does it say?' he asked at last.

'I don't think it is necessary for you to know.'

Nicholas felt tempted to snatch the letter from Staley's hand and read it himself. The man's disdain was infuriating.

'At least it's in Latin and not Dutch.' Staley appeared to take pity on Nicholas, or perhaps he just enjoyed toying with him. 'Pemberton is making marriage arrangements for his eldest daughter. He was negotiating with Lord Titheredge, a staunch supporter of the King's, but he has changed his mind it seems and now prefers Van Dorp.'

Lord Titheredge – Nicholas vaguely remembered Lettice referring to a family visit to his country estate in Hampshire. Of course, he could never have been in the running for her hand, but still, the news pained Nicholas more than he had anticipated. *After pride comes a fall*, he could hear Abigail telling him.

Staley frowned and his voice became graver. 'He then says that since their friend's visit to England is now assured, he would like to cement the union of our nations with his own daughter's wedding. There must have been other, more important communications we have missed. Who has assured Pemberton that the Prince of Orange is set to invade and why are they so confident of his success?'

'Perhaps they overreach themselves,' Nicholas said hopefully, then, seeing Staley's expression, added, 'The pamphleteering of the Dutch is winning over the people and I am sure Pemberton is involved, if not in the writing then in the dissemination of their lies.'

'What do you think we were questioning his man about?' Staley replied testily.

'And what has happened to Isaac Smith?'

'That is not your concern.'

'Except it is,' Nicholas exclaimed. 'Isaac is innocent of any wrongdoing and I care for the fate of a fellow Christian, as any decent man should.'

Staley looked amused. 'Are you enamoured of the blackamoor?'

'Of course not.' Nicholas swallowed down his anger. If Staley was trying to bait him, he would not rise to it. 'I may know more about Isaac than you think.'

'Pray tell.' Staley surveyed him quizzically.

This time, Nicholas was not going to give up his information so easily. 'What about my cousin, Father Matthew? You still haven't told me who betrayed him.'

'Let me reseal the letter,' Staley said with a sigh.

Nicholas waited impatiently while Staley painstakingly refolded and resealed Pemberton's letter. Finally it was returned and Nicholas slid it carefully into his bag.

Next he was made to wait again while Staley got out his tobacco, inhaled a large pinch of snuff and then blew his nose with a red handkerchief. Nicholas drummed his fingers on the desk until Staley looked pointedly at them with raised eyebrows.

Leaning back in the rector's chair, Staley gazed up at the ceiling. 'What if there was no betrayer? No Judas in your midst.'

'What do you mean?'

'At the time of your cousin's arrest, several Harcourts were being pursued. One of them was particularly important to our mission. Though of course every one of them was vital.' Staley gave him a condescending smile. 'This particular Harcourt had information that, had he been forced to give it up, would have led to the destruction of our network in Britain. A decoy was needed. Another Harcourt to stand in for that one. Your cousin offered up himself.' Staley blew his nose again. 'Father Matthew was remarkable under questioning; not only did he throw them off the scent of the other Harcourt, he also managed to convince them that he was innocent of any involvement in the fabricated plot. Not to mention keeping you and your father safe.'

A wave of nausea swept up from Nicholas's stomach to his throat. He knew the kind of questioning Matthew would have been subjected to and how extreme the torture must have been for Staley to consider his fortitude exceptional.

'But he hid when the soldiers came.' That day was still as vivid in Nicholas's mind as if it had taken place only the week before.

'Of course. It wouldn't have worked if he'd handed himself in to the constable, would it? An anonymous letter was sent, informing the authorities that Father Harcourt was in residence at Measham Hall.'

Nicholas felt like punching Staley's sneering face. How could he tell his father that Matthew had willingly submitted to his own destruction? That all those whom Father had suspected of betrayal were innocent, while Matthew had exposed them to danger? Forcing himself to remain calm, he addressed Staley.

'I've brought you this letter and you have admitted that Matthew did the Jesuits a great service. Surely my father should be released from your threats of exposure?'

'*Ad maiorem Dei gloriam.* Have you forgotten that all we do is for the greater glory of God?'

'Worming and lying don't glorify God.' Nicholas spoke through clenched teeth. 'And neither does extortion.'

'We do what we must. Your cousin was honoured to die in the Lord's service.' Staley shook his head as if in sorrow. 'We haven't finished with you just yet, Master Hawthorne. As you have pointed out, Pemberton is most certainly involved in the pamphleteering that is doing the King so much harm. You must deliver this letter and discover what you can in Holland. It is useful to have you in Van Dorp's house. The man must be wealthy for Pemberton to want him as a son-in-law and wealth ensures connections to power, if not power itself. Find out who else among the King's advisors has moved their allegiance to the House of Orange.'

Nicholas thought of Churchill, but could not bring himself to say another word to Staley. Rising from his chair, he marched out. He might be Staley's dog, but he would not come to heel.

Mr Van Dorp may have been the fortunate possessor of the richest and most extraordinary villa and gardens Nicholas had ever seen, but he was not, Nicholas couldn't help feeling, a suitable husband for Lettice. For a start he was at least twenty years older than she was and while he knew that was not a disadvantage to many men's minds, he did not think Lettice would find the considerable distance in ages favourable.

If he had been handsome, perhaps she would not mind so much, but Van Dorp was a singularly ugly gentleman. His starched collar was no substitute for the absence of a perceptible jawline and the stiff material appeared to be the only thing preventing his face from melting into his neck. His discoloured teeth followed the direction of his chin in slanting back towards his throat. They were also housed in a mean little mouth with thin, colourless lips. Van Dorp's nose was probably his best feature, but the small eyes perched above it were at too close a proximity. Nicholas couldn't bear the thought of this man pressing kisses on beautiful Lettice. And he was convinced she would find her betrothed very dull; it was hard to imagine Van Dorp laughing, attending the theatre or discussing novels.

Nicholas was unable to elicit anything much in the way of light conversation from Mr Van Dorp. Neither was he to be drawn on his own political allegiances or anyone else's, though judging by the number of orange trees in his hot-house, his support for Prince William was plain to see. From the talk that Nicholas could follow, the Dutch seemed to be more concerned with the threat from France and a new war with the French than affairs in England. Nicholas asked Van Dorp if he had many English visitors.

'My plants are of interest to people from all over the world,' was all Heer Van Dorp would say.

The gardens consisted of a series of squares boxed in by high hedges, giving each one an air of privacy. Walking through them was rather like being in an enormous maze. Each square had its own special feature. In one was a grotto made entirely out of shells. Another had the most unusual plants growing out of and around elaborate rockwork. Most pleasing to the eye were the plantings of tulips arranged in formal patterns, but with petals of a great medley of colours: yellow, crimson, purple and white.

Although he was at liberty to roam the grounds as he pleased, Nicholas was never alone, for there were always gardeners or servants nearby and he was conscious of being watched. He hoped to search the outbuildings for a printing press, but was never able to enter them without someone appearing at his elbow with an offer of assistance, steering him in another direction.

It was also frustrating not being able to explore the United Provinces properly. He would have liked to travel by barge to Amsterdam and Leiden, but Pemberton had told him to hurry back with an answer. There was also Staley to consider.

As he wandered the house and grounds, awaiting Van Dorp's response to Pemberton, Matthew's deception weighed heavily on Nicholas's mind. At times he was filled with fury that Matthew had willingly abandoned them and not only that, he had also exposed them to terrible danger. He would have to tell Father in person and when he was in an angry humour, he held this against Matthew too. Now he sympathised with Father's frustration when Matthew had refused to take the oaths that might have saved him. Father's lack of reverence towards his brother's martyrdom was also more understandable.

But then, Nicholas couldn't help admiring Matthew's absolute devotion to his Maker. He was proud of his uncle's bravery and knew Matthew believed he and Father and Crewe were all as courageous and devout as he was. Matthew would not impose a cross too heavy for them to bear, he told himself, though he suspected Father might disagree.

A week after his arrival, Van Dorp handed over a letter for Pemberton and Nicholas set sail back to England. On his way from the docks, he stopped off at Fenchurch Street, but Staley was not in London and stony-faced Mr Northleigh was unsure when he would return. He had left no instructions.

How typical of Staley to be so aggravating. What was he supposed to do with the letter? He couldn't delay giving it to Pemberton indefinitely.

Taking a private room at an inn nearby, Nicholas sat down with the folded parchment. It had a thick seal with Van Dorp's crest imprinted on it. A candle glowed on the table by his elbow. What if he prised the seal off with his knife and then warmed the back enough to stick it back on? He picked gently at the wax with a fingernail. It was stuck fast, the paper rising with it. Without Staley's chemicals there was no way of removing the seal without tearing the paper.

He held the letter up to the light as Staley had done. Fine lines of densely packed writing sloped across the page, but they weren't clear enough for him to read. He scratched his head with frustration. It wasn't his fault if Staley was absent and had failed to tell him what to do.

Given his business interests, Pemberton was bound to be kept up to date on the ships crossing the Channel. It would be unwise for Nicholas to pretend he had been delayed by bad weather. Pemberton might even have been alerted to his presence in London already. There was nothing else for it: he would deliver the letter and hope to discover its message afterwards.

Pemberton was clearly pleased with the contents. He opened the letter in Nicholas's presence and read it with a look of increasing satisfaction.

'Good news, sir?' Nicholas asked.

But Pemberton only nodded and folded the letter away into his waistcoat pocket.

'My daughter is currently in town; say nothing to her of your trip to Holland. I do not want my competitors in trade to get wind of it and you know what women are like – they must tell everyone they meet of everything, no matter how inconsequential.'

Nicholas couldn't see how Lettice might convey information about her father's business to his competitors, but agreed not to speak of his recent journey.

There was still no sign of Isaac, but he didn't want to show too much interest in him in case he aroused Pemberton's suspicions.

How sick he was of all this subterfuge. His life seemed to be comprised of ever-increasing webs of lies. When he thought of Robin, working nearby in his honest trade, Nicholas couldn't help wishing that Ellen had been his mother. But then, no one was quite what they seemed, and Ellen too had her secrets.

Lettice was in the dining room when he came down for breakfast the next morning, feeding slices of apple to a large grey parrot through the bars of its cage. The delight radiating from her face when she saw him almost broke Nicholas's heart.

'Isn't he beautiful?' She indicated the bird. 'Sent all the way from the Americas.'

Nicholas examined the parrot with equal enthusiasm. 'I should like to make a sketch of him. But must he be always kept in a cage?'

'For the time being. I hope eventually to train him like a hawk, so that we can let him fly around the gardens in Kent.'

They both watched as the parrot shifted from one foot to the other on its little perch. It gazed back at them warily with its round black eyes. They were standing so closely together Nicholas could feel the rise and fall of Lettice's breast against his arm as she breathed. She smelt of spring flowers and a slight feminine muskiness. Forgetting his high principles regarding Platonic or Seraphic friendships, he had a sudden urge to pull her to him and press his lips to her smooth pink cheek. How could such loveliness be destined for the rusty arms of Mr Van Dorp?

'Have at your bum!' the parrot screeched, making them both leap back, startled, from his cage.

'He speaks.' Lettice laughed and Nicholas joined in, relieved she was not so delicate as to be affronted.

'You will have to teach him better manners before you release him to your neighbours.'

'*La dildo, dildido,*' the parrot sang as if in reply.

'At least that is harmless nonsense.' Lettice gave an arch smile and Nicholas couldn't be sure if she knew the word's meaning or not.

'I hope your future husband will let you keep such a free-speaking bird,' he said without thinking.

She laid her fingers on his sleeve for a moment. 'Would you allow me such pets if you were my husband?'

Again, he couldn't be sure if she was sincere or merely teasing him. He decided to continue in a playful vein. 'I would be so completely your slave I would make a sorry cuckold of a spouse.'

'If you were my husband, I would never betray you,' she replied with mock-indignation.

'I could never be worthy of your devotion.'

'Then you will have to perform further heroic acts in order to earn it.'

Nicholas felt then like the greatest coward on earth. Far from being heroic, he was creeping around, spying on her father and acting as an emissary for her marriage to a man he was convinced would not appreciate or nurture the sort of woman she was. It was cruel to keep her in ignorance of her fate, yet it was not his place to inform her.

He needed to discover exactly what was in that letter, but for all he knew, Pemberton had burnt it by now. How frustrating it was that he had carried it all this way and still did not know what it said. He would have to make another foray into Pemberton's study; the trouble was Pemberton now spent much of his time there. He clearly found it a place of refuge from the rest of the household, which was still struggling to maintain the seamless organisation it had enjoyed when Isaac was in residence, for the man seemed to fulfil the duties of a steward as well as a secretary.

As if summoned by the devil, Pemberton himself stepped into the dining room.

'Good morning, Father.' Lettice gave him a solicitous smile. 'Did you sleep any better last night?'

'A little, my dear, a little.' Pemberton pressed the bridge of his nose as if to relieve some pressure there. He was still only a shadow of the robust, cheerful man, Nicholas had first been introduced to.

'Her Ladyship has gone to visit her mother,' Lettice informed him, then, turning to Nicholas, added, 'Lady Calverton is unwell again.'

Pemberton rolled his eyes and called for the footman to bring him a cup of whey. Nicholas noticed that he was wearing the same waist-coat as the previous day. Might he have left the letter in its pocket?

'Lady Margaret would do better to stay in the country,' Pemberton remarked, turning to a copy of the *London Gazette*, which had been left on the table.

As Pemberton reached to pick it up, Nicholas was sure he could see a corner of the letter sticking out of his pocket. Pemberton was sitting at the head of the table, with Nicholas and Lettice on either side of him. If he could be sufficiently distracted, it wouldn't be hard to tug the paper from his pocket, but it would take the skill of a pickpocket to purloin it without either Lettice or her father noticing. He looked up at the parrot, willing it to squawk some obscenity, but it was standing on one leg with its eyes closed.

On an impulse, Nicholas leant across the table, knocking Lettice's pot of chocolate towards Pemberton. The lid was dislodged and thick, brown liquid cascaded over the newspaper towards his lap. Nicholas had hit the pot with enough force to send a few drops upwards and to his delight, a couple landed on the rose-pink silk of Pemberton's waistcoat. Leaping to his feet, Nicholas applied his handkerchief to Pemberton's vest, while Lettice and the servant, who had finally appeared, did their best to stem the tide of chocolate before it reached his lap. Pemberton himself sat as if immobilised while the others fussed around him.

'Please forgive my clumsiness,' Nicholas said, enclosing the letter within his handkerchief and stuffing the two into his own pocket.

'Thank goodness the chocolate had gone cold, at least,' Lettice said reprovingly.

'It may stain, though,' Pemberton grumbled. 'I'll change my clothes and you can take these to be washed,' he told the boy, whose own coat had also acquired a spattering of chocolate.

Nicholas could only pray that Pemberton was sufficiently distracted not to look immediately for his letter.

Complaining that this was why he preferred to breakfast alone and that these sort of accidents never occurred when Isaac was at home, Pemberton left the room. Making his excuses to Lettice, Nicholas followed swiftly after. As soon as he got to his own chamber, he opened and read the letter. It was, like the earlier one, written in Latin. Van Dorp accepted the generous dowry his future wife would bring with her and thanked Pemberton for promising a portion of it in advance. This would, as agreed, be used towards the provisioning of merchant ships for their mutual friend's new enterprise and thus help to ensure its success. The peace and prosperity of both nations would benefit from their alliance.

Nicholas's stomach turned. If Staley was correct, Pemberton was helping to fund the Dutch fleet and Lettice's marriage was both the pretext for the transaction and its prize. If there were to be a Dutch invasion of England, or even a war with France, as the talk had been in Holland, Pemberton would be implicated. That Lettice was to be wed to a man entirely unsuited to her in age and character was neither here nor there.

Pemberton's voice rose through the house; he was shouting for his boy. Fearing he had discovered the disappearance of his letter, Nicholas ran back downstairs with it. By this time the dining room was empty and he was able to drop the letter onto the seat of Pemberton's chair. The parrot flapped his wings and bowed his head. Nicholas put a finger to his lips as he backed out of the room, praying the bird wouldn't expose him. The parrot's eyes seemed to expand and contract, almost as if he were giving a conspiratorial wink.

As Nicholas reached the door, however, it let out a low whistle. 'Pretty fellow,' it cried, fanning out its tail.

Nicholas collided with Pemberton's page, who was entering the room behind him.

'Sorry, sir,' the boy said, sidling round him. 'Just looking for something for His Lordship.'

'Can I help?' Nicholas asked. Then, waving at the parrot, added, 'I was examining this extraordinary bird.'

But the boy had spotted Pemberton's letter. He held it aloft with a triumphant smile, gave a quick bow and raced out. He was in such a hurry, Nicholas could see no reason why the page should mention bumping into him to his master. The parrot gave another whistle and Nicholas also hastened away.

He went once again to Fenchurch Street and left an urgent message for Staley. The schoolmaster still had no idea of the man's whereabouts or when he would return. Nicholas wondered if he ought to seek another audience with Petre, but without Staley's confirmation that the letter referred to a planned invasion by the Prince of Orange, it did not seem conclusive enough to share with the dean and he did not even have the actual dispatch in his possession, but could only relate the contents. He didn't want to raise a false alarm or make a name for himself as some fantastical braggart and besides, he'd rather not become any more deeply embroiled in the whole miserable spying business than he had to.

Trinity term sped quickly by. Although he was still viewed with mistrust by many of his fellow scholars, Nicholas had accrued a small circle of devoted students, whom he enjoyed teaching. In mid-May, however, the King stirred up more hostility towards himself, and papists in general, by sending the Archbishop of Canterbury and six bishops to the Tower for signing a petition against his Declaration of Indulgence, which they refused to read out at church services. In taverns and coffeehouses, it was all anyone spoke about. As far as most people were concerned, the arrests of Church of England bishops were proof that James was becoming a tyrant, intent upon destroying English liberties.

Despite the tensions in England, Nicholas decided with relief that he must have been wrong about a Dutch invasion after all. Nothing came back from Staley, not a letter or a messenger, and Nicholas dared to hope that he had moved on from this particular intrigue. It was possible Crewe had managed to call Staley off, or perhaps he had gone too far in tormenting someone else and they had run him through with a sword. Nicholas would feel no pity for Staley if that were the case.

He and Lettice continued to correspond on matters philosophical and literary. Conscious that his letters were probably inspected by Lord Pemberton or Jane, Nicholas was careful never to stray from strictly academic discourse, though Lettice also wrote very amusingly about her sisters and acquaintances. No mention was made of any betrothal and he could only assume that her father had still not informed her. Part of him could not help hoping the wedding had been called off. Perhaps if the invasion wasn't going ahead then neither was the marriage.

At the end of term, he returned home to Measham Hall. He had anticipated some awkwardness with Father, not having seen him since his astonishing revelations. But as soon as they were together again, custom overcame novelty and his eyes, so habituated to seeing Father as a man, resumed their comfortable perception. He and John Thornley avoided one another and Nicholas pushed any thoughts of where Father might be during his frequent absences firmly out of his mind.

He had been waiting to tell Father in person what he had learnt about Matthew and, knowing Father would be both hurt and angry, he chose his moment carefully. They were walking around the gardens together one evening, discussing where the cuttings and seeds Nicholas had brought from Oxford would be best planted. The June air was laden with the rich and soothing scents of roses, syringa and honeysuckle. Nicholas tried to ensure Father was in the best possible frame of mind by admiring his latest additions to the physic garden and, as Father led him through the new beech grove, agreeing that there could not be anywhere in the world so beautiful as Measham.

'Let's sit for a moment.'

Nicholas stopped by a stone bench and when they were seated side by side, Father with a lit pipe in his mouth, he recounted all that had passed over these last few months and what Staley had revealed – that Matthew had chosen to sacrifice himself in order to save another priest with the same alias. As first, Father refused to believe what he called 'a damned pack of lies', but once his ire had abated, he conceded that it was in keeping with Matthew's character to martyrise himself.

'And he shielded you from prosecution,' Nicholas pointed out.

'I would expect no less.' Father threw the stick the dog had dropped at his feet. It tumbled along the path, pursued by Artemis. 'Are you freed now, from this Jesuitical espionage?'

'I've had no communication from Staley since April, so perhaps I am.'

Father put his arm through Nicholas's, hugging it to his side in an unaccustomed act of affection. 'I do hope so. I pray every day for God to keep you safe and not to deliver on you any punishment for my sins.'

The sun was dropping behind the hill and choruses of birdsong and clacking frogs rose up all around them.

'"May the gods of the underworld free us from war",' Nicholas said. '"And let those who want to fight, do so in their own fields."'

'What's that from?'

'An antique play called *The Frogs*.'

Father nodded. 'I shall always think of that now when I hear them croaking.'

They returned to the house to find Crewe beaming from ear to ear. 'The King and Queen have been blessed with a prince,' he announced. It was some time since Nicholas had seen the old man look so happy. 'A baby boy safely delivered on the tenth of June.'

The following Sunday, Nicholas and many of their servants accompanied Father to a thanksgiving service at Measham church. Copies of the service, as ordered by the King, were handed to those of the parishioners who could read. Most followed the prayer, where they were asked to offer up thanks that, 'although their manifold sins had most justly provoked God into taking so many of the Royal Progeny', he had remembered mercy, 'and begun to repair their former losses by renewing fruitfulness to the Queen, and giving birth to a Royal Prince.' They faltered, however, when it came to the lines about God having preserved the King 'from the madness of the People' and Nicholas could hear some shuffling and grumbling along the pews.

As the congregation filed out of the church, there was much whispered discussion as to the feasibility of the Queen having been delivered of a boy child at so convenient a time.

'According to her own ladies, the Queen's breasts didn't swell as they should and not one of them has seen so much as a drop of milk come forth from her,' a well-informed matron told her companion.

'And no one was allowed to touch her belly,' her friend murmured. 'I reckon as it were all padding.'

'Cuthbert says they'd a few infants ready to be smuggled into the Queen's chamber through one of them secret passages that runs under the palace,' another woman said over her shoulder, forgetting discretion in her eagerness to join in the conversation.

'That's right,' her husband nodded. 'Some noble's bastard, no doubt. There's enough of them.'

Nudged by his wife, Cuthbert saw Nicholas and his father standing just behind their neighbours and coughed. A hush fell over the little group until they were clear of the porch and out in the churchyard, where they enthusiastically resumed their demolishment of the Queen and her supposed fruitfulness.

'Even if they saw the child come out, they can't say for sure who put it in.' Cuthbert, clearly delighted with his own wit, was holding forth as Nicholas and William passed them.

'Ignorant fools,' Father ranted as they walked home. 'They repeat the malicious slander spread in unlawful newsletters as though it were gospel. I wouldn't even wipe my arse with those sheets. To think of all the Queen has suffered: married off to a foreign prince and sent to a hostile country when she was scarcely more than a child – she is said to have cried for days, you know – and then, after all the babes she has lost, when she finally brings forth a healthy prince, everyone claims it is not hers, even though she gave birth to him in a room packed with witnesses.'

Father was walking so fast they had left the servants some distance behind, which was a relief to Nicholas. Father's sympathy for the Queen's predicament seemed decidedly womanish. It was peculiar to think Father had been delivered of him. So peculiar, he did not dwell on the thought for long. In balance, he supposed Father's compassion was a virtue. Perhaps he was the more complete person, being both male and female.

When, on 29th June, the bishops who had been sent to the Tower by the King were acquitted by a jury, the whole country erupted in celebration. There were fireworks and Pope-burnings in Leicester and Derby. The difference between these and the muted festivities for the new prince's arrival couldn't have been starker. The King may have spent thousands on a spectacular firework display over the Thames for the Queen's up-sitting, but it was the triumph of English law and English bishops that impressed the people, not the recovery of the Queen from a birth most chose to doubt had even occurred.

Conjecture as to the true parentage of the Prince of Wales only increased. Now it was suggested the infant had been smuggled into the Queen's chamber in a warming-pan. 'Of all ridiculous things,' Father spluttered.

Nicholas was disturbed to see pictures, brought over from Holland, that depicted Father Petre and the Queen side by side, rocking the baby's cradle, Petre's hand clasping one of the Queen's breasts.

'She doesn't even like the man!' Although Father did not hold a high opinion of the King, he had become a fervent supporter of the much-maligned Queen.

Nicholas wondered what part Lord Pemberton might have played in spreading these tales and their accompanying illustrations.

As the summer progressed, rumours about a Dutch invasion also grew. There was speculation that the Prince of Orange's fleet would land in Yorkshire and Father feared his army would try to take the Midland counties on their way down to London. With this in mind, he decided to bury their most valuable jewels and plate in the garden to keep them safe from marauding soldiers on both sides.

'I found this among Matthew's things,' he said, coming in from overseeing the digging. Nicholas was in the library reading a recent book by Robert Boyle entitled *A Free Enquiry into the Vulgarly Receiv'd Notion of Nature*. Father placed a gold necklace on the table beside him. 'Thought you might be interested to see it.'

'What is it?' As Nicholas picked up the chain, an oval locket slid off it and onto his lap. He held it for a moment before prising the clasp open with his fingernails.

'The miniature of Lawrence Gascoigne, Matthew's friend.'

'The man you believe told Staley about you?'

'That's right, the man I was supposed to marry.'

Nicholas stared at the picture for a few moments before taking it over to the window to examine it more closely. He turned to Father, his eyes wide. 'This portrait, it's an exact likeness of Staley, or Mr Waddington, or whatever name he goes by now.'

'Are you sure?' Father peered over his shoulder at the young man gazing out of the picture, his watery blue eyes archly downcast and his rosy lips parted in a slight pout.

'His wig is more modest now and he is older of course, but otherwise it is unmistakable.'

'Matthew said that was his own hair.' Father tapped the locket frame with a muddy fingernail. 'He was willing to take the Hawthorne surname if we married. He must enjoy changing his name; I wonder if his character changes with it. How he managed to exert so much influence over my brother, I'll never understand. It was Gascoigne who first persuaded Matthew to attend St. Omers. They met in Paris, you know. Matthew said Gascoigne was devoted to him and would do anything he asked. But Gascoigne didn't have a vocation; he was not a priest.'

'He talks like a priest,' Nicholas said, thinking of his last encounter with Staley.

Father shrugged. 'Like a Jesuit, you mean? Doesn't necessarily signify he's ordained.' Turning away from Nicholas, he leant into the alcove, his eyes fixed on the roses growing beneath the window. 'Maybe it was Gascoigne who convinced Matthew to sacrifice himself. How do we know his story about this other Harcourt is true?'

Nicholas thought back to Staley's expression and tone of voice when he spoke of Matthew. 'I don't believe he pushed Matthew towards the scaffold,' he said slowly. 'Though he has always treated me with contempt, he could not conceal his admiration for Matthew's courage. When he said Matthew was remarkable under questioning, he sounded entirely sincere.'

Father sighed. 'Matthew never spoke of Gascoigne. I thought they had ceased all communications years ago.'

'Perhaps they had,' Nicholas said softly. 'Who knows where Staley got his information from.'

For the first time since they were introduced, Nicholas hoped for another encounter with Staley. The wretch would not look so smug when he was unmasked. Nicholas imagined telling Staley just how disgusted Matthew would be by his former friend's extortion. How low he must have sunk to threaten Matthew's family. Staley could no longer pretend his motives were honourable, for Nicholas understood it was jealousy and spurned love that drove him.

But later, when he reconsidered the prospect, he was not so sure of Staley's motives. The man's religious zeal had seemed genuine. Staley was more likely to repeat the phrase he had used before and insist that he did what he must for the glory of God. Nicholas was not so confident he would ever successfully ruffle that peacock's feathers.

As autumn approached and Nicholas was preparing to return to Oxford, the King announced a general election. By the time Nicholas was settled back in his room at Magdalen, the former heads of the college had also been reinstalled. All this came too late to win back any popularity the King might once have enjoyed and he was forced to call the election off again because of the threat from Holland. Now, most people concluded, it was not a matter of whether the Prince of Orange would invade, but of when and where his navy might land. By mid-October, news spread of an alarming report from the English ambassador at The Hague; the Dutch intended 'an absolute conquest' of England, he warned.

Nicholas wished he had tried to get an audience with Father Petre in order to warn the King, though the proof he'd had was thin and he doubted anyone would have taken him seriously. He waited expectantly for a message from Staley, but nothing was delivered. Then, reading through a week-old copy of the *London Gazette* in the refectory one morning, Nicholas came across an alarming announcement. The body of a man, believed to be a Mr Gilbert Staley, had been dragged from the Thames. The man's throat had been slit. He had been identified by one of the King's advisors at Whitehall for whom he worked occasionally.

Reading the article again, Nicholas was gripped with dismay. When Crewe had told him he would do what he could to silence their oppressor, he surely hadn't intended such desperate measures? Or might

Part III: Becoming a Man

Father, in his grief and anger, have sought revenge on Gascoigne? He quickly chastised himself – neither Father nor Crewe were murderers. There were bound to be many others who wished Staley dead. There was so much violence abroad, he could have been killed for any number of reasons. Nicholas ardently hoped that if the murder was political, he was marginal enough in Staley's affairs not to become a target himself.

Leaving the library the following afternoon, Nicholas bumped into Doctor Paterson, whose advice he had sought over Ned's treatment. The doctor was both dishevelled and distressed. Half his long beard had been pulled out and his gown was torn.

'I have just been subjected to the most dreadful violence by soldiers,' he told Nicholas, wringing his hands.

He was not the only scholar to have complained about being abused by the troopers that had been billeted on Oxford and Nicholas, who had been keeping out of the town since he no longer had to consort with Ned's Roisterers, extended his commiserations.

'You are aware, no doubt, of the great many brothels that have opened since the arrival of the soldiers.'

Nicholas shook his head, wondering if Doctor Paterson still assumed he was the one who had caught the pox.

'I was merely attempting to warn the men of the dangers in store for them should they be lured into such places,' Paterson continued. 'But they are common knaves and would not heed me.'

'I am sorry to hear that, sir.' Nicholas had not realised Paterson was so zealous. He did have a wild-eyed look about him, but perhaps that was only the temporary result of his encounter with the soldiers.

'Did you read my paper?' Noting Nicholas's blank expression, Paterson added, 'On the transportation of whores. I have placed a copy in the library.'

'I have not had the opportunity yet.'

Paterson looked disappointed. 'And your friend, is he cured?'

When Nicholas explained that Ned had died, Doctor Paterson sighed. 'He must have been too far gone for the mercury to drive out the disease.'

Nicholas, whose doubts about the use of mercury had only increased after witnessing Ned's reaction, frowned.

'You must join me in preaching to our sergeants.' Paterson placed a hand on Nicholas's arm. 'Your friend's demise will make a good example for them. Think of the lives you might save.'

Not wanting to join Paterson in a bloodied chin and tattered clothes, Nicholas declined this invitation, pleading other duties.

'We'll lose more men to the French pox than to Dutch swords, you mark my words,' Paterson called after him as he hurried off.

As the weather grew colder, the condition of the nation grew hotter. Hostility towards the King's army increased with the arrival of further troops from Ireland. Before William's forces had even set foot in England there were battles between Catholic and Protestant regiments. Fifty men died in Portsmouth after a skirmish between the Duke of Berwick's regiment and Irish foot soldiers. The Scottish troops were equally disliked by the English populace.

Then, to his delight, Nicholas received a request from Lord Pemberton. Jane and Lettice were in London, due to travel back to Kent to join him. However, there were so many soldiers on the roads he feared for their safety. He had his own servants to accompany them, of course, but both women had insisted on having none other than Nicholas as their travelling companion and protector.

Nicholas immediately wrote back to say it would be an honour to accompany Lady Pemberton and their daughter. Always pleased to see Jane, Nicholas told himself that the eagerness with which he anticipated being in Lettice's company was purely that of a fond friend. His sudden sense of elation at knowing she prized his presence above all others was merely his old longing for a sibling and had nothing to do with any passions of the heart. He knew she was destined to be another man's wife and would not elevate her above her sisters in his affections.

'The soldiers do at least ensure the post is delivered,' Jane noted wryly, looking out of the coach window.

Although there were many soldiers on the road, the impending invasion seemed to have improved their discipline somewhat, or perhaps it was the Pemberton crest on the coach doors that encouraged their officers to keep them in order.

'And yet you would not let me go to Hounslow to see His Majesty's forces training on the heath.' Lettice turned from Jane to Nicholas, who was sitting opposite her, and the sulky frown that had clouded her fair complexion cleared instantly. 'It has become one of the sights of London.'

'As you know full well it is not a place for respectable ladies.' Jane also looked across at Nicholas, lowering her voice as though she could exclude Lettice and her maid from their discourse. 'I was told the tents were full of lewd women there to debauch the soldiers.'

'The King was present most days and there was feasting and fire-works,' Lettice retorted.

'That was the employment of powder for war, not entertainment,' Jane said disapprovingly.

'Since everyone complains about the cost of a standing army, we might at least be entertained by them.' Lettice rolled her eyes at Nicholas, as if assuming he would take her side in the argument.

'I believe there was a great deal of sickness among the soldiers this summer,' he said in a placatory tone.

'It was excessively hot and very stormy. I have never been so relieved by the arrival of autumn.' Jane took out her fan as if to demonstrate her reaction to the heat.

'And yet the news that arrived with the changing season has been so very disturbing.' Lettice pulled on her shawl, elbowing Jane in the ribs.

'Indeed?' For a moment Nicholas expected her to announce her betrothal and his heart pounded in his chest.

'The Dutch invasion?' Lettice looked at him with surprise.

'Of course.' He smiled and shook his head. 'I thought perhaps you were referring to family concerns.' It seemed clear Lettice knew nothing of her future marriage.

'I was speaking only of the weather.' Jane snapped her fan shut.

Nicholas was dismayed by the continued animosity between two women he held so dear. Travelling with them was not turning out to be as enjoyable as he had anticipated.

'Has Isaac returned home yet?' he asked, hoping at least to change the subject.

'Returned home to his Maker,' Lettice said dryly.

'His ship was lost at sea,' Jane said sorrowfully.

'What ship?'

Both women answered at once. Isaac had been on his way to Barbados; he was overseeing some trade business for Lord Pemberton when his ship went down in a storm.

'His Lordship must be distressed to lose such a valuable servant,' Nicholas said, struggling to keep his voice level. He could not believe Pemberton would have willingly sent Isaac on such a long voyage unless it was to get him out of harm's way. If only he had never mentioned Isaac to Staley, Isaac might be living still.

For once the ladies were silent. Jane opened her fan, flapping it rapidly up and down in front of her face. Lettice turned to the window. Only the maid let out a sob, and Nicholas was moved to see that her eyes at least, were as full of tears as his own.

→ Chapter Twenty-Three ←

November 1688

Nicholas and Prudence scrambled up the hillside behind an excited Richard. All around them the air resounded with the roll of drums and the clarion call of trumpets. The insistent tunes throbbed through Nicholas's veins, setting his blood alight and propelling him on to the summit. He took Prue's hand, pulling her up with him. But even the rousing drumbeats and piping hautboys could not prepare them for the sight that met their eyes when they reached the cliff's edge.

Spread out across the Channel was a mighty armada, stretching as far as the eye could see. The grey November sky was filled with sails, like row upon row of laundry pegged out on a giant's washday. There must have been at least three hundred ships and they had all hoisted their colours. The orange, white and blue striped flags of the Dutch prince, along with his orange pennants, flew brazenly atop the masts, borne aloft by an easterly wind.

The whole of the Straits was filled with vessels of every size. You could almost have leapt from one ship to another all the way from Dover to Calais. Great warships flanked the smaller craft and as they passed Dover Castle their guns thundered monstrously, sending reverberations through Nicholas's chest. He grabbed Richard and Prudence, shielding the children beneath his arms. Crowds were amassing around them, their gasps and cries fluttering feebly in the wind as the Dutch drums kept up their triumphal beat. The children wriggled free of his protective embrace to watch the spectacle below.

As the gargantuan fleet sailed by, Nicholas took out the prospective glass Lord Pemberton had lent him and put it to his eye. Through it he could make out merchant ships packed with cavalry and draughthorses, carts and artillery. Soldiers lined the decks in parade formation. There must have been thousands upon thousands of men in total.

'The wind favours them,' a man at his elbow observed. 'I heard our fleet is stuck in the Thames Estuary, unable to move.'

Nicholas doubted the English forces would be capable of holding off an invasion of this magnitude even if they could engage them. Despite the months of rumour and speculation, it was hard to digest the enormity of the scene before him. Lord Pemberton said James's court was in a state of panic and disarray. Nicholas wondered how many men were likely to desert the King's army and join the Dutch.

'So much for the King's Catholic wind keeping the Dutch fleet from our shores,' the woman beside him sneered. 'Seems Prince William has God's blessing now.'

'Is it true? Are we being invaded?' Jane demanded as soon as they returned home. She was sitting by the fire with a piece of embroidery that did not look as if it had advanced since the previous afternoon.

'It's the biggest fleet ever,' Richard shouted, holding his arms out wide as he ran towards her. 'It filled the whole sea.'

'Liar lick-dish,' Doll said scornfully, rising from her seat at the virginals. She had refused to come out with them, preferring to stay at home and practise her music. She was becoming almost as accomplished a musician as Lettice.

'It's true.' Prue's voice was filled with wonder. 'I never thought to see such a thing. 'Twas like a painting of a seascape.'

'They sailed on westwards, so the rumours about them landing in Margate or Ramsgate were wrong,' Nicholas addressed

Lord Pemberton in a more accusatory tone than he had intended. All sorts of destinations for the Dutch fleet had been proposed in recent weeks, from Scotland to Essex, and Nicholas wondered if Pemberton might have been one of those deliberately misleading the King and his navy.

'We must make peace with the House of Orange.' Lord Pemberton shook his head. 'We cannot return to the strife of the late civil wars.'

Nicholas handed him back his prospective glass. 'They are certainly well-prepared. The reports from France were correct in this; there cannot be a greater army in all Christendom. Whatever the King's enemies here say, the Dutch aren't gambling on an English welcome.'

Nicholas had seen, through Pemberton's spyglass, the words on the banner hanging above what could only have been the Prince of Orange's frigate. *For Liberty and the Protestant religion.* He knew many Englishmen were ready to gather behind that flag. If James failed and William was accepted, it would mean the end of Catholic toleration.

Jane looked up at Nicholas, her brow furrowed with concern. Richard curled up beside her like a pet dog, resting his head on her knee so that she was forced to return the embroidery to its basket. She stroked his hair absentmindedly.

'Your father will take it hard.' She spoke softly.

They all looked expectantly at Nicholas. He shrugged and sighed.

'If the French come to the King's aid it will only magnify our sorrows.' Pemberton sat down opposite Jane, on the other side of the fireplace. 'Better to arrive at a peaceable accommodation.'

'Perhaps I should join the Kentish regiment.'

The sense of exhilaration Nicholas had experienced that afternoon as the martial music called to him still lingered in his heart. Surely it was his duty to take up arms in defence of the King. He would feel like a coward if he did nothing while his country was attacked.

Pemberton looked horrified. 'Their commander is deeply unpopular here. He has struggled to find those who will take a commission.'

'I could join a different regiment.'

'Did you see the fleet?' Lettice appeared in the parlour.

'You are looking better, my dear.' Pemberton smiled at her indulgently.

Lettice's parrot, which had never got to fly through the gardens as planned, had been found dead in the bottom of its cage that morning and Lettice had been so upset she'd retired to her bed. 'I sought consolation in prayer as you suggested, Father. I know it is wrong to grieve excessively for an animal.' She perched on the arm of his chair.

'Good girl.' Pemberton patted her arm.

'And how was it?' she addressed Nicholas.

'Magnificent,' he had to admit.

'Nicholas wants to fight them.' Richard pranced around the room, thrusting an imaginary sword back and forth.

'That is very brave of you.' Lettice smiled up at Nicholas, her eyes bright with admiration.

'Very foolish, more like,' Jane responded quickly.

'I advise patience,' Pemberton said. 'Wait to see how things fall out before rushing to take up arms.'

Nicholas nodded. His feelings towards his host were contradictory. He strongly suspected the man of treason, yet Pemberton had always treated him with amiable generosity. And while Pemberton was arranging an underhand marriage for his daughter, he also appeared to be a gentle and loving husband and father. It was clear from his subdued manner and careworn appearance that he was weighed down with grief at the loss of two of his sons, and though this was never alluded to directly, it elicited some sympathy from Nicholas.

Freed from the obligation to spy for Staley, it was easier to enjoy life at Pemberton Manor and Nicholas was not in any hurry to exchange its comforts for a life of hardship and savagery. But then, how could he hide away indoors while his King and his religion were under threat? How disappointed Matthew would be if he chose comfort and security before his duty to God.

He spent the next week with the Pembertons, deliberating over what he should do. The whole household was avid for the news, which Lord Pemberton relayed to them as soon as he received it. On 5th

November, as if to mark the Gunpowder Plot, the Prince of Orange's army came ashore at Torbay. Some days after that, Pemberton read out a pamphlet he had been sent, describing William's entrance into Exeter. The family listened spellbound to the account, which listed regiments from all corners of the globe. Richard was especially enthralled by the 'Laplanders in Bear Skins taken from the Wild Beasts they had Slain, with black Armour and Broad Flaming Swords'.

When it came to the account of 'Two-hundred Blacks brought from the Plantations of the Netherlands in Surinam, dressed in embroidered Caps lined with white Fur, and plumes of white Feathers', Nicholas looked across the table at Lettice and their eyes met in recognition of the book they had discussed about the African prince, Oroonoko, who had been taken to Surinam.

'There were "Fifty Gentlemen, and as many Pages to attend and support the Prince's Banner, bearing this Inscription, GOD and the PROTESTANT RELIGION. After these Rid the Prince on a Milk White Palfrey. Armed Cap a Pee, A Plume of White Feathers on his Head. All in Bright Armour, and forty-two Footmen Running by him"', Pemberton continued.

Richard clasped his hands together beneath his chin. 'I wish I could have seen it.'

'Will they march on London, Father?' Lettice asked, her voice a mixture of fear and longing.

It was difficult to read of such pageantry without desiring to see it for oneself. As events progressed, it was also hard not to admire William's troops, who were said to be more disciplined and respectful than the King's roguish army. If it had not been for their differences in religion, even Nicholas might have been tempted to switch his allegiance, especially when the news came that King James, having marched to Salisbury to meet the enemy, had run back to London while William's army was still over sixty miles away. It was said the King was suffering from nosebleeds and had given in to a shameful panic.

More and more officers were defecting to Prince William's side. Included in their number was Lord Churchill, Henry Calverton's friend. Even King James's own daughter, Anne, was now supporting her sister and the House of Orange. Nicholas heard with alarm that the towns of Leicester and Derby had declared for the invader. He waited anxiously for word from Measham Hall, afraid they would be attacked by the violent anti-papists who were, according to the newsletters, rioting in several cities, burning down Catholic chapels and schools.

The Queen fled with the infant prince to France. The following day the King also tried to escape, but was detained not far from Pemberton Manor by local fishermen who had been searching any boats big enough to cross the Channel, knowing they might find wealthy Catholic refugees on board to rob. His Majesty was held at the Queen's Arms in Faversham for several days before being rescued and returned to London where, to Pemberton's surprise, he was met by great crowds of well-wishers.

'It would have been better for us all if he'd got away,' Pemberton grumbled. 'As it is he has allowed his wife and child to become hostages to Louis. Now he will be even more at the bidding of the French.'

Support for the King did not last long. Especially after the Irish troops in his army were disbanded and left to find their own way home. All over the country, stories were being spread of murderous Irishmen on the rampage, of streets running with blood and women and children murdered in their beds. In London it was rumoured that the papists were planning to burn the city to the ground, just like in '66. Even Nicholas grew concerned for Robin and Ellen, until Pemberton let slip that, in truth, it was the Protestant Londoners themselves who were lighting bonfires and crying that they should not be put out until the Prince of Orange came to town.

'Your father's scheme has been a great success,' Pemberton told Jane as they sat one evening in the parlour. 'My donation was worth every penny.'

'What scheme is that?' Jane asked warily.

Nicholas was sitting in an alcove, attempting to read the first volume of a French romance lent to him by Lettice. Perhaps the original would have been more entertaining than the English translation, though he doubted it. The subject matter of *Artamenes* was a bit fantastical for his taste.

Lettice and the younger Pembertons had all retired for the night and he had been about to follow them, but now he waited to hear what Pemberton would say next. His host was in unusually jovial form, perhaps thanks to the wine they had been drinking since supper. The same wine that, along with the flickering candlelight, was not helping Nicholas in his reading.

'Using the post office to distribute letters about the Irish threat.' Pemberton chuckled. 'He's got them circulating throughout the land; it's quite masterful really.'

'And is it true, about the massacres?' Jane asked.

'Of course not, but it's got everyone up in arms and shown James's supporters that they don't stand a chance. The papists are lying low, quaking in their holes, while the people search for murderous French and Irishmen.'

Jane gave a little cough and Nicholas looked up from his book to see them both turn towards him.

'No offence intended towards your father, Nicholas.' Pemberton nodded over at him before returning to Jane. 'But the lad understands how things work. England is much better off under the Prince and Princess of Orange. They'll soon restore law and order.'

Were it not for the letter from Father that had arrived that morning, assuring Nicholas all was well at Measham, he might have found it hard to contain himself. As it was, he bit his tongue and managed a wan smile.

Father wrote that he and Crewe had spent the previous months working hard to endear themselves to their neighbours. This, along with his own regular Sunday attendance at church, was keeping them safe from papist-hunting mobs. They were aided by a general confusion as to the source of the threat – some said it was the French, others the

Irish. The whole of Derbyshire, as well as the neighbouring counties, were armed, however, ready to support the Prince of Orange. Nicholas should stay where he was until peace was restored. It would be perilous now to travel up to Derbyshire, not only because of the unrest, but because snow and ice were making the roads near impassable.

Nicholas closed the book and placed it on the windowsill. Taking the candle he had been reading by, he made his excuses and went up to his chamber. Once in bed, he sat up for a long time, ruminating on what he had heard. Getting home might be difficult, but returning to Oxford seemed equally unconscionable. How could he ever respect himself if he slunk back to his books and vegetables at the university? To continue his position there under a new regime would make him a craven scholar. He could not while away his time in idle comfort, when better men than he were risking their lives to defend their principles. If ever there was a time to take to the field and use what skills he possessed to fight for his faith, it was now. Only a coward could hear the lies being spread about his Catholic brothers and do nothing.

⇢ Chapter Twenty-Four ⇠

20th December 1688

I t was a bitterly cold, overcast day, but at least it was dry. Desperate for some time alone to plan what he ought to do next, Nicholas borrowed a horse out of Pemberton's stables and went for a ride through the estate parklands.

The King was currently in residence in the same county, in the town of Rochester, ignominiously dismissed from London by the Prince of Orange who had ousted the English troops and moved his own Dutch Guard into Whitehall. According to Pemberton's sources, James was expected to slip away to France, successfully this time.

Nicholas was tempted to ride straight to Rochester to offer his services to His Majesty. After all, his grandfather had fought for Charles I, he had a duty to uphold his namesake's honour. And yet, he found his previous night's bravado waning in the pallid morning light.

Lord and Lady Pemberton were unanimous in their insistence that the noblest action for any Englishman was to remain at home and work with the Prince and Princess of Orange. To follow King James was a fool's errand, as his failure to withstand the invasion proved. And Nicholas had to admit they had a point. He was not a soldier at heart; did he really want to fight for a sovereign who could not even command the loyalty of his own people? He knew Father would also oppose his going.

But then, witnessing William's invasion fleet had reignited the passion he once felt for his religion. How could he ever forget Matthew's last words to him: 'you are one of God's angels. Continue to do His work and be His messenger. There is no greater calling.' Matthew had never been deterred by the hostility of his fellow Englishmen. He had faced calumny and persecution with the greatest bravery.

Nicholas's deliberations were broken by the cantering of hooves down the track behind him. A small horse and only one from the sound, but being driven hard. He brought his own mount to a halt and waited at the side of the path.

Lettice's grey mare appeared, her rider wrapped up in a hooded cloak. Slowing, the horse came to stand beside Nicholas's and the rider pushed back her hood to reveal a very different Lettice to the composed young woman he had grown so fond of. She had torn the headpiece from her hair and her face was flushed and wet with tears.

'What's happened?' Nicholas asked in alarm.

'I am to be sent to Holland.'

She looked suddenly as if she might collapse and fall from her saddle. Nicholas swiftly dismounted and went to help her down from her horse. Leaning forward into his outstretched arms, her whole body shook with great sobs so fierce they reverberated through several layers of wool, from her chest to his. He clasped her tightly, his face pressed against her neck, her hair tangled with his own. The musky, honeysuckle scent of her perfume made him feel quite giddy.

'Don't cry, my honey sweet, please don't,' he found himself saying, his words muffled against her soft skin.

Then she slipped through his arms to stand on the ground and he turned quickly to catch her horse's reins.

'Father is marrying me off to some Dutch partner of his in trade. He always said he would consider my happiness first in any match he arranged, but now it seems I am simply to do his bidding and my desires carry as much weight as a porcelain vase or a crate of oranges.' As she spoke, she gripped his riding cloak between her hands, addressing the buttons on his jacket with impassioned outrage.

The horses began to browse the dry grass beneath the hedgerow, unconcerned by human affairs. Nicholas was stricken with guilt for the part he had played in arranging her marriage. If only he had told Van Dorp some story to put him off the match. It wouldn't have mattered what lies he invented, anything to preserve Lettice from unhappiness.

'I thought Father intended me for someone else.' She twisted one of his buttons. 'A match much more to my liking, with a suitor who has my stepmother's blessing.'

Looking up, her eyes fixed intently on his, her meaning could hardly be mistaken. His heart was beating *quadrupla*, knocking against his ribs. He swallowed, trying to slow his whirling thoughts.

It was true, Lord Pemberton seemed to look favourably on him, though Jane had never given the impression she approved him as a suitor for Lettice. She was always quick to interrupt their conversations and evidently disliked them being left unchaperoned. Unless that was only for propriety's sake.

Nicholas realised that, for Lettice's reputation, he must get her home as swiftly as possible. It would be damaging for her if they were found alone together as though they had arranged a secret rendezvous. Certainly, it would not help persuade her parents that he was an honourable candidate for her hand.

'Let us return to the house,' he said, placing his hands on her shoulders. 'Lord Pemberton is a reasonable man; he will not force you to marry against your will.'

'I am never going back there. I told Father I would not marry his Mr Van Dorp and he threatened to lock me up until I remembered my duty.'

'Perhaps he spoke in anger,' Nicholas said uneasily. 'Jane will take your part.'

'Jane does Father's bidding.'

Ignoring the scorn in Lettice's voice, Nicholas insisted, 'Jane will know how to placate your father, to bring him round.'

But Lettice only shook her head wildly. 'Do you love me, Nicholas?'

Her question caught him off guard. 'I love you as a sister,' he replied automatically.

She dropped her hands from his chest and pulled her cloak tightly about her. 'I thought your feelings for me were stronger than that.' Her voice was thick with tears.

'Yes.' His voice spoke out before reason could stop it. 'Of course I love you.' Staring up at the network of branches arching overhead, he rushed on, 'I have never allowed myself to entertain any amorous notions regarding you, but had circumstances been different I would have considered it the greatest joy on earth to be your husband.' The word sounded foreign to his ears. It seemed fantastical to think of Lettice as his wife and he her lord and master. He lowered his gaze. Something rustled in the undergrowth, but it was only a robin sifting through the dead leaves.

'We could elope. Once we are married my parents will accept you.' The radiant smile had returned to her face and her eyes glowed with excitement.

Wishing he could share her confidence, Nicholas felt nonetheless that he must remind her of the reality of things. 'I am base-born and a papist.'

'You are also the sole heir to a substantial estate and descended from a noble lineage. If you convert to the Church of England, imagine what you might achieve. Lord Calverton esteems you greatly; he could get you a position in the new order.'

'You have been giving this some thought.'

Her ambitions for him were disarming. It seemed she had his whole future mapped out and in the opposite direction of the route he had just been planning.

'Haven't you?' Lettice sounded disappointed.

Nicholas needed some time to compose his thoughts. He turned towards the horses, who were working their way down the hedgerow. He didn't want them taking flight. If they lost them, they would be in serious trouble.

'Why would Lord Calverton have any influence with the Prince of Orange?'

She gave a little laugh. 'Lord Calverton and my father have been working with our new ruler for months. Keeping him informed of preparations at Court for the invasion, the movement and recruitment of troops, the King's vacillating moods.' She regarded him more earnestly. 'They were only doing what they believed best for the good of the country.'

Nicholas stared at her in amazement. 'How do you know all this?'

'They pay no attention to a girl and are careless in their talk. Besides, I know their cypher.'

'You have read their letters?'

'I was looking for parchment and came across the code along with a letterbook hidden in an old desk in Edward's closet. A clever place to conceal them, for Ned never did any writing. It amused me to decipher them. I had hoped to discover some information relating to myself. Perhaps that is vain, but since no one consults me, how else am I to learn what lies in store for me?'

Having grown up in similar circumstances, Nicholas had only sympathy for her predicament, but he didn't like to show this. He felt foolishly inept in the light of Lettice's knowledge. Staley would have done better employing her as a spy.

'And Prince William's success has ensured you will be married to the Dutchman.'

'Not if you marry me first.'

'I cannot forsake my faith,' he warned her.

He could feel Matthew's spirit hovering at his elbow, hear Matthew's voice whispering urgently into his ear, *Noli oblivisci*. He shook his head. The wind was jostling the branches beside him, that was all.

Lettice looked crestfallen. 'This is the wrong country and the wrong time to be a papist,' she said flatly.

Nicholas stroked the flank of her horse, noticing for the first time the packed saddlebags. 'It was right under our King.'

Lettice kicked a shard of ice that lay across a puddle. 'You aren't planning to follow him, are you?'

'I thought you were keen to see me join the King's army?'

'I was only teasing you.' She moved towards him. 'As your wife, I would be willing to run away to France with you, but you don't have any connections, no family or land there, do you?' She raised her eyebrows hopefully.

She was a conundrum – he was never certain when she was in earnest and when she was toying with him. For such a young woman she was very shrewd. Her plump lips were half-parted and looked so inviting he couldn't resist planting a kiss on them. Her breath smelt of cardamom seeds, so aptly named 'grains of paradise'. Her mouth, warm and succulent, opened for an exchange of long and passionate kisses.

Who knows where these might have led if a pheasant hadn't clattered up into the air behind them. Nicholas felt a slight tremor in the earth, followed by the thundering of hooves. A group of riders was racing towards them in a cloud of mud and snow. He and Lettice sprang apart.

'Quick, we must flee.' She ran to her horse, grabbing its bridle from his hands.

He seized her round the waist to restrain her. 'We will never outpace them.' If they were her father's men, it would look much worse for them if they bolted.

'They might be Irishmen,' she screamed in sudden terror.

'Halt. Stay where you are,' one of the riders shouted in a distinctively English accent.

Nicholas recognised the purple livery now; they were Pemberton's men all right. At least that was better than being accosted by soldiers, or so he hoped.

'You mustn't blame Nicholas,' Lettice implored her father. 'It was I who followed him.'

Pemberton turned to Nicholas, his pale face flushed with anger. 'Is this true?'

Nicholas hesitated, torn between gallantry and truthfulness, then silently assented.

Lettice dropped to her knees in front of her father. Raising her hands, her palms pressed together in a position of prayer; she looked like a supplicant out of a Greek tragedy. Her disordered hair flowed across her shoulders, while her skirts cascaded in silky rolls over the chequered stone floor of the hall. Nicholas wondered if he should join her there, like a couple before the altar.

Jane, standing just behind her husband, let out an exasperated sigh.

Pemberton reached his hands out to his daughter, his voice gentler. 'Do get up, my dear. These dramatics really won't do.'

'Promise you won't send me to Holland to marry some old Dutchman,' Lettice insisted.

'Mr Van Dorp has a large house in Amsterdam as well as his country estates. You will have everything you could possibly desire.' Pemberton took her hands in his. 'He will be a kind and generous husband, I guarantee it.'

Lettice remained steadfastly kneeling. 'But I have given my heart to another. A young man whom you love as a son, whom you have already welcomed into our family. He has gained the respect and esteem of all who meet him, Lady Jane and her parents not least. He has an old title and lands to inherit; he will bring honour and wealth to our name.'

'The bastard?' Letting go of her hands, Pemberton grabbed her by the wrists and hauled her to her feet. 'Do you think I would marry my daughter to a papist son of a whore? Those romances you read have turned your wits.'

'Ralph, please.' Jane put a restraining hand on Pemberton's arm.

'If he was a king's or a duke's bastard you would have no such reluctance,' Lettice cried out, undaunted by her father's rage.

Shocked by the change in Pemberton and smarting under his words, Nicholas bit back the urge to expose the hypocrite's own illegitimate son. Overriding his resentment against her father was his admiration for Lettice's indomitable spirit. By God, he would elope with her if she wanted him to. Father would welcome her to Measham Hall and he would find a way to make her happy.

'Nicholas.' Pemberton was pointing at him. 'Why don't you tell my foolish daughter who it was who brokered her marriage deal?'

Nicholas realised all at once why Pemberton had sent him to Van Dorp. He had been the instrument, not only of an international intrigue, but also of a domestic one.

'I was only the messenger. I played no part in the negotiations.'

'You brought me an excellent report on Mr Van Dorp. You were in raptures over his gardens and his hot-houses.'

'You knew?' Lettice stared at Nicholas with a look of such agony he felt the image would be forever imprinted on his heart.

'I carried a letter to Mr Van Dorp, but I did not know the contents,' he lied.

'Oh, come now.' Pemberton had regained his composure. 'You knew full well the purpose of your errand. This whimsy my daughter has conceived that you are her suitor is all in her own head.'

How Nicholas loathed Pemberton. The man was as slippery as an eel. He wished now that he had run off with Lettice before Pemberton's men caught them. Why had he let the stigma of his birth constrain him?

He looked directly at Lettice. 'If I never considered myself your wooer it was purely because I did not think myself worthy of a woman as noble-spirited and intelligent as you are.'

'No.' Lettice returned his look with tear-filled eyes. 'You do not love me well enough. For all your flattery, that is the truth of it.'

Jane tapped her walking stick on the ground. 'Lettice, dearest, listen to me as one who endured an unhappy first marriage to a man only a few years my senior. Mr Van Dorp understands your ambitions to host assemblies and would support you in such endeavours. He is a great advocate for learning in ladies. You will find him far more generous and indulgent than any youth.' She moved cautiously over to her stepdaughter as if towards a wild animal. 'Please believe me when I tell you I have only ever had your best interests at heart and would oppose this match if I thought it would end in your unhappiness. Even if that set me at odds with your father.' Jane glanced at Pemberton, a look that was equal parts warning and admonition.

'You will become the most feted woman in Amsterdam and London.' Pemberton gave Lettice a forced smile.

Part III: Becoming a Man

The four of them stood in uneasy silence for a moment. Nicholas was paralysed by an agonising mixture of conflicting emotions. He knew that what Lettice wanted was for him to throw himself before her with a passion to equal hers. To promise her that he would outdo anything Mr Van Dorp could offer her. But it would be another lie. He could not compete with Van Dorp in wealth or status. He could not provide Lettice with the sort of society she longed for, especially not now with King James ousted. Even if he were to steal her away from her father, what kind of life could he offer her then? His conscience would not let him make the grand gesture that her heart and his were calling for.

Lettice nodded slowly. 'I should have known it.' She addressed Nicholas in a voice loaded with outraged pride, 'You're just another grovelling slave to Rome. A puny whey-faced boy without the courage to act like a proper man. Go off and fight for your papist King, lick the boots of the French tyrant.' She threw up her arms as if shooing him away. 'Go and play with your popish trinkets. Why should I sacrifice myself for such an asshead?' Gathering up her skirts, she ran upstairs before Nicholas could say a word in his defence.

He turned to see Jane looking at him with embarrassed pity.

'Leave my house, you ungrateful cur,' Pemberton said softly. 'Before I set some true-bred dogs on you.'

'I have tried everything, Nicholas, but Ralph is adamant, he will not have you under his roof any longer.' Jane clutched her shawl around her shoulders with one hand while the other rested on her walking stick. Her face was bone white.

'Go back inside, My Lady; it is too cold for you out here.' Nicholas had the strange sensation of re-enacting a scene from his childhood, only in reverse.

Jane ignored his entreaty. 'Ralph spoke in anger, as a father. I'm sure his attitude to you will soften once Lettice is safely wed.'

'I hope she will be happy in the United Provinces. They say the Dutch are a sober, pious people. I cannot picture her there,' Nicholas said anxiously. He didn't know if Lettice was reconciled to her marriage or had merely retreated in order to plan her next move. And though he loved Jane, he couldn't help wondering if she was influenced in her promotion of Mr Van Dorp by her poor relationship with Lettice. Jane was a good and kind woman, but she might still be eager to rid her flesh of the thorn that was her eldest stepdaughter.

'Just wait,' Jane said. 'One day you will hear of the celebrated Madam Van Dorp, patroness of the most esteemed writers and hostess of the most sought-after assemblies. Perhaps you will even be invited to attend one.'

Nicholas had to smile. He could indeed envision the scene Jane painted.

A servant joined them on the front steps. He was carrying a travelling bag.

'I've had Daniel pack what you will need most for the journey,' Jane said. 'I thought it would be easier for you if your trunk is sent directly to Measham Hall. I did my best to get you a horse, but Ralph won't allow it.' She untied the purse that was hanging from her waist and gave it to Nicholas. 'Take this, with my blessing. And write to me as soon as you are safely home.'

'You are very kind.' Nicholas shoved the purse into his jacket pocket with some embarrassment. He did not like to count the contents but he was in need of funds and couldn't afford to refuse her gift.

Jane let go of her shawl and placed her hand over his. 'We seem destined to be parted because of others' misconstructions.' She squeezed his hand. 'I shall look for a wife for you. A woman with the influence and qualities to reunite us all.'

It would take godlike powers to achieve that, he thought. He stared out over the magnificent gardens. The fountains were dry and the canal glittered with its icy covering. Such wealth was achieved with pragmatism, not love. Taking his leave of Jane, Nicholas hoisted the bag onto his back. He had no desire to remain a minute longer in Pemberton Manor.

Something flew over his shoulder to land on the grass near his feet. For a moment he thought Pemberton must have set an archer on him but, bending down, he saw that it was a shuttlecock. He turned to look up at the house. Richard was standing on the balcony, waving goodbye. He smiled and waved back. There at least was one Pemberton Jane had influenced for the better.

As he began to walk the road to Canterbury, Nicholas went over and over that morning's events. Lettice had turned to him for help and he had failed her. Should he come back that night and try to rescue her? Would she even want him to? Come to that, did he really want to? He understood that her words had been spoken in anger, but he was still wounded by the ugliness of them. He didn't believe now that they could ever reconcile their religious differences. She considered it a sacrifice to marry him. Real sacrifices were the kind made by men like Matthew, with no thought of worldly gain. If wealth and status were so important to her, she was better off with a man like Van Dorp.

Part of him still suspected she had cast him as her Romeo because he had the looks and the background for the role, not because she genuinely wished to be his wife. Perhaps she believed herself to be his Juliet, but for how long could such an amour last? At least Father would be pleased if he heeded his advice by acting with more restraint than his parent seemed capable of.

The wind had picked up, bringing with it cold gusts of rain. He would need to seek shelter soon. From the comfort of a good inn, with a tankard of ale before him, it would be easier to work out what he should do next. And once he had decided, he would have to write to Father and let him know where he was bound. Though deep in his heart, he already knew it would be France, for he could not spend the rest of his life feeling like a coward.

After a few miles Nicholas came to a village. It was already growing dark and candles had been lit in every window as a precaution against the Irish threat. The one small inn had its windows boarded up. Nicholas kept on walking until the road had narrowed to little more than a mud track overhung with trees and hedged in by brambles. It was gloomy, but at least it offered some protection against the driving rain. He wished now that he had stolen a horse from Pemberton's stables. The bag on his back seemed to grow heavier with every step he tracked through the claggy mud. By the time he got to Rochester, the King would probably have departed. Hopefully he'd be able to secure a safe passage to France.

Suddenly he felt a tugging on his knapsack so violent his feet rose off the ground. He put his hand to his sword hilt as another hand descended on it. Just managing to keep a grip on the handle, he tried to swing round but was held fast by the bag strapped to his back.

'What've we got here?' A strong odour of onions and cabbage was exhaled in his face along with the rough male voice.

His bag was released, but just as quickly a knife was put to his throat by Onion-breath. A big, burly man with violence in his eyes and a wooden club in his hands stepped out from behind an oak.

'I am a friend of Lord Pemberton's,' Nicholas said, trying to keep his voice calm and steady. 'He will not take kindly to this treatment of me.'

'Is that right?' Onion-breath sneered. 'And what's your name?'

When Nicholas told them, the large man grunted. Out of the corner of his eye, Nicholas was aware of Onion-breath nodding, then, just before blackness descended, he saw the club flying towards him and felt a terrible crack against his skull.

As he came to, Nicholas watched a spider crawling across a low ceiling covered in cracked, smoke-browned plaster. When he managed to move his head and look around, he found he was in a small room, probably the parlour of a cottage. A fire glowed in the grate beside him and a man was sitting at a table facing the only window. Daylight had come, so Nicholas must have passed a whole night here.

The man's figure looked vaguely familiar, but it was hard to tell who he was from behind. He seemed to be preoccupied by the hailstones rattling against the windowpanes. The air reeked of vinegar and, touching his scalp tentatively, Nicholas discovered that the smell came from the damp bandage wrapped round his aching head. There was no sign of his sword. He slipped his hand into his pocket only to find it empty – Jane's purse had been taken as well.

The man at the table stood up, blocking the window. When he turned round, Nicholas blinked. But, the apparition, instead of fading, only grew more real and now it was coming towards him. It sat down on the edge of the low bed and Nicholas pushed himself away from it, his back against the wall. The straw-filled mattress rustled and sagged under the extra weight, suggesting more substance than might be expected from an ethereal being.

'No need to be afraid.' Isaac's voice was as full-bodied as his appearance. 'That was quite a blow Tom gave you, but you aren't among ghosts, not yet anyhow.'

'They said you had died at sea.' Nicholas's mouth was parched and his muffled words rolled around inside his bound skull.

'Hmm, well, I needed to disappear for a while.' Rising, Isaac lifted a large jug from a dresser and filled a cup with ale. 'Here, drink this.'

Nicholas gulped down the warm beer gratefully. 'I'm very glad to see you alive and well,' he said, wishing he felt better himself.

'Are you?' Isaac gave him a hard look.

'Of course.' Nicholas shifted uncomfortably. 'But where am I?' He hoped his assailants weren't about to reappear.

'In a cottage belonging to Lord Pemberton.' Isaac rubbed his hands, holding them out in front of the fire. 'Not far from where you were apprehended.'

'Those were his men?'

'They're a little rough but know how to do as they are bid.'

Nicholas looked desperately around the room. Isaac now stood between him and the only exit – a bolted door. In his present condition he didn't like to try his luck at tackling the man. Especially when he didn't know who lay in wait outside.

'Is this intended to keep me from Lettice? Kidnapping is an extreme measure if that is the case.'

'Don't worry, he isn't shipping you off to his plantations.' Isaac appeared amused. 'Though your treatment would not have been so violent had it not been for your little adventure yesterday.'

'What, then – does Pemberton mean to prevent me from following the King?'

'Quite the contrary. However skilled you are as a swordsman, I don't believe you pose such a threat to the Prince of Orange that you must be locked away.' Isaac gave him a sardonic smile, before turning to stare out of the window again. The noisy hailstones had turned into soft flakes of snow and Nicholas was grateful for the quiet. 'We understand that you have been employed in spying on us.' A note of bitterness crept into Isaac's voice. 'Your friend Staley was most informative on that score.'

'I have no friend by that name,' Nicholas insisted, wondering what else Staley might have said. Surely it wouldn't have been in his interest to disclose what he knew about Father.

'Well, now you must put your services to use for a different master.' Moving the chair so that it faced Nicholas, Isaac sat down again. 'Go to Rochester and join King James's entourage. We need someone to monitor his movements. If he stays in France your work will be easy enough, but if he decides to send forces back to England or to Ireland, you must inform us, giving exact information as to the number of troops, when and where they plan to arrive.'

Nicholas could hardly believe his ears. Just when he had thought himself free of spying he was being told to resume a role he hated. Not only that, but Isaac was asking him to become a traitor to his own side. Pressing his fingers to his pounding temples, he tried to marshal his thoughts. There was a way out of this – he would play along in order to secure his freedom, then once he was safely in France, he would be out of Pemberton's reach. Isaac's chair creaked as he leant back in it and a spasm of pain contorted his face.

'I heard you were arrested,' Nicholas said. 'I hope Lord Pemberton managed to secure your release before much suffering was inflicted upon you.'

Slowly stretching out his legs, Isaac gazed heavenwards. 'I have been avenged.'

'Did you kill Staley?' Nicholas stared at Isaac with reluctant admiration.

'I am not a murderer,' Isaac said with an injured air. 'It didn't take much to get Staley to reveal all he knew. The man was more addicted to gaming even than Edward and had accrued more debts, for all he was a priest.'

'So, he was a Jesuit?'

'After a fashion. He was not as pious as your uncle, by any means.'

'My cousin, you mean,' Nicholas said, but a wave of despair broke over him, knocking the breath out of his lungs, for it was clear Isaac had discovered his family's secrets. It wouldn't be enough to leave England, not unless he could get Father out as well and would he ever consent to leaving Measham Hall? What a curse his parent had delivered on him, that he must be forever at the mercy of other men.

Isaac was observing him with a mixture of pity and impatience. 'It's thanks to Staley, or should I say Gascoigne, that you got such a fine education. He intervened to ensure your uncle's wishes were honoured.'

Nicholas leant forward, trying to ignore the pain in his head. 'But it was my great-uncle Percy who sent me to St. Omer. Staley – Gascoigne only accompanied me there.'

'Rather fortuitous, don't you think? Your great-uncle may have wanted you to have a Catholic education, but he's far too mean to part with any money on your behalf. Staley – we may as well use that name as any other – befriended him in order to maintain a connection to your family. Despite his other faults, Staley was devoted to your uncle Matthew.'

'And Staley told you all this?' Isaac was surpassing Crewe in his store of knowledge.

Isaac smiled. 'Everyone needs a confessor. It's a case of knowing when to listen and how to ask. You have some way to go in acquiring these skills, but I'm demonstrating for you what can be achieved.'

'That's all very well, but I don't imagine you relied on words alone to extract Staley's confession,' Nicholas said irritably.

'One can't be too delicate about these things, though force must only be used as a last resort and for the greater good. Too often it elicits false testimonies.'

'I suppose Staley thought the same.' Nicholas shifted back against the wall again. 'Before you had him killed.'

'That wasn't my decision, but in terms of security it was a wise one.'

'Lord Pemberton must have wanted to punish the man who abused his son.' Nicholas watched Isaac carefully, but his reaction was disappointingly calm.

'Edward told you, did he? Well, if you think that information is going to get you out of our mission, I'm afraid you are mistaken. It will not damage Pemberton's reputation and his wife is already aware of my parentage. The knowledge we have about your father, on the other hand, that really would make life unpleasant for your family. You'd lose everything.'

'So, you're stooping to the same tactics as Staley. I did not take you for an extortioner,' Nicholas said indignantly.

'Surely you have learnt by now that is how the game is played. We will hold the information about your aberrant parent in reserve, only to ensure you carry out your part of the bargain.' Isaac gave him a reproving look. 'This country will be better off under the Prince and Princess of Orange. We are ensuring English liberties are preserved. You might work for that without coercion.'

'And Staley claimed he was working for the glory of God. It seems you all like to consider yourselves saviours.'

'I'm being pragmatic,' Isaac said. 'William and Mary are more likely to keep the peace here.'

Nicholas slumped back, feeling defeated by Isaac's remorseless logic. 'Why did you send me to see Petre?' he asked, as much out of curiosity as anything else.

'We needed verification of the Queen's condition. Knowing that we could no longer wait out King James's reign for a Protestant to return to the throne made matters more pressing. We also wanted information on who else was currying favour with the dean. It was a useful exercise – to see how reliable a messenger you might be.'

'And the pamphlets spreading rumours about Petre fathering the Queen's child – was that Pemberton's handiwork?'

'Lord Calverton was involved in the writing and importing of certain pamphlets, and I too made some modest literary contributions.' Isaac looked rather pleased with himself. 'Surely you must agree that a war of words is preferable to physical bloodshed.'

'Lying is better than the truth, that is your argument?'

'Sometimes the truth needs embellishing.'

'What about those who suffer because of your false claims, the Queen for instance?' Nicholas demanded, remembering Father's outrage on her behalf.

'I suspect the Queen will be much happier in France, as will the King. Surrounded by those of the same faith, they can enjoy a very comfortable retirement. Though I fear Louis will not be content to leave England in Dutch control. We just have to hope Prince William does nothing to provoke him.'

'Lettice said she found evidence that Lord Pemberton had been spying for the House of Orange for months.'

To Nicholas's surprise, Isaac chuckled. 'The letters in Edward's desk? So, the little mouser discovered them, did she? Nothing of much importance was kept there, certainly nothing that matters now.'

Initially offended by Isaac's irreverence towards Lettice, Nicholas recalled that she was, in fact, his half-sister. 'You wield a great deal of influence over your father. And he allows you a lot of freedom.'

'Lord Pemberton knows that I am always working in his best interests,' Isaac replied firmly.

Nicholas suspected that the rest of the family were ignorant of Isaac's elevated position, or perhaps they chose to ignore it. Edward certainly wouldn't have been capable of filling the role he played. Nor, come to think of it, would Nicholas himself.

'How do you expect me to discover all the King's military plans?

I don't have any connections at Court,' Nicholas said, overwhelmed by what was being demanded of him.

'A personable fellow like you will have no trouble finding a patron. You speak good French and know how to fight – as your encounter with the highwaymen proved. We have every confidence in you.' Isaac smiled benevolently and refilled their cups with beer. 'Besides, His Lordship will help you purchase a commission in James's army if necessary.' Going over to a chest, he took out two purses and dropped them onto Nicholas's lap. 'Or use this to fund your way into the King's circle, whichever is the most direct route. We can arrange further funds, but first you must prove your value. You'll have to find a private messenger, someone you can trust, preferably unlettered. Address all correspondence to Mr Laurent, at the sign of the Fighting Bear in Covent Garden.'

Nicholas was astonished to discover that between them, the leather bags contained over three hundred pounds in a mixture of coin and bills of exchange. The money would certainly make his task easier, if not any more palatable.

'Make sure you divide that up and secrete it about your person,' Isaac advised. 'I have got you a horse. Now, *vogue la galère*! You must bestir yourself and get to Rochester.'

Despite himself, a flicker of excitement ran through Nicholas. He was still going to France as he had planned, only on horseback and with money in his pocket. He might get out of spying yet, but if he couldn't rescue Father, at least Isaac was a more agreeable intermediary than Staley. It seemed he was destined to be trapped in a web spun, if not by the Fates, then by the actions and ambitions of other men, but perhaps in that his life did not differ so much from those of Lettice or Isaac.

'And what about you?' he asked. 'You can't stay hidden away in a rural hovel forever. The Pembertons can't manage without you, for a start.'

Isaac laughed and then winced. Placing a hand on his ribs, he stooped to pick up a log and throw it on the fire. 'Having miraculously survived the shipwreck and made my way back to shore, I shall return to the bosom of my family.'

'And yet they treat you like a servant,' Nicholas pointed out, thinking of his own position at Measham Hall.

'Ralph Pemberton has promised to set me up in my own establishment. He will always ensure I am well provided for.' Isaac's voice grew uncharacteristically sombre. 'But it is true, he leans very heavily on me.' He raised his eyebrows. 'As you know only too well, a son must serve his father, for he owes him loyalty and obedience.'

Nicholas couldn't help being moved by Isaac's fidelity. 'We are brothers in hostage then, both pledged for our fathers.'

Isaac raised his cup. 'Here's to the misbegotten, bantlings and bastards.'

'Stall-whimpers and love-brats.' Nicholas drained his beer. 'A toast to us by-blows.'

Acknowledgements

Huge thanks to all at Duckworth Books: Matt, Pete, Sophie, Danny, and especially my editor, Rowan Cope, for her invaluable work on the different stages of this novel and Sarah Lambert for her perceptive feedback. Thanks also to copyeditor, Becca Allen, and designer Dominic Forbes for the beautiful cover.

As always, my heartfelt thanks to Colin Teevan, most insightful, inspiring and supportive of readers and husbands.

The Messenger of Measham Hall is dedicated in memory of my father, Robin Dewhurst, 1st May 1934 – 24th June 2021.